**150 YEARS STRONG**

DAVID **C** COOK

# JOIN US.
# SPREAD THE GOSPEL.
# CHANGE THE WORLD.

We believe in equipping the local church with Christ-centered resources that empower believers, even in the most challenging places on earth.

We trust that God is *always* at work, in the power of Jesus and the presence of the Holy Spirit, inviting people into relationship with Him.

We are committed to spreading the gospel throughout the world—across villages, cities, and nations. We trust that the Word of God will transform lives and communities by bringing light to the darkness.

As a global ministry with a 150-year legacy, David C Cook is dedicated to this mission. Each time you purchase a resource or donate, you're supporting a ministry—helping spread the gospel, disciple believers, and raise up leaders in some of the world's most underserved regions.

Your support fuels this mission.
Your partnership sends the gospel where it's needed most.

**Discover more. Be the difference.**
**Visit DavidCCook.org/Donate**

# PAPER CUT

# PAPER CUT

*A Novel*

**RACHEL TAFF**

*wm*
WILLIAM MORROW
*An Imprint of* HarperCollins*Publishers*

PAPER CUT. Copyright © 2026 by Perry Circle LLC. All rights reserved. Printed in the United States of America. No part of this book may be used or reproduced in any manner whatsoever without written permission except in the case of brief quotations embodied in critical articles and reviews. For information, address HarperCollins Publishers, 195 Broadway, New York, NY 10007. In Europe, HarperCollins Publishers, Macken House, 39/40 Mayor Street Upper, Dublin 1, D01 C9W8, Ireland.

HarperCollins books may be purchased for educational, business, or sales promotional use. For information, please email the Special Markets Department at SPsales@harpercollins.com.

hc.com

FIRST EDITION

*Title art courtesy of Shutterstock / Street Boutique*

Library of Congress Cataloging-in-Publication Data has been applied for.

ISBN 978-0-06-338039-4

25 26 27 28 29 LBC 5 4 3 2 1

*For Mom and Dad*

# PAPER CUT

# LOS ANGELES, CALIFORNIA

*May 2022*

MY MOTHER NEVER LETS ME FORGET THE DIFFERENCE BETWEEN HER fame and my infamy.

Diana Golden, the idolized, the feared, earned her fame by gracing the world with her artistic contributions to photography.

As for me, I gained infamy by killing someone twenty years ago. Someone I once loved.

"You're next," Malin whispers in the wings of the Orpheum Theater. She pats my arm, like she's done hundreds of times before, but there is no warmth in her touch. She's just doing her job, and now it's time for me to do mine.

A cheerful voice trills over the sound system. "Please welcome the acclaimed memoirist of *Rattlesnake*, the hero of a generation, Lucy Golden!"

Somewhere inside, I must be telling my legs to move, because I hear my heels clacking against the stage floor, quickly drowned out by applause. Once I adjust to the lights, I take in the audience assembled in the historic theater, packed in tight like sardines. A swift adrenaline rush ensues. Malin booked me for this event, cheekily titled "She Slays: An Evening with the Media Mavens of Modern True Crime." Two thousand of my closest friends shelled out half a month's rent to hear the riveting ins and outs of my well-told tale. Compared to the scale of Crime Con, it's shaping up to be a quaint affair.

My name sticks out in the program, next to a *Los Angeles Times* crime reporter, a pair of comedy-crime podcast hosts, and the creator of the latest hit show about a female vigilante who Lorena Bobbitts every Harvey Weinstein figure in showbiz. Yet again, I'm the only one who knows what it's like to live through something the others pretend to understand. But you know the old saying: Mother knows best. If she's taught me anything, it's that you can't say no to your fans.

From fifth row center, the best seat in the house, Mom winks at me like she's a femme fatale in a black-and-white film, her favorite role to play. I've learned a thing or two about the spotlight, having lived in her shadow for all my thirty-five years, but tonight I'm reminded of my deficiencies and all the ways I fail her.

My success in the arena of true crime and my modest but mighty fanbase are not enough. This world is beneath her, meant for housewives in Middle America who consume real-life horror stories while they Windex their windows in their ho-hum subdivisions, not for the wealthy elite who buy my mother's photographs to grace the walls of their Vail chalets and Nantucket cottages. Her epic love affairs with rock stars and tech tycoons may inspire more online discourse than her photographs, but she insists her dating history's irrelevant to her legacy. *My daughter caters to another audience*, she tells her important friends. She puckers her lips when she says *daughter*, like she's tasted something sour. Every time, I smile at her graciously. At least she claims me as her own.

I toss my bangs out of my eyes and scan the room. I recognize several faces from the press, then spot Julian, his phone glued to his ear, standing in the back. I flash my signature Cheshire cat smile at the audience of primarily women between the ages of sixteen and sixty-five who devour tales of gruesome murders and insidious cults to alleviate their own anxieties. I linger on the neon outline of a rattlesnake splashed across the electric-blue cover of my memoir, held in the hands of everyone as far as I can see. Included in the price of admission for this special evening of gore and female rage is one paperback copy of the book that landed me here—the success of which is my biggest blessing and my biggest curse. They hold my words close to them, like they own them, like they own me. Because they do. Another copy perches on the podium, turned to page fifty-four as I requested.

"Thank you for being here tonight." I adjust to hearing my voice distorted through the speakers. "Thank you for your support all these years. Before we get started, I thought I'd read a passage about the first time I visited the Oasis." The fans salivate like their favorite band's teasing them with the first few chords of their smash hit. "For old times' sake," I tease, savoring their collective held breath. They laugh, right on cue, ready to rock.

I trace my finger down the page, but before I can begin, I hear a bang.

I look up to see what's causing the commotion.

It's a man, charging down the center aisle toward the stage.

I've never seen him before. He's not one of the regular Lucy Golden haters who would love nothing more than to burn me at the stake. The crowd's panicked whispers swirl around the theater. My pulse quickens.

The intruder bellows his threats. "Shame on you!" Spittle flies from his vile mouth and settles on his protruding chin. He points right at me. His other hand's stuffed into the pocket of his Members Only jacket, camouflaging what I assume is the gun that will end me. Men like him believe this torment is what I deserve for what I've done. Will the pain be dull or sharp as the bullet rips through my abdomen?

For a long time, I've been curious to know what it feels like.

A woman shrieks and dashes toward the exit, unleashing hysteria in the crowd. A domino effect we're all acutely primed for these days— fleeing at a moment's notice, triggered by a single, loud disturbance in a packed theater.

But there's a problem. I can't move or speak. All I can do is picture my demise.

Headlines and news segments of this man's mug shot next to my author portrait. Fans mourning the loss of a feminist savior. Naysayers rejoicing victory at last. Armchair detectives sliding the conclusive puzzle piece into place. My life's work boiled down to quotes pulled out of context to accompany cliché posts of desert sunsets. In one fell swoop, my entire existence narrows into obscurity.

Once the intruder makes it to the front row, I look down from my place onstage and wish with every fiber of my being that I could make him understand why I had to do it.

Why I had to lie.

Two security guards barge through the double doors at the back of the theater. Relief floods over me as they tumble down the aisle and, at last, restrain him.

"Slut!" Red-faced and blubbering, the stranger roars as he's taken away. "Man-haters! All of you!"

My mother lifts her hand to cover her open mouth. I can't help but be touched by her distress. Funny to watch her try on maternal instinct for size. An unflattering fit—it's never suited her.

The murmur of the crowd surges. I kick myself for letting fear take hold. I've always done what's necessary to ensure I take the details of what really happened that night to my grave. What's the harm of a little white lie if it saves so many and grants me the esteem I deserve? I suppose only the fraying of my nerves when vultures like this intruder circle and wait for my corpse to fall, spent and splayed on the pavement. No doubt my decades-long deception would provide a decadent feast.

A trickle of sweat slides down the small of my back. I sense the audience's eyes on me, all blinking like a school of aquarium-trapped fish. My hand trembles as I touch the page, trying to find my place, so I can pick up where I left off, like nothing happened.

*Because nothing did*, I tell myself. *Nothing at all.*

Through the deafening silence, I hear them.

"We love you!"

"Screw him!"

"Keep going, Lucy!"

My fans shout out their reassurances. Applause breaks out. I lift my head to take in the magnificent display.

They believe me.

AS A HERD, WE WALK THREE BLOCKS TO A NEW RESTAURANT ON Seventh and Grand. The place hardly feels luxurious when a tent city's up in flames down the street, but the patrons ignore the ugliness over industry chatter, absinthe drips, and caviar toasts. When Julian and Malin launch into a discussion about the latest publishing scandal, Mom tugs on my elbow. Her perfume of vetiver and fig wafts toward me. "Touch-ups?"

The restaurant bathroom is wrapped in wallpaper resembling a Rorschach test. Mom saunters up to an enormous brass mirror. I gasp when I see how much my mauve lipstick has worn off.

"Fuck." I frown at my appearance. "Why didn't you tell me?" My fair complexion still appears dull despite the $220 retinol serum I just charged to my Amex. I fuss with my bangs, never the right length no matter how often I complain to my hairdresser. As I examine my profile, I consider how pronounced my jawline might be if I got filler at a med spa or if it wouldn't be noticeable enough to merit the indulgence.

"Don't be so vain." Mom powders her poreless milk-white T-zone with her Chanel compact. "Try this." She unearths a gold tube from her Celine tote. "This color will work better on you than on me."

Something about how she offers the lipstick to me—although a kind gesture in theory—serves as a reminder of her superior beauty. It's the precise occasion to compliment her.

"I doubt it," I say as I swipe it on my lips. "It's a great color on you."

The little girl inside of me beams at the thought of holding on to a tube of my mother's lipstick. I imagine her perched at her three-paneled vanity, back in Coronado, as the sunlight streams in from the bay window, bounces off her perfume bottles, and highlights her cheekbones. She will eternally be the most stunning woman in the room.

"Couldn't they have hired better security?" Brushing off my praise, Mom never breaks eye contact with her reflection as she voices a litany of grievances, a habit of hers I somehow forget about when we're apart. "Who is even running this circus? You shouldn't associate yourself with something so low brow. The Goldens are better than that."

I'm still adjusting to our new arrangement, with my mother as my temporary adult roommate. Three months ago, Mom called out of the blue from Coronado to propose the idea of living together. I hadn't heard her raspy voice in months. Flattered she asked, I immediately agreed, even before she explained that she was preparing a show for a gallery in the Arts District conveniently located five minutes from my loft. But she was the only one who was truly there for me during that hellish autumn and the subsequent trial, so I let myself daydream about the bond we'd forge, the grand times we'd have. To my dismay, most nights, she leaves me to fend for myself. *Catching up with old friends*, she claims. More likely, she's seeing a new man who's high-profile enough to make her sign an NDA. Often, she finds me on the couch when she returns to the loft—if she returns—and badgers me while I make us a nightcap. *You should get out more, darling*, she'll say, then click her tongue. *Wasting your youth, are you?* It's been years since we've spent this much time together. It makes me feel sixteen all over again.

"I'm only looking out for you, doll." Mom takes the lipstick back and snaps it closed. "You can't let that guy rattle you."

"It's not a big deal." I brush her off and remind her I've been through worse. "I'm used to it."

Mom arranges the slope of her oxblood curls and grins at her reflection: a job well done. "Coming?"

"Right behind you."

As the door swings closed, I adjust to the deafening silence, in sharp contrast to the purring of fans only an hour earlier as I signed their fresh copies and their original paperbacks, marked with the wear of multiple reads. I brace myself against the sink and count my shallow breaths. In and out.

No one should ever get used to vultures circling above, waiting to swoop in and attack.

I pull out my phone and examine the photos Malin snapped of the event. I select the most flattering one to post, with my chin slanted at the right angle. I craft a caption to summon the right amount of concern, but also to convey that I have everything under control. My fans will like that.

> She Slays 2022 was one for the books!
> A note to my fans in attendance: We appreciate your patience and solidarity. Conversations are under way to prevent disturbances of a similar nature in the future. Rest assured; your safety is my number one priority. XX

Ping! The response is immediate. One of the regular haters nabs the first comment.

> TexWatson86: You reap what you sow.

Thankfully, my most loyal fans come to my rescue.

> FunkyJunkie716: You're so brave.

> MMophead_99: OMG! So scary! TFG you're OK.

> LizzieBorden23: Our hero.

Like magic, I can breathe again.

A HOSTESS WITH BOTCHED LIP FILLER LEADS US THROUGH THE sleek and soulless restaurant. We pass a marble bar where a well-dressed couple pays more attention to each other than to their craft cocktails. As the man runs his hand up the thigh of his wife or girlfriend or mistress, the impulse to be weakened by a stranger's touch surges through me. I let it pass.

The lights are impossibly low. I wonder if Mom might deign to wear her reading glasses in public or use her phone as a flashlight to read the menu. Instead, she cranes her neck over the menu, smashing her buxom chest against the table. "The gallery space is incredible," Mom gloats. Malin knows the critic covering her show's opening and Julian knows the gallery owner and I know I'd kill them all if I could get a drink faster.

At long last, the aspiring actor moonlighting as our waiter brings our first round. I never thought I would like martinis, but since Mom moved in, it's become our little ritual. I've adapted to the bitterness of the olive, but I'm still adjusting to this kind of intimacy with her. It, too, is intoxicating.

"Moules frites, a dozen oysters, and shrimp cocktail for the table," I tell the waiter. Mom makes a face, a silent protest of my indulgence. She can eat a whole feast without gaining an ounce, a gene I tragically did not inherit.

Julian takes a swig of his scotch. "The sirloin. Well done." Julian hands over his menu. "I detest seafood."

"To each their own." Mom rubs Julian's arm, likely in order to judge the thread count of his suit and check if he's still wearing a wedding ring. He is, but that's never stopped her before.

Malin proposes a toast and raises her glass of Sancerre. "To the continued success of *Rattlesnake*!"

Mom sings out, "Hear, hear!" Half of her martini disappears down her gullet.

"I appreciate that, Malin," I say. "But I thought tonight's meeting was about next steps."

My job as a fixture in the true crime landscape keeps the lights on, for the most part, but as of late, the lucrative offers are few and far between. My unimpressive stack of half-finished manuscripts and mounting credit card debt have become increasingly difficult to ignore. The *New Yorker*'s declaration that I'm the "premiere voice of post-

9/11 California noir" feels like a distant memory, because it is. Malin and Julian lured me here under the guise of an exciting opportunity sure to revitalize my career. Their elusive promise of good news better deliver. I make a silent prayer that relief is on the horizon.

"What's the latest?"

"Just wait. You're not going to believe this." Malin glances around for eavesdroppers. "Isaac Coleman reached out. He wants to make his next documentary all about you."

The brininess of the cocktail coats my throat. I struggle to swallow before I can respond. "Wait, the guy who solved the Buckhead Butcher cold case?"

"He's sensational," Malin raves. Her years in California have obviously scrubbed away her Scandinavian cynicism. "He forced the police to take another look and pegged the real killer."

"We binged the whole series in a night," Julian adds, subtly reminding Mom of his marital status. "He just signed a huge streaming deal."

All the blood rushes to my head. "Isaac's a big name right now. I'll give you that."

Malin twists the back of her diamond hoops and leans in, conspiratorial. "He said you are the prime example of how true crime has evolved. Isn't that thrilling?"

The three of them watch me expectantly while the waiter delivers our appetizers. Vodka splashes onto my wrist as I fiddle with the olive. I'm intent on taking control over anything, even a stupid garnish. The awkward silence is made even more uncomfortable as it's scored by the clangs of cutlery and dishes being rearranged on the table.

Mom dunks a shrimp into cocktail sauce. "This will give your fans, new and old, what they really want. Inside access."

"You knew about this?" I ask her, then turn to Malin. "You told her before me?"

Mom nudges me. "You know it's impossible for Malin to keep a secret from me, doll." Mom is the generous benefactor who foots Malin's exorbitant fees as she alternates between family friend and paid employee. Even though Mom doesn't understand my career, she deems publicity a necessity for anyone bearing her last name.

Malin continues. "I also arranged for you to appear on *The Remy Olsen Show*!"

Mom gushes. "Oh my God, I love Remy Olsen!"

I slurp back a Rhode Island oyster. It irks me that Mom's acting like she's impressed. "Mom," I sneer at her. "Didn't you say daytime TV is a death sentence?"

She winces at me calling her "Mom" in public. "I would never say that."

"You're leaving out the best part," interjects Julian, rubbing his hands together. "I spoke to your publisher about Isaac's offer." He pauses for dramatic effect, and I consider tightening his tie until he turns beet red. "If you sign on to this doc with Isaac, they will commit to publishing an anniversary edition of *Rattlesnake*. A whole new print run, cover, nationwide tour, the works." He smirks, pleased with his negotiating skills.

Hope balloons in my chest. My publisher showed interest in publishing a special edition when the fifteenth anniversary of the crime came around until a popular podcaster tried to cancel me for my interpretation of the Michelle Carter case. The whole fiasco went viral, and the opportunity was extinguished before contracts were drawn up.

"Isaac's fan base is huge," Malin chimes in. "*This* is how we get the TikTokers involved, how we push the Gen Z fans who only watch streamer docs off their asses and into bookstores to buy your book. Your engagement has plateaued because your story is twenty years old. Isaac will make it new again."

She must know how badly her words sting. I chew the inside of my cheek, acidic from the mignonette. I hate to admit that she's right. Late at night, after I read the messages from my dedicated fans, I check the forums, an itch that demands to be scratched. It's impossible to forget the things the trolls call me: *has-been, lunatic, whore.* That is when they deign to mention me at all. Now Isaac's the next big thing, and for some unknown reason, he's willing to fold me into the warmth of his spotlight. Somewhere inside, Mom's old refrain echoes: *Take a risk—it won't kill you.* On the contrary, I think it might.

"Lucy," Julian says, "you're being given another chance, a way to take back the narrative."

"But Isaac Coleman's taking over the narrative!" I blurt out. Trusting anyone in the media with my story has long proved to be an arduous task. The hour-long specials portray me as someone I no longer am—a lost little Lolita, forever encased in desert dust and disaster, sixteen until the end of days. Or worse, they make me into the villain. "Look, it's not what I was expecting. This is a bit of a shock."

Malin wrinkles her nose, flustered by the confrontation. It makes her look weak. "Hey, we have your best interest in mind." She taps my hand like I'm a petulant six-year-old on the brink of a tantrum.

"Right now, this is the move," says Julian. "Isaac wants to work with you. This is the comeback you've been hoping for."

If I manage to suffer through the documentary, I'll climb the next rung of the ladder. I'll exhale when my credit card statement arrives every month. I'll reach a new audience. My fan base will multiply many times over. Maybe this time I'll be so untouchable, no one can drag me down.

But the twisting in my gut isn't elation about the possibility of advancing my career. If Isaac is as brilliant as they say, I will need to be careful. I will need to keep him in the dark.

"Fine." I put Malin and Julian out of their misery, amused to watch relief wash over them before I deliver my caveat. "I'll hear what Isaac has to say, but . . ."

They exchange a weighted glance, hanging on with bated breath.

"No promises." I lift my drink to my lips, ready to forget this whole evening.

When everyone acts like you have no power, it's important to remind them that you do.

# LOS ANGELES, CALIFORNIA

*June 2022*

THE NIGHT BEFORE I'M SUPPOSED TO MEET ISAAC, MOM AND I WATCH Isaac's documentary *Buckhead Butcher*. I've seen it twice already, once last fall when it premiered and again the night of the She Slays event, in the privacy of my bedroom, but I'm not about to admit that out loud.

Isaac's omniscient voice is woven throughout, but we never see his face. For some inane reason, film critics liken his unoriginal narrative device to speaking on the audience's behalf, asking questions they'd ask and, effectively, removing himself from the film. But all I can obsess over is the hack whom the voice belongs to. What does he want from me?

While I plow through spicy fusilli in large spoonfuls, Mom barely touches our spread of Jon & Vinny's takeout. She's too busy blurting out her every thought in three-minute increments.

When the first victim helps a stranger with directions in a creepy parking garage, Mom literally gasps. "My God! What an idiot!"

"Do you think *he* did it?" she squeals about the surly brother-in-law, then the lead detective, then finally the school counselor. Just as Isaac's textbook misdirects intended.

When the credits roll, the fusilli is gone and so is my belief that I can go through with this. The Buckhead Butcher took the lives of seven housewives who parked their cars at the wrong places at the wrong times and tragically never made it home because they'd been caught in his trap and subsequently hacked to bits. The murderer was your run-of-the-mill sociopath.

But Isaac broke him.

Isaac knew when to give him the floor and let the maniac take the credit he believed he'd earned. He crafted a windy narrative and shot from the hip with some cheap tricks, but there's no way the person now forever known as the Buckhead Butcher will ever be seen as redeemable.

"So, Isaac's not half bad," Mom says, delivering her review.

I exit out of the streaming app and toss the remote into the recesses of the couch. "Whatever."

From the velvet green armchair, Mom stretches her twiglike arms up then coils her long waves into a hair clip. "This will be great for your brand."

"My brand," I repeat, dubious. I know for a fact Mom despises the word *brand*. *Destroys all integrity to boil an artist down to a box.*

"Your brand bought you this loft, didn't it?"

Before Japanese record-listening cafés and craft breweries for the hipster elite ran rampant in the Arts District, I took a generous sum from a studio that made a mediocre but solvent feature film about that summer and bought this two-bedroom loft. Only Odette, fresh from overpaying for the mid-century modern bungalow she landed in Venice, thought it was a worthwhile investment at the time. Oceanside living did not appeal to me. I'd had enough of that.

When I don't answer, Mom hounds me. "You're intimidated, aren't you?"

"He knows what he's doing," I snarl at her in the dark. "But so do I."

I polish off the last of my martini, even though a tension headache's brewing. Mom snorts, unconvinced.


THE FOLLOWING AFTERNOON, THE JUNE GLOOM OUTSIDE COMplements the depressing confirmation that Isaac is beloved by critics and the public alike. At a red light at the Vermont and Melrose intersection, I hate-read glimmering write-ups and chug my second coffee, even though I'm set to meet Isaac at a café. Acid festers at the top of my gut. I force my eyes to open wider than usual.

When I see a glowing rave on the popular Buckhead Butcher forum posted by TexWatson86, I can't help but laugh. Of course Isaac's fans comprise my most avid haters, busy fawning over his "uncanny grasp of a female victim's psyche." The driver behind me lays on their horn, alerting me that the light's turned green. I soar across the intersection and promptly spill the remainder of my coffee all over the center console.

Thanks a million, Tex.

In my periphery, I make out the copy of *Rattlesnake* from the She Slays event on the passenger seat. I reset my jaw, crippled by the story it contains, the one I'm now supposed to relive to lend some boy genius new material. Throughout my entire career, I've placed the utmost importance on owning my narrative, captaining my ship. My most popular talk on YouTube is about the significance of first-person accounts. This impostor went to film school. He grew up in Calabasas. He has no idea what it's like to go through what I went through.

Then I remind myself, his numbers don't lie. If I play this right, they'll be my numbers too.

By the time I find parking off this drag of Santa Monica Boulevard between East Hollywood and Silverlake, I'm fifteen minutes late to meet Isaac. I figure my tardiness is expected—most people in Los Angeles run twenty minutes behind and blame traffic or parking without social repercussions. I refuse to admit I'm late because I'm still recovering from watching his Emmy-nominated crock-of-shit triumph. The coffee shop's quiet, the hush punctuated only by a twinkling of indie music and keyboard clacks of aspiring screenwriters.

Bent over an espresso cup and an iPad, Isaac Coleman fits in with every other pretentious asshole on the Eastside. He has one of those haircuts where the top half is floppy and the bottom half of his scalp has a tight shave. A disturbing reminder that we're composed of skulls and bones. A rectangular blazer looks comical on top of his lanky frame and costly vintage T-shirt. His jeans glide over Blundstone boots that have never seen a speck of dirt. He looks younger than me, maybe by only a couple years, but he appears at home among his trendy surroundings.

A coil of envy snaps inside me. He's in the phase of his career when he thinks this glow is going to last forever, but I know what it's like to be that sparkling young visionary. When you're labeled a "genius" too young, be wary. It comes with an expiration date.

"Lucy." He greets me like he's run into an old friend, sets down his iPad, and gestures to the chair opposite him. "Please."

After an awkward exchange during which he insists he order and pay for my drink of choice, Isaac delivers his made-to-seem-casual, generic preamble. "Thank you for coming." As I sip my matcha latte, he looks at me like I'm about to ingest poison. "Oh, by the way, I just listened to your commentary about the Idaho case, you know . . ." Isaac looks up like he's trying to remember the name of the victim. It's fun to watch him flounder. He gives up quickly. There is hope yet. "Anyway, I appreciated your perspective. Insightful."

"Mm-hmm." I search for an empty compliment. "And I find your films . . . interesting."

"Oh?" Isaac adjusts his glasses. "I didn't know if you were aware of my work."

*Buckhead Butcher* dominated the true crime news cycle for the better part of last fall. "Hard not to be."

Isaac's expression is indifferent, but his neck flares pink with satisfaction. Every artist is the same. They refer to their meager offerings of ego as their "craft" instead of what they are: commodities. Fan their ego and they'll give you what you want in return. That's Hollywood for you.

"I can imagine you have a lot of questions," he says. "But first things first. I want you to know that if there's ever a moment in this process when you question my methods, know that my guiding principle is to tell the truth."

This guy must be kidding. According to his IMDb, he started out in reality television. "I appreciate that, but I already told my story."

He holds his hands up like I'm accusing him of petty theft. I refrain from pointing out the irony. "You told it beautifully."

When I spot a copy of *Rattlesnake* among his pile of papers, I suddenly feel naked. Isaac catches my line of sight and plucks my book out of his things. "But you wrote this when you were seventeen, eighteen, published it at nineteen. All the wounds were still fresh. You couldn't have been in the right state of mind to recount it all with a level head." His wording reminds me of the language the lead prosecutor used, as if my brain had been scrambled and I had no ability to decipher up from down, let alone comprehend what I'd done. It makes me want to kick Isaac in the mouth. As he flips through his copy, two dozen Post-its stick out like red flags. "Given your position now, I'm sure you will find, if you haven't already, a new perspective that will be enlightening."

He chose that word on purpose, trying to throw me off my game. I glance around at the other patrons, who are lost in thought, and the baristas constructing flowers in oat milk foam. I search for anything to hold on to that might ground me again, but I can't stop from floating back to that night, back to the chain-link fence in the Vortex parking lot, resigned to let the darkness engulf me.

"So, my process," he continues. I resist the urge to groan. "You know as well as I do that investigations run very differently today than they did back then. I'll do my part, tell the story, but we will work closely together. So, it's key to the success of this project that you and I trust each other."

"I don't trust anyone."

"Given your history, I understand that, but I believe, in time, I can earn it."

He might be used to getting what he wants, but he doesn't understand how far I'll go to protect the lone shred of peace in my life that remains. "Let me ask you something," I say. "Why me?"

Isaac moves his espresso cup onto its tray as if he storyboarded the action, then launches into his pitch. "I see your story as a cautionary tale of a young girl, of nature versus nurture. When the world failed her, she fought back. She triumphed. She became an unlikely hero at the ripe age of sixteen. It's universal. It's timely, especially today. Now look at you, all grown up. If I didn't know what happened to you, what you did, who your parents are, and I passed you on the street, I might think you're just another striking woman in this city."

I blush and instantly loathe myself for being susceptible to his flattery.

"See, you are so much more than that," he says. Out of habit, I watch his Adam's apple, analyze it, imagine how it tastes. *Tart or sweet. Grass or rain.* "You turned what happened into a career. You changed the discussion. You paved the way for what true crime is today. Color me impressed."

I will not be swayed by a man who, if he gets his way, if I let my guard down, could destroy everything I've accomplished. "Why you?"

Isaac claps, pleased, prepared to answer the question. "Because you need me. You might not want to admit it, but your profile's waning. Your fans will move on, if they haven't already. If you don't reintroduce yourself to today's true crime buffs, you're out of luck. I have direct access to the ones who matter and will keep you afloat. We do this right, and we're both sitting pretty. I'll make another hit. You'll reap the benefits of book sales and secure yourself another few years in the limelight. Isn't that what you want?"

His correct assumption stings. "I haven't agreed to anything."

"I'm not sure what they told you." Isaac cocks his head to the side like an innocent pup. "I'm making this documentary with or without you," he declares, like it would be ludicrous for him to consider my participation mandatory.

This is a setup. I want to fire Julian and Malin. I grit my teeth so hard they might crack. I want to run as fast as I can, but something stops me.

The night in the greenhouse all those years ago stops me.

I sip my latte to regain my composure. "If I say yes, what would that entail?"

"I'll bring a small crew, as small as possible, to ensure you're comfortable, and we'll talk."

I can handle an interview. I've weathered countless interviews, from expert journalists and late-night comedians to law enforcement officers and magazine fluff writers. "I will need to approve the questions ahead of time."

"This is a conversation."

*Jesus.* "A conversation." I perform, like the puppet he wants me to be. "With you?"

"And others, of course." Isaac scribbles in his Moleskine notebook, and it immediately reminds me of Arthur's. "I'll design a shooting schedule that follows the narrative I have in mind and stagger conversations with several people from your past over the course of filming. I'm thinking three weeks, more if we need. How's Monday after next for a start date? Your team said you were available."

I worry my heartbeat's loud enough for him to hear. "Who wants to talk?"

"You may have your own idea about how it should be done," Isaac lectures, in a condescending manner I don't appreciate. "This is a methodology that works for me. You'll see, by the end, why."

"You didn't answer my question."

"Don't you think it's fair everyone gets the opportunity to tell their stories too?" His fingers brush mine as he reaches across the table for a napkin. "That's what you always say, right?" He wipes his patchy five-o'clock shadow and crumples the napkin between his naked fingers. I bet he'd say he's married to his craft. He tosses the soiled napkin into his empty cup.

"So, are you in?"

DURING THE TWO WEEKS BEFORE SHOOTING BEGINS, JULIAN hounds my lawyer daily for updates on the doc contract and irons out the anniversary-edition deal with the publishers. Isaac sends a disturbingly chipper kickoff email, and it reads like everyone else but me is in on the joke. Malin replies to me privately, listing off a series of questions that I may be asked, trying to justify her inflated fees. The questions blink on my computer screen, taunting me. Questions I refuse to answer in the privacy of my bedroom, let alone say into a mic pack. But I need this to work. It has to work. The alternative is not an option.

I'm well aware of the fact that most viewers are going to compare photos of my parents and make their judgments of who I grew up to resemble the most. They'll point to Max's nose and Diana's heart-shaped face. They'll drool over Mom's buttery skin in those old music videos until they stumble upon Odette's *Rolling Stone* cover, baring it all, lithe and ferocious, and forget all about me.

So I drop several hundred on a Hydrafacial and two grand updating my wardrobe with effortless, minimalist pieces. My hairdresser trims my bangs and gives my color a refresh. I ask the nail technician for a sophisticated taupe. When she asks me what shape I want—coffin or almond—I choose the latter.

If I'm going to grace the living rooms of America and beyond, I might as well look my best doing it. I model each new look in the full-length mirror in my bedroom and assess my appearance from all angles.

I will make them look at me. I will not be forgotten.

*Production Day 1*

# DOWNTOWN LOS ANGELES

ISAAC ARRIVES TEN MINUTES BEFORE OUR AGREED-UPON START time. When I invite him into my downtown loft, I see he's not alone. The whole crew lingers behind him, arms full of equipment, sleeves full of tattoos. A lanky cameraman snaps his gum at me. One woman with a shock of blue hair sticks out in the jumble of men.

Isaac enters without introducing his crew. "Morning."

I step aside to let these pests invade my home. I'd figured Isaac would want to film at a studio, but he insisted we start the process here, that it would be more intimate. "I was just about to make some coffee."

"Black's fine," Isaac says before I offer him any. He strolls across the loft in his Blundstone boots and begins to dissect every object I own. His first stop is my bookshelves on the far brick wall, meticulously arranged by genre, then author. Isaac plucks the French edition of *Rattlesnake* off the tallest driftwood floating shelf and flips through it absentmindedly, as if it is nothing more than an ancient magazine at a dentist's office.

"Anything I can get you?" I ask the woman, who is organizing a stack of papers. "I'm sorry, I didn't catch your name."

"Oh, right." Isaac places the French edition back on the shelf and skims the back of Alice Bolin's *Dead Girls*. "Lucy, meet my assistant—"

"Sloane," she says, finishing Isaac's sentence. She smiles, tight-lipped, apparently unaccustomed to Isaac recognizing her, but there's a flicker of personality beneath her reserve. She's pretty, with graceful features, but she's chosen to obscure every delicate part of her. A trail of spiky earrings crawls up her ear, and she's fresh-faced save for the jet-black eyeliner smudged on her lash line, an oversized ripped sweater and baggy jeans slung over her slender frame. And of course her hair, electric blue and shagged, is hard to ignore. The kind of marker to suggest she's tried and maybe succeeded in rejecting the expectations placed on her.

"If you need anything during the shoot, anything at all, Sloane's your girl," Isaac informs me. "Coffee, a break, issue with scheduling—call Sloane, okay?"

Of course, the one woman on Isaac's payroll has been assigned as my go-to. God forbid I order around some unsuspecting Chad to fetch me tampons. I cross to the open kitchen to retrieve some mugs. "So, coffee? No coffee?" Sloane's lips part, and I recognize that look—she's starstruck, befuddled that the real Lucy Golden is talking to her, I'm sure. Sloane fails to respond to my offer, mindful not to take up too much space, as assistants are advised to do in this town, even though her boss can't be that much older than her. I know how foreign it feels for strangers to pay you any mind when you moved through your entire childhood invisible.

Mom emerges from her bedroom, making a grand entrance, her wide-leg trousers swishing with each step. She introduces herself to Isaac and holds out her hand like she's expecting him to kiss the ring. "Diana Golden."

"Pleasure." Isaac shakes her hand. Her face falls when she realizes he's wearing a faded concert T-shirt from Odette's first stadium tour. He registers her expression. "Hope she's doing well. I'm a big fan."

At the mention of her estranged elder daughter, Mom makes no attempts to mask her brutal death glare and joins me at the counter. She side-eyes the camera crew's lighting choices and performatively gulps down her array of Chinese herbs. Isaac confers with his crew about the setup, assessing how best to control the morning sun coming in the floor-to-ceiling steel-framed windows as it slices across the concrete floor.

A black stream of coffee fills the pot and perfumes the air. Mom mutters under her breath, "You think filming here is a good idea?"

"Not really something I can discuss at the moment," I whisper back.

Mom grazes her black-cherry nails along her neck. I sense she wants me to offer up information about Odette unprompted, but her patience wears thin. "Have you spoken to her lately?"

"A few weeks ago." I'm careful about how much information I pass between them. "She's back at the beach."

"You didn't think to inform me?" She watches the camera operator test the white balance against the windows suspiciously.

I start to apologize, but Isaac calls out to her before I can. "Diana, I would love to find some time for you to participate."

A smug pout forms on her painted face. "I'm due at the gallery," she announces, ignoring his request. In seconds, she plucks her Prada bag off the hook by the door, waggles her fingers in a wave, and flees.


BY THE TIME I SETTLE INTO THE GREEN VELVET ARMCHAIR THAT'S been carefully staged by the window, then in front of the desk, then back at the window again, my coffee's cold. Isaac asks my permission to begin, with a lift of his eyebrows. I acquiesce. It's showtime.

"Well, here we are," says Isaac.

"So it appears."

Isaac taps his foot in deep concentration, his copy of *Rattlesnake* open and cracking across his lap, so worn the spine's bound to break.

I cross my legs; I'm conscious my image is taking up Isaac's frame, aware of the people who will see this one day. I imagine them bingeing late into a Tuesday night, iPads pulled up to their noses. The glow of the blue light illuminating their bedrooms as they consume my life's tragedy before they drift off to a Trazodone-induced sleep.

"So, you live with your mother, Diana, these days?" Isaac attempts to break the ice.

"She's staying with me, actually." I make the distinction. "Temporarily."

"How would you describe your mother's romantic life growing up? From what you can remember."

"Romantic life?" I hesitate, unnerved by Isaac's question and clear preference for his subject's mother over his subject. I'm appalled he thinks his obvious pandering is how he'll earn my trust. Still, I consider my answer. Mom's relationships with men were even more transactional than the ones she fostered with her muses, undoubtedly feeding the fame machine. I offer my textbook response to this common inquiry. "A lot of men entered and exited her jewel-box bedroom throughout my childhood. I suppose having children with two different fathers gave her another way of looking at the opposite sex. Purely for function, to satiate a certain need. A few of them stayed longer than others. Some came back around after they'd been gone for years, wrongly assuming they could change her. Some tried to play stepfather by disciplining us or taking us out for ice cream. Most ignored us."

I shift in my seat, on edge, wondering if my response sounded too forced.

"How did the fifteen-year-old you think about love?" Isaac asks.

I'm amused Isaac's treading so lightly, interested in my adolescent brain's understanding of something so trivial. "I asked Mom about love once when she kicked an old boyfriend out of the house. I'll never forget it. She said, 'It is the nature of man to assume he is God's gift to the world, believing himself superior because of the violent knot that hangs between his legs.' I was six."

The assistant camera operator, a scruffy guy wearing a beanie, attempts to clear a tickle in his throat without the boom mic picking it up.

Sloane scribbles something on her clipboard, and Isaac shifts his focus, nodding. Steam rises in me at this secret exchange. I can't resist asking the question that woke me up at two a.m., when the green-house floor often materializes in my mind's eye. "Hold on. Can I ask you something?"

Isaac looks up from Sloane's clipboard, as if he's been caught passing notes in a middle-school classroom. "What is it?"

"Will we . . ." I hesitate. Sloane gapes at me. "Are you planning to shoot in the desert?" It took me a long time to trust my intuition again, but I somehow know with every fiber of my being that I will be forced to return to that patch of earth I once knew as home. Whether Isaac drags me there by the neck or I go willingly, into the burning ring of fire.

"Yes," Isaac confirms. "At the end of the shoot, we'll go to the Oasis."

That word, that encompasses so much of me and my nightmares, my wanting, stabs at my eardrums, and swiftly, I free-fall. Tumbling backward, past rattlesnake skins and dandelions, the night that changed everything and the red wool blanket. I can almost hear their voices, the women I used to call my sisters, singing their siren song. Back to where I swore I'd never set foot again.

"Lucy?"

I realize that I've totally missed whatever he just said. I smile, trying to disarm him with some charm. "Sorry, can you repeat the question?"

"Can you close your eyes for me?"

I laugh. "You're kidding, right?"

"Indulge me," Isaac says, grinning crookedly. "I want you to go back to the beginning, to the day the Fowlers moved onto Marina Avenue. The day that started it all."

If he wants a performance, that's what he'll get. I'm Diana Golden's daughter, after all. Isaac will be eating out of the palm of my hand in no time. If he's not already.

I think back to that day, the sun on my face and ocean breeze tangling my hair. The Hotel Del towering over the Coronado coastline, towheaded surfers launching their boards into the Pacific waves. Sunburned kids dragging their beach toys along the shore, their little feet hot on the sand. Back then, the summer of 2002 appeared picture-perfect, but now when I look closer, I see the cracks. I taste the salt, the paranoia.

All along, that summer had teeth. It promised to bite, and it did. It swallowed me whole.

"Okay," Isaac says, seemingly satisfied by whatever misty introspection my face emotes. I flip my eyes open, hell-bent on doing what I do best.

Telling stories.

"Comb through your memories . . . what you saw, what you heard, what you believed." Isaac tries to hypnotize me back there. "Take your time. What do you remember?"

"I remember everything," I say, because as much as I will myself to forget, I do.

# CORONADO, CALIFORNIA

*June 2002*
*72 days before*

In the nine months since that tragic Tuesday morning, Coronado found a way to keep going. We kids returned to school, and the adults returned to work. We wore brave faces. We shopped for our groceries on Sundays and rolled our garbage cans to the curb on Thursdays. To an outsider, it might have appeared as if everything was normal, how it was before, but without fanfare, without saying it out loud, we started to lock our doors.

When the Fowlers arrived that summer, we could no longer pretend nothing had changed. Rumor had it the Fowlers had fled their native Manhattan abruptly and bought the pink house sight unseen. The family's striking presence on our block, their marked claim on the pink house I coveted, reminded us that we, too, were susceptible to the dangers of the world beyond our little island.

I pretended to adjust my bike seat as movers unloaded the boxes inside, sweating. I glimpsed a few rigidly polite smiles the father aimed at them. The kind that signaled, *I'm a nice guy, I swear, but we don't need to engage in small talk.* He was tall and lean, handsome in that anonymous, white-collar way. He sorted through the boxes on the front porch, scanning the labels. His presence irritated me, but I quickly chalked up my distaste to envy. There he was—a father, a husband, a man who stuck around.

The wife wore a fitted powder-blue tracksuit and a matching wide visor that obscured her face as she surveyed flowers in the garden. The son stretched out on the porch swing, bulky headphones framing his dark hair. He was tall like his father, focused like his mother. He had a brooding quality to him I was unaccustomed to witnessing in boys my age, perhaps the effect of an East Coast boarding school or a premature misreading of *Catcher in the Rye*. I had wondered what it might be like to encounter an elusive boy next door—or, rather, a boy across the street— all summer. I'd heard about these mythical creatures in pop songs and watched them in the romantic comedies Odette flipped past on TV. To suddenly see one, alive and well, unnerved me. To see one so comfortably taking up space in the pink house, my beloved pink house, stung like an act of betrayal.

The pink house was one of those white-picket-fence numbers with lush garden beds, storybook shutters, and an American flag flapping in the wind like it was ripped out of a Pottery Barn catalog. The house was built for a family like the Fowlers, intended for a nuclear unit I'd never been a part of. I'd always loved it, for as long as I could remember. It was the same shade as a shell I once stole from the ocean floor. I spent hours sitting on our front porch looking across the street, turning that shell over in my palm, rubbing it smooth, daydreaming about what it might be like to have a father who mowed the lawn and pressed Band-Aids to my scraped knees, to carry on with the sense of calm achieved from living in that kind of splendor every day. That was the life the house across the street offered.

It existed just out of my reach.

MARTINI IN HAND, MOM RIFLED THROUGH HER BUSTING-AT-THE-SEAMS closet. The synth of disco from her record player pulsed through the sea breeze drifting in through the bay window. She bounced her hip to the beat of the song with a seductive, knowing ease.

"Is now a good time?" I asked from the doorway, hoping she'd pull me into a hug and congratulate me on a job well done.

Spinning around, her colorful caftan hovered behind her and the camera slung around her neck swayed. I knew from the second our eyes met: praise was not in my near future. "Why not?"

I plopped down on the settee and helped myself to a bowl of cherries. "The new neighbors arrived," I told her. "In the pink house."

She extracted a vintage Halston from its hanger and tossed it onto the bed. "Pray tell."

"Word is they're from New York." The tartness of the cherry puckered my mouth. "Manhattan. I can't imagine what they've been through. It must have been awful. I mean, can you even imagine? I wonder if they know anyone who . . ."

The electricity in the air shifted. I looked up to see an incredulous sneer on Mom's milk-white, heart-shaped face. "You're stalling, aren't you?"

It was difficult to mask any shred of anxiety from Mom. Although she occasionally guest lectured at art colleges around the country, she didn't believe you could teach art. *You either have it or you don't.* I worried that was how she looked at me—like I was one of her admirers destined for mediocrity and a string of disappointments.

In what I liked to think was a calculated move, I had written a tall tale about a road trip with my father behind the wheel. Aside from craving her praise for the writing itself, I hoped the mention of my father might spark empathy within her and she might finally tell me what I deserved to know—who my father was and why he'd left me behind. I was on the precipice of turning sixteen, and all summer, all my life, I'd begged her for answers to questions she refused to indulge.

"Well, did you like it?"

Mom gestured to the stack on her bedside table. I went to retrieve it and gulped when I saw her red pen marks scattered across the first page. "You know, I can just call Pauline." She rifled through more gowns. "There's no shame in getting into the workshop that way. It's what a lot of people do."

I could tell by the way she said *people* that she meant *untalented nobodies*. Pauline Donovan, an awarded novelist, opened up applications for her writing workshop to exceptional high school students in the San Diego area. I'd spent the summer agonizing over piece after piece for the application, due in a matter of weeks. Every single one, Mom rejected.

"I don't want a handout," I said for the twelfth time. "Maybe I'm not ready."

Mom settled into the throne of her vintage chaise and lit a joint. "Criticism is important for any artist to hear."

"That's easy for you to say!"

"I've had my critics," Mom said, and searing pain flashed in her emerald eyes. "You remember that *Chronicle* piece? Philistine . . ." She pursed her lips, revisiting the single dreadful review in her otherwise revered career.

I scanned the pages for any phrase I could salvage. "Just tell me what I need to do to get better."

"She wants to know what you have to say." Mom exhaled a cloud of smoke. "You had the audacity to lie."

"So you've never posed a model for the shot that you wanted?"

Mom rolled her eyes. "Lucy, think about my exhibit from '97. The series of my former lovers in the shower. Without my interpretation, it could be deemed pedestrian, but it dove right into intimacy. To be an artist, you need to have a voice."

I dropped my chin and spoke my worst fear into existence. "Maybe I'm not like you. Maybe I don't have a voice."

"Well, it's better you find that out when you're young."

I felt like I'd been slapped. "But I want it. Doesn't that matter?"

Mom kept it cool, her voice as husky as her idol Barbara Stanwyck's. "You can't expect to engage your audience if you're not active in your own life. Take a risk. It won't kill you."

The papers turned sharp in my hands, as if they could slice my fingers clean off. "I thought this was a risk."

She discarded ash into her jade ashtray. "Everybody *wants* it. You have to have the goods to back it up. A great artist takes chances. You hide in your shell, cower in your room, check off boxes like a little school mouse, make up ridiculous stories that lack substance, and then you expect a pat on the head. You observe life, but you don't live it. Just think, earlier, you gawked at the neighbors from New York, but did it ever occur to you to introduce yourself? To step in frame? If you choose to be a coward, your art, if you can call it that, will suffer."

I stared at a spot on the rug, ashamed to fall apart in her presence. Mom rolled her neck and offered a bold suggestion. "Listen, if you want to try, take advantage of your youth while you can." She scanned me up and down. "Start with your outfit."

"What's wrong with this?"

"You're not a kid anymore. Someone might notice you if you stop dressing like one."

I tugged at my cotton dress, mortified. It was a shapeless mauve blob. My white sneakers were partly untied, tinged with dirt. My dishwater-brown hair hung past my shoulders, without a bounce to speak of. She was right. I did not possess a single ounce of her luster. I saw the way men looked at my mother. Then there was her work, her iconic photographs, each collection more arresting than the last. I couldn't fathom how I was related to her.

At the time, I believed the reason I failed to live up to her standards was simple: I was not hers. No, I was my father's daughter.

"If you want to tell a great story one day, you can't wait around for things to happen to you." Mom nursed her shrinking martini. A bitter-sweet charm emanated from her, the air hazy with smoke. "You have to be brave."

# DOWNTOWN LOS ANGELES

SLOANE SLIDES A PIECE OF PAPER ACROSS THE COFFEE TABLE BE-tween us. It's a copy of the photograph of my father I kept hidden in my nightstand throughout my childhood. To this day, it's one of Mom's biggest sellers. The photograph defines her early aesthetic, the off-kilter framing, the generous use of negative space. The subject's positioned in front of a cloudless sky. A prismed geometric shape sits above his right shoulder. I never could quite make it out. On the back of the original, my mother scribbled "MAX, 1985" in her messy scrawl in blotted ink. The year before I was born.

I trace my thumb over the dark-haired figure with piercing features and a five-o'clock shadow. The man who made me. Back then, it was the single piece of him I owned, the lone proof he existed, apart from the heaving lungs in my chest. I slide it back across the table and nod at Isaac to get on with it. I need to appear self-assured but *never* defensive. A fine balance to strike.

"What did you know about him before that summer?" Isaac asks.

"Only his name," I say, monitoring my expression. "How would you formulate a person made of flesh, bone, habits, and eccentricities from a five-by-seven image taken before you were even born?"

"I don't know that you could . . ." Isaac replies, bristling at my po-etic reply. "So, what did you tell yourself back then?" he prods. "About your father. Who was he to you?"

"You know the phrase 'absent father'?" I muse. Isaac blinks at me. "You know, 'do you have an absent father? Is your father absent?' Like he's home sick with the flu, with a daytime soap blaring in the background, and therefore, he cannot raise his hand when his name's called to declare himself present. I always struggled to find the correct response when someone asked me that. Did he tuck me in with a bedtime story and show up at my dance recitals, watermelon-colored carnations in hand? No, never, but he made his presence known. When I looked in the mirror, all I saw was this stranger. Even now. The uncanny resemblance can't be denied. I always knew there was this *other* inside me, a facet that did not match my mother or my sister. Something powerful. So, I hated him, and I wanted him. There was no separation between the two impulses. Only one and the same."

We let my admission simmer for a moment. I relish it briefly—the sizzle of my performance.

Suddenly, Isaac signals to the camera operator to cut. The crew starts to break down their gear.

"I'm sorry, are we done here?"

"For today," Isaac announces without ceremony. The sound guy encroaches on my personal space to untangle me from the mic pack.

How had I only managed to capture his attention for a sliver of time? I gave him pure 24 karat gold. In a flash, I imagine Isaac canceling the documentary altogether. My publisher pulling out of the anniversary edition. My inevitable fall into obscurity imminent.

"I thought we were filming until six." I glance at the clock on the wall. It isn't even noon. "I cleared my whole day for this."

Isaac and Sloane exchange an indecipherable glance; then he hands his things to her to pack up, like he's a kindergartner unable to keep track of his lunch box. Isaac motions me over to my corner desk.

Pouting, I cross my arms in front of my chest. "What is it?"

Isaac clears his throat. "I told you this was a conversation."

I squint at him. "Go on."

"The thing is . . ." Isaac scratches his neck, and red lines appear instantly on his skin. "You need to loosen up. It sounds like you've rehearsed all your responses."

"How could I have rehearsed when you didn't let me know the questions ahead of time, huh? Riddle me that."

"You're coming across . . ." Isaac bites his bottom lip, searching for the right word.

"Spit it out."

"Come on, 'absent father,' 'jewel-box bedroom,' 'watermelon-colored carnations in hand' . . ." He condescendingly quotes me back to me. "Tell me you just made that up on the spot and I'll back off, but it's important that my work is representative of real-life conversations, revelations in real time. I'm not a gorilla who calls action for some overly choreographed, prewritten soliloquy so you can push your PR machine's agenda. My work is about authenticity. All you have to do is speak your truth."

I ignore the sinking feeling in my gut. Sure, maybe I'd stolen a line or two from something I'd written on my very own laptop, but so what? I resented his implication that I was somehow shielding him from "my truth."

"Tell me, Isaac," I say. "Why do you want to do this now? What is it you're looking for?"

His mouth twitches. "I have reason to believe there's new information about this case."

I force a smile. "What new information?"

"Remember what you agreed to, okay?" Isaac turns away from me to fold his director's chair. A crew member takes it from him before he can finish, like he's the queen bee and all these people-pleasing worker bees slave away and submit to his holy ways without protest. He lays a hand on my shoulder and stoops slightly to meet my eyes. "You need to trust my process."

ONCE ISAAC AND HIS CREW LEAVE, WITH THE REMINDER THAT they'll be back tomorrow for round two, the loft stills, save for the wails of the air conditioner. It's quiet enough for Isaac's offensive insinuation and thinly veiled threat to somersault around my brain.

I can see the trailer now, narrated with an over-the-top voiceover. *"You thought you knew everything about this crime, until now. Tune in for the explosive new findings in the Lucy Golden case."*

I need to get out of here.

I pull my shirt over my head, disgusted by the dank sweat in the armpits, and toss it into the hamper. In the bathroom, I blast some new music that a fan recommended to me, lather my skin, and scrub away Isaac's infantilizing approach. He should be so lucky to capture a single minute of my time. When I step onto the bathmat, I change the speakers to Odette's fourth album, the one that divided critics.

Diving headfirst into Mom's closet, I search for something to wear to take myself out on the town—high on the idea of slipping into someone else's skin. For my inspiration for the evening, I choose Phyllis, the bored yet bold housewife Barbara Stanwyck plays in *Double Indemnity*. Wearing an anklet is out of the question. Unlike Mom, I do not have Barbara Stanwyck's supermodel legs. Instead, a cream silk blouse hanging in the back of her closet calls to me.

I could just have a drink, so I can feel like a regular person. Not Lucy Golden, hero to many, monster to few. I could tip well and go home at the end of the night. Alone.

I could behave.

TONIGHT'S COCKTAIL BAR OF CHOICE OOZES WITH THAT OLD Hollywood, vintage feel: black-and-white tile floors, low lighting, deep leather banquettes, crystal decanters on display. The place is populated with men who know the difference between bourbon and rye and haughty women who pretend their impeccably styled ensembles are mere afterthoughts. When a barstool opens up, I slide onto it before anyone else can. The bartender wipes down the bar and mutters in my direction. I order a martini, then scout my prey.

A group of talent agent types holds court in a corner booth, fresh off the clock and away from their desks in their Century City sky-scrapers, sleeves rolled up, jackets in a heap. The testosterone's intoxicating even from ten feet away. I try not to stare, but looking at these clean-shaven, aggressive men thrills me. The way they pound each other's backs like they're on a sports field, their muscles pulsing as they suck down craft beer and mezcal. My primal instincts kick in. I'm the one in control here. I'm the woman of mystery, wearing red lipstick, alone at a bar. Loneliness is best served with glamour.

One by one, they recognize my presence. After a brief discussion, one of them is nominated to do their worst. He's generically handsome—dark hair, six feet tall, broad-shouldered. A vacancy lurks behind his eyes that I know too well from looking into my sister's.

"Waiting on someone?"

"Could be," I say. It's like a scene out of a movie. A flirtation that could have been penned by one of their Hollywood clients.

He commandeers the stool next to me. His cologne's woodsy, with a touch of Clorox. The slightest gap between his two front teeth reminds me of an old friend. I push the thought away.

"You gotta admire a woman who enjoys her martinis. Vodka or gin?"

"Vodka."

He scowls.

"You taste the olives more that way."

"Ah, so you prefer it dirty," he says. Even he can't keep a straight face. I laugh, my incisors exposed, testing him to see if he recognizes my infamous smile, the one the press described often during the trial coverage.

"Jeremy." He extends his meaty hand. "You look familiar." Does he see infamous killer Lucy Golden or siren of the summer Barbara Stanwyck? I wait for him to reveal himself. "Do I know you?"

This is what it means to be on the verge of C-list celebrity status. Right now, he's questioning if I'm the intern he ghosted back when he worked in the mailroom at CAA, if he saw me guest star on a Shonda Rhimes show, or if I'm truly a nobody in his sphere of influence.

"No, I don't think so." He answers his own question, because he's either lazy or doesn't care as long as he gets to take me home.

So tonight I'll be the everywoman, safe from the fetishists whom my reputation tempts. Even though I'm enjoying this flirtation, I want to speed past all the pickup chatter and skip ahead. I want to see this man unleash his carnal desires. I want to see him morph into what I need him to be: a wolf in the night.

Suddenly, I feel a set of eyes on me that aren't Jeremy's. I survey the room, but there's nothing out of the ordinary. I shake off my paranoia and blame it on Isaac's cold accusation. I turn back to tonight's play-thing, who has no idea what game he's in for once he rounds the bend and passes go.

I tug on his belt. "Ready?"

Jeremy throws a twenty on the bar with one hand, the other low on my back. His table of coworkers erupts, hooting and hollering. The bartender looks me over, but I'm not embarrassed. The hoopla spurs my animal need for him more. We stumble out of the bar. While he hands the valet his ticket, his mouth is in my hair.

BEFORE HE UNLOCKS THE DOOR TO HIS SPANISH-STYLE LOS FELIZ duplex, his hand's already up my skirt, his fingers like bliss, like fire. I pulse beneath his touch and bite his neck, ravenous with desire. He spins me around. I brace myself against his cluttered counter. He fucks me from behind. I feel hot all over, feverish and feral. This is what I needed. I arch my back. My insides tighten around him.

"Please, Lucy," he says. "Call me Daddy."

My vision blurs. *Motherfucker.*

He knows exactly who I am.

All his mind-numbing appeal is zapped in a flash. This was a mis-take. A stupid mistake made all because of some hack's vague threat. Nothing feels good anymore. He shudders, coming inside me like a teenager. I feel ill, my feet like lead, my body separate from the rest of me. While he ambles to the bathroom to clean himself off, I pull down my skirt and button my blouse. I throw my hair back into a ponytail, repulsed by the sweat that's formed from this act I already regret. He's no wolf—just another vulture, scavenging his way through sick fantasies, talon by talon. By the time he emerges from the bathroom, shirtless, in his boxers, with a satisfied expression on his face, I've gathered my things.

"Where are you going?" he whines.

I walk over to him slowly, to tease his craving for round two. He grins as I get closer, reaches out to paw my breast through my blouse. To his horror, I pivot, knocking over his costly bar display. I'm intoxicated by the crash of shattered glass, louder than I anticipated. A familiar cacophony that rattles me daily. It's invigorating to be the source. To claim it.

His jaw falls open. "What the fuck?"

For good measure, I grab an intact bottle of WhistlePig. A well-earned souvenir for dealing with another scumbag like Jeremy.

"It was just dirty talk! Can't you take a joke?" he shouts as I leave his place. "You crazy bitch! That's aged twelve years!"

I walk three blocks to Hillhurst before I call a car, thrilled by my racing pulse. I take a pull from the WhistlePig and try to relive how it felt the last time, being touched. I used to keep a list of these transitory men. I used to give them monikers: Brit from *No More Heroes*, the Stuntman, the Dominant. I used to care if they called. I used to scheme that one of them, one day, would father my child and buy me a pink house. I used to think that was possible.

When the car arrives, I climb into the fabric-covered back seat, which reeks of Axe body spray. Through my liquor haze comes the tunnel vision. My fingers are tapping away on my phone before I make the conscious decision to tell them that's what I need them to do. I refuse to let Jeremy ruin a perfectly fine evening.

There are some recent likes on my post about the She Slays event. Reposts by the attendees who paid for a picture with me. I like every single one. Familiar usernames comment. A novel-length message from a girl from Ohio who thanks me for changing her life and giving her the courage to speak up. Each ping grants me the momentary serotonin boost I need to keep going and remind myself it's all worth it. They believe me. They need me.

We haven't announced the documentary officially yet, because we're still waiting on Isaac's inane quote about how excited he is to work with me. Still, it doesn't stop me from logging in under my fake account and spreading the rumor. It only takes ten minutes for my comment to gain traction. I strive to focus on the giddiness of the fans, but the vultures find a way in, starved like they always are.

FreddyKrugerFanatix00: There's no way this is true! LG can suck it.

LizzieBorden23: Best news ever! I can't freaking wait.

TexWatson86: About time that pyscho slut's put in her place.

desertdoll692: Will it end in a fairy tale or a bloodbath?!?!

As we barrel toward downtown, a new message pops up. The user's profile picture is a faceless avatar. No posts. No followers. A video's attached. I click on it and see it's of the disruption at the Orpheum. The shooter zooms in on my face, so close the video turns grainy. My blurred image watches intently as the intruder's taken away by security. I hold my thumb over the video to pause it, forever questioning how my expression reads to someone else, how it might read to the others who are still out there. I'm reminded of that sensation from earlier, at the bar, the unnerving suspicion that someone might be following me. I wonder if he's still watching, keeping tabs, trusting, like always, that I'll keep our secrets.

"Excuse me, can you please circle the block a few times?" I ask the driver, paranoid enough to want to verify that the coast is clear. He sighs but complies once I promise him a generous tip, which I will never send.

Back at the loft, as Mom's sound machine lulls her to sleep, I watch *Mildred Pierce* and order enough Thai delivery to feed a family of four.

When I spill short rib on Mom's blouse, I throw it down the trash chute and hope she doesn't notice its absence.

Bleary-eyed and bloated, I tangle myself up in my sheets, a pillow between my legs as I fantasize about the temporary relief of a man there instead, but men like Jeremy only see me for what I've done, for the fantasy I'm capable of fulfilling.

I squeeze my eyes shut, rake through my memories of *Rattlesnake*, and stew over Isaac's warning. Finding out whatever new information this crook thinks he knows is the only option.

The only chance I'll claw my way out of this mess alive.

# CORONADO

*68 days before*

Following Odette's instructions to avoid the ID check, Arthur pulled me through the back door of the Vortex, past the sticker-covered greenroom stinking of body odor. My head on a swivel, I watched Odette, mid-gig, unaware of our tardiness, head-to-toe in leather. Odette inherited Mom's confidence and cheekbones, her late father's stage presence and raven-black hair. With the howl of Janis and soul of Alanis, Odette entertained the twenty-somethings and unwashed teens with fake IDs. Half of them comprised her local groupies and sang along, shrieking the lyrics. The other half were distracted by their own vices making them feel something, anything, or nothing at all.

The bald bouncer with gauged earlobes signaled to Arthur. I wondered if Arthur spent his nights here, after he left the cozy cocoon of our house. A month after 9/11, Mom had returned from a Palm Springs weekend gushing over a photograph taken by "a kid with promise" and designated twenty-five-year-old Arthur Weyland as her apprentice. He traipsed around our house like it was his own, fixed Mom's camera blunders, and inserted his opinion wherever and whenever he could. He was the first man in a while to stick around for longer than a weekend. Though, occasionally, he embraced the life of a nomad, going up the coast for a few weeks, what he called "an experiment in his performance art." Even in his absence, a perpetual token of his manliness remained, like the grease stain his truck imprinted on the driveway. The combination of his solid chest, self-assuredness, and baritone voice made my toes curl with a new, raw kind of panic. When he looked me over, sometimes I liked to believe I sparked a similar chemical reaction within him too.

After depositing me in the corner booth, Arthur snuck away to the bar. I scanned the room, looking for any familiar faces, and waved to Judy Temple, Moroccan-American drag queen and Mom's latest muse currently crashing in our guest room.

Judy sauntered over to me. "Lucy, honey, you're sprouting up like a weed. Looking more and more like your mama every day. Is she here?"

"Migraine," I told her. "Are you singing tonight?"

"Gig uptown." Judy cracked her toothy smile.

Arthur returned to the table with a whiskey for himself and a spiked lemonade for me. Judy shook the ice in her own cocktail. "Up to no good, I trust?"

Arthur smirked at Judy and clinked his glass against hers. Judy kissed me on both cheeks, then returned to her group of friends.

"Your mom said your birthday's coming up," Arthur said.

"Sixteen."

"All grown up."

I forced down a big gulp of lemonade. "You think so?"

He gestured toward the stage. As he turned, I caught a glimpse of a curl on the nape of his neck. "She certainly knows how to command a crowd."

I watched Arthur watching Odette. His lips were so red, like he'd been sucking on a cherry lollipop. I hoped he didn't think I was trying too hard to look like my sister, a feat I would never master, no matter how many outfits I stole from her closet.

The song ended with a fancy flourish on the drums. As the applause thundered, Odette breathed into the microphone. "Thank you. That was fun." She picked up an old guitar out of its case, a classic black Gibson. "This guitar belonged to my dad." Odette plucked the strings as she introduced the next song. Envy poured out of me. She was lucky she owned something concrete of her father's that she could hold in her hands. "This one's for him."

My mother met Jesse Quinn when she was Odette's age— nineteen. After she lost her parents, she took her sizable inheritance and her long legs from Coronado all the way to Sunset Boulevard and walked right into one of Jesse's shows at the Whiskey a Go Go. He completely missed his cue because he couldn't take his eyes off the redhead in the crowd. He'd found his muse.

Everyone idolized Jesse and Diana, but they only knew each other for a year before a housekeeper at the Chateau Marmont found his body, cold, in the bathtub of his drug-laden suite. Another star lost to the 27 Club. Soon after, Mom pivoted to photography. Her first exhibit made a huge splash in LA art circles and her enigmatic persona quickly became part of the cultural zeitgeist. The dead rock star's pregnant girlfriend's private photographs became synonymous with Jesse's gone-too-soon legacy and effectively launched her career.

Arthur traced his finger around the rim of his glass. "So, tell me. How's the writing coming along?"

"It's not."

"Shame." Arthur stretched his arms back, using his hands to support his head. A sliver of his black Moleskine poked out the top of his shirt pocket. He never went anywhere without it. "You don't know how powerful you are."

"Powerful?" The proclamation rang false in my ear. "I'm not the one with rock-star blood in my veins."

"You can't create anything if you pretend like you don't have any effect on the world around you." He put his large hands on the dingy table separating us. "I see you. You affect me."

"I do?" I ducked my head into my chest in disbelief. "Why are you so interested?"

"Are you kidding?" Arthur's stony face grew more expressive as he swirled his whiskey. "Maybe your father's not Jesse Quinn, but if he's one of the long-lost great loves of Diana Golden, I'm nothing but interested."

"Because you wish you were one of them?"

"You've got some wild ideas." Arthur laughed off the suggestion as preposterous, but it was unclear why he clung to my mother the way he did. Was it because of her reputation as an artist? Or did he want to take her to bed and fuck the feminist rhetoric she preached but did not follow right out of her?

"Isn't she old enough to be your mother?" I shot back.

"First off, age is a bullshit construct," Arthur lectured. "You're fifteen—most people would say that makes you a child. Do you feel like a child?" I shook my head, and he pressed on. "Second, I am many things, but being one of your mother's lovers is not one of them." He glanced over toward the bar, where a gaggle of girls in bandana tops checked him out. "So, where is he, then? Your old man."

I searched my vault of lies for something to say that might keep him intrigued. "He's in jail," I blurted out. "For hurting women." I regretted it as soon as I said it.

"Isn't that what all men do," Arthur quipped. I set down my glass, taken aback. "Sorry. I shouldn't have said that." He looked young as he apologized, remorseful about dipping his naughty hand into the cookie jar. "Why did you just lie, Lucy?"

It happened rarely—someone accusing me straight to my face of lying. Usually, I was able to slip in and out of fact and fiction without raising any alarm, but Arthur saw right through me. "Sometimes I'd rather tell the story I want to tell."

"Instead of admitting you know nothing?" Arthur tapped his pack of Parliaments against the table. I nodded. "You should know the truth, don't you think?"

A shiver crept over me as the chords to the next song rang out. "This is my favorite song," I said.

"Then go dance!" he shouted. I remembered Mom's task of stepping into frame, participating. That's what he brought out in me. Boldness. Honesty. I took his glass of whiskey and threw it back, forcing it down as it burned my throat.

Buzzing, I stomped onto the dance floor and let the crowd swallow me. Arthur's stare spread warmth across my back like I was sinking into a hot bath. Odette belted out the bridge and lured me under her spell.

A hand on my waist jerked me out of the trance as delicate and thin as a spider's web. I knew it was Arthur before I met his inscrutable eyes. He jumped around to the beat like a guy who had been to hundreds of concerts in his youth.

"Hey!" I shouted. "Would you call this a risk?"

"What?" he yelled back. I was grateful he hadn't heard me. A far cry from the wallflower I usually was, I pulled him in to dance with me, then reached up and tangled my fingers in his hair. I gawked at his jaw, scarred and sharp, curious what it might be like to graze my lips against the edge.

Arthur leaned down toward my ear. "What the hell's gotten into you?" Sweaty bodies swam around us. I backed away, embarrassed, but he pulled me closer, into his barrel chest. I looked over his shoulder and found the Fowler boy from the pink house across the way leaning against the old jukebox. He was looking right at me. I blinked, thinking I'd imagined him, but I hadn't. He made no attempts to hide that he was staring, inspecting Arthur's manly hands on the small of my back.

I felt like I might faint. I extracted myself from Arthur's grasp and slipped out of the bar. Odette's howl faded as the heavy door slammed shut behind me.

I ran across the empty street, into the gravel parking lot where Arthur had parked his truck. I raised my finger to my neck. My pulse was building, electric. Alive. That's what this all meant. That's what all my favorite songs and books were about. That's what I was hunting for. I knew I could write the hell out of that feeling. I just had to capture it.

A minute later, the thud of Arthur's heavy boots shifted the gravel. Each step deliberate. The streetlights flickered.

"You're something else." He advanced toward me. Back on the dance floor, I had been totally and utterly in my body, of my body, for my body. But in that moment, I might as well have been sitting on top of the chain-link fence around us, watching it all happen below, a passive spectator.

He dropped his cigarette, embers red and glowing. I swallowed, questioning what it would be like to kiss him. Did I want it to happen, or did I want to say it happened? I trusted I would feel something different than I had on that mall bench last fall when the kid from the tennis team stuck his tongue down my throat and I marveled that people took pleasure in such an act. But I found pleasure in the idea that I could seduce a man of Arthur's experience.

"I don't want to go home," I told him.

"I could take you somewhere." Arthur pressed his thumb onto my wrist's pressure point, between the tendons. "But I have to warn you. It's a place that will change you."

All the blood in my veins swam toward that pressure point, where his grasp held me captive. "Where?"

"Forget it." His eyes gleamed like fool's gold, potential buried in the irises. "I'll take you home."

Wherever he wanted me to go, I would follow. "No, let's go."

Without giving him a chance to take back the invitation, I hoisted myself up into the passenger seat. I watched him in the side mirror as he adjusted his jeans. He pulled himself into the driver's seat and started the engine.

He yanked the gearshift, backed out of the parking lot, and turned onto the street. I gripped the door handle and watched the Vortex shrink in the rearview mirror.

"Hey, you trust me, don't you?" he asked with a tenderness that pierced my worry.

He leaned over me to retrieve matches from the glove compartment, then drove through the streets in silence. Smoke from his cigarette congested the truck cabin. The memory of our brief intimacy hung in the air, like a bright, bloated balloon, begging to burst. I couldn't deny the power this new buzz gave me, to be close to someone, to surrender.

AN HOUR LATER, HEADING NORTH UP A LONG STRETCH OF I-15, I WATCHED rows of windmills whirl. I rested my head on my hands against the window and studied my warped reflection in the side mirror.

"I wish I looked like her instead, like Odette," I said. Arthur scoffed. "What?" I shoved his shoulder.

Arthur steadied himself, clutching the wheel. "Sure, Odette's stunning, but you're beautiful."

No one had ever called me that before. I assumed he'd be embarrassed by this sudden confession of attraction, but I couldn't read his expression in the dark cabin.

"Besides, there's more depth to you," Arthur continued. "You're a raw nerve. You're bound for something bigger." He fixed his gaze on the horizon like he could see my bright future up ahead. I tucked my knees under me and let out a yawn. My eyelids grew heavy, yielding to the lull of the highway.

"Hey, why don't you get some rest?" He stepped on the gas, and the truck roared, dragging me into sleep.

I swear I asked him where we were headed.

If I had opened my eyes, if I had insisted he take me home, I'd be a nobody. Of this I am sure. But I slipped away, and he pressed on the gas, changing the course of my life forever.

Just like he promised.

A MURDER OF CROWS SWARMED ABOVE, SOARING ACROSS THE EARLY MORNing sky, croaking a warning, but it was far too late. An omen ignored.

My back ached from the hard metal beneath it. Wrapped in a red wool blanket, I struggled to sit up. When I moved, lizards scattered in all directions. My head pounded. For the life of me, I couldn't remember how I'd gotten there—to the back of the truck, to the desert, to the morning, but then I saw I was not alone.

"She looks just like him."

"The first one's finally here."

"It's time."

The chorus of voices belonged to a small huddle of strangers. Euphoric smiles spread across their sun-kissed faces, their stares fixed on my every move.

"What's going on?" My voice sounded tinny in the arid expanse.

A figure parted the group down the middle, heading straight toward me. I took in the wild sight. At last, there was the enigma I'd drawn in my mind's eye, long ago, sketched from the slightest of clues.

There was no mistaking it. It was my flesh and blood, my father. Max.

As dawn broke, he pulled me off the truck, whiplashed, anew. He seemed to be part earth, less human and more animal than I could understand, like the universe was designed for him and him alone. The sun rose, bloody orange and salmon pink, as my feet hit the dusty ground with a ceremonial thud.

"It's you," I said.

I saw myself in his sloped nose, his down-turned eyes, his long fingers. He'd aged, of course, since my mother captured his image in that photograph more than sixteen years ago. His wispy hair, grazing the back of his tunic shirt, had faded to silver. Specks of white dotted the patchy facial hair on his angular face. He was older than I thought he'd be, a decade older than Mom. Even I, a daydreamer savant of sorts, never once imagined I would first meet my father in a desert at dawn, surrounded by strangers dressed in plain clothing.

I tried to make out Arthur's expression, but the sun obscured my sight. Only hours ago, he drank with me in that dingy booth at the Vortex, all the while knowing where my father was and plotting our reunion. How had Arthur found him?

"Where are we?" I asked, desperate to banish the aching in my head.

"The Oasis," Max said. I memorized the cadence of his voice, low and masculine, like he was a cowboy of the Wild West. The lines around his eyes crinkled in a satisfying, weathered way. With my hand still in his, Max spun me around.

The wind breezed past as he guided me through the compound, two cozy caramel-colored adobe structures sunk heavily on the desert floor amid coarse Joshua trees and fragrant juniper bushes. A colorful collection of chairs, picnic tables, hammocks, and tarps were arranged on the rocks and dirt between the houses. A baby-blue Airstream trailer was tucked behind the house on the right. Behind it all, a large glass greenhouse glimmered, alight with activity and blooms. The sunlight bounced off the roof, creating a kaleidoscopic luster. There was an apparent holiness to the grounds, as if the compound had magically sprouted up from the core of the earth long ago. I turned back to Max, and he smiled at me, his face open with curiosity.

A rowdy group of young children, half a dozen or so, half clothed, tore out of the house on the left and charged through us, breaking our handhold. Their laughter reverberated in the vast landscape. Max cheered them on. They whooped in response, reveling in the blaze of his attention. It was infectious, and I let myself ease, softening in their joy.

Max stooped to the eldest girl's eye level and spoke to her like the loving man I always hoped he'd be. The girl looked to be about ten years old. I'd learn later that her name was Susanna. She twisted her hips from side to side, listening to him, until she took off running toward the greenhouse. The other children followed suit. The place was populated with women and children. The only men present were Arthur and Max. I wondered if this imbalance was the reason why I felt so calm. Why it felt so peaceful.

I looked back to the truck. There was no road to follow. No other buildings as far as I could see. We were alone out there, unsupervised, pioneers on Mars. I felt the farthest away from home I'd ever been, a stranger on foreign soil, clueless about what it all meant, but I couldn't help it.

I was transfixed.

# DOWNTOWN LOS ANGELES

REGRET OVER THAT LAST GLASS OF WHISTLEPIG SKEWERS INTO ME. I
examine the purple bags under my eyes in my reflection. A knock on
the bathroom door competes with the rhythm of the pounding in my
skull.

"Lucy," Sloane calls from the other side of the door. "We're ready
for you." I dab another layer of color corrector under my eyes and pray
Isaac's team will light me generously.

Yesterday wasn't my finest hour. Sure, I'm a little rusty, but I'll
pull myself together, because that's the only way to get through this
intact.

"Was Max who you expected him to be?" Isaac shows no apprehension about saying my father's name. It's jarring to hear it aloud in
the loft.

"Hard to say," I reply. "To spend my whole life until that point
only having my imagination fill in the blanks for me, it was difficult to
match any of my childish ideas to a person."

Isaac purses his lips. I grow self-conscious that I'm still not giving
him what he wants. In the same breath, I resent my desire to please this
pretentious asshole. Still, I offer him something to make it sound like
all of my musings are spontaneous. The last thing I want is to appear
rehearsed. Rehearsed means one thing in my line of work.

Guilty.

"I wonder if that was part of the problem."

Isaac sits up. "How do you mean?"

The leftover alcohol pulses uncertainty into every cell. "I designated a kind of"—I search for the right way to describe it—"a mystical quality to him before I ever met him."

"But you felt a connection to Max?" Isaac asks. "Was that immediate?"

"At the time," I admit. "Our first real conversation opened me up to the possibility that I could finally understand that other part of me. The part I never knew how to embrace." I wipe a bead of sweat off the back of my neck, dizzy with paranoia that I still sound studied.

"Are you feeling all right?"

I scour my brain for a better excuse than picking up the wrong stranger at a bar and the hangover my thirty-five-year-old body can't tolerate without a session of hot yoga, a cold plunge, and a day of Victorian bedrest. "I didn't get much sleep last night."

Isaac grants me no sympathy for this plight. "I've been meaning to ask you a favor."

"Go on."

"I want Diana to participate in the documentary, but I haven't been able to get a hold of her."

"True crime isn't her thing." I take a long sip of water, which my dry mouth immediately absorbs. "Besides, she's busy with her exhibit."

"The interview can be anywhere, on her schedule. Here, or preferably back in Coronado, at your childhood home. That would fit my vision perfectly." Isaac's eyes turn glassy, like he's watching the final product on a big screen. "Would you talk to her for me?"

"Mom doesn't talk about that summer," I tell him. I remember once, Mom said her stardom was due in part to her curated allure. There's a calculated difference between the things she shows in her photographs and the things she conceals. *You always want to leave them wanting more.* "But I'll talk to her."

"Thanks, Lucy." Isaac sighs, relieved. "You never know—it could be a good thing for you two. For your relationship."

I bristle at the implication that our relationship needs anything it doesn't have already. I watch him settle after this request, and I ache, witnessing how easy this ordeal is for him, despite how torturous it is for me.

He goes on. "Now, the incident at the She Slays event—is that kind of harassment something you deal with often?"

"Any public figure does." I remind him of the throngs of people who devote themselves to me, well-intentioned and otherwise. "But the true crime community is unusual. The parasocial relationships my fans form with me are often intertwined with their own experiences of trauma. It's easy for them to project whatever they're going through onto my story and get confused."

"Still, you're participating in this documentary, which will only bring more attention. You invite this chaos into your life," Isaac says, as if this is a great thesis statement he can't wait to prove.

"A long time ago, I made a decision," I say. "I'm not going to disappear. I'm sure that would make everyone more comfortable, if I sat back and let the headlines gather dust, but why should I be the one who slinks away like a wounded animal and never poke my head out of the ground? My fans *respect* me because I have a voice. I have something to say."

Isaac sighs, like it's a great gesture of generosity to give my soapbox moment any airtime. I dig my fingernails into my palm, punishing myself for waxing poetic.

He moves on to questioning me about each of Max's followers. Recounting each of their names is an odd practice and takes some getting used to, like I've forgotten how to tie my shoes. It's troubling to hear their biographies according to Isaac: their hometowns, ailments, bouts with addiction, scrapes with the law, little traumas, runaway tales, and absent parents.

"Anyone ever reach out to you?"

"No one legitimate," I tell him. "Sure, over the years, there have been many claims from people who say they were at the Oasis, but you can't go down that rabbit hole or it'll drive you mad. People like that just want their fifteen minutes of fame."

"So you haven't been in touch with anyone from the Oasis?" he asks again, stupefied. "This whole time?"

"No," I snap, unsure what he's implying. "Why would I be?"

Isaac takes off his glasses and rubs his eyes. Without them, he looks younger, a little boy lost. He takes a dramatic breath, and I prepare myself for what's coming next.

Finally, he lays it all out on the table: pictures of the others. The lost ones.

My gut stirs. I panic that I'll see the remnants of last night's Thai food on the coffee table in seconds, but my hangover is not to blame for this overwhelming dread. Trusting myself after everything that's happened takes concentrated effort. I push away the doubt and voice my sneaking suspicion aloud.

"So, that's what this is all about." I look up from the photos of the haunted faces spread out on the coffee table as Isaac's mission crystallizes. "You want to find them."

"Don't you?"

I turn to the window, gazing through the portal to the bustling concrete city below. I consider each of the ones we lost, the secret of their final moments blown away in desert dust.

"They deserve to be brought home and laid to rest properly," Isaac presses.

I wish with all my might their souls found peace in the darkness. "While I'm pleased to hear you're not one of the naysayers, surely you understand there's a very good reason why finding them is impossible."

"Their families deserve answers."

Shivering at the thought, I warn him. "I'm afraid you're on a fool's errand."

"Their bodies are still out there, Lucy." Isaac smiles, and I realize his smile is flat, straight across, a line, not a half-moon on its side. "If what you say is true, they have to be, right?"

The room stills, but inside my chest, there's a riot, begging to be heard.

"No one is ever really lost," Isaac says. "As far as I'm concerned, we just haven't found them yet."

# THE OASIS

*67 days before*

It looked like we were heading straight into the sun until the low rolling hills of the landscape revealed themselves. I struggled to keep up the pace and get my mind off my thirst and the little nails pounding in my head. Sweat pooled on my back as we ascended higher into the desert, passing lizards bathing on the rocks.

I tried and failed to picture my mother by this man's side. I couldn't have invented someone more different from all the other men who paraded in and out of our house—the cultured suits, the edgy rock stars, the foreign art collectors.

"I want to hear it from you," I said, thrilled I was able to go straight to the source. "How you met Mom, why you split, how you found this place, what you're all doing out here, everything."

Max rubbed his beard. "Are you happy, Lucy?"

I stepped over a boulder in the path. "How do you mean?"

Max grinned, and I could see how similar our smiles were. Mom always teased me for having a Cheshire cat smile, a quirk I hated about my appearance, but seeing the same shape on Max's face filled me with exorbitant gratitude. "I want us to get to know each other. Isn't that the most important thing about a human being? If they're happy?"

I considered this, but the correct response eluded me.

"I've caught you off guard." Max held up his hands, like he'd touched a hot stove. "I tend to get ahead of myself sometimes. It's just so exciting to finally meet you."

I relaxed, relieved he seemed to have spent just as much time daydreaming about our meeting as I had. "You have no idea."

"So that's why you came here?" Max asked, forging ahead in front of me.

I tried to remember exactly what I'd told Arthur in the parking lot. "No, I thought we were going to explore, look for inspiration, you know. This place, you . . . it's all new to me. I couldn't have even dreamt it."

"It is a special place."

"Are you . . . happy?" I asked him.

"Yes," Max replied without missing a beat. "We all are here. Especially now."

I picked up my pace to keep up with him. For all the discussions we'd had in our home about creating art, I didn't remember a time when we questioned if it ever made us happy, if we even made each other happy. Creating was about saying something important, making a name for yourself, building a fortune, achieving acclaim, striving for genius.

"How do you know?" I propped my hands on my hips, my heart beating fast from the exercise and his presence. "Maybe that sounds silly, but . . ."

"It's okay," he assured me. "You asked what we do here, and it's really quite simple. I created the Oasis as a safe haven for unconditional belonging. We belong to each other, to this place, to the earth itself." He waved me over, then put his pointer finger to his lips and turned to take in the vista. "Listen now."

I looked out at the sweep of endless desert, as far as my vision allowed. It took a few moments for me to hear what he meant—the music in the breeze through the sand. The vibration of the land echoed its history in wordless song. I could have stood there like that for hours, and it would have felt like only minutes passed, as I soaked up the peace implanted into the hallowed terrain.

"Biologically, humans are drawn to vistas like this," Max said. "From the high ground, we can make sure no enemies are in pursuit, hunting us. From here, we feel some semblance of control in an otherwise uncontrollable world. When you confine yourself to fluorescent-lit offices inside skyscrapers, you can't see when enemies are approaching. You're blind to everything around you. That's what happened in September. If those in the outside world had been more connected to themselves, to the universe, if they'd been more aware of the space they occupy on the earth, they would have survived. They would have been ready to face the danger head-on and act."

I looked out, trying to take in this lesson, but my mind wandered back to the Fowlers and how they might feel about Max's little theory. A chill spread across my back as I recalled the boy's intense stare at the Vortex.

Max started walking again. The shuffle of our shoes against the sand scored our hike. "Every night, we observe the sun setting to honor our connection to the cycles of nature. We release the day that's gone by and leave the past behind to maintain peace for the future. If you strengthen your character and learn self-discipline, one day, you'll understand."

Distracted by the mention of that night, I brimmed with curiosity, imagining how they all came alive under the stars. Still, I had plenty more questions for him that he hadn't yet answered. "But isn't it just as important to know where we came from to understand where we're going?"

He laughed, and I noticed his violet-blue eyes, how they reminded me of my own. "Ah, my little poet," he said with a tenderness that touched me. I hadn't even told him I wrote. Or had I? Perhaps he saw my capability in a way Mom had not. "You do love your words, don't you?"

My stomach knotted. I felt an urge to press him more, but Max suddenly threw his arm out in front of my chest to stop me from going any farther. A distinctive rattle rang out, a back-and-forth humming like a sinister pendulum. Up ahead along the path, ten feet away, a rattlesnake lurked on a flat rock. Max looked at me, a crease between his brows. Petrified, I dug my fingernails into his arm as I imagined the worst.

Max squeezed my hand, a kind gesture that cast out all the fear left in my body. A minute later, the rattlesnake slithered its way across the path and disappeared into the vegetation. We were headed back toward the compound when Max said, "A rattlesnake bit me once."

"What did you do?"

"Stay calm. If your heart rate increases, the venom works its way into your system faster." He reached down to pick up a branch in the path and tossed it into a bush. "For all its majesty, the desert can be cruel." He spoke with a strange remove—I realized he hadn't answered my question. He only told me what I was supposed to do.

I considered what might have happened if I had been bitten out there in the middle of nowhere. No one back home knew where I was. I had no idea how long it had taken us to get here from Coronado. I didn't even know where we were. Even if I left right then, what difference would it make if I made it home at three in the morning or noon tomorrow? Part of me resented my goody-two-shoes tendencies.

Did I really have to tell anyone where I'd gone?

AS WE HEADED BACK TO THE COMPOUND, I COULDN'T IGNORE MY HEADACHE any longer. Max suggested I was dehydrated. He jogged off toward the adobe house on the right and ducked his lanky frame into the doorway.

I walked up to the rest of the group, huddled together in the yard. There were about twenty of them including the children. I felt like the new kid on the first day of school. They openly gawked at me. I searched for Arthur's familiar face, desperate to know how this was all possible, but he wasn't there.

"Welcome," a gap-toothed girl said. She used her hands as a visor to observe me.

I returned a reserved smile, uncomfortable with the attention. "I'm Lucy."

"We know," she replied, tilting her head as she continued her assessment. "I'm Fiona. This is . . . everybody. We've been waiting a long time for you."

"A long time," a nymphlike woman repeated, running her hands over her sizable baby bump. She introduced herself as Eden.

"How long have you been here?" I asked.

They turned to each other, like I'd asked to understand an inside joke.

"One day, you'll understand," Eden said, echoing Max, then narrowed her gaze at me, which reminded me of the peculiar authority of my mother's lens. Looking back, I know she was waiting for me to root myself into their sacred ground.

I STUDIED THE BACK OF ARTHUR'S HEAD LIKE HIS TANGLE OF CURLS MIGHT hold the answer, nipping him in the heels as he strode toward his truck parked in the dirt. "How the fuck did you find him?"

He looked back toward the others congregating around the picnic tables, the melodic highs and lows of their storytelling traveling across the airwaves. "Keep your voice down." Arthur tugged the passenger door open, dug through the middle console for his cigarettes, then leaned against the truck to light up, too unbothered to even close the door.

I slammed it shut to get his attention. He barely flinched. "You owe me an explanation. Why are you acting like there's nothing crazy about all this? Why is he?"

He sighed. "You asked to come."

I felt nauseated. I couldn't remember when I'd last eaten. "But how long have you known?"

"About Max?" He scratched his head. "He wanted to see you."

"Why didn't you tell me?" I shoved his chest, which did nothing. He was rock solid. "What's wrong with you?"

"Don't get hysterical." He stepped back. "Here, take one. It will calm you down."

I snatched the pack from him. He was right. I needed something to suppress my anger. "Why did you ask me all those questions about him if you knew where he was? *Who* he was?"

He cupped his hands around my cigarette to light it, protecting the flame from the relentless wind. "He asked me to bring you here, but I wanted to see what you knew first. If you wanted to be here. You asked for this." His features drew together in a disapproving shape. He didn't understand why this omission mattered. "Diana has no right to keep your father from you. He's a brilliant man. You deserve to know him. He deserves to know you."

I took a drag. The smoke cut my throat. "Start from the beginning." I was always one step behind him, like a child who was taught the whole word before learning the letters.

"Isn't this what you wanted?" Arthur stepped toward me. The closeness and the nicotine made me dizzy. He ran his fingers along my forearm. "I did all this for you."

He was right. I wanted this. Arthur had gone against his mentor's wishes for my own benefit. Max wanted me there. That had to be worth something.

"The Oasis is exactly what you need." He sucked on his Parliament like it was candy between his teeth. "You have a chance to step into who you truly are. Your father's here, right in front of you. This is the inspiration you've been looking for."

I looked back at the group, at Max holding court. The display of glee. He was their king. That much was clear. They appeared content, this family of strangers, strung together by their mutual love for what, I wasn't yet sure.

"Okay, I'll stay." I dropped the cigarette into the dirt. "Thank you, Arthur. For bringing me. I . . ." A cry threatened to emerge from my throat, but I managed to collect myself, choking back dust. "I'm sorry for doubting you."

"I know." He assured me I didn't need to elaborate. He understood how much it meant to me to find Max at last. "I know."

I watched the others retreat into the house on the left to avoid the highest sun of the day. Max tipped his hat and disappeared into the house on the right alone. I twisted my shoulders to stretch my back and looked toward the dirt road, considering the route that had brought us there.

"So, what do you think?" Arthur asked. "About Max?"

I sipped water from a canteen, trying to equate my well-worn day-dream with the man I'd walked beside on the path, who wanted nothing more from me other than my happiness. "He's more than I ever hoped for."

# DOWNTOWN LOS ANGELES

AFTER A GRUELING MORNING OF ISAAC INTERROGATING ME ABOUT Max's theories, we break for lunch. Isaac and his crew congregate outside to refuel on nicotine and food-truck burritos. I pass by them with a polite wave. I tell myself it's good that I'm trying. I need them to like me. Or better yet, fear me.

My stomach's a pit, but filling myself up with anything right now will only make me tired during an afternoon of mind-numbing inquiries. The pang of hunger will keep me sharp and prevent me from sounding media-trained, God forbid.

I hang a right on East Third Street, pass a tattoo shop, and decide it's time I pay a visit to Mom at the gallery. I want to bring up Isaac's interview request before I lose my nerve.

I enter the courtyard of the Hauser & Wirth complex, survey the eclectic lunch crowd at Manuela, and linger by the outdoor sculptures. I call Mom twice, but she doesn't pick up. When I'm about to peek through the exhibit doors, she emerges and steers me away from the entrance into the center of the courtyard, at the feet of a massive ironwork.

"Darling," she huffs. I can tell where this is going. "I'm right in the middle of it."

I swell with need, contemplating the best strategy to take. "I have a favor to ask."

She crosses her arms in a power stance. "What can I do for you?"

"Isaac told me you haven't responded to his request to be interviewed for the documentary."

Mom laughs. "Oh, I responded, darling. I told him no." She looks past me and mouths an apology to the gazelle-like gallery director waiting for her return.

"Well, I was just wondering if you might reconsider," I manage. "For me."

"You know I have no interest in going down that road." Mom sighs, like this request exhausts her more than a Hollywood spin class. "Now, is that all?"

I ball my fists, annoyed with myself that I ever agreed to do Isaac's bidding in the first place. "It's fine. Forget it." I wave it off like her refusal means nothing to me, but the tiniest dagger pierces my gut. She can't grant me one small favor. "I actually came by because I'm dying to get a sneak peek."

"That's sweet of you." Her emerald eyes glint in the afternoon sun. "But I never show my work until it's done."

Another one of her edicts—I should know better. "I'm sure it's all fantastic . . ."

"It's not about that," she snaps, and tosses her long, dark red waves. "Would I ever interrupt your flow?"

I shake my head, cringing at myself for committing this cardinal sin.

"Hang in there, okay?" Mom squeezes my hand, and I'm reminded of her power, how one simple touch once worked on me like a sedative, back when I needed to be numbed most. "Why don't you go see the new exhibit in the other gallery?" She throws the suggestion out over her shoulder as she retreats from me. In seconds, she's prattling on to the gallery director as they disappear behind the clouded glass, leaving me alone again.

THE EXHIBIT AT THE FRONT OF THE BUILDING FEATURES A DAN-ish artist's large-scale paintings of faces over which webs of red string and something resembling spaghetti stretch in maddening patterns. The effect is unnerving. I'm meant to see the person's face underneath, but the parts have been concealed and disfigured beyond recognition. I meander through the maze of stark white walls and loiter in front of each piece with a thoughtful expression, like Diana taught me.

I let myself daydream about the documentary going exactly the way I want it to go. Isaac's new-information ploy is only a bluff, but his involvement produces an uptick in my online following. I picture the cheerful call from Julian telling me the anniversary edition has hit the bestseller list. I play out a scene in my head of Mom and Odette reuniting at an ornate dinner party I'll host in my renovated loft with an impressive mix of authors and critics who are now my dearest friends.

"Fuck!"

The cursing yanks me out of my fantasy. The volunteer stationed in the gallery flinches. His fingers fly to his lips in a shush formation. I follow his gaze and surmise that the noise came from the next room.

I round the bend and recognize Sloane immediately. It's difficult to be innocuous with that mop of blue hair. She apologizes to the volunteer and makes a show of turning off her phone. She tenses as I approach.

"Please be mindful of the other patrons," the volunteer says, then turns on his heel and leaves us.

Flustered, Sloane excuses herself. "Shit, I'm mortified you witnessed that."

"What are you doing here?" I study her. "Isaac didn't ask you to babysit me, did he?"

"What?" Sloane looks genuinely surprised at the suggestion, but I wouldn't put it past him. "Of course not. My friend does the social media for this place. I told them I'd check it out."

I can hear Mom's disdain in my ear. *The imbeciles who think they know how to market my art . . .*

I observe the piece Sloane is viewing: an abstract sculpture that resembles little more than an anthill. "What was that all about?" I ask. "Did this . . . inspire something in you?"

"God no." Sloane laughs. "It's just . . ." She clutches her brick of a phone in one hand. "Forget it." She unzips her dark backpack and drops her phone inside. We fall into an awkward silence, just looking at the anthill sculpture.

"Modern art's the worst," I offer.

She breathes a sigh of relief. "Totally."

I check my watch. We're expected at the loft in ten minutes. It occurs to me that she could very well be doing Isaac's dirty work and making calls to people from my past, cajoling them into speaking on camera. What I wouldn't give to take a peek at her call log.

"Well, we should be getting back," I announce. "Do you want to walk with me?"

WE PASS ARTS DISTRICT BREWING, AND THE SMELL OF HOPS WAFTS out onto the sidewalk. It doesn't take long for Sloane to pitch me her film idea. She appears nervous, rambling a mile a minute, stumbling over her words. "So, it's basically a meditation on identity in the digital age. Anyway, I'm raising funding for the feature version now. I can't believe Isaac took the time to watch the short. Most people don't care about the future of the gopher who fetches them coffee."

"How long have you worked for him?" I attempt to sound casual.

"I came on for prep a few months ago. Before that, I worked for this showrunner who was a nightmare. She said she was going to let me shadow this season but only hired me to shuttle her son back and forth from soccer. Her show got canceled. Serves her right. She lacked vision."

"Wow, that sucks," I commiserate, distracted by the idea of Isaac prepping for far longer than I even knew about the doc. "How do you like this gig?"

Sloane bites her chipped black nails. "Oh, it's so much better when the people you work for actually have the goods to back it up. Isaac's a genius."

"You really think so?"

"Without a doubt. I'll gladly attach my name to whatever he does." I gulp, unsure how to bond with Isaac's number one fan. She rushes to fill the silence. "I mean, assistant life still has its drawbacks, but it can't last forever, right?"

It takes me a minute to realize she's waiting for me to assuage her anxiety, which I find odd. "You'll catch your break," I promise, even though it's more likely she won't. So few do.

"Thanks." She stops biting her nails, like the idea of self-improvement is plausible. "Perseverance and patience."

I imagine the affirmations she says into the mirror every morning, the unoriginal trick a therapist tried to teach me years back before I fired her. Still, I admire Sloane's delusional drive, one of many requirements needed to succeed in this city.

"Plus," she continues, "I'm not sure I should even say this, but I've devoured *Rattlesnake* countless times, so it's exhilarating to be even a small part of this project. To work with you is literally a dream. I mean, not *with* you with you. *For* you."

I catch her in my periphery. This little admission of her fandom gives me all kinds of ideas.

"It's so inspiring to witness what you've been able to do with your platform. After everything you've been through, you're so brave," she gushes. "Sorry if I made that weird."

"You didn't," I tell her. "It's nice to know someone in the crew is on my side."

Her shoulders relax. "Well, if there's anything you need, just let me know. That's my job."

I'm about to take her up on this offer and persuade her to hand over whatever Isaac thinks he has on me, but I think better of showing my hand too soon. This is a long game. Playing my cards right will require "patience and perseverance."

By the time we make it back to the loft, everyone's waiting for us. It's jarring to come back to a roomful of strangers in my home. I close the door behind Sloane and twist the deadbolt in place before returning to the hot seat. Sloane slips inconspicuously back to her post by Isaac's side and grins at me when we start up again, elated that she's shared an afternoon with her idol. Isaac's oblivious to our little exchange.

Cozying up to Sloane might just be the ticket.

THAT NIGHT, MOM THINKS I'M WRITING.

"Good on you," she coos as she slips off her Gucci loafers by the door. I detect a hint of condescension, but I only point to my laptop. She theatrically tiptoes to her bedroom. If I can't interrupt her flow, she should grant me the same courtesy.

When her door closes, I abandon my desk, pour myself a glass of WhistlePig, and flip the TV on, volume low. I find *Body Heat*, one of my favorite movies, airing. I toil over Julian's latest email. The publishers are in the process of mocking up a few covers for the anniversary edition—do I have any ideas I'd like to share? He tells me they want to fast-track the printing and need the foreword in six weeks. He asks if I can swing a draft in that timeframe with filming. *How's that going, by the way?* My daily interrogations an afterthought.

Instead of analyzing Kathleen Turner's prowess, I fix my stare on the place I avoid. The place where I can't hide.

There on my computer lies a blank document that I'm supposed to magically transform into a spellbinding explanation of what the past twenty years has meant. A self-effacing monologue that's unforgettable, tear-inducing, yet sharp as glass. I shiver as I come to the same old conclusion.

I'm not good enough.

That's why Mom's interest in me is guaranteed to lapse any day now. No doubt she'll return to Coronado the minute the exhibit's done, and we'll go back to our monthly check-ins. We'll revert to our empty promises that we'll take a trip up to Paso Robles for a wine weekend. She'll forget to tell me when she's in town until after she's left, supplying me with vague excuses about how busy she gets. *I simply ran out of time, doll!*

I should brainstorm. I should take one of my hundreds of books off a shelf and find examples. I should reread *Rattlesnake.*

Instead, I give in to my baser instincts and search for Isaac's assistant online. When I find her, I swipe through her picture carousels: a vintage-glass set at the Rose Bowl Flea Market, a shadow on a sidewalk, the super bloom last year, a thrift-store haul, the back of her head as she walks along the Venice canals, blatant self-promotion of her short film. The images make me pity this small-town girl with unoriginal dreams and a cliché aesthetic. It shouldn't be difficult to worm my way into her sphere. I switch over to my fake account to catch her latest update—a post-workout selfie with the hashtag #yogaeverydamnday in neon letters.

I look up the yoga studio that Sloane has tagged in her post, then check the forum. Fifty new comments have been made since my last visit. News of the documentary sparked discussions anew. The armchair detectives agonize over every detail, comb through the weather reports, and skim records for a land deed. Someone claims their uncle Stuart spotted the truck in Utah. Another draws comparisons between Max's background and Keith Raniere's. I roll my eyes at the imbecile boasting about buying the original wool blanket off eBay. But one exchange gives me pause.

MurderSheSold812: You think Isaac Coleman won't dig 'em all up? If anyone can, he can.

TexWatson86: Not without LG, but we all know she can't be trusted.

Case_Exhibit_: Dude, the bodies don't exist. They never did! LOL

Highhhpriestess516: Of course they EXIST! They have names and families who loved them. They deserve justice!!!

TexWatson86: That selfish bitch won't lift a finger if it doesn't serve her own interests.

Highhhpriestess516: Misogynistic much?! Get off that bandwagon. #ibelievewomen

Case_Exhibit_: Once a fame whore, always a fame whore.

TexWatson86: The truth will set you free.

I glower at those six words until my eyes water, until the letters don't spell out anything anymore. They appear defective. Gibberish or a foreign language.

TexWatson86, what do you know about freedom?

## THE OASIS

*67 days before*

A bell rang out—loud and celebratory. As a herd, the women and children dropped what they were doing and swarmed to the source. Eden grabbed my hand. Goose bumps rose on my arms as we joined the others in a large circle around the perimeter of the greenhouse.

Slowly, Max lifted his head.

Necks back and eyes wide, we watched the day turn to night. Everywhere I turned, a streak of pink, a tear of orange ripped across the sky. I'd never seen a sunset with the moon hanging so low, kissing our heads. The greenhouse flourished, the hues of the setting sun projected through our reflections, distorted by the glass. Magnificent and brilliant, the splendor seemed to exist purely for our amazement.

Once the sun disappeared below the horizon, the heat dissipated. The women whirled about, loosening up in the darkness. I looked around at the people in Max's community. They appeared unburdened, without weight on their shoulders. I wondered what it might take to be like that.

AFTER DINNER, MAX LIT THE CAMPFIRE WHILE THE WOMEN HELD THE LITTLE children nuzzled against their chests. Arthur draped the red wool blanket from his truck around my shoulders. Enveloped in his sandy musk, my cheeks grew warm from the fire. I was excited for whatever might come next.

Once we all settled, Max cleared his throat. "Since we have a new face here with us tonight, I think it's time to tell her what we're all about."

They laughed playfully at this, and I smiled awkwardly, missing the punch line of the joke.

"Why don't we tell a little bit of the story of the hero?" Max said. This phrase brought the whole desert into silence. I felt special, and I wasn't sure what to expect from this campfire story, but I promised myself to commit every word to memory, so I could transcribe it all later.

Max stared into the red-hot flames as he spoke. "Our purpose is to live out the story and bring the New Kind into the world, to share it only with those who dare to listen. To pass it on to the generations to come so that they may keep the tradition alive long after our earthly bodies have left this plane. Our pursuit of wholeness frees us from the wanting."

My eyes grew watery from the smoke as I listened to the rich cadence of Max's voice.

"Ronnie," Max called to a freckled, lanky young woman. "Tell us how we came to learn it."

Ronnie traced figure eights in the dirt with her feet. "We don't have to. The story is innate in the soul of every human being, part of the collective unconscious." She spoke with a chain smoker's rasp, which gave the effect that she was well beyond her years. "As etched into us as our thirst."

Max directed his attention to Beatrice, shy and twenty-one, next to me. "And how does the outside world treat it?"

"Mankind does not revere the sacred nature of the collective unconscious." Beatrice gathered the bottom of her dress, thumbing the hem. "War, politics, money, consumerism—all of it stems from those in their shadow selves."

Max passed the baton. "Eden?"

Eden required no prompting other than her name. "Here at the

Oasis, we bring the collective unconscious back into balance, where it belongs, so the outside forces of evil cannot break it." Eden placed a hand on her swollen belly and angled her head up toward the sky again. "Here, under the kindness of this moon, we brave the Underworld so we may know the Light."

"You can too," Susanna said from her post beside Eden. She hugged her knees to her chest. "You don't have to be afraid anymore."

I struggled to follow what they were saying, the holy-sounding words framed around lofty ideas I couldn't grasp. I bit down on my tongue and reminded myself that I was a visitor, and Max had plenty of wisdom to share. After all, his people oozed with satisfaction in a way I did not.

LATER, WITHOUT WARNING, MAX RETREATED TO HIS HOUSE. ARTHUR QUICKLY followed. My hand lifted into a wave that went ignored. Aching to hear my name on their lips, I watched the two of them kick dirt around the doorway, hands in pockets. The light of the moon cast ghoulish shadows of their tall forms.

"Come on, dear," Eden said. "When Max leaves the fire, that means it's time to turn in. Arthur is on watch tonight. He'll keep us safe."

Eden led me into the women's quarters. The space was worn-in, but there was a warmth to every dusty nook and cranny. Cream-colored curtains draped over the open window in the kitchen.

Wordlessly, in the dim light of a single bulb, Eden handed me a cotton nightdress from a rack of clothes and waited while I changed. In the hallway, we passed a dark green trunk and stacks of blankets like the red one from Arthur's truck bed. The large back room had mattresses strewn about the floor like a big, cozy nest. The rest of the women filed in, the children tucked in beside them.

I watched Eden's pregnant stomach rise and fall, envisioning the fetus coiled up in amniotic fluid. Ronnie let out a wheezing snore, then turned on her side. Her bare breast exposed. The night breeze traveled through the small window, a welcome relief on the napes of our necks.

Once they all fell asleep, I rose, tiptoeing between the mattresses to peer outside. Max and Arthur were still there, in the doorway of the other adobe, all crossed arms and sinewy muscles while the fire roared on. Like the whip of a lizard's tail, Arthur sensed my gaze and looked in my direction. I slunk down, my back against the wall, curling my toes under so I wouldn't wake Fiona, fast asleep inches away.

Somewhere out there a coyote howled, ferocious and feral. Animals had it easy. They didn't concern themselves with what others thought. They cried out into the darkness whenever they needed to be heard.

"FOLLOW ME," EDEN WHISPERED.

I stirred, disoriented by how deeply I had slept. We stepped out of the house as the day was breaking. The tie-dyed morning sky clashed with the colorless landscape beneath it. Somehow, I already felt capable of missing this place I understood so little of.

I followed Eden inside the greenhouse, which she unlocked using a key she pulled out from the pocket of her dress. A cloud of humidity hit us instantly. Everywhere I looked, there was a new sign of life. Fat, bloodred tomatoes, zucchini on the vine, fragrant herbs. Misters rained down on the plants, underscoring the whole greenhouse with a melodic *swish swish*. In the center there was a circular platform made of stone that looked like it had been there for centuries.

"It's magical." I smiled at Eden, but her expression flattened. She had not brought me there for my own amusement.

"This is how we sustain ourselves," Eden said. "This is what keeps us from depending on the outside world. It's crucial for us to be self-sufficient."

"So you never leave?" It was hard to feel trapped out there when land stretched for miles on all sides. No fences keeping us in or others out.

She flipped open a control panel and turned on the misters in the back row. "Why would we?"

"How do you . . . ?" I struggled to find a polite way to ask.

"Make money?" Eden sighed, disgusted by the concept, not weighed down by the realities of it. "You don't need as much as everyone says you do . . ."

"How did it start?" I asked, desperate to know. "How did you find Max?"

Eden tucked my hair behind my ear. "For anyone who needs a home like ours, Max provides refuge. For expectant mothers, like me, needing a safe place to raise a child. For those who have endured the ugliness of the outside world. For the children—the New Kind, we call them. Even to girls like you, who have been mistreated. Max generously takes us all in to show us real joy," Eden said, weaving through the pathways, inspecting every crop as I followed. She pressed her fingers into the soil beds, checking the moisture. "It's only a matter of time."

"Until what?"

"September was one of the last stages."

I cleared my throat, which still felt unbearably dry. My thoughts shifted again to the Fowlers in the pink house, but my old life felt a million miles away. "You mean September eleventh?"

"On that day, Saturn and Pluto were opposing. That won't happen again until the year 2020." She mentioned this factoid like I should already have known the placement of the stars. "Nature tells you what to expect. You just have to pay attention. Once the outside world is destroyed, by war, by greed, by ignoring the sacred cycles of the earth, we will be in the Light. Thriving."

I rounded my shoulders, self-conscious in the thin fabric of the nightdress, processing this premonition. "So Max is the hero? In the story?"

"He's the only one who has braved the Underworld and made it into the Light. Now he's gracious enough to teach all of us how to reach that place of wholeness. You, too, can be a hero, Lucy. You're so special." She regarded me for a moment, like she was memorizing the location of my freckles, as if they were the planets she praised. "You look so much like him." Eden touched my cheek. "You see that now, don't you?"

I did feel safe there, in Eden's gaze, her pregnant stomach between us, with the glittering, clear dome above. For the first time in a long while, I wasn't dispensing white lies, desperate to craft the perfect image to make whoever was looking see me in a certain light. I could belong simply because I was Max's daughter.

That, in and of itself, was magic.

WHEN MAX BID ME FAREWELL, HE KISSED MY FOREHEAD. "SAFE TRAVELS, MY little poet."

At this kernel of acknowledgment, I couldn't ignore a deep exhale from the little girl inside.

"A word of caution," Max said, one eye on Arthur's truck, ready to depart. "Now that you know our story, promise me you'll keep your eyes wide open? Remember what we taught you."

"I promise."

The kids skipped their way to us, bunches of wildflowers in their grubby fists.

"Beautiful, isn't it?" Susanna handed me a desert flower, her farewell gift. "Beautiful," she repeated, like she enjoyed how the word tasted. The poor thing didn't yet understand how much that word would plague her as soon she graduated from child to preteen, how she'd be doomed to inspect her reflection and agonize over the pressure to be just that. I realized she might not meet that same fate if she grew up in a place like the Oasis, surrounded only by people who lifted her up.

AS WE DROVE AWAY, THE LOW TILT OF THE RADIO BLURRED A CONSTANT STATIC. Arthur smoked his cigarettes in lazy succession, one after the other.

I focused on the dirt road ahead. It looked like if Arthur drove much farther, we'd fall off the earth. I braced myself for the nothingness that death advertises, terrified I never made my mark. But of course, the top of the hill was merely that—the top of the hill. There was earth again, catching the wheels of the truck and us along with them. A long stretch of road rolled out beyond the hill: paved highway, street signs, and blinking traffic lights ahead.

It wasn't the end of the earth at all. It was the outside world.

I borrowed a scrap of paper from Arthur's center console and jotted down my musings on Max's vast wisdom, the desert air, the mystical greenhouse. Arthur insisted I read it to him. I complied, mortified and elated he cared enough to listen. Once I finished, I unclenched my white-knuckle grasp on the door handle.

"Feeling okay?" Arthur asked, his expression soft with worry.

"I . . ." It was becoming increasingly difficult to hide from him. "I'm overwhelmed. By all of it."

"You're onto something." He reached over to comfort me, putting his hand on my leg. I collapsed under the weight of feeling close to him again, hoping this meant he hadn't forgotten our near kiss. "Let me read whatever you write next. We'll work on it together." The familiar distress plowed through me, just as blatant as the need to have my words studied and adored. "Don't let anyone else read it." He fingered the pocketknife on his keychain. "Trust me. Your mom would be upset with you for lying about where you were."

"I won't say a word."

I tried to stay awake, to memorize the route and his touch. I worried if I moved an inch, he'd retreat, forget he ever called me beautiful, and a stifling ache would take the place where his hand had once been.

# EAST HOLLYWOOD

THE SVELTE INSTRUCTOR AT YOGI SOL REMINDS THE CLASS TO RELAX our brow bones and ruminate on our intentions. I keep my focus trained on the door—willing Sloane to show up and justify the effort of rolling out of bed and onto a rubber mat at 6 a.m. Just my luck, she never appears.

By the time we're on the third sun salutation, I'm fuming—an adverse effect of intentional breath and movement. Of course, staging a run-in with the documentary filmmaker's assistant is a ridiculous idea. The old man next to me huffs, mouth open, and I'm tempted to scold him for not using his ujjayi breath properly. As I lie in corpse pose during Savasana, I welcome the temporary relief of the ice-cold lavender-doused towel on my forehead and meditate on the agony I'll endure if Isaac discovers what really happened that summer, and the kicker: how long I'll have to wait to find out if I'm completely screwed.

After the students exchange namastes, I scan the room again, but there's no way I could have missed Sloane. The girl has bright blue hair. The doorway's jammed with foot traffic. I make it into the refreshing blast of AC in the lobby and return my rented mat, then feel a tap on my shoulder.

"Lucy?"

I turn around, half expecting to meet a fan. I feign shock at the sight of Sloane, her blue waves swept into a lazy topknot, an all-black workout set squeezing her curves.

"Oh my gosh!" I smile. "Can't believe I'm running into you here!"

Sloane hikes her yoga mat higher up the crook of her arm. "I know! I'm surprised I haven't seen you here before."

"First time," I admit too quickly. "Great intro deal."

Sloane slips off her sandals and puts them into one of the open cubbies. "Well, stick with it and you'll get addicted. I couldn't even get into crow pose a year ago."

"Awesome." I pretend like balancing in crow pose is on my vision board too. "You know, I'm impressed—working out before the job and everything." I try to make it sound casual, but I don't know if I would buy my beatific grin either. "So, what's Isaac got in store for us today, anyway?"

Sloane scrunches her nose and glances at the door to the studio as the next class files in and sets up their mats. "You know, I really can't say . . ."

"Oh, come on." I reach out and touch her forearm. "I'm only joking."

Sloane glances around as if Isaac has a mole planted in the studio. "For the record, I wish I could tell you . . ." She rolls her eyes. "But you know Isaac and his *process*." We share a half-hearted laugh at Isaac's expense. Sloane slides her backpack into the cubby, taps on her phone, then tosses it on top of her things. My stomach turns over, mimicking flip dog.

"I better grab a spot," she says, heading toward the studio door. "See you later, Lucy."

I take a long gulp from my water bottle, determined to act naturally as I seal the deal, praying that her phone won't lock. "We should hang out sometime—take a class or grab a drink."

Sloane turns back to me, one hand on the door, and her face brightens immediately. "How about this weekend?"

I shrug. "Friday?"

She beams; then she's gone. As the teacher greets the class and the Zen music emerges from the speakers, I glance over to the front-desk employee, who's distracted, convincing a customer to dish out two hundred dollars for leggings. As discreetly as I can, I turn to the cubby wall and tap Sloane's phone. The screen's already locked, but her calendar for the day blinks on her home screen. Yoga at 7 a.m., then scheduled at 1 p.m.: "Interview with TF."

The music inside the studio changes to an upbeat pop bop from the nineties, and my heart jumps in sync with the tempo. I put Sloane's phone back, slide on my sunglasses, then head out, pleased that my little stakeout proved to be fruitful on the first try.

If Isaac thinks I'll resort to groveling at the feet of a man whose family's favorite pastime is souring my name, he's in for a rude awakening.

There's no reason to apologize to Theo Fowler. He played his part; I played mine.

LATER THAT DAY, I'M BACK AT THE LOFT, STAGED IN THE GREEN armchair, though we might as well be in an interrogation room from a film noir set given Isaac's line of questioning today.

"So, it was understood that you wouldn't be telling your mother where you'd been?"

"My mother didn't keep me on a leash." I recall the mornings when hours flew by, when the words unfurled onto the page with little effort. I forgo the memories of Arthur brushing his thumb against my shoulder when he passed through the living room on the way to fix Mom's latest camera blunder. The stolen glances. The hour he spent beside me as I wrote on the porch and he scribbled in his elusive black Moleskine. When I asked what he was working on, he only laughed and told me to keep going. "I wrote and rewrote with more focus than I ever had. I spent the first few days after I returned obsessing over a new piece that I thought would be perfect for the workshop application, all about my brief stay at the Oasis."

"So you went from being admired as Max's daughter back to being invisible."

"I wasn't invisible to Arthur."

"What were things like at home when you returned?"

When I stood on our street, I hoped Mom, Odette, and Judy would come running outside, wanting to know where I'd been all weekend, who I'd been with, craving every detail of my travels. When you're a young girl, your deepest desire is that someone will show curiosity about your inner world. I remember the sting when I walked through the front door and realized no one was home.

"As normal as ever," I say. Sloane nods at me to go on, like she believes our little moment in the yoga studio might earn her a producer credit. "Odette was leaving for LA to start her residency at the Troubadour. Judy was working her gigs and modeling for Mom. Mom was preparing for her annual summer bash. But like Max promised, I saw the outside world in a new light."

"Go on."

I summon the weighted days I spent comparing the world I knew with the Oasis, probing every interaction for confirmation of Max's theories, looking for something in Theo Fowler that never existed.

"No one else saw the danger on the horizon."

# CORONADO

*59 days before*

Mom's party guests, in billowing dresses as though they'd just flown in from a shopping spree at a Marrakesh market, sucked down her lethal margaritas. Judy and her friends, each one bearing a chosen name more eccentric than the last, parroted Diana as they blew kisses: "Darling!"

I was refilling drinks and eavesdropping when the Fowlers entered through our front gate. The son took in the scene with a curious grin. The husband and wife wore matching summer whites and seemed startled by the eclectic crowd. The wife clutched a platter of summer pasta. As Mom took it from her, the wife, Melissa, introduced herself, then her husband, Colin, and son, Theo. I delighted in learning their names, like they were dolls in my very own pink dollhouse, further detailing my daydream of the perfect nuclear family. I pretended it was the first time I'd noticed them.

It didn't take long for Colin to gush. "I have this art buddy back in New York who would scream if he knew I was standing in *the* Diana Golden's yard right now."

Mom simpered. "Oh, you really don't have to say that!"

Odette grabbed a beer out of the cooler and popped it open. Immediately, Theo's eyes traveled to her bare stomach, her tight-as-can-be jeans slung low on her hips.

"Was that you playing the other night at the Vortex?" he asked.

"Yup." Odette toyed with the beer wrapper. I flinched, worried he'd mention seeing Arthur and me on the dance floor that night.

"You sounded sick. Kind of like Garbage."

"Theo!" Melissa yelped.

Through gritted teeth, Theo told her, "It's a *band,* Mom." I suppressed a laugh. Theo caught this and smiled at me. A single lock of hair fell into his face.

"What part of New York are you from?" I asked.

"Upper East Side." Colin popped an olive off the charcuterie spread into his mouth, then joined Melissa on a wrought-iron bench, and draped his arm over his wife's shoulder. His fingers absentmindedly played with her long blond hair.

Odette dipped her head back in misery. "I'd give anything to live in New York."

"I've done some time in Manhattan," Mom interjected. "So, you decided to leave after 9/11?" I clenched my jaw, humiliated she'd dare say anything.

Melissa patted Colin's leg. "We just needed a fresh start."

"I'd always wanted to live in California," Colin said.

"By the way, I wanted to talk to you about establishing a neighborhood watch," Melissa said to Mom. "I'd love your help."

I braced myself for a sharp-tongued reply. Mom sipped her margarita and squared her feline eyes at her new neighbor. "There's nothing to worry about here. We're a *beach* community."

"I know it might not be your cup of tea, but I promise you," Melissa pressed, "I only want to protect our families."

Clearly bothered by Melissa's claim on the neighborhood she'd lived in all her life, Mom clocked the untouched grill. "Oh, Colin? I have a job for you!" Soon, he was sporting a yellow apron I didn't even know we had.

When they couldn't find the tongs, Theo and I were nominated to run over to the Fowlers' to retrieve some, even though the act of grabbing tongs hardly required four hands. I felt childish given how easily Mom offered me up, like I was incapable of fraternizing with kids my age without her intervention.

At the threshold of the Fowlers', I paused, curious how the pink house might be altered as soon as I stepped beyond the arched doorway. The interior was exquisitely decorated in blinding white, apart from pops of seafoam and coral. Luxury in every corner.

"Shoes off," Theo ordered. I slipped off my sandals and placed them next to his sneakers in a cubby organizer. He strolled through an archway into the kitchen. As he rummaged through the drawers, disrupting the meticulously organized system, I noticed a wedding portrait hung in a mercury glass frame. A handsome man in the center appeared to be rattling off a toast as Melissa and Colin raised their champagne flutes. I was about to ask Theo who the other man was, when he appeared next to me, tongs in hand.

"So, at the Vortex . . ." Theo asked. "Is that guy your boyfriend?"

My stomach dipped. "Nope."

Theo stuffed one hand in the pocket of his jeans, then made a proposition. "Want to blaze?"

ONCE THEO RAN THE TONGS BACK OVER TO OUR HOUSE, WE SETTLED INTO HIS backyard, illuminated by strategically placed lighting. Neat rows of flowers lined the perimeter of an exactly square lawn opposite a kidney bean–shaped pool. I dipped my feet into the water, picturing Max roughhousing with the little kids, Eden tending to the greenhouse, a week more pregnant than I'd last seen her, starlight on her skin. Perhaps I no longer required the comfort of escaping to the pink house's fantasy anymore, now that I could daydream about the Oasis and Max, my own father.

Theo placed a wooden box on the tile and dug out a little bag of pot.

He rolled up the joint, licking the edges to seal it. The pink flash of his tongue made me unsteady.

"Do you do this a lot?" I asked, nervous about how I'd respond to the drug. I'd only smoked once before, at Odette's birthday party in the spring, when I coughed up nothing but ash.

"They tried to put me on these drugs last year when . . ." He trailed off, then lit up the joint. "But pot's better."

Theo was someone who had experienced life on a deeper level than I had. He needed substances to cope with the traumatic nightmare that was 9/11. Despite his troubles, he told me he was bound for Stanford on a swimming scholarship in September. Before I went to the Oasis, Theo Fowler was everything I'd ever imagined wanting. Impressive on paper, handsome, worldly, with experience that might rub off on me.

"So, what's the deal with your sister?" he asked, out of the blue.

I'd heard this question before, and without a doubt, I'd hear it again. Of course our entire interaction had been a ruse to get to Odette.

Theo noticed my scowl and cracked up. "Whoa! Guess I touched a nerve!"

"It's unbelievable!" I ranted. "She's so cold, but you can't deny she has this *effect* on the opposite sex."

"I meant no offense by it." He handed me the joint and held my gaze while I inhaled. "Just trying to get to know you."

I tried to decode the words that we weren't saying, hyperaware that his thigh was mere centimeters from mine. I was suddenly in possession of a tantalizing story I normally would have indulged, but I felt the need to keep the Oasis sacred and all for myself.

"Listen, I'm supposed to meet up with some people," he began. I felt the urge to make myself disappear. I'd been reading too much into our interaction. I passed him back the joint and scrambled up to go.

To my surprise, he extended an invitation. "Hey, why don't you meet me tomorrow night? I've been meaning to have a local show me the beach."

"'The beach is closed to the public after sunset.'"

He flicked the ash into the pool drain. "That stops you?"

BY THE TIME I MADE IT BACK HOME, MOM WAS HOLDING COURT, MAKING A mess of the kitchen. She was drunk but happy—the best combination for her and everyone else around her. Colin pulled on the belt loops of Melissa's white linen pants. She leaned her head back against his chest and gave up her needless task of cleaning up another woman's house. I was watching them, in awe of their attraction, when Arthur tugged on my arm.

Nothing, technically, had occurred between Arthur and me, yet guilt about sharing a joint with Theo and fantasizing that someone like him could desire me crept in. I couldn't fathom Mom ever feeling a dash of guilt for seesawing between two men, but then again, I didn't know for certain if either of them wanted me that way.

I followed Arthur outside. By some miracle, no one else had found their way inside the carriage house. At first, I noticed his black Moleskine lying on the drafting table and contemplated if I could swipe it, until I saw what was beside it. A new set of prints had been laid out. Portraits and landscapes and abstract film blurs of the Oasis, all in a cool, arresting black and white.

There was one of me, taken from afar. I hadn't noticed Arthur with his camera at all that night. The shadow of the fire loomed large in the sand, while my expression appeared as a question mark, an unfinished puzzle. The wool blanket was wrapped around my shoulders, my eyes glassy as I turned over the story of the hero inside my mind. Raised by a photographer, I'd grown accustomed to having my picture taken, but it was invigorating to be captured by someone else's lens. By Arthur's especially.

A wave of worry surfaced. "Mom hasn't seen these, right?"

"Of course not." Arthur touched my shoulder and shook his head. "She never will. This is ours, Lucy."

I picked up the portrait, careful not to smudge it. I wanted to pore over that night, to make sure it was as luminous as I remembered. "Is it hard for you to be away?"

Heat rippled off his skin. "Sometimes."

"You're not a very good liar," I teased.

"Not as good as you."

I hated that I ever admitted my penchant for lying to him. My tongue felt foreign, furry from the joint. "The neighbor across the street asked me out." I knew it might be a stretch to call Theo's invitation to the beach a date, but I wanted to test Arthur.

"Are you trying to make me jealous?"

"Are you?"

"Jealousy is for people in their shadow." He took a step back from me. I fell prey to the sway of my nerves, second-guessing his every move. The haphazard dance of wanting him as he pulled away made me light-headed. "That kid's only a distraction from your work. Your writing's getting stronger. The Oasis changed you, didn't it? Like I promised." He grabbed my wrist and pressed his thumb between my tendons. "If you ever go back, you'll learn to be braver." He dropped my hand and gathered his photographs. "Anyway, your mother's collection's about wrapped up. She won't have much use for me anymore. I'll be heading back to the desert tomorrow night. For good."

A lump rose in my throat at the threat of Arthur being in the desert without me. I might have gotten away with a weekend but disappearing for longer seemed improbable. In a few days, it would be July. I needed to submit my workshop application by August, and school would start only weeks after that.

Arthur returned his covert Moleskine to his shirt pocket, slid the photographs into a manila envelope, then sealed it shut.

WELL AFTER TWO A.M., I FOUGHT MY NOISY BRAIN FOR SLEEP. MY BODY WAS racked with overwhelming apprehension about what might happen if I met Theo on the beach. If I could slip into mundane adolescent rebellion, it would be like my illicit trip to the desert never happened.

If Arthur left for good, whatever flirtation I'd conjured up between us would be nothing more than a lark I'd embellish at sleepovers. Whatever magic existed in Max's Oasis, a far-fetched fairy tale no one would ever believe.

The doorbell rang. I rolled over, exhausted, and hoped someone else would send the late-night guest bothering us away. But the doorbell wouldn't stop ringing. I threw the blanket off me and ambled into the hallway. I turned the deadbolt and opened the door to find Judy in her favorite red wig, now lopsided and matted, flamingo-pink heels in her hand. The last I'd seen her, she'd left our party and headed off to a night-club in Hillcrest for a gig.

"Where's Diana?" That's when I noticed the welt on her cheek, bruises on her collarbone. She'd been beaten. Brutally. "They took my house key, my purse, everything . . ."

"Oh my God." I ushered her inside. She yanked her wig off, exposing her damp cap. I'd never seen her without her vivacious spirit. It scared the hell out of me. I raced back down the hallway and barged through Mom's door without knocking. "Mom!" I shook her, but she wouldn't budge. "It's Judy."

She mumbled, "Tell her I'm asleep."

"She needs you. Someone hurt her." I watched as she slowly opened her eyes. Her gaze flitted over to her settee, where her favorite film camera was laid out. "Mom?" I pleaded.

"It'll be fine," she moaned. "I'll handle it tomorrow." She flipped over, turning her back on us.

I rummaged through the hallway closet for a spare towel, to soften the blow.

"You know how she is with those margaritas . . ." I said as I returned to the living room.

Judy took the towel and sighed, like she'd known disappointment was coming. Some of her press-on nails had fallen off. The remaining digits of fire-engine red appeared inappropriately bright under the circumstances. She must have fought her attacker off. Tooth and nail.

"How about I draw you a bath?" I offered.

Judy waited in the hallway while I ran the water in the tub. I pulled the first-aid kit from the medicine cabinet and placed it on the counter. I thought of the first time I'd met Judy, when I came home from school to her performing "The Man That Got Away" as Judy Garland's *A Star Is Born* played in the background. Mom cheered her on from behind the camera. "She's a star! Isn't she?" Mom clicked the shutter. "Look out, Broadway!"

Looking at Judy now, half out of drag, her face swollen and pulsing, my heart ached for her. I wanted to understand why someone would hurt her. How the world could be so cruel. I didn't need to look far for the danger Max had warned me about. I'd found it right there on my doorstep.

"I can take it from here." Mom's throaty alto startled me. I turned to see her in the hallway—her silk robe wrapped around her slender frame, her favorite film camera hanging from her neck. She placed a hand on my arm and dismissed me. "Go to bed, Lucy."

I wanted to protest, but there was no leniency in her demand. I took one final look at Judy. Her lip quivered, but I never saw a single tear of hers that night. As soon as I stepped out of the bathroom, Mom clicked the door shut behind me. I held my breath and tried to make out their conversation through the wall.

"I tried to tell them," I heard Judy say. "I told them I was born here. I said I'm an American too, but they didn't listen."

*58 days before*

The day after the party, Mom materialized in the kitchen, raccoon-eyed, her slip hanging off her shoulder. She rubbed her temples and waited for the coffee to revive her.

"Mom, what did the police say?"

"About what?"

"Judy!" I shouted. "Where is she?" I'd checked her room that morning. The bed had been made; her suitcase was missing from the closet. "Did you file a report?"

She took a mug out of the cupboard and poured the coffee. "I took care of it."

"You did?"

"Believe what you will, darling." She slunk back down the hall.

"But wait." I went after her. "Don't they say the first twenty-four hours are the most important? Do they have any suspects? Anything?"

"You watch too many movies."

SOMETHING INSIDE ME SNAPPED. I NEEDED TO BECOME THE KIND OF ARTIST who took risks. I needed to take a stand when someone like Judy was targeted, like Max would do for his people. I needed Mom to trust I had something to say. I needed to learn more from Max, to soak in all he had to teach me. I needed to be the girl who would join the boy from New York at the beach.

Desperate to leave my cowardice behind, I charged into Odette's room to ransack her closet.

Only five minutes later, Odette appeared out of nowhere, lunged toward me, and snatched a hanger out of my grasp. "What the fuck are you doing?" She pointed to the vest I was wearing. I'd been caught red-handed. "And wearing?"

"I'm sorry, okay?" I knew she'd tired of this exchange, which we'd had countless times before, but I couldn't help it. I was desperate for whatever pixie dust she possessed to rub off on me. "I have nothing to wear. I'm meeting Theo tonight."

Odette sighed, then grabbed her makeup bag. "Come here." She sat me down on her unmade bed and went to work.

"How did you know you were in love?" I asked, remembering her with her spiky-haired drummer, leaning against the side of the house, his pierced tongue in her mouth.

She cackled, smudged my eyeshadow in the process, then licked her thumb to fix her mistake. "I'm not in love. I'm fucking him." Odette pumped the mascara wand in and out of the tube. "There's a difference."

"Well, it seems like he's in love with you."

"The dude's in love with himself." She instructed me to open my mouth, applied a petal-pink lipstick, then handed me a tissue to blot. Conversations like this, when Odette tolerated my infiltration into her Technicolor world, were rare. I wanted to be her friend so badly. "He's not even coming to LA. He can't stand not being the front man, so he's sulking." Odette tossed her leather show pants into her suitcase. "Real men take what they want and don't apologize for it."

I inhaled sharply. There was a stark contrast between the juvenile crush I'd developed on our new neighbor overnight and the spiral I felt in my gut whenever Arthur spoke to me. One was pure and perhaps even possible; the other was inconceivable.

She knelt down to zip up her suitcase. "Would you help me with this?" I could hear the edge in her voice, and I was well aware that our allotted bonding time would soon expire. I obliged her and sat on the bulging suitcase as she struggled with the zipper.

"Odette," I said. "I need to tell you something."

Finally, the zipper gave. Her mind was elsewhere, and I knew she hadn't heard me. I wanted to find a way to keep her there, but nothing could stop her. For better or worse, my sister believed she had more important things to worry about than me.

As soon as Odette left, I snuck back into her room, swiped the bottle of her jasmine perfume that she'd forgotten on her dresser, and tucked it into my backpack. I froze when I heard the familiar, muffled murmur of Mom's husky voice and Arthur's baritone in her bedroom. I was eager to make out their conversation, but then Arthur appeared in the doorway. I wished I had the power to freeze him there, to keep him for myself, to stop him from leaving too. He looked me over, sizing me up like some cattle at auction, anxious for the slaughter.

THEO POINTED DOWN THE FOGGY MASS OF SAND AT THE ICONIC RED PIPETTES visible in the post-sunset haze. "What's that down there?"

"The Hotel Del," I told him. "Some people say it's haunted."

Out of nowhere, Theo grabbed my hand. Every vein in my body ignited. We took off running toward the dark blue waves. Ten yards away from the coastline, he let his hand fall.

"I've never been in the Pacific before," he said.

"I've never been in the Atlantic. How does it compare?"

"I don't know yet."

He worked the buckle on his belt and tugged off his jeans. I was thankful for the cover of night to disguise my blushing face. He left his jeans in a heap on the sand, jogged to the waterline, and pulled his shirt over his head. The large knot of his spine contracted and released. When he realized I wasn't behind him, he walked backward and shouted over the raucous waves.

"You coming, Golden?"

"That water's freezing."

He dove into the waves headfirst and surfaced seconds later, shrieking. "Shit!"

"Told you!"

"What are you waiting for?" he called out. I imagined water droplets resting on his long lashes, wishing I could see them up close. He waded through the water, his palms grazing the salty spray of the waves.

Dry-mouthed, I slumped down onto my knees and dug my fingers into the sand. Before I went to the Oasis, this invitation would have been enough for me, to be a placeholder in this red-blooded boy's summer before his grand life plan was set to begin. The realization began to crystallize in my mind. His was a call I could not answer.

Once Theo had tired of the Pacific, he trudged his way back up the beach. I watched him dress and couldn't tear my eyes away from his slick skin. He joined me on the sand, water dripping from the ends of his hair. Before I could make up an excuse to leave, he locked his mouth to mine. I reared my head back, but in one swift movement, he pulled the back of my neck closer. The churning in my chest deepened. He sank his teeth into my bottom lip, and I felt a pang of hunger for something more.

Was this it? Was this feverish kiss the inspiration that was supposed to bring me closer to my highest self? An alarm went off inside me. I pulled away and fled, leaving Theo there to dry off alone.

He was the last person to see me before I disappeared.

I SPRINTED BACK TO THE HOUSE, THE TASTE OF THEO'S DISAPPOINTMENT LINgering on my lips, humming and raw. I was not what he wanted me to be. I couldn't stop thinking about Arthur's photograph and the way he'd captured me. A tormenting thought persisted: I kept imagining the weight of Arthur's lips on mine instead of Theo's.

Max was right. Now that I'd stepped foot in the Oasis, my eyes had been opened to the disasters and evils of the outside world. Terror was right on our doorstep, ringing our doorbell, beaten and bruised. The horror of 9/11 couldn't be ignored now that Theo and his parents lived across the street, now that Judy had been targeted because of the way she was born, the way she lived her life.

Theo and the writing workshop and my mother's superiority and the false allure of the pink house and this island of surveillance and terror—they were not the answer. Everything would be better if I returned. In the Oasis, I belonged.

I heard Arthur's truck before I saw it. Engine rumbling low, radio static ticking, loitering in front of our house. My heartbeat pounded in my ears. I rapped my knuckles on the passenger window.

"Wait," I said. "Take me back."

Without a word, he shifted the truck into gear, like he'd expected me all along.

WHEN WE BREAK FOR LUNCH, I TAKE REFUGE IN MY BEDROOM, WELL aware of the crew's presence on the other side of the wall. I'm in the middle of my chopped salad, scrolling through Theo's company website, when I hear the front door clang closed. The vibration echoes through the loft. I check the clock—1 p.m. on the dot.

Sloane knocks. "We're ready for you!"

I rush to the door and crack it open an inch. "Is someone else here?" I keep up the charade, acting like I'm oblivious to who's around the bend.

Sloane glances toward the living room, where Isaac's standing by, surely wanting to capture my look of horror once I see who he's invited into my home for a little reunion.

I EMERGE FROM MY BEDROOM TO FIND MY LEATHER ARMCHAIR IS occupied, now placed beside the green velvet one, the original hot seat. Even though I'm prepared, it's disconcerting to see Theo Fowler as an adult. The promising value he possessed as a teenager has been steadily polished in the last two decades, but I can still spot the wear and tear. He has a combed haircut, rounded shoulders, a crisp blue suit, and a gut he thinks he's disguising that's squeezed by his belt. There's still that same superiority, an awareness of his tax bracket that clashes with an oh-so-delicate, put-on air of suffering.

"Take a seat, Lucy," Isaac says, instructing me to sit in the green chair beside my old neighbor. "About time we get started."

I know from my online search that Theo's already divorced, onto his second marriage and second round of kids. He works under his dad at a firm in Dallas. He's adopted hunting as his latest hobby— venturing into Hill Country with his beer-gutted, SMU-educated good ole boy buddies on long weekends. Privileged by day, perhaps shaken by nightmares of me when the sun goes down.

"Theo, thank you for coming today." Isaac can pull out the charm whenever the situation warrants it. "I know this can't be an easy subject to revisit, so I appreciate your cooperation. What made you decide to participate?"

"Last year, my mother was diagnosed with MS," Theo says. "Every day presents a new set of challenges. I worry about the case making headlines again. Stress isn't good for her condition. It's important someone from our family speaks out." He blinks at me, vigilant, so I express my condolences.

"I'm sorry. I was unaware Melissa had fallen ill . . ."

Theo hangs his head. "She tried her best to protect you."

"I've always been vocal about appreciating your mother's efforts—"

Isaac interrupts me. "Theo, can you paint the picture for us? What was the summer of 2002 like for you?"

"My family had just been through hell. We experienced a devastating loss on 9/11. It was a challenging time." Theo pauses and pounds his chest with his fist, like he's a firefighter who defied the odds. "Everyone knows now that things had gotten . . . messy back in New York, so we left and went to Coronado. We all agreed to move on. Things were finally looking up. I was set to swim at Stanford in the fall. My parents were getting along again. But when the Goldens entered our lives, it wasn't so easy to leave the past in the past." Theo directs his sobering gaze to Isaac, like I'm not even in the room. "My mother led the search and devoted herself to bringing Lucy home safely. In turn, Lucy ruined not only my reputation, but my entire family's. We've never been the same."

When I look at him, the fury in my chest intensifies. He fails to mention that Melissa started the neighborhood watch in the first place to protect her precious boy, not to bring me home. A what-if occurs to me. If I had never returned to the Oasis that night, would Theo and I be the ones living in the pink house on our little island, playing husband and wife, arguing over dishwasher cycles and refereeing holiday squabbles between the in-laws? The possibility of an alternate reality suggests regret, but it's a simpler existence, one in which I'm nobody but somebody's wife. There's a reason why I did not pursue that path. I was meant for something greater.

"Listen." I begin my rebuttal calmly. "I had no control over what the press—"

"This isn't about the pariahs in the press," Theo says, determined to make his point. "When your book came out, it was all the proof I needed that you didn't care one iota about what happened to us. You used our family's dirty laundry as color for your little manifesto. You capitalized on our tragedy to entertain your loyal readers. Isn't that your specialty?"

"Tell us, Theo," I hear Isaac say. "How were you impacted?"

"Our family will always be associated with a vicious crime. To be implicated . . ." Theo's voice cracks. His easy slip into vulnerability makes me embarrassed for him. I feel the urge to remind him he's being filmed. "I lost my admission to Stanford. My swimming career ended before it could begin. My parents don't speak, to this day. I don't know how to quantify how it affected the past twenty years, but suffice it to say, I am not the same person I was before that summer. I'll never get that back."

I take the opportunity to make my point. "You work for your dad's firm now, don't you?"

He adjusts his tie around his neck. "I don't see how that's relevant."

"How could it not be?" I say. I see Sloane pop her head up from behind the monitor. Her smirk is contagious. "Once again, they came to your rescue and bailed you out. No matter what kind of messes you make, they'll make sure you move through life without holding yourself accountable."

He folds his hands in his lap and leans toward me. "As a father now, I can't imagine a scenario in which I wouldn't do everything in my power . . ." He trails off again, as if overcome with emotion, conjuring the nightmare in real time. "I would do *anything* to protect my child." He clears his throat but can't resist. "I know that's difficult for you to understand."

There it goes—that snide arrogance parents exude when speaking to the abominable childless adults who can't possibly fathom the gravity of such a thankless burden. I want to slap him.

"I was hurting," Theo goes on. "After everything that happened in New York, I wasn't thinking clearly. I own my part in it." He puts his head in his hands. "I made a lot of mistakes back then. I'm sorry for what happened to you, Lucy. I really am. I absolutely hold myself accountable for my childish larks, but you seem to forget I was just a kid with a crush on the girl across the street."

Suddenly, the last twenty years dissolve in an instant. I see past the slicked-back hair grazing his shirt collar and see the boy in the pink house. I'm transported back to that night on the beach. I'm back sitting beside him, my tongue in his mouth, searching for the kind of high only the desert supplied.

Theo interrupts my train of thought. "I didn't deserve for my name to get dragged through the mud, but I've moved on with my life. I'm grateful I had parents who helped me get to where I am now. I've made peace with it all. Now who is going to hold you accountable, Lucy?"

I clench my jaw. "Excuse me?"

He straightens his posture. "What about the lives you've ruined, besides your own? When are you going to take responsibility for what you've done?"

I cross my arms in front of my chest. I wonder if this is the extent of what Isaac has in store for me—one public stoning after another. Sloane looks away, like she can't bear to watch Theo attack my character. Maybe she is on my side.

Theo Fowler can say whatever he likes, but I did not destroy him. I did not break his bones and set them crookedly back in place. The exact outcome of his perfect little life was there the whole time. The boyish finger pointing outward—his first impulse, even still.

You can speed up fate, but you cannot determine it.

# PARAMOUNT STUDIOS

MALIN TAPS HER FRESH SET OF ACRYLICS AND INSPECTS THE HANDI-work of the lip-pierced makeup artist hired for my appearance on *The Remy Olsen Show*. Today, I'll be captured by two sets of lenses: Remy's, aimed to please Midwest housewives and Nielsen ratings, and Isaac's, designed for his precious process.

"More blush," Malin determines. She digs through her giant Louis Vuitton bag, and I'm hoping she's going to hand me whatever prescription drugs she has floating around the bottom of it. She doesn't. Instead, she retrieves eucalyptus lotion, slathers her hands, and offers me a dollop.

Isaac roams the dressing room in a caffeinated flurry. "How'd you talk me into this?" Sloane follows him with a water bottle, trying to get him to calm down and hydrate, but he persists in his circles. "It's too soon."

"You agreed, Isaac," Malin reminds him. "It's good press for you too."

"I despise the press," Isaac snaps. He stops in his tracks, causing Sloane to narrowly miss running straight into his back.

I try to assuage him, because his nerves are only exacerbating mine. I rub the lotion into my hands. "Well, you said you wanted to know what my life is like now."

"Remember this one's live, so stay present," Malin says to me. "Answer like I told you, okay?"

When I nod, my head movement prompts a grunt from the makeup artist.

"Hey!" Isaac tightens his grip on the map of the Paramount Studios lot that's balled up in his fist. "No premeditated PR tactics."

Malin smirks, an unspoken faith that all the media training she's instilled in the Golden women over the years won't fail us now.

A moment later, a handler confers with Sloane. "Ready to meet Remy?"

Isaac instructs his head cameraman, Derek, and his crew to capture our preshow meeting with Remy. The Daytime Emmy–winning host appears more plastic in person than she does on TV. I search for the serious journalist she used to be underneath her cakey makeup to no avail.

"Lucy, wonderful to see you." She shakes my hand. I can tell she's not looking at me directly, but rather my hairline. Perhaps a trick she's learned after decades of interviews.

"Thanks for having me back, Remy." A few years ago, for her NXIVM coverage, I filled in as a last-minute replacement, an expert on high-control groups.

Remy delivers her tired catchphrase without a drop of irony. "Thanks for trusting us."

A PRODUCTION ASSISTANT GUIDES ME TOWARD A BEIGE COUCH on set. Malin always requests for me to be preseated. If you enter while the camera's rolling, you risk the possibility of a less-than-warm welcome by the studio audience. It turns out they're too distracted by the show's warm-up comedian to notice my arrival, and Malin's right, yet again.

The studio's freezing, but the stage lights combat the chill in full force. I wish I were wearing a more breathable top. Isaac and his crew are busy negotiating for space with Remy's production team. Sloane lurks like Isaac's shadow, whispering in his ear. He shoos her away like a gnat. Finally, Remy takes her position in her armchair. The director counts us down, and then we're off.

When the cameras blink red, Remy introduces a video segment detailing the ins and outs of my case. As I wait, I count the stripes on the assistant director's shirt. This tactic, an old Malin trick, makes my expression appear neutral and thoughtful. The video ends, not a moment too soon.

"Well, Lucy," she starts. "Thank you for being here today. How does it feel knowing it's been *twenty years* since that fateful summer?"

I tuck my hair behind my ear, showcasing my understated yet elegant choice of small gold hoops. Every move has its purpose. "It's difficult to wrap my head around, Remy," I tell her. "But the more time that passes, the more grateful I am."

When Remy raises her perfectly microbladed eyebrow, no wrinkles appear in her shellacked forehead. "Grateful?"

"I understand that must sound strange," I explain. "I am forever marked by what happened to me. But through it all, I was given a platform. I'm able to tell my story. Countless others are never granted that opportunity."

The studio audience responds with respectful hums.

Remy takes the segue. "Now you're telling your story in a new way," she says. "Isaac Coleman, the acclaimed documentary filmmaker, known for *Buckhead Butcher*, has selected you as his next subject."

"That's right, Remy." I smile at Isaac, whose hands are shoved in his pockets, his posture suffering. "We're working together on a documentary." I make sure to position it as a joint venture. "I'm also thrilled to announce I'll be releasing a special edition of my memoir, *Rattlesnake*, updated with a new foreword exclusive to this edition. Fans are going to love it."

The audience claps, but it feels thin in my ears. Not as spirited as I imagined it last night when I was tossing and turning.

"Fascinating," Remy replies. "What are you hoping the world will gain from revisiting your story?"

"Thank you for asking that," I say. "It's no secret that there has been plenty of controversy—"

Remy jumps in. "Well, surely you can understand the frustration surrounding this case." I blink at her blatant interruption of the flow of our conversation when we're live. She takes my pause to mean I have no idea what she's referring to, which is frankly condescending. "There *are* unanswered questions. The *missing bodies*, for starters . . ."

"I . . ." I hesitate, appalled at her audacity to mention the missing bodies. I catch sight of Malin in my periphery, nodding at me to go on. I quickly pivot back to Remy's original question and hope no one notices my lapse. "Well, Remy, I hope that today people will hear my story for what it is and monitor their own internalized misogyny. The media's handling of the case at the time . . ." I pause, unsure about breaking Malin's cardinal rule in bringing up something that wasn't part of the preinterview, but I suppose Remy's already done that.

Remy eggs me on. "The Hal Jacobson fiasco."

I bristle just hearing his name. His reptilian snarl springs to mind. I consider my public annihilation by the notorious journalist Hal Jacobson to be one of the worst hours of my life. I'd just published *Rattlesnake*, and he argued against every word I'd written. His evisceration gave the casual haters matches and perpetuated the problematic accusations with an arrogant spray of gasoline.

*If you were so remorseful, why didn't you turn yourself in?*

*Is that what you think grief looks like?*

*Do you consider yourself a sexual deviant?*

*What did you leave out of your little diary?*

The ten-minute video garnered a couple million views online. I scroll through it sometimes, critiquing my bumbling responses to Hal's targeted character assassination.

"At the time, I didn't know any better," I tell Remy. "Hal justified humiliating me by saying he was a fair journalist. As a man in a position of power, his account was deemed more credible than that of the nineteen-year-old girl who'd lived through it."

"That didn't age well," Remy agrees, pursing her lips like she's proud of her radical feminism. I resist the impulse to pick this response apart. It doesn't matter what level of woke was accepted back in the early aughts. It was always wrong. "Especially given the allegations of sexual misconduct against Hal Jacobson that were made public during Me Too by former female staffers."

"It's validating, yes." I give her this point. "His mission to vilify me was irresponsible journalism, at best. My sexuality *and* my innocence shouldn't have been up for debate. The court reviewed the evidence and made their ruling. My name had already been cleared. When a man makes it his mission to discredit a woman's word, and the public listens, there is nothing more dehumanizing than that."

"I find it heartbreaking," Remy replies, as her manicured hand floats to her chest. "You are a hero to so many. So many women since have pledged their support to you, regretful of the ways they might have slandered you back then. You're so strong and brave, but in the Oasis, in the press . . ." Remy delivers the melodrama so the network can use this clip for previews. "People forget you are a victim too, don't they?"

Max's old refrain immediately comes to mind: *There are no victims.*

I pause for dramatic effect, like a cry's lodged in my throat. It's not, but no one who's watching will know the difference. "I'm a free woman today for a reason. I know without a doubt, my purpose is to give a voice to the voiceless."

Touched by this, Remy sheds a tear. Her overflow of emotion sends the studio audience into a frenzy. I crack my Cheshire cat smile to solidify their fandom and cap off my performance. There, by the main camera, Isaac claps his hand on Sloane's shoulder, satisfied by something I can't put my finger on. This electric spark of all the eyes in a room being on you—there's no comparison. Looking for a spectacle, folks? Let Lucy Golden entertain you.

I'm lucky it's fashionable to believe women these days.


*Silverlake*


AFTER THE TAPING, SLOANE TELLS ME SHE'S SUPPOSED TO MEET SOME friends at Bar Stella and to "swing by." I feel a pang of insecurity that this assistant already had plans when I asked and now I'm the one tagging along. I remind myself that this girl fawned over me. I've never intentionally socialized with a real fan before. I reapply my lipstick, a more daring shade of burgundy that I will have to constantly touch up, but it's important to lead with an appearance of strength.

On the way to Silverlake, I check my Instagram and already I've amassed three thousand more followers since the show aired. They're ticking upward by the minute. While the TexWatson86s of the world lick their wounds, my fans rave over the appearance. One of them edits a snappy compilation of the footage. I repost it and exhale as the likes accumulate. The comments on the Hal Jacobson interview double down with support for me, cancellation for him. Whatever Isaac might have up his sleeve, I can manage. Befriending Sloane will be too easy.

Keep your enemies closer.

The car rattles down the freeway. I glare at the back of the driver's hairy neck. For a moment, I panic about this anonymous person I've handed my life over to without a second thought. Then the road catches, and the ride evens out. I check my lip lines in my phone camera again and buzz with the potential of the evening.

I can be Lucy Golden tonight, and for once that could be a wonderful thing.

I SHOVE MY WAY THROUGH THE PACKED BAR. I SYMPATHIZE WITH the bartenders, destined to manage the meek whims of transplants asking them to make the bartender's special because they don't know themselves well enough yet to know what they like. I wait as the boys hit on the girls and the girls hit on the girls. I always find it sad when I observe this mating ritual from the outside. I want to tell them to lower their expectations. There's nothing lasting to be found in a bar flirtation—a fuck, if you're lucky, or even better, a free drink.

A huddle of twentysomething girls poses for pictures, and instantly, I feel my age when the flash goes off in the dark bar. Squeals of passionate promises to meet each other for brunch follow. It's obvious they'll never go, because that's not the way friendship in Los Angeles works. I used to believe it did. Years ago, I frequented this exact bar with the actress who played me in the movie about that summer, but our friendship fizzled out a couple months after the premiere. Now I know she only pretended to like me so she could imitate my gestures and provide some colorful anecdotes during the press tour. I made the grave mistake of introducing her to Odette, and the rest was history. She realized, or maybe she'd always known, any cachet she might glean from the Goldens was best found in my rock star older sister. Odette was even a bridesmaid in her Big Sky, Montana, wedding. Yet another feather to add to Odette's stacked cap of superiority. Since then, I've stopped trying, preferring my own company to the forced intimacy of surface-level companionship with women who have nothing in common with me.

After the bartender hands me my martini, I find Sloane on the back patio, a sexy and narrow sanctuary with overhanging trees. She's posted up on a far iron table, alone. When she sees me, she makes a big show of greeting me with a hug. Rocking me side to side.

"My fucking hero," Sloane says, and pulls me down next to her. "Can you believe today actually happened?"

"Oh, we don't need to talk about that."

"How can we not talk about it?" Sloane slurs. "You were absolutely brilliant!"

I clock her watery Paloma, a quarter left, a myriad of glasses on the table. "You think so?"

"Even Isaac was pleasantly surprised."

"He said that?"

The bar is too loud. Sloane either ignores or doesn't hear my question. "I'm so glad you came out."

"Thanks for inviting me." I relax into the wall behind me. "So, are your friends in the bathroom or—"

"Oh, yeah, sorry, they just bailed for a *warehouse party*." She punctuates the phrase with air quotes. "Not my scene anymore, you know?"

"Right." I squint at her, trying to assess who this woman is exactly. Daily yoga, a ban on warehouse parties, smudged eyeliner, eager to please. Her put-on tough exterior is only an act. "Not my scene either."

"You'll meet them next time." Her phone lights up, and it's like she's Pavlov's dog, immediately consumed with the text. "Sorry. Always on the clock, you know."

I fake sympathy, but I'm dying to know whatever it is Isaac's texting her at this hour. I debate how I can steer the conversation toward something I can use without raising suspicion.

"So, how do you think the shoot is going so far?"

"Good. Really good," Sloane says as she replies to her text. "You know, it's still early days."

"Meaning?"

Rudely, she makes me wait for her to press send and gulp her cocktail. "Oh, I wouldn't want to overstep."

I force a casual smile. "Well, now you have to tell me."

"I mean, you crushed Remy, so that's great." She pauses. "That'll be great. The response from today alone—"

"But?" I prod her. Sloane chews on her fingers, delaying her response. "What is it?"

"It wouldn't kill you to open up more," she spits out, eyes squeezed shut, like she's ripping off a hangnail. "You're coming off less rehearsed than you did at the beginning, which is something, but there's not really much *new* that you're giving us. The reunion with Theo Fowler yesterday—I'm not sure if you've been told this before, but . . ."

"Go on."

"I'm not saying this personally, but your refusal to acknowledge what the Fowlers went through may make you come off a tad unlikable."

I roll my eyes. "I've been called worse."

"Well, and maybe that's just it. You're so tough that viewers might find you unrelatable. Maybe you should try to look at your past through a bit more of a critical lens than you usually do. Dig deeper. You might surprise yourself."

I suppress a scoff. What right does this assistant have to give me direction? Does she honestly think I haven't looked at my past through a critical lens? That's all I do. That's what I'm known for. I tamp down the anger bubbling up inside me and plaster on a brave face.

"Thanks for letting me know," I tell her. "It can be hard to read Isaac sometimes."

Sloane nods in agreement, realizes she's chewing her nails again, and forces herself to stop.

"So . . ." I can't believe I'm resorting to this, but I feel like I have no choice. I'm getting nowhere. "What is he planning to do to find the missing bodies anyway?"

Sloane stares at me, doe-eyed. It's obvious she knows more about his schemes than she's letting on. I wonder now if Isaac pushed Remy behind Malin's back to mention the bodies. I wouldn't put it past him. He's arrogant enough to believe after twenty years he will be the white knight to save the kingdom. He'll find out soon enough: it's a lost cause.

"You can tell me," I press her. "I won't rat you out."

Sloane slurps down the remainder of her drink. "I just don't think that's my place."

"I mean, you're as much a part of this production as anyone else." I try to butter her up. "Just because you're an assistant doesn't mean you're not important."

"I appreciate that," she says with zero appreciation. "Isaac's process is really important to him, though. If you knew what he had planned, that could compromise his whole narrative."

"I care more about this project being a success than he does. If you let me know what he's planning, then I might be able to make it even stronger. Have you considered that?" Sloane falls silent, and I realize I've gone too far. I need to turn this around. Quickly. "You know what?" I polish off the last of my cocktail. "That's enough work talk."

"Totally. I'm so fried." Sloane relaxes, flips her blue shag. "Besides, never in a million years did I think I'd be out with the one and only Lucy Golden. We should celebrate."

"Another round?" I offer. "My treat."

At the congested bar, I slip the bartender a fifty-dollar bill to cut the line and order a round of cocktails and tequila shots. Before I return to our table outside, I drop a little something special into Sloane's Paloma. I didn't want to resort to this, but desperate times.

"Come here," Sloane says, after we take our shots. "Let's take a picture." She tilts her head toward mine and outstretches her arm to capture us. Neither of us smiles with our teeth. From the outside, we must look like just another pair of Hollywood hopefuls on a Friday night, drunk on our delusions.

SLOANE RENTS A STUDIO IN WEST HOLLYWOOD, AT THE INTER-section of Willoughby and Stanley. When I can't find her keys in her gargantuan bag, she apologizes over and over.

"You don't have to do this," she says, her arm limp and sweaty around my neck. "I'm so embarrassed. I don't know how I got so wasted."

"Don't worry about it, babe," I tell her. "Just tell me how to get in."

"It's easy." She points to the window on her first-floor apartment. "Take out the screen and we can hop right in. I do it all the time."

I prop her up against the stoop and follow her instructions. An intruder's dream, the window screen slides right off. I duck down to make my way inside, then open the door for Sloane. Her head lolls. She won't remember a thing. It could have just as easily happened to anyone. She'll wake up in the morning, fuzzy-brained and confused, humiliated for not being able to hold her liquor. It will be a good lesson for her. People never watch their drinks as closely as they should.

"You're such a good friend, Lucy," she slurs.

If she even remembers I was here, Sloane will recall only how lovingly I took care of her.

Careful not to disturb her, I drag her to her unmade bed. She mumbles another apology before she passes out slack-jawed, legs sprawled, platforms still on. My heart races until I hear a steady snore. Now I just need to find something I can use to make this night worth it.

I tiptoe into the tiny hallway and flip on the bathroom light. I grimace at the ring of scum in her tub and the dirty yoga clothes hanging from the curtain rod. The bathroom light allows for just enough visibility in the four-hundred-square-foot apartment for me to find her desk/kitchen table, covered in papers.

I use my phone's flashlight to sort through the mess. It's hard to even know what I'm looking for—a schedule, a contact list for interviews, anything that can point me in the direction of Isaac's schemes. I flip through the papers one by one. It's an impressive collection of research on the case, sure, but nothing I haven't seen before. Just book reviews, old news articles, magazine interviews, the missing poster, the court transcript in a heavy binder. The photos of the others that Isaac showed me the day before.

It dawns on me: Perhaps Isaac's only bluffing and he's clueless. He has no new information to blow the case wide open. He doesn't have a prayer, because how could he? There's nothing I need to worry about. That night will stay buried, where it belongs.

I'm returning the piles to the way I found them to the best of my ability, when a scrap of paper falls out of one of the binders and floats to the floor. I kneel down to retrieve it, holding my breath as I flip it over. Sloane's written an address with a Westside zip code. It's dated at the top, only two months ago. Underneath, Sloane's underlined a name. A name I've never heard before.

_Ivy Peters_

The room purrs, and the hairs on the back of my neck prick me wide awake, sobering me up after the evening's cocktails. Sloane stirs, and I freeze. I can't push my luck any further. I pocket the note and get out as fast as I can, exiting the way I came, like I was never there.

# THE OASIS

*57 days before*

"My little poet," Max greeted me as I stepped down from the truck cab. Arthur tapped the truck hood, satisfied at his job well done. The little kids ran to me, shouting, exposing their assortment of lost and growing-in teeth, pulling my hand to chase the sun with them.

"Eden, Fiona," Max called out. "Look after her, won't you? Show her the ropes?"

Eden smiled. "We'll see to it."

Max squeezed my shoulder. "Everything here is designed for your growth. We only want what's best for you."

Fiona squealed and threw her arms around me. "You're going to love it here."

"WE SHARE EVERYTHING," FIONA EXPLAINED. "CLOTHES, BELONGINGS, WHAT have you. Max says you lose your materialistic inclinations when everything's shared. That junk will lose its meaning, trust me."

I followed Fiona and Eden into the women's quarters as they outlined the rules of Oasis living. Fiona took my backpack and placed my things inside the dark green trunk in the hallway. I ran my hands through the clothing rack of nightdresses.

Fiona pulled out the cash I'd taken from Mom's wallet. Eden pocketed it. "I'll get it to Max."

I acquiesced, but when Fiona took out my journal, I had to protest.

"I should hang on to that. I'm going to talk to Max about writing down the story of the Oasis."

Skeptical, Fiona looked to Eden to determine her next move.

Eden winked at me. "I'm sure we can make an exception for something like that, right, Fiona?"

Fiona waffled. "Sure, but you should know we take all these rules seriously, so don't get used to exceptions." Fiona ushered me into the women's sleeping room, where Ronnie was feeding one of the youngest a bottle. "We all do our part in helping with the children." Fiona plopped down in front of Ronnie and the child. She pulled me down to join them.

The child reached for me. Ronnie asked, with purple bags under her eyes, "Want to hold him?" Ronnie transferred him to my arms, then leaned her head back against the wall and yawned.

"You'll get the hang of it," Eden reassured me. "Don't worry." I was surprised by the heft of the child, who couldn't have been much more than six months old, but I warmed to his sweet-smelling skin, the tiny fingernails. He grabbed the ends of my hair. "Now the kitchen," Fiona said. I hooked the baby onto my hip and followed them.

Eden toured me around the kitchen and summarized how our days were structured. "So, every day we tend to the crops in the greenhouse. We all pitch in. We take our daily walks, which are good exercise and help clear the mind. Let's see . . . There's our sunset ritual. Every night, someone's appointed to mind the camp while the rest of us sleep."

The little boy relaxed into my chest, winding down post-bottle. Ronnie appeared in the doorway and took him back without a word.

Fiona looped my arm through hers. "I'll take you to Max for your session."

"My session?" I asked. "What's that?"

"You'll see." Fiona squeezed my side and headed to the door. "It's spectacular."

"Wait." I stopped her at the threshold. "I'll need my journal, then, right?" I turned back to Eden, who held the journal against her pregnant stomach.

"One last thing," Eden said. "It may seem strange, but it's essential that we all remain pure here. There are no secrets between us and you're not to do anything with your body that could taint it. Understand?"

"HERE WE ARE," FIONA ANNOUNCED AS WE ARRIVED ON MAX'S DUSTY STOOP. A rusted directional sign was hung beside the door in place of a doorbell. "You're so lucky you get to start at the beginning."

My heart pitter-pattered at the idea of being alone with Max again. I turned the notebook over in my hands, fidgeting.

"Don't be nervous," Fiona said. The door opened, and Max appeared, his lips turned up in a cocksure smile.

"Fiona." He dismissed her and stepped back to let me inside. The space was modest, a copy of the women's adobe, but it was colorful. A large wooden bookcase covered the main wall, crawling with books and cacti and a collection of gathered treasures. There were two futons and a simple chair arranged in the center of the room on top of a faded orange rug. A little kitchenette was tucked into the side and a bare hallway led to the back of the house.

"Have a seat." Max gestured to the chair. I did as I was told. He hiked up his work jeans, rested on one of the futons, then reached into his shirt pocket for a bag of sunflower seeds. He offered me some, but I declined. I couldn't imagine how awkwardly I'd fumble cracking them open with my teeth in front of him. He, on the other hand, did that expertly, spitting the shells on the wooden floor.

"Thank you for inviting me back," I said, clueless about what these sessions entailed.

"I always knew you were meant to be here." Max smiled. "So, what have you got there?"

"Oh, nothing."

"You're clutching that awfully close to your chest for it to be nothing." He pointed at my white-knuckled grip on my journal.

"Oh, well, I just mean it's nothing special. Not yet."

"You shouldn't say that about your own creation." Max whistled. "Does your mother tell you that?"

I shrugged.

Max popped another seed into his mouth and splintered it between his molars. "You shouldn't be so willing to take her word for it."

I watched him as he sucked the salt off a seed. "I was wondering, now that I'm back, what you thought about me writing about the Oasis? Maybe I could be the historian. Keep a record."

He sucked on his bottom lip, assessing the offer. "You would have to understand our story like it's your own."

"The story of the hero," I recited.

"The story of the hero." He whistled again, through his teeth. "Well, if I'm going to trust you with such an important role, you will have to trust me too."

"Of course," I swore.

Back then, I believed that perhaps this was my purpose—to become the official keeper of Max's philosophies, to spread his word like gospel through the ink in my novice pen.

He crushed the shells into a pile under his heel. "It all starts with the sun, you see. We spend the day bathed in its Light. It helps us see our path. Illuminates how we can survive, what plants to grow, what food to eat."

Realizing he was already dictating to me, I grabbed the pen strapped to my journal and flipped to the first empty page. I raced to copy it all down.

"This evening, like every other since the beginning of time, the sun will set in the west. Tomorrow morning, you will see the sun rise in the east. But how did the sun get there? How did it manage to go from the west to the east in the arc of the night? I haven't seen it. Have you?"

I caught up transcribing and panicked as I realized he'd asked a question, but he wasn't waiting for my dull response. He was selecting his words, carefully.

"Have you ever seen the sun travel across the sky with a Herculean gust of wind at its back?" He crossed one boot over the other, staring up at the ceiling as he monologued. "The sun disappears every evening behind the horizon and crosses through the Underworld."

I bristled at this word—*Underworld*. They'd said it a few times. I didn't like how it sounded, but he spoke as if he were a guru of some sort. I trusted that what he said he believed to be true.

Max kept going, unaware I'd briefly been someplace else. "Every morning, the sun rises from the shadow world. Every day, this is a victory. Here at the Oasis, we work with our shadow selves, confront them, know them intimately."

I vibrated with nerves. "How do I do that?"

"You recognize faults," Max explained. "Those of your own doing and of others. If you see someone out of alignment with our way of life, breaking their promises, you come and tell me. For all of us at the Oasis to remain pure, we need to be held accountable for our actions. Accountability makes us stronger. You, too, will be observed by the others."

"So I need to tell you if I see someone doing something wrong?"

Max lay on his side and propped his head up with his hand to look at me. "I'm not like your mother. I'm not interested in grading you for what you deliver. I want you to tell me if someone isn't upholding their end of the promise to honor what we stand for here, so I can guide them back to their path. If you do that, if you remain pure, you'll be rewarded. You'll make it into the Light too. You'll achieve wholeness. Out there, in the outside world, those people, they don't love you. They don't see you for how special you are or for *who* you truly are. They only care about themselves. We're a real family. We take care of each other." Max sprang off the mattress and gave my hair a tousle. "That's all for today, my little poet."

He left the sunflower seeds in a crumbling dust pile and snaked down the hallway. I set down my notebook and swept the shells into the palm of my hand. I stepped out of the adobe house and sent the shells flying into the dirt. I clapped my hands, trying to rid them of Max's spit, the brittle salt, the harsh woodiness of the shells, but there remained traces, impossible to dispel.

FIONA BROUGHT ME BEHIND THE AIRSTREAM WHERE ARTHUR STAYED AND showed me the cowboy tub. She'd already filled it up halfway with the hose. "Get in," she directed me. "This is part of the cleansing."

I glanced around to see if anyone, namely Arthur, could see us, but the coast was clear. I covered up my body as much as possible as I stripped down. Fiona just giggled.

"You have nothing to be afraid of." She took off her own clothes and climbed into the tub without an ounce of self-consciousness. "We all have bodies. They're just temporary anyway."

I fumbled into the lukewarm water and scooted my back against the tub, gazing up at the barren sky to avoid Fiona's stare.

She splashed me and laughed. "I have to admit I'm kind of jealous you get to start all over. In my first session, I just cried the whole time." Fiona kicked her legs out to float on her back. "It was so freeing to realize that everything I struggled with before finally made sense. The poison I put into my body separated me from my potential. The reason why I wasn't happy back then is because I wasn't here."

"What about your family?" I asked. "Your friends back home?"

"Everyone here is my family," Fiona insisted. "Where we come from doesn't matter. Max doesn't like us to dwell on the past or the people who don't understand how important our work is. It'll get easier. Worry is a part of the outside world's conditioning."

I traced the water with my hands, considering what this rule meant for me. It was better if I didn't think about Mom or Odette, if I didn't stew over the family I wasn't talented enough to be a part of. I didn't want to feel indebted to Coronado anymore. I was tired of feeling invisible.

She propped herself back up, her hair sopping wet. "How old are you?"

"I'm almost sixteen." I dipped my head back to get my hair wet too. "A couple weeks away."

"Then you'll be my family too." Fiona grabbed my hand under the water. The gap in her teeth seemed to expand with joy at the idea. "One day soon."

When Max and Fiona reminded me to leave the past in the past, when the children's affection warmed my spirit, when Arthur's touch weakened my knees, I forced myself to stay fixed there, in the desert, in the present.

Until, of course, it became impossible.

# DOWNTOWN LOS ANGELES

EVERY TIME I TRY TO EASE MY MIND AND FALL BACK ASLEEP, THERE'S Fiona against the flame, howling in the wind.

The glowing red letters of the clock on my bedside table tell me it's three in the morning. Too late to take a sleeping pill if I plan to be alert for filming. So now I'm a sitting duck, resigned to pretend to be asleep for three more hours. I grope my twisted covers searching for my laptop. The battery's still warm from a few hours ago when I tried and failed to find any information about Ivy Peters. Nothing concrete materialized, and it's driving me crazy not knowing why this person's name and address were in Sloane's apartment among the research on my case. I located the address and only found an unassuming house in ritzy Brentwood that hasn't been on the market since the seventies. Since when does someone in this day and age have zero online presence? I log back in to the forums to double-check I haven't overlooked a mention of her by some sleuth. I clench my jaw when I see that there are a flurry of new comments. I scroll to the original post that sparked the new activity.

The photo attachment loads pixel by pixel as a chill spreads across my back. The quality's poor, sources of light bleeding across the frame, but there's no doubt it's me. Last week, at the cocktail bar, with the silhouette of Jeremy behind me. I'm laughing, martini in hand, and at first, I'm distracted and pleased by how much I look like Diana in the way I hold my glass, the way I tilt my head just so.

Then I see how TexWatson86 captioned his post.

TexWatson86: "If I could take a bite out of his flesh there, then I'd really taste him, his flesh and blood."

*The nerve of this troll.* I can't help but scroll through the responses. My whole face is aglow in the blue light, eyes wide open and tears instantly pooling from staring too hard.

CalPally917: The slut looks like she doesn't have a care in the world. Man-eating ice queen can't keep her legs shut.

GeorgyaLeaf109: Gah, this makes me sad. Why can't she move on? Have a normal relationship? It's so desperate. Doesn't she want to be a mother someday?

JoJoYesteryear83: Isn't she like 40 now? That ship has sailed. Given her track record, I'd say that's for the best. No need to pass on that crazy to the next generation. Some people are not meant to be mothers.

Case_Exhibit_: At it again, eh, Golden? LMAO That guy must have a death wish.

LizzieBorden23: Don't slut shame. This is 2022. She's allowed to do what she wants. Hasn't she been through enough?!

OllianderTeee888: I'd take her for a spin. It's always the dangerous ones who are legendary in the sack.

I press down on my chest, trying to squeeze out the wrath, the restlessness, but the tactic doesn't stop me from consuming every comment, every insult, every defense given on my behalf. With each one, I feel my insides calcify. I tell myself I will read until the hurt dissipates and the words lose all meaning.

I will keep reading until I feel nothing, once again.

# PAPER CUT

ALL THE POWER I HELD ON FRIDAY DURING THE *REMY OLSEN* TAP-
ing transfers back into Isaac's hands as soon as I open the door. His
genius idea for the day's filming is to follow me in my day-to-day life.
He's given himself permission to film my Zoom meeting with Julian
about the anniversary edition. Sloane comes over to my desk while the
crew's setting up and hands me a fresh cup of coffee.

"Thought you might need some extra caffeine today," she says in
a teacher's pet kind of way, like she wasn't loose-limbed in my arms
forty-eight hours earlier.

"Wow, thanks." I take the offering. "So Friday was—"

She cuts me off. "So much fun, right? We have to do it again." She
laughs awkwardly, like she didn't send me a string of apology texts Sat-
urday morning for acting like a sloppy freshman. She lowers her voice,
so the crew can't hear. "Maybe yoga next time, though? I haven't had
that much to drink in a while."

"Really?" I blow on the coffee. I play it off like it's no big deal.
"Happens to the best of us."

She smiles, overflowing with gratitude. There's no reason my number one fan needs to feel embarrassed about her drunken night out
with Lucy Golden. The less she knows, the better.

"WELL, WHAT DO YOU THINK?" JULIAN ASKS OVER ZOOM, AND IT
sounds like a bad line reading. I click open the file to see the first pass
at the anniversary edition's cover design. The second cameraman hovers over my shoulder, and I have to pretend like this invasion of privacy
is normal.

The first option is a film photograph of a young girl's silhouette
against a campfire, but there's something artificial about it, computer
generated. The next one closely resembles the original cover, except
the color scheme is no longer neon—instead, it's been updated with
a moody, thriller palette, gory and ghoulish in bruised purple and
oxblood. The third one sends a charged pulse through my blood-
stream.

It's an illustration of the greenhouse, so uncannily captured, it's like the artist was there that night. The moonlight slices through the side. Silhouettes hover in a circle around it, giving the effect of a holy glow. I reach out and touch the screen in a trance. I can hear it, the sound of the glass breaking. I relive it, my whole world falling apart.

"Lucy?" Julian's voice blares through the computer's speaker. "Are you still there?"

"Yeah, yeah, I'm here." But I couldn't be further away. "Listen, let me sit on these for a day or two and I'll get back to you. Okay?"

Julian clears his throat. "I thought you'd be excited."

"I am, Julian." The pressure of the cameras makes me feel like I'm acting in a B movie. "There's just a lot going on right now. With filming and—"

"Have you even started the foreword?"

It takes me less than two seconds to decide it's best to fib about my lack of productivity in that department. "Yeah, it's been all-consuming."

"Want me to take a look?" Julian's voice jumps an octave higher. "Let me give it a read before we send it in."

"No, you can't," I say, too aggressively. I'm sure he knows I'm full of it. "I'd rather get it in better shape first."

"Well, what's your take?"

"My take?" I stare at the ceiling as panic swells inside me.

"The publisher wants to know your approach," Julian says. "It's going to affect the rollout. The marketing, the tour. What are you going for here?"

I become locked in on the image of myself reflected back on my computer screen. Again, I'm reminded of the toll it takes to constantly refresh my narrative, like I'm an aging pop star spinning the wheel of reinvention, in desperate need of a new aesthetic. Of course, my story, as it's been told, is not enough. If I plan to keep profiting off my life's tragedy, I have to find a fresh angle, a new thread to pull. I run my fingers over the keyboard, wishing I could disappear beneath it until this is all over. Until I make it through filming. Until Isaac gives up and moves on. Until I ensure my secret's safe, yet again.

# PAPER CUT

ISAAC DECLARED THIS DAY OF PRODUCTION "A DAY IN THE LIFE," YET promptly secured location rights to the Last Bookstore, as if I went there daily. Isaac shoots footage of me in the high-ceilinged bank turned bookstore, perusing the crime shelves in the vault. He interrogates me like he's on a witch hunt, expecting me to drop a spell book from my cloak.

"Let's talk about the online discourse," Isaac says, adjusting his unironic beanie.

I groan. "You want my commentary on the hellhole that is the internet. Really?"

Isaac smirks, then hands over his beloved iPad. "No, I want your commentary on this." It takes me only a second to realize he's pulled up the forum on his screen, gone right to the photo of me with Jeremy at the old Hollywood bar. The puritans have come out in droves since I last checked. Another hundred comments amassed.

"Just another day in paradise," I joke as I hand back his tablet.

"But all the names they're calling you . . ." Isaac scratches his head.

I shrug. It's hilarious that he thinks I'd break down on camera about being slut shamed by a bunch of vitamin D–deficient bullies. "All of that is just noise. People can say whatever they want about me, and trust me, they have, and they will."

"But someone took this picture of you, posted it online to cause a stir, and you're not disturbed by that?" Isaac asks in disbelief.

"Why should I be?" I toss my hair over my shoulder. "You wouldn't believe how many people take photos without asking or acknowledging that I'm a human being. No, to them, I'm just a monkey in a zoo. Come one, come all!"

Isaac takes a step back and nearly runs into the shelf behind him. It's amusing to watch him squirm like this. "So this doesn't scare you?"

"*Scare me?*" I scoff. I can't believe I have to remind him. "I've been through worse."

ISAAC FINALLY CALLS CUT TO WRAP FOR THE DAY, AND THAT'S when the diatribes about the internet gossip come to life. At last, I hear what Isaac's crew really thinks of his latest subject. Unbeknownst to them, I'm in the next aisle over, engrossed in the first chapter of a Shirley Jackson classic and well within earshot when they delve into their slandering.

"Turns out she's a freak—in more ways than one!" Derek jabs, then barks orders at his assistant to pack up the cameras.

"Seriously, what do you think she smoked to believe all that shit about the Light?"

"Ooh, the Light!" A rumble of snickers.

The sound guy quips, "How 'bout it, Sloane?"

"Please, I could never join a fucking cult."

A siren blares inside me when I hear Sloane joining in. Each pitch of their laughter confirms it: I'm on my own here. Now I see myself through their eyes: the crew, Isaac, Sloane, my supposed fan and wannabe friend. I know who I am to them. It doesn't matter how many designer clothes I buy, how many books I sell, how many fans I accumulate, how many talk show hosts I charm. It doesn't even matter how many anonymous men I pick up in bars or how many trolls admonish my promiscuity online. I will always be, first and foremost, the dumb girl who joined a cult, as if it were a conscious decision. In their minds, I was the fool passing by an enclave of strangers in the desert who said, "Sign me up! While you're at it, please fuck up my life."

Isaac's grinning when he passes the aisle, but he stops in his tracks when he spots me. He doesn't tell the crew to settle down, watch their mouths, or respect me. I think I detect the faintest bit of remorse in his expression, but maybe I'm only imagining his having a conscience.

ON MY TWENTY-MINUTE WALK HOME, I DECIDE TO PUT IT ALL out of my head. Screw the documentary; screw Isaac and his badmouthing crew. Screw Sloane pretending to be my friend. Screw the online viper who believes all it takes to break me down is to call me a slut.

How fucking original.

# PAPER CUT

To soothe my fraying nerves, I start up one of my favorite true crime podcasts to catch the latest of an amateur's attempts at cracking a cold case from the nineties. I'm digging through my bag for my lip balm when I come across it again: the scrap of paper I took from Sloane's apartment. I read the name and address for the umpteenth time.

The late-afternoon sun beats down on my forehead. I pause in front of a Buddhist temple and listen to the podcast host obsess over a minute detail. I consider the way she looks through court records, interviews eyewitnesses, relatives, and old boyfriends, scans online databases, and draws conclusions from disconnected data points.

Any old armchair detective could figure out exactly why Ivy Peters was relevant to my story two months ago during Sloane and Isaac's elusive "prep." So why can't I?

# THE OASIS

*54 days before*

Eden, the unofficial guardian of the greenhouse, detailed what each plant needed. "Here, we grow what we eat."

Fiona checked the soil of the tomato plant and chimed in. "We're not indebted to the consumerism of plastic bags of takeout food. We stay pure in our bodies."

The others buzzed around Eden, working away, bees in a hive, but Ronnie remained still. With a glassy look in her eyes, she idled by the center stone platform, an empty watering can in hand, until Eden prompted her to continue the lesson and return to work.

"At the Oasis, we are valued, not turned away, for our magical ability to create life," Ronnie recited, staring off into space as she tended to the herbs.

After finishing our work for the day, Fiona ushered me to Max's adobe for another session. It was quickly becoming my favorite time with him. He told me story after story that I'd transcribe. He'd lived what felt like more lives than any human being ever had. He'd traveled the globe, worked with his hands, healed many, stared death in the face, and thrived despite the suffering he'd witnessed and endured. That gnawing hunch that he'd long held the key to my artistic purpose had been con-firmed. At first, Max's curiosity about me caught me off guard; then, over time, I began to expect it and even felt entitled to his interest.

"That's why you came here, isn't it?" he asked that afternoon. "To find inspiration?"

I squirmed under the pressure that I might not pass his test. "All I know is to look for it, to recognize it, and then to capture it. That's what my mother's always taught me."

"Ah," he said, like he'd solved a riddle. "What does capturing it bring you?"

"Well, that's the problem," I said. "I'm still working on the captur-ing part. Mom says I embellish too much, but I guess I hope what I bring to the table can be just as meaningful as Mom's photographs or Odette's music. If I'm able to capture something in a meaningful way . . ."

"Then you would belong." Max finished my thought. "So, your art is self-serving." Max asserted his assessment as a matter of fact, not opin-ion. He tossed his sunflower seeds to the side, so he could use both of his hands to gesture. "In an effort to feel like you belong, you jump through hoops for those who tell you that you don't. That's a conditional kind of love. We're not interested in that here." He stood, signaling that it was near time for me to depart. "But the cowardice in you can fade. All those false beliefs, you'll learn to let go."

As soon as he dismissed me, done for the day, I took my cleansing bath with Fiona, then spent another hour translating my shorthand into a more proper legible format to present to him later. I labored more on that first draft than I ever did on my own piece for the workshop ap-plication I would never turn in. As I toiled over it, I worried that I was incapable of understanding the magnitude of Max's ideas and panicked that I was the only one who wondered where the ideas came from. No one dared question Max at the Oasis. I wasn't going to be the first, so I resigned myself to paying attention, believing one day it would all click into place, and I'd understand. He trusted me with his theories, and that felt important.

I took my role seriously, like the Oasis was a place I was destined to be a part of. A crucial part. As it turns out, I was right.

THE OTHERS HAD TURNED IN FOR THE NIGHT, BUT A LIGHT REMAINED GLOWING in Max's adobe. I couldn't wait any longer. Now was my chance to show him my work. When he didn't answer, I pushed open the door and saw it. There, on the simple chair I'd been sitting in only hours before, was a revolver. I'd never seen one up close before, only in the movies. A shock wave ran up my legs and thundered in my gut. I considered that revolver, heavy with menace, dormant on the simple wood, and bristled, realizing its close proximity to the children.

"Lucy?" I heard Arthur call out from the fire pit. I closed the door as quietly as I could. "What do you think you're doing?"

"Nothing." Heart racing, I scampered over to join him. "I just wanted to show Max what I've been working on."

"Now's not the time." Arthur turned a log in the fire with a stick. "He's working with Ronnie in the back. It could take all night."

"Is she okay?"

Arthur chewed his bottom lip. "She committed a fault."

"What did she do?" I cowered, nervous that my innocent act of rebellion could be deemed a fault too. "Is she—"

"Follow the rules and retire for the night."

"It's just . . ." I looked back to Max's adobe; the light flickered, and a pang of curiosity hit me. I longed to know what Ronnie might have done and how Max might guide her back to the path. "Why does Max have a gun?"

Arthur threw the stick into the fire, and it caught flame. "Why would you even ask something like that?"

"I'm not trying to . . ."

"Protection." Arthur snapped another piece of wood in half. "For protection. You have no idea what it takes, all the sacrifices he makes to keep us safe. All of the children safe."

"I'm sorry," I said, hanging my head. "Forget I asked. I shouldn't have assumed." Of course Max needed a means to protect them, out in the open air, from coyotes and snakes and God knew what else lurking on the desert floor. Predators from the outside world could encroach on our land.

"You need to trust him." Arthur reached for me and pulled me into his chest to calm me, smoothing down my hair. "Like you trust me."

I inhaled his scent of tobacco and fire. The pit in my stomach morphed into something else—the wanting. I looked up at him. He moved his hands down to my neck, as if without thought. I'd later come to know that every move he made served a purpose.

His full lips parted, and I thought, *This is it—he's going to kiss me, at last.* I wished I had the artistic skills to sketch him, in the moonlight, the crease in his temple, to memorize him.

He stepped back. The heat of our contact froze over in an instant.

"We shouldn't," he said. He turned back to the crackling fire. I waited there as he tended to the flame, willing him to change his mind, to find a way to prove I was worth the risk.

"Why not?"

"You're supposed to remain pure."


*50 days before*

Without telling the others where we were headed, we took off in Max's old truck. Sandwiched between my father and Arthur in the cab, my skin burned with anticipation, and from being that close to them, for vastly different reasons.

"Arthur." Max rested his wrist on the wheel, a loose grip as he barreled down the dirt roads. "Next time, you tell me right away. You know better."

"Max, please." I rushed to his defense. "I meant nothing by it. I'm sorry."

Arthur leaned his head against the window. I realized I'd never seen him in a passenger seat.

We'd been driving for a half hour when we passed by a couple trailers, though I couldn't tell if they were abandoned or just poorly cared for.

"Now, my little poet," Max said. "If you learn to shoot, you'll reclaim any fear you might have about the gun. We've been talking about bravery, haven't we?"

"Right." I close my eyes, trying to remember the exact wording from yesterday's session. "The hero is the one who chooses bravery over fear."

Soon enough, we arrived at the deep core of the desert. It was wasteland, sandy mountain after sandy mountain of formidable rock, and endless sky. Arthur hopped out of the passenger seat and set up a row of cans on remnants of dead trees as makeshift targets. Max whistled, observing Arthur at work, then retrieved the revolver, the same one I'd seen on the chair, from the glove box. When I followed him out of the truck, my legs felt like jelly.

"Now, it's simple," Max said, after explaining each component of the revolver. He placed it in my hand. It surprised me how much I liked it, the bulk of the metal, the mother-of-pearl handle gleaming. "You'll feel a recoil. I'll show you. Hold your stance." He rammed my hand back a few times to get me used to holding it steady.

Arthur smoked a cigarette, a fat chunk of ash hanging off the end. "Good. Now, you'll see in your sight a little circle, so you can line up your target—"

"I got it," Max said to him, before turning back to me. "Hold your position steady and strong. Be confident. Are you ready?"

I lined up my target, then squeezed the trigger, feeling the kickback in my muscles. The bullet hit the can and knocked it off the stump.

Adrenaline hammered through me. I wanted to go again and again. I wanted to live inside that moment of extremity. A thrill like I'd never experienced.

"That's it," Max said into my ear.

"You're a natural," Arthur agreed.

With the gun still in my outstretched hands, I turned toward Arthur so that I could evaluate how my newfound skill might have altered his opinion of me. But the color drained from his face. In one swift movement, Max grabbed my wrist and aimed the gun at the ground.

"Damn it!" Max scolded me. I'd never heard him yell before. He took the revolver out of my hand, and with it, all the power I had felt moments before dissolved. In its place came shame. "What in the hell were you thinking?"

"I'm so sorry."

Max stomped toward the cans, fuming, the gun waving down by his side, but his anger couldn't be contained.

"First rule of shooting," Arthur said. "Never aim the gun at anyone or anything you're not prepared to shoot."

I covered my mouth. "Arthur, I didn't mean to . . ."

Arthur exhaled a cloud of smoke, and I wanted to disappear inside it. "Let's call it a day, Max." I'd never seen Arthur look so defiant. "We should have prepared her better."

Max charged toward Arthur, challenging him. "So you don't trust me now?" He tapped the gun against Arthur's chest. My reflexes snapped to attention. Hands seized. Jaw locked.

I tried and failed to understand the two of them, their relationship. For all the authority I assigned to Arthur, all the power I gave him, Max was always the one in charge. It was unsettling to see Arthur reprimanded. I was ill-prepared for what came next.

Max cocked the gun and aimed it at Arthur.

"Whoa now." Arthur held his hands up. He took a step back in the dirt. "Take it easy."

Advancing toward him, Max spoke out of the corner of his mouth. "Your lack of trust hurts me, Arthur. You, of all people, should know I'd never let anything happen to you."

Arthur backpedaled to the truck. "Of course I trust you." His frame hit the door with a thud.

A bead of sweat trickled down my neck. I didn't know how to stop Max's taunting. I squeezed my eyes shut, hoping that when I opened them, it would be over, but still, Max held Arthur up against the hood of the truck, the end of the barrel inches away from his temple.

"Are you watching this?" Max said to me, pressing the gun to Arthur's head. "This is what happens when you let your shadow control you."

Arthur cowered, the white of his throat exposed, vulnerable.

"It doesn't matter if I pull the trigger, Arthur." Max pressed the gun farther into his temple. "Your body is temporary. If you fear what might happen to it, if you think you're powerful enough to control the inevitable, you'll never beat your shadow. You'll never be the hero."

Arthur closed his eyes. Tears squeezed out against his will.

"Do you hear me?" Max shouted, demanding a response. "Did you learn your lesson?"

My whole body tingled, needles poking my skin.

"Yes, Max," Arthur said.

"Well then." At last, Max lowered the gun. Arthur held the place on his head where the gun had been and bit his tongue.

Max placed the revolver back in my hand. "Go again."

### 42 days before

The day before I turned sixteen, Ronnie ran away.

"Ronnie!" We shouted her name and scanned the horizon.

The night before, she'd been assigned to watch the camp. Since her cleansing session with Max, she'd been stoic, quiet. That morning, we expected to find her waiting by the extinct fire, whistling her folk tunes, a tired grin on her freckled face.

As soon as we realized she was gone, our chores for the day were quickly abandoned. We organized the hunt. Max and Arthur drove off in their trucks, eight tires spinning into the dust. She couldn't have gotten far on foot.

Fiona and I were assigned to scour the trail of our afternoon walk.

"I don't understand what all the fuss is about," I said, my muscles straining against the incline. "She probably just went out for a little bit. She'll be back any minute now."

"We have to remain pure, Lucy," Fiona replied. She picked up a stray long branch in the path and used it for a walking stick. "She knows better."

My heart squeezed. "Maybe something happened to her."

"Like what?"

"I don't know." I searched my imagination for a plausible explanation. "Animals, hitchhikers. Maybe she was just homesick."

"This is her home," Fiona snapped. "She was supposed to watch over us, and she failed."

"She'll come back."

Fiona scoffed. "Don't you get it? If she leaves like this, she can't come back. She will never get to the Light. She knows how special our mission is—if she doesn't, then she's one of them." She gestured to the horizon, the outside world.

I stopped in my tracks. I almost asked her, *So we're never supposed to leave?* But it wasn't worth it. Fiona was as loyal to the cause as anyone at the Oasis. I didn't want to say anything that she could report back to Max as a fault. "Then why are we looking for her?" I asked. Fiona didn't answer me.

That night, after a quiet fire, I dreamt I found Ronnie a couple miles from camp, her feet blistered and raw, shoulders toasted pink. Dizzy from sunstroke, incoherent apologies tumbling from her parched lips. Max, the loving leader, forgave her misstep, nursed her back to health, set her back on the path to wholeness. We all watched in awe as he freed her of the evil of the outside world and made her clean once more.

When I woke up the next morning, Ronnie was nowhere to be found. Her mattress lay empty.

No one mentioned her name again.

ISAAC SHOWS UP TEN MINUTES BEFORE THE CREW'S SET TO ARRIVE for a full day of rehashing Ronnie's escape. I wonder if his early arrival is designed to keep our conversation private for his sake or mine.

"Any chance you're susceptible to bribery?" He gestures to the sizable carton of Sidecar doughnuts in his hand.

"Depends." I take the carton from him and place it on the counter. "Did you get the huckleberry?"

Deadpan, he quips, "Only one way to find out."

I oblige him and pluck the purple-glazed doughnut from the box, though I'm sure I'll regret the sugar crash in an hour.

"I apologize for my crew's behavior yesterday." Isaac delivers his little prepared speech as I bite into my treat. "I should have stepped in and cut it off. I feel awful about it." He stares at me while I chew.

My mouth goes dry, but I still fight back. "Do you feel awful because they were making fun of me or because I overheard them?"

He pulls out a stool from the kitchen island and picks out a butter-and-salt doughnut for himself. "It won't happen again, I promise." He extends his other hand. "So, how about a truce?"

I take it, even though my fingertips are sticky from the glaze and I have no intention of letting my guard down. "Sure."

"Thanks." He tears off a piece of his doughnut and gobbles it up.

"Anyway, I'm glad we have the chance to talk." Of course his truce comes with strings attached. "Any progress with Diana?"

I turn on the faucet and wash the sugar off my hands. "She's not interested."

Isaac takes off his glasses and pinches his nose. "Did you even try?"

I feel the urge to scream as I dry my hands on a dish towel. "What is it that you even want from her? This documentary isn't about Diana Golden. This is about me, right?"

I study a fleck of glaze clinging to his bottom lip. He slips his glasses back on, readying himself to go on the defensive. "I want her to speak on *your* behalf," he says. "She was there through the whole trial. She's the one who met Max first. Don't you ever think about that?"

I toss the dish towel on the counter and take a slow, ragged breath.

"Lucy, this is important. I'm not trying to upset you—"

I cut him off and busy myself with cleaning up the mess from his sad excuse of an apology. "I'm not upset." I'm about to go on when the doorbell rings, and Sloane pokes her head in.

"Come on in," I call out.

As the crew files in and sets up for the day, Sloane hovers in my vicinity. Her anxious energy's palpable. I'm sure Isaac clued her in on his morning mission. She probably picked up the doughnuts herself, but she doesn't come right out and apologize for chiming in with the rest of the crew. I'm not sure why it bothers me so much. I'm the one pretending to befriend her. It doesn't matter what she thinks of me anyway. She's a means to an end.

"Want to go to the seven o'clock flow tonight after we wrap?" Sloane asks, rocking back and forth on her heels. "Toni's teaching. We could grab a bite after."

I detect the quiet desperation on her face as she delivers this casual invitation. "I have plans."

It's refreshing to not have to lie about that for once.

## Brentwood

I STUDY THE SCRAP OF PAPER AGAIN, DOUBLE-CHECKING THAT I have the right address. Next to the multimillion-dollar new builds on the street, the modest split-level sticks out like an act of defiance. Wind chimes twinkle on the front porch. Overgrown bushes line the brick-and-stone facade. I put on the parking brake for good measure, make my way to the front porch, knock, and prepare myself for the likelihood that this little mission will be a waste of time.

I hear a man grumble as he turns the deadbolt. "Hello?" The man is in his eighties, sporting oversize wire-rimmed glasses and a hunch under his worn gray cardigan.

"Good evening, sir," I say, plastering on a polite smile. "I'm wondering if I could have a few minutes of your time."

"No solicitors," he huffs.

"I'm not selling anything," I assure him.

"Doug?" a woman calls out from inside. "Doug?" The man turns toward her call, his shoulders hunching farther.

He starts to close the door. "Now's not a good time."

I stick my shoe in its path. "I'm not trying to bother you. This is about Ivy Peters."

His expression softens. "You're with the documentary folks?"

"Yes, I'm one of the producers." My name's on the tip of my tongue, but I blurt out an alias instead, hopeful he won't recognize me. "Liza." I extend my hand, impressed with my spontaneous improvisation.

He takes it gingerly. "Doug."

"We just have a few follow-up questions," I promise. "This won't take long."

"Doug?" the woman inside calls out again, and then I see who the voice belongs to. A woman, the same age as Doug, appears in a wheelchair behind her husband. Her eyes are frost blue, white hair permed. "Is it her?" Her soprano jumps an octave. "Is it Ivy? I told you, honey! I knew she'd come back!"

MINUTES LATER, I'M SIPPING ENGLISH BREAKFAST TEA ON A plastic-covered floral couch in the cluttered living room of Doug and Helen Peters. Helen's veiny hands shake as she brings her own tea-cup to her crusty, magenta lips. She watches me with suspicion. Doug wheels her into the adjacent kitchen of granite and ornate cabinetry from the nineties and parks her chair in front of a window looking out on the sun-dappled backyard.

"She'll be back tomorrow, my love," Doug tells her as he places a shawl around his wife's fragile shoulders. My heart races—I'll be able to get a hold of her tomorrow. I'll come back after filming, and I'll get to the bottom of this. When Doug returns to the living room, I pretend like I've been busy admiring their artwork. I realize that there are no photographs, no family portraits, no evidence of a beloved daughter at all. He settles into a gingham-patterned recliner.

"Did I hear you correctly?" I search his cloudy eyes for confirma-tion. "You said Ivy will be here tomorrow?"

Doug looks back to his wife to ensure she's out of earshot. "You have to understand, my wife isn't well."

I set the teacup on the antique coffee table in front of me. "I'm sorry to hear that."

"Helen's never been the same, but these past few years, it's . . ." He pauses. "It's easier to pretend that she's coming back. Tomorrow. Always tomorrow."

I dig a notebook out of my purse and play producer/fact-checker. "Now, can you confirm the last time you spoke to her?"

"I told all this already to that young fellow," Doug protests, and I think maybe he's onto me, but I have to play it cool.

I nod sympathetically. "We like to be thorough. Given the circum-stances."

Doug sighs. "I haven't seen her since she was seventeen, but she called us a few times for money after she left. I sent it to her. Other-wise, I could only imagine how she was going to get it. The last time must have been '84. It was spring, I remember. She was living in some shoebox in Hollywood with a whole host of shady dope fiends. We did everything we could to track her down, even thought we had a few leads over the years, but she's always evaded us. My wife's never given up hope, but I let go a long time ago."

"Why's that?"

"She doesn't want to be found," Doug says.

"I understand this might be a difficult question to answer," I say, treading lightly. "Can you confirm, for the record, if your daughter ever was part of a group called the Oasis?"

"Impossible," Doug says sternly. "There's no proof that she was ever at that nut farm. I told that fellow it was only a rumor. I don't want her associated with it anymore. She was gone long before all that came out anyhow. Besides, Ivy's never been that kind of girl."

The dagger twists deeper into my gut—the arrogance as strong as Isaac's crew members, as Sloane, adamant that nothing like that could ever happen to them. They aren't susceptible. They're invincible, stronger than girls like me.

"I don't mean to be insensitive." I adjust my tone. "How did those rumors come about if they aren't true?"

Doug clears his throat, which turns into a nasty cough. I wait impatiently as he blows his nose into a hankie. "For a brief time, she stayed at a shelter, St. Joseph's in Culver City. I suppose some other girls from there wound up in that deranged cult, but Ivy was a good girl. A well-meaning girl."

I take note of the shelter's name. "Is there anything else you can tell me about her? We want to make sure we paint the full picture of who she . . ." I hesitate, unsure if I should assert her existence in present or past tense. I decide to appeal to the lighter side of things. "Is."

Doug appears grateful I made that distinction, though it seems like he believes the opposite. "As a kid, she never misbehaved, never talked back. She'd play outside for hours growing up. Come back to us with skinned knees, dirt in her hair, without a care in the world." He chuckles to himself, remembering. "She was a seeker, and she made the mistake of getting mixed up with the wrong people. She was wrestling with things she did not share with us. I know that now."

"I noticed you don't have any photos of her?"

"It got to be too hard to see her every day," he says. He opens a drawer in a side table and pulls out a small black-and-white photo. "Then it started to confuse Helen—Ivy frozen at seventeen. She'd be sixty-two today."

He hands the photograph to me, but it's so faded that it's hard to distinguish her features beyond curls and a round face. I trace my thumb over her, this missing girl, and feel something bitter wrench in my gut.

"I'm going to need that." He points to the photograph. I snap back to reality and hold it out to him. He takes it and returns it to its drawer. "If she wanted to be found, we would know more today than we do."

A few minutes later, Doug walks me to the door, and I feel listless. Before I go, I ask Doug one more question. "You said Ivy ran away when she was seventeen. How come?"

Doug's grip on the doorknob whitens. "It's time for you to go. I need to give Helen her medication."

"Please," I tell him. "If there's any chance that it could help . . ." I adjust my tactic. "I promise we'll do everything in our power to find out what happened to Ivy."

I can see it in his poor posture. He may deny the likelihood that this team of filmmakers can get to the bottom of Ivy's disappearance, but even the decades of silence haven't robbed him of his last drop of hope. He doesn't want to die without knowing for certain. Rifts may rust, photographs may be taken out of their frames to soothe the ache, but a parent will always want to hear the story of their child's life, to know it by heart.

"I'm not proud of it," he admits. "I kicked her out when she got herself into trouble and that was that. She never forgave us, a stubborn thing, just like her mother," he mutters to himself before he returns to his ill wife and checks another day off the calendar.

### *Downtown Los Angeles*

THAT NIGHT, MOM MODELS AN ARRAY OF OUTFIT OPTIONS FOR HER upcoming exhibit opening. I spread out on the couch, nerves still raw from my visit to Ivy's childhood home in Brentwood, contemplating how she figures into my story. I look up the shelter, St. Joseph's, and decide to head there early tomorrow before filming. Helen's mystified stare is stuck in my head like an eerie refrain, and I wish I could silence it.

Mom strolls back out to the living room in an asymmetrical bronze blouse and knee-length leather skirt, two pairs of heels in her hands. Her cheeks are flushed.

"How about these?" She steps into the chunky bronze heels first. "Too matchy-matchy, right?" She kicks them off without waiting for input. "Did I tell you I'm missing a blouse? The cream silk Carolina Herrera. Have you seen it?"

I remember the borrowed blouse I wore the night I met Jeremy, the one I stained and threw down the trash chute, the one in Tex's photo. Mom could easily discover this if she deigned to look into the online chatter, but I don't have the courage to confess. "Bummer," I say. I catch a glimpse of the now-empty Sidecar doughnuts carton sticking out of the recycling bin and remember Isaac's request. "So, Mom, I wanted to ask you something."

She takes a seat at the dining table, so she can clasp the strap on her other heel. "You can borrow something for the opening, but I need to choose first. It's my night."

"No, it's not that." I watch her turn her foot from side to side as she assesses the heel. "I'm wondering if you've had a chance to reconsider the interview."

Mom tosses the bronze heels in my direction, discarded for their inferiority. "You can have those." They tumble under the coffee table. "What interview?"

"Thanks," I say. "For the documentary." I twist the ends of my hair as I try to make it sound like no big deal. "We could go to Coronado together, shoot at the house."

She fusses with the bow at the neck of her blouse. "We've been over this."

I tuck my feet under my lap and reconsider my approach. My chest burns as I take on Isaac's plea like it's my own. "It would mean a lot if you could show up for me, just this once."

"Just this once?" she hisses, then stomps back to the dining chair and removes another pair of heels. "You don't think I've shown up for you? After everything I've done. I was the only one who held your hand through that fall." She pauses, and I'm taken aback by the mention of that dark period. We never talk about it, so sometimes I wonder if I only imagined it: the agonizing pain, the middle-of-the-night spirals, the loss of what might have been.

Already, this conversation is getting away from me. "I appreciate all of that, Mom. I really do. I'm just hoping you might be open to talking about that summer on the record after all this time."

"Is Isaac getting to you?"

I study the weave of the throw blanket on my lap. "Of course not. I understand you think saying no might be what's best for you, but maybe it would be a good thing for us, to talk about what happened, for real." I surprise myself with this admission. Doug's piercing regret did a number on me.

"Why are you attacking me?" She pushes off from the dining chair. Its screech across the concrete floor wrings my insides out like nails on a chalkboard. "What have I not done for you?"

I pull the blanket around me, deeply lamenting sticking my neck out. I wish I could take back the last five minutes. "I'm not attacking you, Mom. I'm grateful for everything you've done for me."

"Why do you care so much what Isaac wants?" She flicks her long waves in my direction. "He's using you. He's going to lose interest when he realizes there's nothing new to say. The shoot will end, then everyone will move on with their lives. Will you be able to do that?"

"It's a job. It will be good for my career."

"Are you sure that's the only reason?"

I bite my tongue. Hard. Mom slinks toward me and joins me on the couch. She pulls my head into her lap. She runs her icy fingers through my hair. I want to melt into her milk-white skin. I want her to agree to do whatever I need her to do. I want her to tell me it will all be okay.

"How about this?" she says. I look up at her, marvel at her perfect chin, her curved eyelashes. "I'll let him shoot opening night, hmm?"

I turn on my side, so she doesn't see my disappointment when I lie. "Thank you. That's all I want."

# CULVER CITY

THE OVERWORKED FRONT-DESK ATTENDANT SIGHS AT MY REQUEST. "It's policy," she says. "I can't give out that kind of information." She smacks her gum, bored, blending in with the gray, beige, and tan furnishings of the St. Joseph's women's shelter.

"You don't understand. I'm her daughter." I spew out the backstory that I crafted on the highway like an out-of-work actor on her way to an audition. "My mother is at a memory care center and her doctors have asked me to make a timeline of her life."

"Then you need to tell your mother to come here herself," the woman replies, clicking away on her massive, decades-old desktop computer, playing solitaire until her lunch break.

"I'm telling you"—I'm grasping at straws—"my mother's unwell, unfit for traveling. Ivy Peters. She was here in the late seventies. Could you just—"

"Excuse me, did you say Ivy Peters?"

I turn around to find a nun in her sixties, habit and all, considering me, her wrinkled hands clasped together in front of her robes.

"Yes, that's right," I confirm. "Did you know her?"

"I'll take it from here," she says to the front-desk attendant. The nun swipes the file from her colleague's desk and beckons me to follow her into a sad excuse for a chapel. A couple pews face a modest altar.

The nun introduces herself as Sister Ruth and gestures for me to join her in the front pew.

"I'm sorry to hear your mother is unwell," Sister Ruth says with a deep sincerity. Part of me feels guilty for lying, while part of me is intrigued to find out how Sister Ruth would smite me if she knew. "I've prayed for her for a long time."

"Thank you," I say, playing along. "I'm doing my best to honor her legacy and document her history, so it's not forgotten."

"That's a very loving thing to do," Sister Ruth says. "How can I help?"

"What can you tell me about my mother? Did you know her?"

Sister Ruth nods. "Strange, but I always had a feeling about that girl. I had just taken my first vows when I came to St. Joseph's, and it wasn't too long after that when she fell into my care."

"What was she like back then?"

Sister Ruth sits back. "She was spirited—a little like you, in fact. Questioning everything, passionate." I smile, unnerved by her assessment of me, her comparison too. "I took a liking to her quickly, too quickly." Sister Ruth grabs for her rosary, thumbing the beads, transported to a different place.

"How do you mean?"

Sister Ruth abandons her internal prayer and returns to the chapel. "She taught me an important lesson about expectations. I had to leave it up to the Lord. We had a whole plan in place, but Ivy was headstrong."

My gut instinct says this is a lead. "What plan?"

Sister Ruth details exactly what kind of trouble Ivy had gotten herself into. "If she only realized she was a baby herself back then . . ."

I glance at the file in her hands and swallow. "What did she do?"

"She refused to proceed with the adoption, played us for fools." She shakes her head. "Two days after the baby was born, Ivy ran away."

"But where did she go?" I'm chomping at the bit to learn more.

"She never told you this?" Sister Ruth looks at me quizzically. "Maybe it would be best if I gave her doctor a call."

"Doctor?"

"At the memory care center . . ."

I picture my own mother, Diana, what she must have felt when Jesse died and she was pregnant with Odette, looking for a safe haven, a way out.

"Miss?"

"Oh, sure. My mother's doctor." I snap back into my role, but I can tell she's questioning my intentions. I need to get out of there and fast. "You know, I don't have a card for him. Do you have a piece of paper? I'll just jot down the information for the center."

"I'll be right back." She leaves the room, and in a noncharitable act, she takes Ivy's file with her. I'm gone by the time she returns.


## Malibu

DRIVING TO MALIBU MAY SOUND GLAMOROUS, BUT IT'S ANYTHING but. With one hand on the wheel, Sloane speeds down the Pacific Coast Highway past the Annenberg Beach House. Out the window, the slate-blue ocean makes me feel unmoored. Yes, it's beautiful, but the ocean has always daunted me. I don't like to think about what lies beneath, what's out beyond. I bear down on the door handle, torturing myself with what might happen if Sloane took a sharp left into oncoming traffic.

Isaac thought it might be best if we drove separately from the rest of the crew today, but I'm wary of spending the hour trapped with Sloane, simulating intimacy, especially after going out with her Friday night. I'd rather be home, unraveling what Sister Ruth told me about Ivy. I keep thinking about Max's promise—the refuge he provided for expectant mothers—and the possibility that a naïve girl like Ivy took him at his word. She fit the bill: an outcast, estranged from her overbearing parents, with a desire to carve out a path for herself and for her child. Perhaps she was one of his early followers, and that's why

Isaac deemed Ivy and her mysterious disappearance important enough to investigate.

I know better than anyone. People don't just disappear.

Sloane rolls to a stop at a light, narrowly missing the car in front of us by mere inches. I press my heel into an imaginary brake. "So, how long has it been since you've seen Odette?"

I fiddle with the window switch, debating if it would be better for the window to be open or closed in the likely event of a collision. "Uh, Christmas, maybe?"

"So you're not close?"

"I wouldn't say that." I blanch as a motorcyclist with a death wish zooms by. "She's had a lot going on."

"Must be hard to watch someone you love struggle," Sloane says.

Of course it's hard to witness her descent into the rabbit hole of drugs by way of sex and rock 'n' roll, but she's still Odette. During the trial, she was ordained the next big thing, the daughter of the legendary Jesse Quinn and the glamorous Diana Golden, the sister of the cult killer. There was never any doubt about her talent. All the greats wanted to collaborate with her, from Amy Winehouse to the Rolling Stones, and they did, until they didn't. Until all her charisma and that insane voice of hers didn't make up for the effort required to get her in front of a microphone, onstage, and guarantee a pulse when she rolled over in her hotel suite the following morning. As her career escalated, her gold star tarnished: canceled tour dates, a public affair with a married Oscar-winning director, drunken episodes, cocaine, heroin. The tabloids ate her up and spat her out, regurgitating her hereditary addiction issues in cyclical waves. There'd be mentions of me sometimes, a quirky footnote for the public to chew on. The bitterness of my story added another layer of complexity. I held on during her twenty-seventh year of life, panicked she'd join the club with her father, blessed with his talent, cursed by his demons. Watching from the sidelines, I envied how easily her troubles supplied her work with a glamorous edge. *You can't separate the art from the artist,* Mom always says.

We lean to brace against the bend in the road. Sloane pulls over and parks on the right side of the Pacific Coast Highway.

"What are we doing?" Cars whip by, well over the speed limit. "Her place is in the canyon." I tap my chest and my pressure points, but paranoia quickly takes hold. Sloane must have pulled over to confront me. I panic over the possibility that she knows what I found at her apartment that night, or maybe Doug told Isaac about his little visit from a producer named Liza.

Sloane turns the car off. "We're filming at the pier first." She unbuckles her seat belt and turns to face me. "Hey, are you okay? You're all pale." She digs through her back seat and hands me a water bottle.

"I'm surprised you care," I snap before I can think better of it.

"Of course I do!"

"Well, you're on the clock."

There's a reason it's unsustainable for me to maintain relationships with the women I meet. I can't blame them for not sharing my life experience, for failing to understand why I did what I did, but I also can't relate to the vanilla Hinge dates and job interviews and petty drama over a weekend in Santa Ynez wine country. I can't relate to the casual assurance that we all will one day wind up married, be fertile well into our thirties, successful, and thus, crowned as "having it all." There's no way either Sloane or I could catch up to the other or meet in the middle. So I'm not sure why I'm even sulking about Sloane, who has her own self-serving interest in delivering me to Isaac vulnerable and raw for the camera. Something about her reads as a walking contradiction, which I hate to admit makes me the faintest bit curious what it might be like to be her friend for real, not for sport. I remind myself that, only two days ago, she questioned my sanity for falling into a trap specifically designed for my seizure. She's just like all the rest.

"I'm sorry," Sloane says. "I hate that you heard us talking like that the other day. It was unprofessional, not to mention cruel. I know it's no excuse, but it's not easy pretending to be one of the boys. On or off the clock, I do want what's best for you, Lucy. I mean that. I hope we can still be friends."

I feel my walls waver, though I ache to build them back up to where they've always been. She's doing exactly what I would do—playing the part, climbing the next rung of the ladder to the top. I have to respect her for that. "I'm perfectly fine on my own."

"Well, if you change your mind, I'm here."

I flip the mirror down and touch up my lipstick. She's right. I look like a ghost.

THE MALIBU PIER IS A TOURIST'S PARADISE. RESTAURANTS FLANK the start of the long dock, where green juice cocktails go for twenty-two dollars a pop. At the very end, there's a chic, overpriced shop and café. I find something comforting about the structure's brazen interruption of the ocean. It's a weekday during June gloom, but Malibu's iconic pier still manages to attract tourists and locals alike. Isaac's crew is set up halfway down the pier, and he frames his shot like I'm a buoy in the middle of the Pacific, surfers weaving around my talking head, bobbing in the waves and the late-morning fog. He positions me exactly where he wants me on a bench, jogs out of the shot, and unceremoniously kicks off the interview with an inquiry that should come with a warning label.

"Do you have any idea what happened to the surviving children?" Isaac asks. "Where they might be?"

My eye twitches. Isaac should really learn the art of easing his subjects into difficult topics of conversation. I surmise that he thinks disarming me will make me slip up. Part of his process, perhaps.

The children's little faces have faded into the recesses of my memory in the past twenty years. I don't like to dwell on their what-ifs. They get to me the most.

"If they were lucky, they were adopted by loving families and don't have a clue where they came from and lead normal lives. If you have any decency, you'll leave them alone."

"And they've left you alone?"

I blink back any discomfort my face may have betrayed. "Come again?"

"I'm having trouble tracking any of them down," Isaac admits. The weight of this revelation sinks in. So none of the children have come forward. I picture an imaginary line crossing through the possibility that they have anything to do with Isaac's promise to blow my world to smithereens.

Bending to Isaac's direction, I then rewind twenty years to my sixteenth birthday. I seethe thinking about the girl I used to be, who dove in without understanding for certain what lurked beneath the surface, which creatures might harm, how to avoid the jagged rocks.

The girl who swam into the deep end and never opened her eyes in the salty, stinging water, because she trusted what she was told.

## THE OASIS

*41 days before*

"Happy birthday, Lucy."

Arthur handed me a bunch of wildflowers. I took the cluster from him and pretended to blow it out like a birthday candle. The grounds were still except for the flapping shift of feasting birds in the distance. Everyone else would be asleep for another hour.

"Thank you." I planted a kiss on his cheek. "I thought maybe no one would remember."

"Oh, I remembered."

"You know, I was worried about you the other day, with the shooting lesson," I told him. "Fiona said you're resisting Max."

"You never need to worry about me." Arthur shoved his hands in his pockets. "I'm counting on you to be ready to take this next step."

I relaxed into his undivided attention, no one else around to witness us. "You're right. I'm ready."

WE NEVER HAD MUCH SUGAR AT THE OASIS—MAX CONSIDERED IT IMPURE FOR our bodies—but sometimes Arthur snuck back candy bars from his occasional trips into town for supplies. The kids stashed the contraband in the corners of the sleeping room where it was dark, so the chocolate could harden enough to eat. On this special occasion, Eden and Fiona baked me a cake from a box Arthur picked up from a gas station. I swore to them it was the best birthday cake I'd ever had.

It wasn't. Birthdays were among the rare occasions when Mom showered Odette and me with attention. Mom always made us her favorite angel food cake. She'd mix together Cool Whip, coffee, and Heath Bar bits and slather it on once the cake had cooled. No doubt it was some eighties diet hack of a cake, but it was my favorite. This was the first year I wouldn't have a slice with her, legs swinging off the kitchen counter as she sang "Happy Birthday." As angry as I was at my mother for keeping Max from me for so long, I missed her for the few seconds it took to blow out the lone candle on my icingless cake. I felt a stab of guilt picturing her in the carriage house, wondering where I was. The little kids plowed through the dry cake in fistfuls, and I pushed the thought of her outside of myself.

All day, Arthur kept an eye on me wherever I went. My awareness of his surveillance charged every cell in my being. After the cake had crumbled and the children were put to bed, Arthur told us a story about meeting Eden in Los Angeles. It was unnerving to imagine her in concrete, in the same city as Odette, among the nightclubs and billboards on Sunset.

"She was a sprightly little thing," Arthur joked. "Outside Vons urging me to sign a petition. What was it for again?"

Eden tried to recall. "Refugee efforts? Wait, no, that oil spill in—"

Max interrupted Eden. "There are dangers, more than we can see, facing those outside the Oasis."

Arthur dipped his head, annoyed. Eden shifted toward Max reverently, settling in to listen. Whenever he went on his darker rants, we wrote it off, justifying it as Max's revisiting the Underworld, carrying all of its pain. Much later, I'd realize the convenience of this explanation, an excuse for his behavior at the ready.

"Lucy, you're sixteen today," he said. The sparks from the fire crackled as he spoke, scratching his head obsessively, like a tick was lodged in his scalp. "You have what it takes to make the journey, to belong to the Oasis."

Everyone around the fire looked at me as I took in Max's assertion of faith in what I could offer. "We love you, Lucy," sang a chorus of their voices.

"We're so happy you found your home," Fiona said.

With a cue from Max, Eden led us in an old folk song. I tried my best to memorize the words, but I was distracted by the tips of Arthur's fingers at the base of my skull, twisting my hair over and over, a melodic beat to his touch. The blanket of night concealed this forbidden show of affection. Arthur was careful. He knew a moment before Max looked over at us to take his hand away and pretend he was rearranging the firewood.

When Max finally stood up to retire for the night, Arthur volunteered for night watch. As the rest of us began to turn in, Arthur invited me to join him later.

"A special surprise for you," he promised.

I pretended to fall asleep alongside the others and escaped into the fantasy in my head. I'd studied it in movies and dissected it in passages in books, which I underlined and reread in the comfort of my childhood bedroom, curled up in sheets, the bedroom door locked in shame. Still, my stomach dropped at the idea that what I told myself I wanted to happen would mean breaking my promise to Max.

I waited for everyone's breaths to slow and even. Before I snuck out of the women's adobe, I searched through the green trunk for Odette's jasmine perfume and sprayed it on my wrists, pressed it on my neck, the backs of my knees, on my chest underneath my white nightgown. I could follow the rules. My body was pure.

I could behave.


THE PRIZED MINUTES THAT PRECEDED OUR TIME IN THE TRUCK BED WERE THE most charged with desire. I stirred with excitement and fear, oscillating between the two until the silence was too much to bear. Arthur grabbed my hand, and I traced the lines of his teal-blue veins on his wrist, pumping him full of blood, making his firm body warm. I was too nervous to look at him directly; instead I fixated on the edge of his Moleskine and felt a pang of longing to know what it was he wrote inside. If he mentioned me and imagined this moment like I so often had.

When we reached the truck, he dropped my hand so he could retrieve the red wool blanket from the cab. The same one I'd woken up under earlier that summer. He draped the blanket over the truck bed, then hopped up on the bumper.

"Lucy." He pulled me up. "Whatever happens between us"—he stooped down to meet me at eye level and trailed my collarbone with his fingers—"no one at the Oasis, especially Max, can know. Understand?"

I shuddered, searching his sea glass eyes for reassurance. "I thought you said . . ."

He grabbed my face with his gruff hands and kissed me, greedy, urgent. As guilt funneled through me, knowing this would be deemed a fault in Max's eyes and taint whatever purity I might have had, I let him. I gave in to the wanting, embracing my shadow.

An impulsive flush of warmth spread through me. It was our secret. Arthur and I had been drawn together for a reason that even Max didn't need to be a part of. No one had to know. I was sixteen now. I could take a risk.

It wasn't like kissing Theo, passing energy back and forth like a tennis match. Arthur overpowered me in every way. I rushed to drink him in, but I couldn't keep up. He cradled his arms around the small of my back and lifted me up.

When he laid me down on the blanket, his body hovered over mine. My breath quickened. The chill of his hands shocked my bare skin. I felt little pricks of ice against my torso as he undressed me quickly like he couldn't wait another second. The blunt unzipping of his jeans.

"You smell like heaven," he said. He kissed me again, his chest now bare, his pants in a bunch around his ankles. I wanted to keep him there and press my mouth onto his longer. I would have been happy to be kissed softly and held on my sixteenth birthday, far away from everything I'd been raised to think mattered. But we weren't there to hold each other. He didn't crave my mouth in the same way I romanticized the curl of his cherry lips. He was a man, with a barrel chest matted with hair, a raging need in his core to release what needed to be released. I realized later that I was a vessel, his vessel, for the moment and nothing more.

When I didn't protest, that was all the permission he needed to take me. Max's rule to remain pure, Arthur's twenty-five years on my fresh sixteen—the facts disintegrated. I wanted to participate in the primal act of the wanting, or at least be present in a rendering of it.

During the act, I floated above us there, above the dirt, above the steel of the truck. Watching it all from a distance, like a nymph hanging on the edge of a star. Down below, a young girl was ushered into womanhood, entered into a game she didn't understand well enough to play with ease.

The pain wasn't what I expected. There was no blood, no obvious pool of red to mark the passage of my innocence. There was only the smell. That puzzling mix of Odette's jasmine perfume, his musk, and the sweat the friction of our bodies created.

I waited for it to be over.

We lay beside each other afterward, our edges touching. The dark sky hung over us like a tarp, shielding us from the heavens. I wasn't sure if he would still want me tomorrow now that he'd had me. I didn't know if I wanted the same sensation again, or if I just wanted his return to me to be certain. I only knew I took pleasure in occupying the space beside him like a saved seat, a natural movement of muscle memory.

My thoughts drifted to my mother and the mates she lured into her own bed. She didn't know where in the world I was or what I'd just done. It wasn't so much an act of rebellion, seeing as my mother often reeked of sex, with little apology attached to her Rolodex of lovers. I felt separate from her then, like I was my own woman. No longer a child. Yet there I was, lying beside a man who came into her life first, and I was thinking of my mother as the evidence of his wanting dried on the insides of my thighs. Her hold on me persisted more than I liked to admit.

# PAPER CUT

Arthur extricated himself from the truck bed. I propped myself up on my elbows, watching his naked form dismount off the back. He retrieved his film camera from the cab, climbed back up, and stood over me. With his strong legs straddling me, he arranged the blanket around my naked body, my nipples erect from the cold. I trembled at seeing this foreign angle of his manhood, suspended.

He clicked the shutter. I found it romantic.

I was his muse.

FOR AS LONG AS I CAN REMEMBER, I HELD THAT NIGHT WITH ARTHUR at arm's length, to separate it from the violence that followed. A gnawing inside me begs me to pull it closer and examine it for what it was.

I recall the following nights spent sneaking out of the women's quarters, heart racing, as I waited for Arthur outside the Airstream, straining my eyes in the dark for any sign of movement. For a while, our secret trysts fueled me. I felt a new sense of maturity, like I'd slipped into Odette's grown-up affairs. I gave myself over to him willingly. He taught me how to please him. He shushed me when I moaned, a cloud of danger always above us. I hated that something I wanted was deemed wrong by Max's decree. I asked Arthur, time and again, if we could come clean. If he cared about me, we could have Max make an exception. Arthur always resisted. A few nights, he turned me away. He told me I was too much. Then, the next day, he'd corner me, and I'd forget all about his rejection. My neediness for him multiplied. I'd give in.

Sloane passes Paradise Cove and turns right into the canyon. The dramatic drop-offs to the valley below make the drive more gut-wrenching. Spots flash in my vision. I imagine the car flying off the road, landing in the backyard of a celebrity's Spanish Revival.

"Are you okay?" she asks for the third time.

"I'm fine, Sloane," I lie. "I just need to get out of this car."

Tan, towheaded attendants wave us through the gate. As we make our way down the winding driveway, we take in the gorgeous sandstone buildings, flecked in sunlight peeking through the olive trees. Tucked away in the canyon, this is the place where my beloved sister fights her battle with addiction. To be so lucky.

"Crazy they're letting us film here," Sloane murmurs. She straightens her posture in the driver's seat, her hands at ten and two.

I'm not surprised at all. In Los Angeles, we prefer our breakdowns to be well-documented.

AT ONE TIME, ODETTE MIGHT HAVE BEEN THE ONE VISITING ME IN prison, but I realize this is a prison too, one of her own making. We sip cucumber water underneath a shady pergola with vines threading through the lattice like a basketweave. Odette looks better rested than the last time I saw her, but she sounds manic. She's gained back the weight she'd lost, a reassuring glow in her cheeks. Back in December, she was wasting away in Venice. Her second husband, Diego, the Spaniard with loose royal ties, had left her again. She opened her home to a shady cast of characters who sucked her stash dry. She resembled a wounded bird, not the siren who once strutted across stadium stages in leather pants in the early aughts and belted a high C with ease. I had known I was going to lose her again. I hated when I was right.

She rambles on about the other patients at the rehabilitation center, disguised as a five-star resort. The Reiki healer and yoga teacher's rumored rendezvous in the outdoor shower, the past-life expert's instinct that Odette was once a pioneer in the Wild West, blazing her own trail. As the crew mics her up, I'm a captive audience. There's nothing I love more than watching her perform.

The woman across from me smells faintly of sweat. She hasn't plucked her eyebrows in months. An old pair of Levi's hugs her hourglass hips and a ninety-dollar black T-shirt hangs off her in that intangible, effortless way. Even after everything, all the public scandal she's endured, her nasty divorce from the Marvel actor, the DUI arrests, the failed rounds of IVF, the relapses, I can't mitigate my innate jealousy of her. I still think she is the most beautiful, most talented person on the planet. She will always possess that unattainable spark that makes her irresistible. I can't ever be Mom, but the real tragedy is that I had the potential to become Odette, and I failed.

"Been thinking . . . once I'm out, I'll get the band back together. Touring was the problem, never the studio." Odette raises her arms, covered in bite-size tattoos, gathers her raven hair into a twist, and then lets it fall again. I find comfort in her reliable mannerisms. "I've been tinkering with some lyrics. Could you take a look?"

Honored she wants my praise, I smile. "I'm sure they're amazing."

"I don't know about that." Odette frowns. "How's this whole thing going for you?" She gestures to the camera crew, and I realize she's the first person who doesn't have a dog in this fight to ask me that question.

"There are good days and bad days."

"I can relate." Odette glances at the main building of the rehab, beyond the winding path. "Is today a good day or a bad day?"

I force a smile. "Good, now that I'm seeing you!"

"Bullshit." Her ability to read me feels foreign. So few know the real me, but I suppose I'm to blame for that.

"Well, I'm fresh off reliving my sixteenth birthday. You know, my first time with Arthur."

Odette takes a toothpick out of her front jeans pocket and pops it in her mouth. Her oral fixation since quitting smoking is still as strong as ever. "You could find that exact same scenario on any casting couch in the Valley." She rolls the toothpick around her pink mouth. "Maybe not anymore, but back then." She whistles through her teeth.

A reminder that my situation is no grand revelation. *There are no victims*, the old refrain goes.

"I'm not denying what Arthur did to you," Odette clarifies. "But it wouldn't be the first time a man promised a girl her dreams would come true if she gave him what he wanted. I knew plenty of those men when I was coming up."

"Right." I shift in my seat, dying to change the subject. "Tell me about you. How's the program here?"

Odette details her therapies, her atonements, the crystal work, the Reiki healer's analysis of her blocked energies. "I've responded the most to the inner child work. Learning to parent myself these days. You should know as well as I do Mom wasn't capable of that. Has she reached out to you lately?"

It's not easy managing the estrangement between Mom and Odette. Stuck in the middle of their toxic battle, unsure who to defend, how to shield myself from the bloodshed. "I've been meaning to tell you. She's staying with me."

Odette pauses mid-chew. "Are you serious?"

"Temporarily," I tell her. "She's showing at a gallery near the loft. Friday's the opening."

"Why would you agree to that?"

"Look, I know you're not speaking right now, but I'm sure you can find a way to work it out," I tell her. "Just apologize. She misses you."

"Apologize?" Odette spits out the toothpick. It falls onto her lap. "You have no idea what you're talking about."

I'm flustered by her overreaction. That familiar regret of pushing her too hard returns. Months ago, Mom finally confided in me how angry she was about what Odette said in a *Vanity Fair* interview, claiming Mom rode the coattails of Odette's fame. I'd read the article in question and tried to maintain my Switzerland stance. It was obvious the reporter wanted to spark some controversy and wrangled this slandering out of Odette somehow. She should have known better. You never know how your words might be pulled out of context.

"Did she ever tell you why she missed my first Grammys?" Odette rants. I shake my head. "She was supposed to be my date. I was nominated for Best New Artist. She said she was called for a shoot in Paris that she couldn't pass up, so I went alone. I found out later she was at the Beverly Hills Hotel the whole time. She couldn't bring herself to see me shine for once."

Her account doesn't add up. Mom's always lavished Odette with attention: praising her sublime high notes, offering her clothes to wear onstage, introducing her to the right people, photographing her in the most flattering light. Odette, the rock star, is Diana Golden's greatest work of all.

"Odette." I try to temper her anger. "You've always been the apple of her eye."

Odette juts her well-defined chin. "All my life, I can't remember a time she wasn't picking at me, droning on about my lack of talent, making fun of my performances. It doesn't take a genius to know she saw me as her competition. I finally confronted her and begged her to go to therapy with me, but she refused. She told me I was ungrateful. She told me *I'm* the liar. The truth is she can't look in the mirror and face how much she fucked us up."

"Don't say that." I hear the wobble in my voice. I look over to Isaac and Derek—the camera's trained on our interaction. "She's our mother."

"Oh my God. Knock her down off that pedestal, Lucy!" Odette kicks my chair. Startled, I grab on to the arms and shrink when I spot Sloane, enraptured, gnawing at her fingers. "While you're at it, knock me down too. Do you see where I am right now? Don't you see what I've lost? When this stint is over, I'm going home to an empty house. The constant jealousy needs to stop. It's not good for either of us. I can't live up to your expectations when I'm struggling to make it through every day. Sober. Alive." Odette rips off her vintage Ray-Ban sunglasses so I can see how serious she is about this point. "Every time you let Mom get to you, you're enabling her behavior. You're denying yourself any chance at joy, comparing yourself to either of us every chance you get. You're telling yourself that you don't deserve any better, but you do."

The wind picks up. A cinematic rustle sweeps through the olive trees. My head's spinning, and my mouth feels impossibly dry. I need more cucumber water, but my cup's empty. Odette wipes under her eyes, and I'm bewildered to be the source of my stunning sister's frustration. I'm overcome with the rush of something wild barreling toward me, like a wild fire on the rolling slopes of Malibu. But there is no siren in the distance, no hiss of water-drenched embers, no sign of rescue. Only the roaring flame consuming everything in its wake.

My heart squeezes at her unwavering belief in me—she has no idea what I've done.

When we're about to depart, I find myself stalling, filled with dread to be leaving her side. Meanwhile, Odette chews on a fresh toothpick and dreamily braids her hair, and I equate my presence in her world to a pest, desperate to be acknowledged, even if only by the flit of a hand shooing me away.

When she pulls me in for a hug, I inhale her distinct scent, and I think of her that summer, packing for Los Angeles, kissing her drummer against the wall, trusting she had more important things to worry about besides her little sister.

"Everything's going to be fine," Odette says when we finally part.

How wrong she was back then. How wrong she is now.

# THE OASIS

*40 days before*

"Drink up!" Arthur pushed a chipped mug to my lips, then sucked down his own concoction in two ambitious gulps. With the events of the night before fresh in my mind, I had no desire to get high, fearful that doing so might dilute the memory. However, Arthur must have known if he asked anything of me, I would be hard pressed to disobey. The mixture tasted like dirt. I wondered if I would start seeing dragons approaching from the horizon or waves of Technicolor in my hands, like in the movies. It was nothing like that.

We lounged around the fire pit waiting for it to kick in. Max and Eden had gone on a walk for her session. The others were in the women's adobe, taking respite from the heavy heat. I worried the tea might not work on me, but then my body began to sink, as my head floated, light and flooded with ideas. I couldn't stop the laughter spilling from my lips.

We staggered our departure, weaving behind the Airstream to deflect suspicion in case anyone was watching. Arthur waited for me at the door to the greenhouse. He used his personal key—Eden liked to lock it to keep the kids from messing around with the sprinklers—and we stepped inside. All I wanted was Arthur among the rippling sprinklers, bees, hummingbirds, and juicy strawberries. To devour it all, namely him.

All the while, my own act of betrayal, this secret I was keeping from Max, festered.

Arthur climbed on top of me, the damp stone of the greenhouse floor beneath my back. He tore off Odette's stolen shorts, pushed my underwear aside, and touched me between my legs. I was still sore, but I bucked against his hand. This time, I stayed inside my body. I responded to his every move, running my teeth along the slope of his bare neck.

If I could take a bite out of his flesh there, then I'd really taste him, his flesh and blood.

He pulsed against me, a jolt in his shoulders as he sank into me farther. We erupted into laughter, witnesses to the sweaty, emboldened blaze of the wanting. Back then, I was sure it was love. It sure as hell felt like it.

How could anything, ever, be purer?

When we returned, the others had taken the tea too, the magic working its way into their bloodstreams. They busied themselves with talk of the galaxies and the ever-elusive journey to the Underworld. I listened, commenting from time to time, conscious of my movements. Everything vibrated on a molecular level. Zigzag patterns on skin, swirls in the dark tan of the dirt.

Max and Eden returned from their walk. My whole body went rigid with fear that he might suspect my lapse in judgment, but Max appeared calm as ever. Now I think he'd drunk a bit less of the tea, or maybe none at all, so he could stay levelheaded. For a man who preached so much about freedom, he had a funny way of holding tight on to the reins of control.

I CAME TO IN THE CHAIR INSIDE MAX'S ADOBE, UNSURE HOW I'D FOUND MY way there.

"My little poet." It took me a moment to recognize Max calling for my attention during another session, the most important one yet.

He dropped to his knees so we could be on the same level. "You are the voice the world needs. Your work will be transcendent and stand the test of time. Bigger than fleeting fame, more valuable than all the money in the world. Do you understand?"

"My work," I repeated, mystified by his confidence in me. When I read a great work, perverse jealousy took flight. A deep saturation of envy, wishing I'd written it. "Do you really think so?"

Max gripped my hands so hard my knuckles turned white. "People in the outside world have told you all your life that you don't matter, that you're not worthy, you're not enough, but you are so much more than you know. That's why you're here. So I can help you reach your potential. I can unlock your mind, don't you see?"

That's what he did. He freed me from my anxieties that I wasn't good enough to meet my mother's standards. I, Lucy Golden, had something to say and the talent to say it so that others would listen.

"It's time," Arthur said. "You must commit to the Oasis."

I followed his voice and saw him waiting in the doorway, a front-row seat.

"I am," I pleaded. "I'm here. I am committed." A cry wedged at the bottom of my throat that I wouldn't let escape. I didn't want to ruin the moment.

Max towered over me. "It's time you prove that to us."


THE SOUND WAS UNMISTAKABLE. A WARNING SIGN.

A rattle.

Convinced my vision was betraying me, I blinked. No, it was really happening. We were in the desert on a different trail than I remembered ever taking. How on earth had I gotten there? Everyone was looking at me. I took an uneasy breath like holes had been punched into my lungs.

"Kill it," Max said.

Across the path, Susanna was curled up on the desert ground, her forehead pink and burning in the afternoon rays.

Next to her, a rattlesnake was poised to attack. The sharp jangle of its tail clamored again. Susanna's mouth twitched. She was trying not to cry. Her life was in my hands. It was a simple task. Man versus animal. The snake was a predator. I could surrender to my instincts or follow the way of my upbringing—walking away and letting someone else deal with the problem. If I was brave, I'd take control.

Arthur rambled into Max's ear, frantic but hushed. "Susanna doesn't need to do this. Let me, Max."

"Kill it." Max pushed Arthur aside. "Save the New Kind. Slay the predator. This is how you become one of us. How you prove you're a master over your own human weakness." Max had coaxed the rattlesnake there and brought us to this spot. He'd taunted it to the point it wanted to attack.

I protested. "But it's just an innocent animal . . ."

"The body is temporary," Max said, a familiar refrain. "The soul is what's permanent."

The rest of them, slack-jawed and eager, watched me for their entertainment. They wanted to see that I'd do anything for the good of the Oasis. I didn't know if I was worthy, but I knew I wanted to be. I was thirsty, my tongue putrid and heavy in my head. A fly flew onto my bare shoulder, but I did not shoo it away. I couldn't. My level of concentration was too high. I could not be pulled in another direction.

With a nod from Max, Arthur relented, pulled the revolver from the back of his jeans, and handed it to me. The mother-of-pearl handle reflected white in the unrelenting sun. The gesture too was loaded, but I couldn't meet his eyes, the whites milky as ever, his pupils unfocused and sluggish from the potent cocktail of whatever was in that cursed tea. I took hold of the gun and recognized the power of it in my hand—the force, fervent and impulsive.

"Kill it," Max said again. Louder.

I wanted so badly for him to feel pride thudding in his chest when he claimed me as his. Intimacy with him was so close I could taste it, sharp as the salt from a sunflower seed.

So I aimed the revolver and squeezed the trigger.

The first bullet hit the dirt. Susanna yipped. By a stroke of luck, the second hit the mark, right between the scaly creature's eyes. There was a peculiar satisfaction in the ripple of the bullet, the breaking of scales.

I released a harrowing cry as I stepped forward and shot it again and again, exposing its cold reptilian blood to the sky. A forbidden boldness that had been stashed away and tucked out of sight for far too long propelled me forward, escaping, claiming space and time.

The others whooped. Arthur rushed to help Susanna to her feet. Her hands were trembling. She shook them, trying to take back ownership over her form.

I examined the revolver in my hand, marveling that a life force could so quickly be brought to a permanent end. I'd never imagined killing a deadly rattlesnake would be so crucial to belonging, to becoming theirs. I turned back to Max, the gun pointed at the ground like he'd taught me. He hid it away in his indestructible dark jeans.

"I knew you belonged here." He took my face in his calloused hands. "It's time to celebrate."

Max marched over to Susanna, pulled her onto his back, and began the return journey to the Oasis, the others at his heels. It felt like we'd exited a theater after a romp of a movie, and we all wanted to reminisce about our favorite parts. The main event already gone by, a memory now that we wanted to replay.

Arthur sidled up behind me and kissed my neck. My breath caught as euphoria rushed to my core, daring one of the others to look back and catch us in the act.

By nightfall, the coyotes would feed on the mangled snake's carcass. Come morning, the vultures would descend to leave no piece of the creature untouched.

I pondered whether people might see me differently when I returned. If I ever returned. I brimmed with elation at the idea. If I never returned to Coronado, would Mom ever find a way to forgive herself? Maybe I could be like a snake who shed its former skin. Perhaps that was the way to be free of her judgments: exist in this sacred desert with the ones who deemed me worthy.

Arthur volunteered for night watch and handed me another cup of tea while the others slept. Blessed with the cover that night granted us, I drank up. In the dank Airstream, I bit into Arthur's neck and traced my tongue over his Adam's apple as if I'd been starved for centuries. I gave my body over to his in the dark.

*Production Day 9*

# HOLLYWOOD

TODAY WE'RE SHOOTING AT MILK STUDIOS ON CAHUENGA, BLOCKS away from Hollywood Forever Cemetery, where the greats have been laid to rest. It's been so long since I've seen one of our living legends, Judy Temple, in person, who is fresh off wrapping a campaign shoot for her viral cosmetics brand. Isaac's production team takes over the clean industrial space. Judy's brand team clears the rose-gold compacts and candy-colored palettes from the product display staged on the scrim. In its place, Isaac arranges me like a doll on a modern white chair, matching the background, while Judy changes her wardrobe in the dressing room.

I'm forced to wait patiently, and once we pass the ten-minute mark, I take out my phone to scroll aimlessly. I see a new direct message from TexWatson86 in my inbox. I should ignore it. I refused to dignify the last attempt on my sanity when he took a photo of me without my permission and sparked a whole debate about my sex life.

*Ping!* Another message from TexWatson86 illuminates my phone screen. I make sure no one can see my screen when I open it.

Another photo appears, but this one is not so easy to distinguish. At first, it just looks like an inconspicuous brick building, but then my stomach drops. I realize it's *my* building, downtown, the windows into my living room. The sheer curtains are drawn, but there's a shadow in the center of the frame—a silhouette, *my* silhouette. The shooter must have been across the street, on one of the rooftops, like a sniper, anticipating the perfect moment to take aim at his target: me.

Pressure rises inside me as I comprehend that TexWatson86, whoever he is, knows where I live. He wants me to know he's watching.

"Lucy?"

I jump out of my skin when Isaac calls me back to earth. I lose my grip, and my phone goes flying across the stage floor.

"Judy's ready for us," Isaac announces. He clears his throat. "You good?"

I'm too wound up to think straight. Is Isaac's method working after all?

"Sloane can take that for you." Isaac points at my phone. Sloane sets her binder down, ready on command.

"That's all right." I snap out of it, scramble for my phone, and slip it into my jacket pocket. I'll have to deal with this later. It's time for me to do my job. "I'm all good."

Sloane and Isaac promptly return to business as usual, certainly questioning my sanity. Judy finally arrives on set. She's all business, sipping her water through a straw, so her trademark red lip doesn't budge. Her assistant recites the rest of her day's packed agenda. Our embrace is brief and unsure, like she's afraid she'll catch a cold.

With her signature honey-blond locks coiffed in immaculate old Hollywood glamour curls, Judy radiates warmth as she flashes her veneers and introduces herself to the camera, though she's something larger than all of us now, larger than herself, and needs no introduction.

Isaac begins his interview with the night of Judy's attack, captured in Mom's 2003 collection, which thrust her into the public eye, her celebrity boosted by the timing and association with my case. The most haunting and most famous photograph was of Judy in the bathroom that night. Judy, with her dress pulled down, exposing her concave chest, still felted with hair. Her cheap breastplate left on the counter next to her treasure trove of drugstore beauty products. The welt on her cheek glistened in the vanity's glow, her expression dismissive, defiant. Her right eye was swollen shut. The bathtub was still filling with water behind her.

A film student at USC saw the photograph, tracked her down, and made an independent cinema verité piece with Judy at the center. The film was paraded through the festival circuit, scooping up all the awards. Judy was catapulted into stardom. She transitioned. She reached icon status. Our Judy. The most public, beloved advocate for transgender rights. A pioneer, an activist, a regular judge on *RuPaul's Drag Race*, an entrepreneur. A Broadway musical about her life is in the works. Last year, she was named one of *Time's* Most Influential People in the world. All these years later, she's graciously worked us into her jam-packed schedule and agreed to reminisce on the summer that changed all our lives.

"You think it never crossed my mind that Diana Golden could make me famous?" Judy answers Isaac's inquiries with the flourish of a natural performer. "Maybe it wasn't the way I wanted to be introduced to the public, but you gotta think through that wish before you rub the lamp. Who would I be then?" She laughs to herself and looks up at the ceiling like she's watching a movie of the alternate path her life could have taken. "An old queen still hustling for tips in bars, scraping by paycheck to paycheck. God bless all those girls. My sisters. Every day, I break my back so girls like me don't have to go through what I went through, so they can thrive without the threat of violence."

At the mention of violence, I find myself indulging in a dark fantasy of what might happen if TexWatson86 finds me alone and unarmed. "It's a damn shame we can't even walk home alone without that threat," I say. "I know how that can be—so isolating and dehumanizing, even."

The sparkle in Judy's eyes fades in a way I'm not sure how to decipher. "I'm not sure I follow . . ."

"I know how it feels to be followed, to have every move I make picked apart," I explain, words tumbling out of me. "As a public figure,

I can never fully relax. What happened to you, the attack, it could just as easily happen to me too."

Judy shakes her head in disbelief. I look over to Isaac, self-conscious I said the wrong thing, but I can't read his face, shadowed by a baseball cap. Beside him, Sloane chews the end of her pen.

I backpedal. "I only mean—"

Judy interrupts me. "Do you ever think about what happened when you went to bed that night? I don't mean your brainwashed logic that my attack was the catalyst that sent you back to the Oasis. I mean, do you ever think about why I was targeted, or about what your mother did from my point of view?"

Given the edge in her voice, I get the feeling we should have had this conversation in private. I replay the exact events of that evening through a cheesy filter like a cheap reenactment. I always comforted myself with the fact of Judy's stardom, chalking up the tragedy that brought her there as a fated means to an end. Sure, Judy suffered, but Mom put her on the map.

"I thought Diana was my friend," Judy says. "She told me she took those pictures as proof for the cops, but she never had any intention of handing them over to the authorities." She shakes her head. "Who are we kidding? Cops, now and then, wouldn't lift a finger for someone like me. Not like they did for you, privileged little white girl. We are not the same. You should know better."

I bite my lip as worry swells. "You misunderstood me—"

Judy cuts me off. "Diana took one of the lowest moments I've ever experienced, a night when I was beaten within an inch of my life for the way I look, for the skin I was born in, for the way I live, and she pointed a spotlight at it. She turned her camera toward all my bruises, my heartache. She displayed it for the world to see."

"Judy, I—"

Judy holds up her hand. I snap my mouth shut. "Many criticize your mother for pulling back the curtain on a community that she doesn't belong to and taking ownership over a miscarriage of justice that's not hers to own. It's mine. Your mother has the audacity to think she deserves the credit for giving me the life I built brick by brick. Looking at that photograph, I see what your mother didn't. I'm not broken. I'm a fighter. I'm more than a brushstroke on her canvas. I'm the reason I'm where I am today. Not her. Now I have fans paying me to entertain them like Judy Garland, you know? But Judy suffered too. That's our plight as artists, isn't it? We turn our pain into material, then hold out a cup for change."

The lump in my throat thickens. I try to take apart what she's saying and what I said in order to put everything back together in a way that makes me feel better, but I can't.

"Your mother is an expert at capturing tragedy and wrapping it up in a bow for profit and praise."

I clear my throat, the impulse to defend Mom as natural as breathing. She's not perfect, but she's taught me everything I know. "She's an artist."

"That's what she does. Recognize the difference," Judy corrects me, then clicks her tongue. "I always thought Odette would be the one to follow in your mother's footsteps, but you . . ."

"What about me?"

"What is it that you do now?"

"Look, I know my job is unconventional, but it's important work. I have a platform."

Judy crinkles her eyes like I've helped her make her case. "See? You're the same as your mother, just with a different job title. You exploit tragedies too, speaking about crimes far more complex than you can fathom. You don't educate yourself enough to know better. But the twisted part is, you do it to yourself. You're out here selling your soul, just like Diana Golden taught you to do, and you think that's what makes you special. Tell me. What good are you bringing into the world?"

She's mistaken. Mom's a creative genius; I can only dream of living up to her accomplishments. I effect change. I tell my story, so the evils I endured are not for naught.

Isaac takes charge, directs Judy to detail her memory of the night of the party before I disappeared and the fallout of my return. I wring my hands and watch her, my cheeks reddening. I hate to admit that I'm still enchanted by her and the way she moves. Sharing the space with her takes me back to those days when I was getting to know her, laughing at her jokes, watching film noir with her, and learning all her best beauty tricks. Heartache slices me in two. I missed her all this time, but I'd not been conscious of how she had made me feel when I was with her. She always made me feel seen. Now Judy paints the artist who gave her a career as a mortal enemy, and me as a poor reproduction.

I want to tell her she's wrong about Mom. She's wrong about me. She has no idea the kind of hell I'd endure if the truth about that summer comes to light. She never understood the danger I was in, and she doesn't question the danger awaiting me now.

AS SOON AS WE WRAP, I HIGHTAIL IT OUT OF THE STUDIO AS FAST as humanly possible. I need to hear myself think. My heart's thudding a mile a minute as I wrangle myself into the driver's seat. I'm on autopilot as I drive, merging onto the freeway without checking my blind spot. A driver lays on their horn. I'm too preoccupied to wave an apology.

It might be possible that Tex is a former muse of Mom's, or an ex, maybe, waiting to see if Mom deems him worthy enough to include in her new show. Or maybe Tex is one of the wolves I took home one ravenous evening, bitter about the rejection. Or he's the brother of a victim who needs traction on a cold case and believes this harassment is the way to go about it. Or he's the obnoxious intruder from the She Slays event, an Oasis loyalist, hellbent on bending me until I break.

I think back to the night I met Jeremy at the old Hollywood bar. I go through the evening, then remember I felt that uneasy chill, like someone was following me, and I waved it off. I remember the quote

Tex pulled from my memoir when he posted that photo of Jeremy and me: "If I could take a bite out of his flesh there, then I'd really taste him, his flesh and blood."

My teeth start chattering at the possibility of who Tex must be, a possibility I'm too scared to entertain.

By some miracle, I make it downtown. At a red light, I pull up Tex's messages, to make sure I didn't hallucinate this threat.

TexWatson86: You can't let your shadow win.

My blood runs ice cold.

I curse myself for not taking Tex's harassment seriously until now. I was so wound up in convincing Isaac that the online chatter doesn't matter that I didn't carefully consider who might be behind the messages, casting him off as another ravenous vulture. I didn't ever stop to think Tex might just be the one man I lost track of, circling, anticipating the perfect moment to appear and tear my whole world apart yet again.

My tires squeal as I make a sharp turn into my garage. My legs move on their own—out of the garage, past the drunken clusters of twentysomethings stumbling out of the craft breweries. Past the peddlers holding out empty palms for spare change. I scan each face. He's watching me right now. He's following me, isn't he?

I glance behind me. A shriek. The source reveals herself. It's just a wannabe manic pixie dream girl squealing at her handsy boyfriend as they exit an Uber.

I clench my jaw as the elevator rises. I imagine he will appear as soon as the elevator doors slide open. Will he grab me? Will his hands grip my throat while my eyes roll into the back of my head? Will he take his sweet time, milking my terror? Or make it quick? An eye for an eye.

My stomach dips when the elevator chimes. I have my keys in hand, ready to defend myself.

I look down the hallway, both directions. The coast is clear. I wish I felt more relieved than I do.

I sprint to my front door, chest constricting, and fumble with the key. Pressure swarms behind me, pushing at my back. I'm being watched, I know it. I let out a sob.

The lock releases. I rush inside and slam the door behind me. My chest rises and falls as I hyperventilate. I lean my head back against the door to find momentary comfort in the shield between the outside world and me.

I hold my breath and flip on the lights, anticipating a masked figure in the kitchen with one of my chef knives raised. But the loft is just as I left it. The air conditioning kicks in, jolting me with its roar.

Mom's nowhere to be found, her Prada bag gone from the hook by the door. I rack my brain, trying to remember where she said she'd be. The Broad for a friend's exhibit? The Chateau for a date with an entertainment lawyer?

Slipping off my heels, I feel for my phone in my jacket pocket, just in case I need to call 911. I slide my chef's knife out of the butcher block and leave it on the counter, for good measure. I race to the window and kick myself for leaving the curtains open all day. Before I yank them closed, I look across the street, scanning the windows of the opposite building for a sign of Tex. A sign that never comes.

I creep through the loft, open the door to Mom's bedroom, but there's nothing amiss. Her bed's made. Her clothes are in the open closet. I shut the door quietly, then check the bathroom. I hold my breath as I rip the shower curtain back, then laugh at myself. Can I be that much of a cliché? I understand him more than anyone. I need to put myself in his shoes.

If TexWatson86 is who I think he is, he wants to rattle me. He's always fed on fear.

Entering my bedroom, I sift through the shadows just in case, but there's nothing. Before I know it, I'm dialing Sloane. After all, she told me I could change my mind. She picks up on the first ring.

"Hey, are you okay?"

I experience a brief moment of relief as I hear her voice, eager to help.

"Could you come over?" I look up at the ceiling, so as to not let myself cry. "I don't think I can be alone right now."

SLOANE BUSIES HERSELF IN THE KITCHEN. SHE PUTS A KETTLE ON the stove for tea. I fill her in as she looks through the cupboards and drawers for whatever magic treatment she thinks will cure my anxiety.

"I have no idea who it could be." Curled up on the couch, I let this lie slip out easily. "He won't stop following me, slandering me online. This can't be happening."

"I can't believe you've been dealing with this on your own." Sloane shakes her head. "I can't imagine how unsettling that must feel and all the talk about being attacked . . . No wonder the interview with Judy sent you down a spiral." Sloane props her elbows on the counter and rests her chin in her hands. Her gaze skims over the lone knife on the counter. "What's that about?"

"I could have sworn he was going to be here when I got home," I admit. Sloane raises her eyebrow. "These fans get wild ideas."

The kettle whistles. "Lucy . . ." she says, full of pity. She pours the hot water into a mug. Drizzles it with honey, then hands it to me.

"I know I sound crazy."

"Don't say that." She joins me on the couch and wraps her hands around her own mug. "You sound exhausted."

"God, you must think I'm a lunatic," I say. "I shouldn't have dragged you over here."

"Don't be silly. I'm just happy you reached out when you needed someone to talk to." She squeezes my knee. "Going back into your past is obviously taking a bigger toll on you than you thought."

"Maybe." I twist my hair around my fingers. "I just need to get rid of him."

Sloane props her legs up on the ottoman. "What do you think he wants?"

I blow on the tea. I may be coming down from a panic attack, but I'm not an idiot. If I tell Sloane about my suspicions, she'd absolutely have me committed. "Who knows? He's an online sleuth. Whatever he wants, it's not important."

"Sounds like it's important to TexWatson87."

"Eighty-six," I correct her. "What matters is he's getting closer," I tell her, panic rising in my chest. "He knows where I live, Sloane. How am I supposed to cope with that?"

We let the quandary hang in the air for a moment.

Sloane pivots to face me. "If he's that dangerous, you should call the police."

"The police?"

"Yeah, I'm sure you have connections, right? A detective you've met through your line of work?" She starts rambling off ideas that make my head spin. "They'll probably have you turn over your correspondence, but they should be able to track him down, right? Get you some protection. I know Isaac has some contacts in the force if you want me to give him a call."

"I don't want Isaac to know anything about this!" I blurt out.

"Why not?" Sloane shrugs. "He already asked you about the photo on the forum a few days ago, and it wasn't a big deal."

"You know the second Isaac catches wind of this, he'll have a field day," I say. "Then the whole doc will hinge on the pursuit of Tex Watson's identity. Isaac will make it some commentary about parasocial fandom in the true crime space and suddenly I will become . . ."

"An afterthought," Sloane says, finishing my sentence.

"Promise me you won't tell him?"

Sloane sets her mug down on the coffee table. "Of course, Lucy. I only want to help."

The more I consider involving the police, the more it sounds like a terrible idea. I don't want them near my case for the exact same reason I don't want Isaac arrogantly cracking open the vault of secrets about that summer that I locked away decades ago. "Besides, stalking cases are dead ends until someone makes a violent threat. The police will only say I'm hysterical."

"Right." Sloane shrugs again. "For all you know, Tex is just a super fan, like you said, with nothing in his life except Crime Con. All the buzz with the doc might have just kicked his fascination with your case into high gear."

I let her naivete and the warmth of the tea ripple through my chest like a salve.

"Anyway, you've dealt with people like this in the past, haven't you?" she asks.

I nod, a chill returning as I recount the instances. In the early days, there were the reporters, amateur and professional, who watched my every move, starved for a scoop. There was the graduate student I met at a reading who showed up at my pharmacy, then the grocery store, and then my doctor's office, until I confronted her. There was the beady-eyed kid who harassed me on the street and tried to throw me in his van and take me to San Quentin. All of them I was able to shake, but TexWatson86 won't be that easy.

"Okay, this is what we're going to do," Sloane says. "Tonight, I'll stay here at the loft, so you can get some sleep. I'll make sure nothing happens to you. You won't be alone, okay? Tomorrow, you'll leave all this mess behind you. If you don't give this guy what he wants, he'll lose interest."

"You think so?"

"We'll be in Coronado soon," she says, sinking deeper into the couch. "You'll need your strength to finish filming with a clear head, without watching your back."

I rest my head back on the couch and pick up the remote to find a distraction. Relieved a plan's in place, at least for now. I tell myself I must have it all wrong. TexWatson86 is no one. It's high time I leave the past in the past.

"Thanks, Sloane, for being here." For the first time in a long time, I mean it. I don't have to go through this alone.

# THE OASIS

*13 days before*

After the usual chores, I made my way to Max's adobe for a session, but the door wouldn't budge. "Max?" I called out, knocking.

A moment later, Max appeared, disheveled. "Fiona needs me right now." Behind him, she was seated in my chair.

"You said we'd talk more about my shadow today."

Max sighed. "Give me a minute, Fiona." She crossed her arms in protest. Max stepped outside to join me on his stoop, not closing the door all the way. She could hear whatever I told him.

"I don't understand." I searched his eyes for comfort. Instantly, I feared he'd found out about Arthur and me, our nights spent together in secret.

"My little poet . . ." Max said in an even voice without his usual affection. "You're one of us now. Your lack of understanding toward Fiona is a sign of weakness. I'm supposed to be able to count on you, right?"

"Right," I replied. "You can count on me, Max."

As Max disappeared inside, I turned back to the camp, my notebook in hand, and spotted Arthur heading off in his truck. I joined Beatrice at the picnic table, the littlest boy fast asleep on her chest. "Where's Arthur off to?" I asked, rubbing the boy's back.

"Max sent him to pick someone up," Beatrice said. "A new girl."

TO DISTRACT MYSELF FROM EVERY MINUTE I WASN'T SPENDING WITH MAX, every second Arthur was gone, I helped Eden in the kitchen. By that time, she was bound to give birth any day. The pool of sweat underneath her dress was an unsettling reminder that the desert climate wasn't the ideal place for expectant mothers. She dried as I washed the various pots and pans, leaning against the cheap laminate countertop.

"I can finish up if you're not feeling up to it," I offered.

She huffed. "We *all* have to do our part."

"How are you feeling?" I asked. "Are you excited the baby will be here soon? Scared?"

Eden wiped down a chipped platter. "Make sure you get the bottom of that pot. Use some elbow grease."

Slowly, the residue on the bottom of the pot began to dissolve. "What are you going to name the baby?"

Eden dropped the plate she was drying onto the floor. It splintered into pieces.

"I'm sorry." I knelt down to sweep up the mess with my hands. "I'll get it." I dumped the rest of the broken plate into the trash can. "Max canceled our session. He's with Fiona. And now Arthur's gone, and I just feel alone again."

Eden winced, wiping her brow. "You're never alone here, Lucy!" It was the first blatant twinge of anger I'd ever seen flare from her, directed toward me, erupting all at once. "If Max canceled, I'm sure he had a very good reason. You've been with him every day for hours for weeks. The rest of us need some time too. Don't be selfish."

Her accusation stung. I took a step back into the counter and dropped the limp wet sponge into the sink. Whatever air that was in the room left.

"You need to do your part, to trust him, or I'll have to let him know you questioned his decisions." Eden softened, pulling me in for a hug, smoothing my hair. "You don't want him to believe you'd go against his word, do you?"

"Thank you, Eden." I sank into her warmth, grateful she was still opening her arms to me, but panicked, more than ever, that I'd be found out for breaking the rules.

ONCE THE CAMP WAS STILL, I READ AND REREAD THE STORIES I'D RECORDED Max telling during our sessions, searching for consolation. A paralyzing fear that I was the one at fault overtook me. I'd betrayed Max by sleeping with Arthur and agreeing to keep our relationship a secret. My body was no longer pure. A lie of omission didn't align with his ideals. My fault was holding me back from becoming truly his, one with my father. Max withdrawing from me that day had to be my punishment. I wasn't who he wanted me to be. I couldn't make it into the Light like the others, because I was cursed with too much wanting, still stuck in the past as my dreams always pulled me back home, to the freefall of Odette's raven hair, to the ring Mom's coffee mug left on the kitchen counter, to the salt in Coronado's ocean waves. I was weak enough to be swayed by Arthur's mouth on my collarbone and command of my waist.

I waited for the light to break through the thin curtains. If I wanted to get back in Max's good graces, I knew what I had to do.

*12 days before*

"I need to tell you something." I twisted my hair in my hands. Max leaned against his door frame. His violet-blue eyes were bloodshot in the early morning sun. "I need to report a fault."

WE WAITED BY THE PICNIC TABLE FOR ARTHUR'S RETURN; HE WAS EXPECTED back any minute now.

"You did the right thing," Max assured me. "I'm proud of you."

Beaming, I leaned into my father's wiry frame and rested my head on his shoulder. My heart soared. Just as soon as I'd tasted that slice of heaven, we heard the rumble of the pickup truck and could make out Arthur approaching on the horizon.

"You're ready, Lucy." Eden waddled over and kissed the top of my head. "Max wants to reward you."

Max always promised that if someone was at fault, he would help correct their path. He would double down on sessions and teach Arthur how to be a leader of the Oasis and right the wrong. Arthur would thank me for wanting the best for him and us. One day, we'd rid ourselves of the wanting and become whole.

"It's time." Eden signaled all of us to take our places.

Arthur stepped out of the cab. I could feel his gaze on me as he joined us in our formation, but I refused to be weakened again. I kept my focus on the newcomer in the back of the truck.

The young woman exited from the passenger side. A frizzy blond mane hung down her back. Max stepped forward and welcomed her to the Oasis. Her face twisted in confusion and awe.

"Lucy." Max called me forward. "You'll look after Amber, won't you? Show her the ropes?"

It was a huge responsibility, an honor only granted to those Max trusted implicitly, a reward for my loyal act. I reached out a hand to my new friend. "You're going to love it here."


AMBER'S FIRST DAY AT THE OASIS WAS BY ALL ACCOUNTS SUCCESSFUL. AFTER her first session with Max, she was shy and reserved. I noticed a pair of bruises on her knees when Fiona joined us for the cleansing. I did not ask her how she got them. That didn't matter, because it happened before, in the outside world.

Touring Amber around the Oasis kept me occupied until nightfall, when Eden offered to show her to the sleeping room. Amber held her hands behind her back, waiting for instruction.

"You better hang back," Eden said to me, and gestured to Arthur, keeping watch by the fire. "Face the fear." We hadn't spoken all day. I relented, and the others retreated to the adobe house. Max had turned in for the night. Soon it was just Arthur and me and the sparks of the fire. An arrangement I knew well.

I was reminded of the power of his presence, but it was obvious something had changed between us. Surely, he couldn't be angry with me for doing what I had to do. He needed to be held accountable for his faults, same as me. I noticed a new Moleskine in his shirt pocket, dark green instead of the same old black one he always carried around, and I wondered where he'd left it, what filled its pages. I waited for him to say something while I observed the fire so intently I couldn't break my stare. He finally spoke, and what he said broke my heart.

"Why did you have to ruin us?"

*7 days before*

I'd been charged with watching all the children in the center of camp while the other women worked in the greenhouse. Max and Arthur had been in session for five days straight. No one was to disturb them. Inside, Max was breaking him, purging him of his faults, making him pure again. Bit by bit.

"What's it like?" Susanna asked.

"What's what like?" I jiggled my knee, but she grabbed my legs to stop them from shaking. She wanted me to pay attention to her.

"The outside world," Paul blurted. "You've been there, haven't you?"

The children looked to me with doe eyes, waiting for my answer, holding on to each other. I considered how Max would want me to respond.

"What do you think it's like? What do you think is out there?" I turned toward the trucks, the world beyond, and it all felt so far away.

"Aliens!" Paul shouted.

"Monsters and bears and burning houses," another said.

"Battles of war!"

"Susanna." I squeezed her hand, inhaling her sweet scent. "What do you think is in the outside world?"

She scrunched her mouth to the side, deliberating. "Snowflakes. I want to see the snowflakes."

"But we can't!" Paul corrected her. He reached out and pinched her arm. She yelped.

"Hey!" I grabbed his wrist. "We don't hurt each other. Ever."

Paul sulked; his cheeks flushed. "But Susanna wants to go out there." The other children audibly gasped, exchanging looks of concern.

"No, I don't!" Susanna leapt up. "I just want to know what it's like. Don't you want to know? Can you tell us, Lucy?"

Before I could respond, we all heard a loud *thunk* coming from Max's adobe, like a chair or a table had been thrown against a wall. All the children rotated toward the source.

"What are they doing in there?" Paul asked. "It's been forever."

"Maybe we should go see," Susanna suggested. Paul rose to his feet, eager for action.

"Settle down now, all of you." I did my best to calm them. "We are under strict orders to leave them be. If you take a seat, if you listen carefully, I will tell you what I know, okay?"

They acquiesced—obedience their default.

"Max is teaching Arthur everything he knows," I told them. "Arthur broke his promise."

"Like a fault?" Susanna's saucerlike eyes grew wide, as if she was imagining what it might take for her one day to go against the grain.

"Right, a fault," I said, eyeing a silhouette passing by Max's window. "Max loves all of us. He's a hero. He saved all of us. He's helping Arthur meet his destiny so he can be a hero himself one day. All of you will grow up to be leaders too."

Paul cupped his hands under his chin, curious. "What rule did Arthur break?"

A shiver traveled down my spine remembering his touch in the Airstream, the pillow of his lips. "That doesn't matter. What matters is Max is leading him back on the path."

"What about the outside world?" Susanna pressed.

In the distance, I heard shouting, but I couldn't make out the words.

I imagined my name in Arthur's mouth as he repented, asked for forgiveness. In that moment, I trusted Max more than I ever trusted myself.

"The outside world . . ." I tried to picture it; Odette's guttural howl from the garage, the ocean, the deep blue for miles, and the bitter lime of Mom's lethal margaritas pierced the haze. "The outside world is full of pain, full of hurt people hurting people, suffering. Here, at the Oasis, we're safe. No one will ever hurt you here. I promise."

The little kids relaxed into this, their curiosity assuaged, but Susanna looked unconvinced. From behind her back, she pulled out a dandelion and handed it to me. I took hold of it and blew—the little buds danced in the wind. Susanna watched, worry swirling in the carousel of her curious mind.

"Snowflakes are kind of like that," I whispered. "Whole one minute, and the next minute they fall apart. They disappear."

IT'S STARTLING TO SEE MY FATHER'S FACE COME INTO VIEW, THE hero of my girlhood dreams.

I wish I were more surprised than I am to see the 1985 photograph of Max, the one I kept under my pillow growing up, as the opening image for Diana Golden's retrospective collection. She resists labeling it her greatest hits album, resentful of the implication that her best work is behind her. Everyone knows what it means if you're digging up your past successes and marketing them as new. Your days as a visionary have gone by.

The cluster of patrons sip their drinks and pontificate, but I can feel their awareness solidify, their curiosity pique. If the spectacle of the infamous killer, Lucy Golden, witnessing her cult leader father's portrait doesn't do the trick, Isaac and his obtrusive camera crew sure do.

Midconversation with Malin and a silver fox, Mom watches me, eager to observe my reaction to her choice, daring me to make a scene. I smooth my dress, which is the color of rust, backless, and way out of my budget, and straighten my posture. From the outside, I must look like the doting daughter, not like a paranoid woman on the edge.

For the standard amount of time that's deemed acceptable, I play the part of pensive art patron. I gaze at the portrait like I'm analyzing her framing, her perspective, her use of negative space. I pantomime experiencing my larger-than-life father through my mother's expert lens, but I'm careful not to look too closely, hardening every emotion that rushes forward. If I let myself truly see him in this way, in her light, I'll collapse. That can't happen here—not now, not like this.

The turnout is impressive. One hundred or so artsy types with palazzo pants, slicked-back buns, and oddly draped European jackets mill about. Permanent lines of scrutiny split their foreheads. I pass by a group of gallerinas in chunky glasses. "I'm really into natural wine lately," one of them says. "Cindy Sherman. I have a huge thing for Sherman right now," her frenemy says.

I polish off the lingering sediment in my wineglass and continue through the exhibit, pretending like I didn't spend the night before obsessing over the identity of my internet stalker. Thankfully, Sloane followed through on her promise. I managed to fall asleep in the middle of our mini movie marathon after countless cups of tea and placating reassurances.

In the next room, a handpicked selection of Mom's muses looks back at me, seducing me, inviting me in for a closer look. The muses I knew so well at times that I thought of them like family, like Judy. Jesse, of course, in all his rock star glory—the one of him smoking outside the Viper Room, the one of him passed out in the greenroom of the Fonda Theatre. Then there are many more muses whose names I lauded and the ones I never cared to learn. The heroin chic models of the nineties, their style now resurrected in the cultural zeitgeist. The sitcom stars who cling to their fifteen minutes and peddle vitamins on the internet.

As I look at the images, Judy's accusation packs a punch. These are the people my mother photographed for her own benefit. Here she is, years later, still reaping the rewards of their beautifully flawed apparitions. Judy believes I'm cut from the same cloth. For as long as I can remember, I wanted to be heralded in the same echelon as my mother, but it's hard to reconcile the fact that Judy didn't mean it as a compliment.

In the next room, there are the iconic portraits of Odette—her first stadium tour, the *Rolling Stone* shoot that caused such a stir. It was Mom's idea for her to bare it all. Despite the estrangement, Mom still doesn't mind showcasing her elder daughter's image. We are among the faces that put food on the table and bolstered her reputation for capturing exquisite messes. I view these photographs of Odette with a renewed sense of understanding of my sister. The reflex to praise her, to covet her slender frame, arrives automatically, but I remember what she told me.

There is pain underneath beauty. A human behind the muse.

Isaac and the crew catch up to me, shifting the focus away from the star of the show. I know that must take the wind out of her sails. Diana Golden's a photographer, yes, accustomed to her station behind the camera, but most people forget she began her whole career as Jesse's muse. Diana Golden, the ultimate inspiration for a rock legend, a hit song on the radio with her name in the chorus. Mom knows how to bring out beauty in others, the tragedy in them too, but sometimes I believe it's her beauty translated, projected onto whoever is in front of her as she clicks the shutter. There's no doubt she relishes stepping back into that role, how essential Isaac's lens makes her feel, how crushing it is when it pans elsewhere and lands on her younger daughter. The one she's always deemed mediocre, at best.

"How does it feel to be here tonight?" Isaac prompts me from behind Derek's shoulder. "Seeing so much of your mother's work, so much of it your own history, does it make you feel nostalgic?"

"Sometimes I confuse the photographs with memories." I pause at the series of Odette and me in the tub. I take in the sight of my little pink body encased in bubbles. An old boyfriend of Mom's, a Getty, crouches on the toilet, lost in a paperback of Yeats, grimacing. "You know, can I still smell the rose-scented bath or is it the photograph tricking me into thinking I remember?"

"Right," Isaac replies, bored stiff by my commentary.

I don't blame him. I'm so used to the reflection of my own face. The excruciating portrait of me when I was six—my front tooth falling out, blood on my freckled chin, evidence of my mother's choice to fill her hands with her camera instead of tending to her daughter's anxieties. Then there's her critically acclaimed series covering the search for me and my trial, called *Before and After*, the portrait of me at seventeen, a week after the trial ended, when I chopped my hair off and dyed it icy blond. I'm leaning against the carriage house door, my face half in shadow, crafting the opening lines of *Rattlesnake* in my brain. It takes me a moment to recognize myself. The lie was fresh on my tongue, and I was wary I wouldn't be strong enough to keep our secret. I want to go back and assure my younger self that the sacrifice will be worth it.

"One of my favorites." I hear Mom's throaty alto purr behind me, purposefully arriving at my side the moment Isaac and his crew take five, like it's unbearable to be captured in the same frame as her pathetic excuse for a daughter.

"Really? I never knew." I rub the back of my neck, panicked Mom can smell my anxiety like perfume. She gulps down a swig of her martini, waiting for me to congratulate her, but I decide to take another tactic, one out of her playbook.

"I saw Judy yesterday."

Mom's silent for only a beat, but I can sense her discomfort. "Did you now? Well, how's our girl doing?"

Nausea tries to grab at me, imagining Mom watching Judy's interview. "She had a lot to say."

"Isaac must really be digging at the bottom of the barrel." Mom laughs. "What does he want with her anyway?"

I shrug, as if her dismissal of Judy doesn't grate. "Provide some background, I suppose. She *was* there that summer."

"No wonder he's desperate for me to talk." Mom snorts, genuinely amused by the idea. As she twirls her olive garnish in her glass, a knot of rage in my stomach tightens.

"Are you nervous about your speech?"

"Why would I be nervous?" Mom snickers. I'm envious of her confidence.

Across the room, I clock Isaac's viewfinder and watch as the panic sets in that he's missing a shot of the two of us together. Mom takes it as her cue to greet the next group of people, side-stepping me with graceful ease.

Before I reach the final room, goose bumps rise on my arms. I can feel it, that sensation of being observed. I know it well. I survey the room slowly this time and spot Sloane rushing around the corner, backpack slung across her shoulder. She maneuvers through the crowd toward me, having been nominated to babysit, I'm sure, as Isaac plays ball with Diana. She hands me a new glass of wine. Her occupational habit of anticipating needs comes in handy just when I need it. I thank her.

"Wild show, huh?" Sloane glances around the room, her cheeks flushed at the sophistication.

"My mother certainly knows how to draw a crowd." I take a sip of the wine, wondering if Sloane thinks being here means she's finally made it.

"Sorry I've been MIA," Sloane begins. "Dealing with a bit of a situation at security."

I turn to face her and see she's bitten her nails down to the quick. "What is it?"

"I wasn't going to say anything, but, well, there was someone trying to get in, claimed they were on the list, said they knew you . . ."

My animal instincts kick in, hackles raised. "Tex Watson?"

Sloane nods, biting her lip.

I think I might liquefy on the spot. "Did you happen to see—"

"I didn't get a good look." She shakes her head. "Don't worry. I explained the situation to the doorman, and he took care of it." Sloane must see the color drain from my face. She grabs my hand in earnest. "That lunatic's long gone. You're not alone, okay? I got you."

I squeeze her hand, unable to thank her or speak at all.

Like a tidal wave, I'm pulled back to that morning. One foot in this world, one in another. I can taste the metal in my mouth.

I can smell the blood in the water.

# THE OASIS

*1 day before*

I'd never seen so much blood in my life.

Half asleep, I stirred when I felt something wet on the floor. I wondered if one of the kids had wet themselves, but when I opened my eyes and saw a dark wash of blood pooled on Eden's mattress beneath her, I knew something had gone terribly wrong. Sweat was beaded on her forehead, her nightgown soaked from the waist down, her face white as a full moon. She was fading fast. "Eden!" I cried out. "Wake up, wake up!"

The women stirred at my cries and leapt into action. Fiona rushed over and propped Eden's head in her lap.

"Get Max!" Fiona cried. "Get Max now."

Paralyzed, I blinked at her.

"Move!" Beatrice shoved me out of the way and ran out of the house, screaming.

Amber ushered the children out of the room as they rubbed their eyes with sleep, confused by the chaos. Horrified, Susanna let out a wail, clinging onto the door frame until Amber pulled her away.

Not even a minute passed before Max and Arthur burst through the door. Arthur looked like he hadn't slept in days, but Eden's state seemed to startle him fully awake. "We have to get her to the truck! Lucy, call the hospital. Tell them—"

"No!" Max shouted over everyone's hysterics. "Everything goes as planned."

"Max," Arthur yelled back. "There isn't enough time."

Max placed a hand on the back of Arthur's neck. "Don't you trust me?"

Arthur hung his head. "She's lost too much blood."

"Remember." Max shoved Arthur into the wall. "You can't let your shadow win. That's when you become one of them, the enemy, a traitor. Every child of the Oasis was brought into the world this way. If you want to belong here, you need to do your part to . . ."

"To keep the New Kind pure," Arthur said, finishing the proverb.

Max leaned his forehead into Arthur's, so they were touching. "Be the leader you say you want to be."

My head was spinning, imagining what might happen if we failed to secure medical attention for Eden and her baby.

"It's time," Max announced. Arthur took this as his cue, and together, they scooped up Eden and carried her out of the house.

"But that amount of blood . . ." I stared at the stain on the mattress and felt dizzy. "That can't be normal."

Beatrice folded the thin mattress in half to dispose of later, unperturbed by the metallic odor. "Max has seen it all before."

Fiona dared me to assert my loyalty. "Max would never endanger the life of his child. He's delivered all of the New Kind at the Oasis—well, after you."

"After me?" I tried to piece it together. "What do you mean?" I shook Fiona's shoulders. I ran through all the details I could remember about Eden and her past. I was floored by how little information I knew for certain. So Eden wasn't a desolate expectant mother whom Max had rescued off the street and generously granted a place of refuge. That was only the narrative they allowed me to believe, and soon I'd realize all the lies they'd ever spooled could come undone with a single tug of a loose thread.

"Max's child," I said, getting used to the idea. Max had fathered Eden's baby. It was all by his design—the New Kind. Max the opportunist.

"So, I'm one of them, one of the New Kind?"

"Yes," Beatrice replied. "You're the first."

"Max is the only one who can bring the New Kind into the world." Fiona lifted her pointer finger toward the picture window behind me. "We raise them in his pure image."

I followed the direction of her dirty fingernail. There they were outside, as if they'd been arranged for this exact juncture, the rosy-cheeked, fiery, and affectionate children of the Oasis chasing what little remained of the night sky.

There were nine of them, Susanna the eldest, six years younger than me. Eden's baby would mark the tenth. Ten more brothers and sisters of mine. They'd been there all along. I'd sung them songs, chased lizards with them, braided their hair. This new knowledge gave me pause. I thought of Odette with her leather corset, low-slung jeans, and power-house voice. She didn't belong to me fully either. At another point in my life, finding out I had nine more siblings and one on the way might have made me feel less alone, but it had the exact opposite effect now. There was no one else like me out there, no one else born of Diana and Max. My mother's resistance toward my father shifted into an eerie focus.

"One day, it'll be my turn to usher in the New Kind. And one day, yours too, Beatrice. You'll be chosen to brave the Underworld," Fiona said.

"We have to go now." Beatrice charged out of the house, reporting for duty.

Fiona hung back when she realized I wasn't following. "Coming?"

"Right behind you."

As soon as they left, I flipped over my mattress to find my journal. I needed to take account of what was happening. History was being made, and I was there to witness it. But when I turned the mattress, there was nothing there. Then I heard something. They were all humming. I recognized the melody as the folk song Eden had taught us around the fire the night of my birthday, before Arthur took me to the truck.

I ran as fast as my legs could take me. The women and children gathered in front of the greenhouse in a circle, the same formation I had found them in when I arrived earlier that summer, months ago now, before this place changed me. I stuck my head through a gap in the circle. They held the red blanket, careful not to let it touch the ground. Humming the ghostly lullaby.

"Grab that end." Beatrice nodded to the far corner of the red blanket. I did as I was told, as the act that Arthur and I committed on that blanket came back to me.

I whispered to Fiona, "What are we doing this for?"

"This is how it's done," Fiona told me between hums. "The birthing ceremony."

I needed to trust, like Eden taught me. If Max had delivered all the other babies before, he must know what he's doing. Eden would survive, the baby would be born, and all would return to normal. Considering any alternative outcome would only isolate me from all the others. I didn't want to be isolated anymore. I wanted to belong. I was one of the chosen ones, the very first of the New Kind.

The humming transitioned into song, open-throated and haunting. "Mother of the water," they sang. "Mother of the soil, bring your new beginnings. Brave the Underworld . . ."

I joined in, singing along, telling myself to stay in the present. *Obey their wishes*, I told myself. Like a lab rat in a maze of Max's design.

We carried the blanket inside Max's house, down the bare hallway, which I'd never explored before. In the empty back room, we found Eden with Max and Arthur. We placed the blanket in the middle of the floor. Eden's cries of anguish must have been the only noise heard for miles. The women pressed wet towels to her forehead and continued with the song. Max took charge of the delivery. Arthur helped position Eden, holding her hand. Max whispered to him along the way. Eden bore down, the mama bear instincts forging ahead.

We waited as each contraction passed. Day turned into dusk. The body heat in that small room did nothing to help my weak stomach. We didn't eat anything all day. I grew nauseated listening to the insistent pleas for Eden to breathe. It reminded me of when I took anatomy in seventh grade and ran out of the classroom during the lecture about lungs. I'd sunk to the floor in the hallway of lockers, forcing breaths in and out, imagining my fragile pink lungs ballooning inside my chest, waiting for them to stop working, waiting for the proof that there was something wrong with me.

As the sun was setting, the cry of an infant rang out. I saw her, the baby, earnest and screaming, her alien body covered in viscera. Her limbs contracted like she wished she could go back inside the womb, where it was safe.

Working in tandem, Beatrice took the child from Max's arms, swaddled her, and took her back down the hall. Fiona signaled to Amber and me to follow and bring the children. I did as I was instructed and took up the rear. I exited Max's house and watched the others proceed in a single-file line into the women's adobe house, but something in my gut told me to turn around. In that moment, I believed it was my devotion demanding I witness Eden's journey to the Light, but now I know a woman's intuition should always be taken seriously.

I knew something wasn't right.

As soon as the last child stepped into the women's adobe, I bolted back to Max's. I knew there was a window into that room on the back side of the house. I'd seen it during the nights I spent in Arthur's Airstream. Out of breath, I crouched down, then gathered the courage to peer inside.

Max caressed Eden's face, pale, sickly. "You did your part." He pressed his lips to her forehead. Her eyes fluttered closed. "Now it's time to go into the Underworld. You must go through it to reach the Light. Only then will you be whole."

Max covered her face with the red blanket; then he held it down.

An animal cry rushed up from my chest, but I could not release it. I covered my mouth. I looked from Arthur's stupefied expression to the weak kicking of Eden's legs, the tremor in her hand sticking out from under the blanket.

A darkness in Max emerged from the depths. Eden's pitiful struggle passed.

My whole body numbed, trying to comprehend how this was possible, but there was all the proof I needed right in front of me. It had all been a lie.

Max was no hero.

That's when Arthur turned his head. Our eyes locked. I slid down the wall. Bile rose in my throat.

A supernatural stillness took over the whole camp, heavy and strange. Eden, the woman I'd admired, who'd treated me with kindness, was gone. Arthur, the bystander, the only love I'd ever known, had let it happen.

Worst of all, my father had killed the mother of his child.

# ARTS DISTRICT

*CLINK. CLINK.*

Mom taps on her wineglass to gain the crowd's attention. A number of other patrons do the same to their own glasses, joining in the symphony. Malin yanks me away from Sloane, into the center of the action. Still stunned, I look back for reassurance, but Sloane's expression flattens as she listens to Isaac's direction. The crew scrambles to capture the speech.

Finally, the buzz of the crowd subsides.

"Thank you. Thank you, everyone, for this very special evening." Mom shows no apprehension about holding court. Her stance is strong, her eyes dazzling, her voice even and clear. Setting the pace, just like she taught me.

"To the team at Hauser and Wirth, thank you for this beautiful space and the invitation." Mom blows a kiss to the gallery director, a tall woman dressed in various shades of cream. "As you can see here tonight, I've taken you back in time to the most pivotal points throughout my unconventional and some might say storied career." The crowd laughs, eating her up. "A life well lived, I'd say, but don't be fooled. It's not over yet . . ."

I take a sip of wine and try to pay attention, but a wave of nausea hits me again. Tex was here, trying to get to me. If Sloane hadn't run interference, he would be in this very room, causing a scene. Malin squeezes my arm. "Are you okay?" I can only nod as a fog of paranoia billows around me.

"So now for the main event." Mom beams as she introduces her top secret film installation. "If you'll join me in the next room, you'll be the first ones to see it. I call this piece *Refractions*."

We migrate to the nearly pitch-black theater room. I sink my nails into Malin's arm and stagger inside. Scowling, Malin deposits me in a corner and saunters off to get a better look.

The film begins. In choppy, quick cuts, scored by synth music, we see sweeping landscapes of Los Angeles and Coronado, then close-ups of hairs on legs, a series of mouths, a dancer's blistered feet in a stark white studio. The music cuts out.

In a splotchy black-and-white film reel, a pair of hands comes into focus, pulling on a rope in long, fluid motions. A faint squeaking of metal against metal ekes out. The camera pulls back just enough to unveil the object that the hands are retrieving: a bucket, rocking back and forth on the line. Water sloshes over the side, overflowing care-lessly. When I hear a low laugh, I know, without a doubt, those hands belong to my father.

The camera pans over and reveals him, wild-eyed, somehow more harrowing in motion. I'm captivated by him as if pulled by a gravita-tional force.

I quickly realize why this sight is so familiar. It's the image come to life—a peek behind the scenes of the photograph I'd kept under my pillow all those sleepless nights as a child, waiting for his arrival and wishing he'd rescue me.

For as long as I can remember, I longed to know what the geo-metric angle in the corner of the photograph was. Now I see, plain as day, that it's the framing of the greenhouse, marking the creation of the Oasis. Back then, the old well was still operational, full of water, constructed to quench the thirst of his people. My father was busy building his desert kingdom piece by piece.

The most sickening revelation dawns on me and pulls me out of

Max's hypnotic trance. Terror wraps around my rib cage. Each constricted breath takes effort.

My mother took that picture at the Oasis. She made this film. She had been *there*.

From behind the camera, I hear her humming. Humming the haunting lullaby I haven't been able to shake for twenty years. The siren song that ushered the mothers of the New Kind to their untimely deaths.

"As nature takes its course"—my mother's voice-over echoes in the projection room—"we can only surrender."

In the dim light, that old sensation returns: the reeling, the knowing.

All along, my mother knew exactly where the Oasis was, because she'd been a part of it, from the beginning.

Heart thudding, I feel my lungs collapse. My knees give out. I release my grip on my wineglass, which shatters on the floor. Heads snap in my direction, accusatory, scolding me for my lapse in etiquette.

My first thought as I fall: *I've made it to the Underworld.*

I learned a long time ago, there's nothing to be found there except darkness.

# THE OASIS

*An hour before*

Only a wall separated us.

Outside, I held my breath, my back against the adobe. Inside, Max crouched by Eden's deceased body. Arthur waited for his leader's instruction.

In a stupor, I managed to stand—my limbs working all on their own. I shook all over like I was the victim who deserved an apology, who needed someone to push the wisps of hair out of my face and rub my back as I drifted off to a peaceful sleep. One of Max's refrains came back to me then.

*There are no victims.*

I repeated it as I staggered across the fire pit. Eden understood this was her fate, and by some outrageous design, she believed her sacrifice would lead her to wholeness. Chest tightening, I knew I had to pretend like I'd witnessed nothing but the miracle of the New Kind. When I entered the women's quarters, the entire camp was silent.

I tiptoed to the telephone hanging on the wall, careful to move quietly. I listened to the dial tone, panicked by the volume. I winced, afraid someone may have heard it. At that moment, the newborn wailed in the back bedroom and I said a silent prayer of gratitude for the diversion. I dialed my home number. It rang twice before the line opened.

"Mom? Is that you? It's me, Lucy," I whispered into the phone. There was nothing on the other end of the line but static. "Mom? If that's you, say something. I'm sorry, okay? I'm sorry I left. I'm out here in the desert with Max. This place called the Oasis. I'm not sure where exactly." I leaned my forehead against the kitchen wall, kicking myself for how careless I'd been on the car rides, failing to memorize the route and register the nearest sign of civilization. "Can you come and get me? Something happened and—"

The hairs on the back of my neck pricked up in alert. Someone was listening. In a flush of panic, I hung up the phone. I spun around and found Susanna, rubbing her eyes red. Her round face was pink and streaked from crying.

"Lucy?"

"Shh, you need to be quiet." I hoped she wouldn't notice the tremble in my voice. "You can't be here right now."

"But the baby won't stop crying." Her bottom lip quivered. "Where's Eden?"

I searched the room for something to give her to soothe her. I spotted Odette's jasmine perfume, the grooved glass bottle inside the open trunk. I grabbed it and gave it to her.

"Hang on to this, okay? Whenever you get scared, just remember it's yours. Only yours." Susanna's face lit up. It had long been ingrained in her that she was not to have any belongings of her own. "Now, do you think you can go back to the room for me? And promise not to tell anyone you saw me, okay? Our little secret."

She folded her arms around me. A lump formed in my throat. When I let go, I swallowed my cry and watched her shuffle back down the hallway, perfume in hand. It was up to me to protect not just me but her too, my little sister.

I picked up the receiver again to call 911, but the phone wouldn't dial out. I knew it didn't matter how loud I screamed. No one outside the Oasis could hear me. The main road was too far for me to walk on my own without them catching up to me. We were in the middle of miles of dirt roads only Arthur and Max could navigate.

I heard their voices, Arthur's and Max's. I went to the window and peered through the curtains. Headlights swung across, carving the outline of my shadow. I ducked and pulled my knees to my chest. An engine rumbled to a start. When the headlights pulled back, I looked out the window and saw Max's truck driving away. Now was my chance. I needed to get the hell out of the Oasis before they found me. Before someone else ended up like Eden.

Before I did.

Adrenaline bursting through me, I opened the trunk in the hallway and grabbed my backpack. Panic took over when I realized I didn't have my journal. Where had it gone? I tried to tell myself I didn't need it. For so long, it had been my lifeline. Now it was tainted with Max's rotten theories.

My only means of escape had to be Arthur's truck. The same vehicle that brought me there would have to take me back. I scampered across the compound in the twilight, heart ticking faster, faster. Soft light peeked out from underneath the front door of Max's house, the structure breathing, pulsing. As the memory of Eden's final moments resurfaced, I leaned over and vomited onto the campfire.

Pulling myself together, I found Arthur's truck unlocked and said a silent prayer of gratitude. I crawled into the truck cab, hunting for the keys, tracing every surface. The dash, the seat, the center console, the floor. No such luck.

I leaned my head back, considering what could be done. The glove box. I shot straight up and popped it open.

Inside, on top of a jumble of papers, there was a handgun I'd never seen before, black, bulky, and menacing. It had to be Arthur's. I was unnerved at the sight of it, but grateful all the same that I now knew how to protect myself from the men who had taught me how to use it. If ever the time came.

Slowly, like I was a bomb about to explode, I shifted into the passenger seat. My hands shook as I retrieved the gun, but then I saw what was underneath.

The word *missing* was emblazoned on the top of the page, with details of my person, last seen in Coronado, a $100,000 reward for information, our home phone number. A photograph of me I'd never seen before. I recognized the dress from Mom's party earlier that summer, the night before I returned to the Oasis. She must have taken it when I wasn't looking.

All this time, I thought I was nothing but a failure to Mom, a nuisance, but she had been looking for me for months. Trouble was, she hadn't found me yet.

My gut twisted. I sensed I wasn't alone any longer. When I turned to the driver's side, I made out a silhouette.

*Tap. Tap.*

My heartbeat pounded in my ears, a rush of blood coursing through me. I shoved the flyer and the gun inside my backpack and slammed the glove box shut a second before the door opened.

"There you are," Max announced, as if unfazed by the events of the last hour. I gulped as it dawned on me that Arthur was the one who had driven off in Max's truck. It was just the two of us now, Max and me. He stepped up onto the foot rail of the truck and slapped the hood. "What are you doing out here all by yourself?"

The only way to survive was to play along. I needed to pretend that I had no idea Eden was dead, her heart thumping one moment and extinct the next. "Oh, I was just—"

"Looking for this?" He hopped down onto the sand and took something out of the inside of his jacket, his face in shadow. I knew before he pulled it out it had to be my journal. "Reading your work, I see now how well you understand the Oasis, better than most. You're meant to be here. You were always meant to be here. I've tried to teach Arthur, to make him a leader, but I have to accept that he'll always be one of *them*." He gestured to the outside world, toward the rest of civilization. "Arthur never belonged here," Max said. "But there's more work to be done, isn't there?"

One false step could mean the difference between life and death. "Right, I wanted to come find you," I said. I hated how high my voice sounded, worried I'd ruin the escape plan. "I thought it was important to record what happened, the birthing ritual. I thought you would want me to write it all down. It's part of the story of the Oasis, and that was the first time I ever witnessed it. I wanted to make sure it reads as authentic as it should." I reached out to take the journal.

He pulled it away, so I couldn't grab it, taunting me. "Follow me."

I had no choice. With my backpack slung over my shoulder, I stumbled out of the truck and followed him as he made his way across the compound, past the fire pit. The bright white of the overhanging stars cast a spattering of light on the camp, like a flock of lightning bugs covering the desert floor. The thought of the two of us, father and daughter, under the cover of night, awake while the others slept, had once thrilled me. Now I was wrought with a nagging need to feel my pervasive fear fully and embrace my role as the hunted. Because the hunted fights back.

I'd wanted to believe the Oasis was intrinsically good, but I'd been a fool. I hated myself for being so stupid. I believed Max because I wanted him to be the father I'd always dreamt he could be. Max had not achieved wholeness. He was not enlightened. He preached constantly about the balance between the Light and the Dark, but he was the evil in the shadow, the devil on my tired shoulder. He used fear to gain control over all of us. All this time, I'd been wondering if the darkness I found inside myself was my fault. No, it was his. That was the answer, the explanation I'd been seeking my whole life. I finally knew who to blame.

Max was getting rid of the women, one at a time.

As I recounted the past weeks in the Oasis and unraveled what I knew now, Max's scheme materialized. Arthur lured women in with his youth and charm. Max bedded them, impregnated them, killed them, then pawned off the child onto his future victims. The New Kind were raised in the Oasis, shaped by his ideals. The New Kind, destined to never know their true mothers, would never know the outside world. The babies were the mothers' gifts, and their deaths a sacrifice they believed would bring them wholeness. I reviewed the faces of the women

I'd slept beside for weeks, who were resigned to their unthinkable fate. On and on, the cycle would continue. Until someone put an end to it, until the machine jammed.

But I was a break in the pattern. I was the first of the New Kind to be born in the outside world, the first to return. Arthur wasn't one of the New Kind, so perhaps he'd been struggling all this time, trying to win Max's approval, to make himself indispensable. If he were to bed one of the New Kind and father a child of the Oasis, would Max have to accept him? Would he no longer be one of *them*?

When we arrived at the greenhouse, Max went to unlock the door, and I caught a glimpse of Arthur's truck key on the chain. He'd taken Arthur's keys—my only way out.

Inside, the fans whirred. I looked over the plants, the misters, searching for an exit that didn't exist. Max turned around to face me, smiling wide like the Cheshire cat. I hated how much I looked like him.

"My little poet," he said, reaching out to stroke my cheek. His hand burned like a branding iron.

"Shall we?" I prompted him, sickened by his skin on mine.

He handed over my journal, then strolled slowly around the planters. Disguising my nerves as best I could, I slipped my backpack off and placed it at my feet, out of sight from Max across the center aisle of planters, unzipping it just enough. The weight of Arthur's handgun in my backpack forced me to consider what I could do to protect myself and the others. I bent down over the planter in front of me—the herbs fragrant and moist—opening the notebook to a fresh page. "Start from the beginning." I tried to stop my hand from shaking as I put pen to paper.

Max stopped in front of a pomegranate tree and plucked a fruit off a branch. "From the beginning?" He used his pocketknife to slice open the pomegranate and offered a handful of seeds to me on the blade.

Cautiously, I shook my head, to which he swiped his finger along the blade and ate the tart fruit himself, watching me the whole time. I knew he was testing me. "The birthing ceremony."

Max nodded, then discarded the rest of the pomegranate into a planter. "Ushering in the New Kind is what keeps the Oasis pure." He made his way back down the opposite aisle. I transcribed his bullshit, my penmanship illegible.

I considered that Arthur might return from wherever he'd gone and open his glove box to discover the gun was nowhere to be found.

"Once a child with my flesh and blood is born into the Light, the mother begins her descent to the shadowy Underworld . . ." Max prattled on with his twisted justifications, assessing the plants as he passed them. "This place becomes the lifeblood that nourishes the Oasis, quenches our thirst, and brings us the harvest in this divinely designed union of the Light and the Dark, as nature intends."

I played along to keep him distracted, while I summoned courage. With his back turned, now was the time to act. I needed to defend myself if I ever wanted a chance to get out of the desert alive.

As quietly as I could, I kneeled to access my backpack, slip my journal inside, and retrieve Arthur's handgun. I nearly floundered from the weight of it, my palms sweating, threatening to let it slip from my grasp. I held the gun down by my side, waiting for the right moment to scare him off. No one else needed to get hurt.

Suddenly, Max stopped in his tracks. Every muscle in my body tensed. He looked up at the sky through the glass ceiling, like he was stargazing and nothing more. "You know, Lucy . . ."

I bristled at his saying the name my mother gave me—a rare occurrence. What happened to "my little poet"?

"I never expected you to come back to the Oasis. I always wished you would. I dreamt of it often. I always worried for you. I feared your time in the outside world would tarnish you, would make you one of *them*. I worried it would diminish the part of you I created. But when you stepped back on our soil, when you took to my teachings like a fish to water, it confirmed for me that everything was falling into place, that the Oasis would thrive with you here. It would continue on. It all became so clear to me. The possibilities of what we could do together."

As I stood there, my bare feet raw and breaking, my body poised to react—to choose fight, flight, or freeze—I couldn't stay silent any longer. I couldn't pretend.

"How could you kill Eden?"

I was grateful for the distance between us, as we stood at opposite ends of the greenhouse that sustained his brainwashed prisoners. I was not grateful for the shadow cloaking half his face. Another mask for his benefit, as he began to realize I'd seen the light.

"You should be careful," he warned. "I would think by now, the first of the New Kind would trust that I have the purest of intentions." I thought of the rattlesnake, how much my father resembled it, slithering and sneaky, ready to shed his skin, pounce on his prey. I shuddered recalling how easily I had pulled the trigger and ended its life.

"You broke my heart, Max," I said. My pulse raced, daring the predator inside me to raise my arm and take aim at the only father I'd ever known. "I wished for you all my life to show up, to tell me who I really am, what I should do, who I should be. If I am capable of having a voice. My mother may not be an easy woman, but I know she must have run away from you for exactly the reasons I'm about to. Because you are a sick, violent man, and you will never, ever hold power over a Golden woman, any woman, or any *child* ever again."

Emboldened by the threat that slid off my tongue, I cocked the gun and focused in on my target—the one who'd taught me how.

He stepped to the right. The moonlight illuminated his face and revealed his shocked expression. He should have known better. After all, I am the daughter of *the* Diana Golden, the idolized, the feared. I'd had her courage inside me all this time, but it had been tempered. I felt it rising then, boiling my blood.

Max howled with laughter like he was getting a kick out of the whole scene. I gritted my teeth, wolflike, preparing myself for what I was about to do, who I would become the moment I gave in to my instincts.

Behind Max, I could make out a shadow on the other side of the door. I could feel the presence of someone else and knew it had to be Arthur. Everything he had said, everything we'd shared, it couldn't have been for nothing. There had been love between us. Despite my recent betrayal, he'd come back for me.

"You're not going anywhere." Max took two steps toward me, so he was in the same aisle. He reached to the back of his jeans and pulled out his revolver, the mother-of-pearl handle lustrous in the starlight.

My chest tightened. There was nowhere to run. I would have to finish what I'd started.

When Arthur pushed open the door, the dominoes began to fall. Max turned toward the sound. I blinked back a cleansing tear.

I squeezed the trigger twice.

*Bang! Bang!*

The kickback sent an electric shock through my system. The first bullet skimmed right over Max's left shoulder and punctured the glass panel behind him. The crack spread, and then the glass disintegrated, shattering all at once. The sound was all-encompassing, the Oasis unbreakable one minute, in pieces the next.

The second bullet hit him square in the chest. I couldn't help thinking he'd be proud, but in chasing his approval, I'd become a killer, just like him.

It's funny when you discover that everything you thought you knew is a lie. You think you've found freedom. Then you look down to see your hands are covered in blood.

# ARTS DISTRICT

"IS SHE OKAY?"

"I told you she was crazy."

"Lucy, can you hear me?"

"Do you think this is part of the exhibit?"

"Someone get the lights!"

I hear them, the voices. They're talking about me, around me, but I'm not there.

I'm back in that first morning in the desert, just before sunrise. The hard metal beneath my back. The lizards scattering, crows cawing in the open sky. I will myself to make a different choice. To know better. To change the course of fate.

The film cuts. The lights in the screening room flicker twice, then burn bright. The stark change is like a siren, alarming and blaring. A new omen. In the chaos, the unnerving cry of a woman crescendos.

I realize it's her, my mother. The one who betrayed me. She sounds frightened, hysterical. "Lucy, can you hear me?"

I find the strength to open my eyes, and there she is, kneeling down over me. Her flawless milk-white skin. Her oxblood waves. The worry she wears on her face is a dazzling sight to behold.

"Oh, thank God. She's awake!" Mom cries out. "Can you sit up for me? Darling, what is it? What's happened?" She takes my head in her lap and runs her cold fingers through my hair. My toes prickle and zing like they've all fallen asleep at once, hardened into one foreign mass.

"Please, everyone, let's give them some space," I hear Isaac say from a corner of the room. The shuffling of shoes, the murmurs of the crowd. Then: "Can you get some water, Sloane?"

I break through the surface and inhale like I've been underwater all this time. Gasping for air. "No, no, no."

The room has been cleared. Only Isaac and Mom crouch over me.

"I should have known." I hear my pleas through each heaving sob. My vision narrows. "It was right there, all along."

"What was, darling?"

"Nothing, Diana," I hear Isaac say. "She's having a panic attack."

Mom's face falls. "So she's making all this up?" Her grasp loosens. My head falls onto the floor. I bite down on my tongue. The taste of metal tinges my mouth. "This is my night, Lucy. Mine. How could you do this to me?" She touches her long pale neck, affected. Her concern for herself quickly upstages all semblance of concern for her daughter. "Of course you had to make it all about you." The clacking of heels. "Get her out of here."

She deserts me on the concrete floor of the gallery to fend for myself, yet again, a meal for the coyotes.

*After*

I looked at my hands, alarmed by what they were capable of, and watched in disbelief as the gun fell onto the tile floor.

I remember the sound of ocean waves in my ears. Arthur spoke to me, but I couldn't understand him. He sounded as if he too were underwater. He shook my shoulders, stooping to my level, but I couldn't focus my sight. He was only a shape.

"Lucy!" Arthur shouted. My vision returned. I'd never seen him look so frightened. But there was something more behind his fear, something deeper. He was looking at me like I was the answer to every question he'd ever posed, like he was in love.

Suddenly, I could inhale. I must have sounded like a swimmer on the brink of drowning, bursting through the surface. Not only could I hear, but the volume was turned all the way up—the ring of the generator, Arthur's voice, clear and pleading, and somewhere out there, commotion.

"Lucy!" He grabbed the gun off the floor and tucked it into my backpack alongside my journal and hoisted the bag over his shoulder.

Max's eyes were still open, as if he were in awe of the stars above and didn't have a cavernous hole in his chest cavity. He looked so small. I marveled that all he was and had been no longer held weight. He was nothing but a mass of flesh, ready to rot, a pile of bones bound to turn to dust. *The body is temporary.*

Arthur pulled me away from Max's corpse, pried the revolver from Max's clutches, and tucked it into the back of his jeans. "Let's go."

"Your . . . your keys."

"What?" Arthur yelled. "We have to get out of here now!"

I pointed to Max's pocket. Arthur grunted and retrieved his stolen keys.

"We need to leave right away. The others—" He stopped before he could bring himself to say it, but it clicked into place without his having to explain further. If the others found out Max was gone, they would stop at nothing until their leader's death was avenged.

He led me to the door. "When I say run . . ." Arthur stuck his head out to see if the coast was clear. "Run." I waited for his cue. We held tight, listening.

The others were gathered around the freshly lit fire pit, conferring about what to do. The little kids cried out, hysterical.

"We need to check the greenhouse," Fiona urged.

"Max?" Beatrice called out. "Max!"

"Where did they take"—Susanna hiccupped between wails—"Eden?"

"Will someone tell me what's going on?" Amber demanded.

"It came from the greenhouse," Fiona screamed. "Why is no one listening to me!"

"It's time," Beatrice said. "It's our turn to protect him. No matter what."

Silently, Arthur gestured to the backpack on his shoulder. I retrieved the handgun from it as quietly as I could. Then Arthur mouthed the command.

*Run.*

Across the camp, the fire now burning at the center like an open wound, I pushed my legs to their capacity, revolver in hand. On a runner's high, my body became electrified, floating right off the ground.

In flashes, I saw their faces—Fiona's scowl, Beatrice, Amber. The kids, my siblings, wore masks of shock, crying.

Fiona charged straight toward us, a knife in her hand, unbothered by the firearms we carried. We maneuvered around her as she sliced at the air. Beatrice flew past the scuffle toward the greenhouse.

As we reached the truck, a bloodcurdling scream rang out. Max's body had been discovered.

The rest of them barreled toward us, like villagers with pitchforks. Susanna, behind the mob in her white cotton dress, held back, bewildered. Frozen. A crying infant in her arms.

That's the last image I have of the Oasis, the utopia I longed for. The last I saw of the people I once thought of as family—their ghoulish silhouettes, backlit by the roaring flames, hurtling toward us, framed in the rearview mirror as Arthur tore away as fast as he could. Only then, when the coast was clear, did I understand what I'd done.

NEITHER OF US SPOKE FOR I'M NOT SURE HOW LONG. AN HOUR, MAYBE LONGer. Time kept skipping, back and forth, up and down. I couldn't hold on to it. The world outside that truck skidded to a standstill. Nothing else existed but us, the frigid air in the cab, and the pitch-black road.

"Fuck!" Arthur slammed his hand against the steering wheel. The horn blared again and again. "Fuck, fuck, fuck," he yelled. I squeezed my eyes shut, but the images of the greenhouse that came to me were much worse. "I should have saved her. She's gone. She's gone."

He pulled off the highway into an old-timey gas station outfitted with retro signs out front, a relic of years past. A pair of flickering streetlamps illuminated the ghostly scene. Most of the gas pumps were out of order, with plastic bags covering the nozzles. Arthur yanked the gear shift, parked, and turned off the engine.

"We should have torn her out of his hands," he said. "We should have told him no even if he threatened us." The corner of his mouth twitched.

"Max's story . . . from the Underworld to the Light." I searched Arthur's face, trying to assess if I could trust his word. "It's been there in plain sight all this time. How could you not have known?"

"Max loved to tell his stories, but you have to believe me, I would never have taken you to that place, to him, if I'd known that this is what he did. He's done so much for me. He gave me a home, a family, when I had none. I can't fathom how he could be that person and a killer. I would have never put you in danger. To think, if we ever, if there's any chance that you might be . . . if we ever . . ."

"I know." I squeezed his hand.

"Lucy, please," he said. "You need to know I love you."

I studied his fingers around mine, and a thousand emotions rushed through me. Arthur had never admitted his feelings for me through anything other than his touch. I wanted to be elated by his admission, but I was horrified by what I'd witnessed, what I'd done. I wished I could bottle up his confession of love and drink it, drown in it, taste it fully, uncontaminated by the poison Max had poured into the well.

"I'll prove it to you, I swear." Arthur twisted my hair in his hands, and I bent to his touch. "You trust me, Lucy, don't you?"

In that moment, all I had was Arthur. I had no choice but to trust that I was all he had too. "I love you."

"I think it would be best if you went back to Coronado." He tossed his keys back and forth. "Alone."

"After what happened, they're going to come looking for me. Oh God . . ." I choked up. I didn't want to think about what might happen to me if the facts of the night fell into the wrong hands. I'd be locked up, my life as I knew it taken from me. Penance for the life I'd taken from Max.

Arthur brought my hand to his lips and held it there. "Your mom, the neighbors, the police—they've been looking for you. They want you back home. It'll be okay."

"I found the flyer." I searched his face, but he didn't reveal an ounce of surprise or remorse.

"When the sun goes up, you'll walk over to that lot and hitch a ride back to San Diego. Tell your family you ran away, but you decided to come back home. Don't mention anything about me, Max, Eden, the baby, what happened in the greenhouse. None of it. It never happened, okay?"

"What about the children?" I could still hear Susanna's cry echoing in my ears. "We can't leave them there. They deserve a chance, don't they?" I knew the women wouldn't let the children go without a fight. With Max gone, the New Kind were all they had left of their beliefs.

Arthur thought for a moment. He looked in the rearview mirror. "I'll call from a pay phone, leave an anonymous tip, and tell the authorities there are children out there who are in danger. No one has to know we were there, but for this to work, you have to go back, Lucy."

My heart ached, thinking of us apart. "But what about us?"

"I will take care of everything. I will protect you, okay? No one will ever find out what happened back there. Once the dust settles, I will come find you. I promise."

I grabbed hold of Arthur, my fists tightening around the back of his shirt, trying to soak in his musk, the sensation of his hands on my back, his lips on my neck. He inhaled in that way he always did when he wanted me, like he was trying to drain me of any air in my lungs.

The only way to survive was to forget it all. I could not stay up at night wondering where the mothers of my little brothers and sisters had gone, what their final moments were like, though the question of who they were swarmed like a hornet's nest, louder and louder in my ear. I needed to forget about the birth of the nameless baby, a day that could have been Eden's happiest, uniting her with the child in her womb after nine long months of cradling her belly and waiting. That moment was robbed from her by my father, the thief. I hated Arthur for putting us in that situation so blindly. I couldn't understand why I still wanted him the way I did, all the lust I once had for him accruing into a monstrous need, like I would die if I couldn't have him.

I wanted to believe he was right, that what happened in the greenhouse wouldn't come back to haunt me. The others in the Oasis would leave well enough alone and unravel the lies Max sold them as gospel in their own time. Arthur would return to me. We would be together like I always wanted. My naïve hope allowed me to untangle myself from Arthur's embrace and head into the night alone.

# CORONADO

I NEVER THOUGHT I'D RETURN TO THE HOMETOWN I LEFT AT NINE-teen, but here I am Monday morning, my sweaty thighs sticking to the vinyl seat, the Pacific Surfliner hurtling forward on the tracks. Isaac thought it would be more cinematic to take the train. After Friday's debacle at the gallery, I'm grateful for the opportunity to skip town.

Isaac peers through his viewfinder expectantly, like I'm going to erupt with emotion over stale saltines and plastic water bottles. "So, how did you finally convince her to sit down for an interview?"

"Who?"

He smirks at me. "Diana." I nearly choke on my water. Isaac can surely tell by the look on my face that I had no idea Mom's agreed to participate in the doc. "She's meeting us at the house later this afternoon. You didn't think I would come all the way to Coronado without her, did you?"

I hide my embarrassment as best I can. "Of course not." I look out the window as if enraptured by the view, but inside, I replay the haunting film from the exhibit. Max's hands drawing water from the well, Mom humming that ghostly tune.

I spent the entire weekend riding the roller coaster of Mom's emotions while trying to get a hold of my own. She came home late Friday night, smashed and weepy, threw open my bedroom door, and wailed about me ruining her special night. As much as I tried to ask her about what I saw in the film, she wouldn't hear it. As she ranted, pacing in circles for over an hour, the fog began to form, obscuring my thoughts, clouding my judgment. She wouldn't stop until I offered *her* an apology. Soon enough, she was back to her old self, giddy about the sparkling write-up of the show in Sunday's paper, and it was like my fainting spell never happened.

But I haven't forgotten what I saw. I haven't been able to erase the film from my mind, or the implication behind its existence. All this time later, for Diana to broadcast this piece of history so widely seems like a gross underestimation of what it might mean to me.

Now, hearing that Isaac's convinced her to participate, she must peg me for a fool. I made a promise to myself a long time ago. I'd never let that happen again.


A DRIVER IN A WRINKLED SUIT STINKING OF CIGARS PICKS US UP at the Santa Fe Depot. Isaac, Sloane, and I take the car while the rest of the crew piles into a van. In a matter of minutes, we're driving over the bridge and crossing the bay. It's odd, this homecoming. I'm surprised by how easy it is to return. No traps await me, only the strong summer sun burning through the June gloom's haze. The island's busier than I remember. Crop top–wearing teenage girls on cellphones have taken over Orange Avenue. My nerves flutter as the driver navigates the traffic circles.

We pull into the circular drive of the Hotel Del, with its manicured landscaping and strategically planted palm trees. The crew are staying in a cheaper hotel across the bridge, but I requested to stay at the Del, the singular pillar of my childhood untainted by that summer. Isaac instructs me to meet them on the beach in an hour.

I pass the long rectangular pool where tanned hotel guests sip cocktails on lounge chairs as their kids play Marco Polo. I spot the famous rocking chairs from *Some Like It Hot*, which starred Marilyn Monroe, my mother's favorite femme fatale of them all.

Relieved to finally have a moment alone, I make it to my room and glide around the beige, white, and blue furnishings of the one-thousand-dollar-a-night luxury suite. Grateful the production is footing the bill, I choke back a vodka from the minibar and pace the room. Stepping out onto the balcony, I take in the slope of sand where it meets the waves. The diamond sunlight skitters across the top layer of water, blue and eucalyptus silver. Children discuss the structure of a sandcastle that will not last the afternoon. Mothers watch over them, book club paperbacks poking out of their designer totes, thighs thick with oil, husbands occupied on the golf course. When I was a child, this ocean held a bully's stance over me, poking at my cowardice. Funny how from above, from this grand historic setting, it looks smaller than I remembered. It's only a beach, a blank slate, as if void of the harrowing discovery made here twenty years before.

A knock jolts me back into the room. I ditch the airplane bottle of hooch in the bathroom wastebasket and skip over to answer the door. I assume it's Isaac with another painful surprise.

When I open the door, there's no one there—only a room service delivery cart boasting an ice bucket, an expensive bottle of champagne, and a hand-tied bunch of wildflowers. I look down the hallway both ways, but there's no sign of hotel staff. I roll the cart into the room, certain there's been some kind of mistake. I'm about to call the front desk, when I see there's a note included and the envelope's addressed to me.

*Why did you have to ruin us?*

The sender left the note unsigned, but there's no doubt in my mind who to blame. The flowers, the question that's plagued me for years—this little stunt has Tex written all over it.

I stomp over to the landline phone. My skin tingles as I wait for the front desk to answer. With each second that passes, I squeeze the note tighter and tighter in my palm.

"Miss Golden, how can I help you?"

"Listen, I don't know what your policy is about protecting guests' privacy, but I'm going to need to move rooms. Now."

A pause. "I'm sorry? Is there something wrong with—"

"The champagne that was sent to my room? I didn't authorize that." I hear how shrill I sound, but there's no time for pleasantries. "I want my things moved into another suite by the time I return. No one can know I'm staying here, got it? All calls are to be blocked. No surprises. No maid service either. Total and complete privacy, do you understand?"

The front-desk employee chokes out an apology and swears to abide by my wishes. I thank her and quickly hang up, certain if I keep going, the lump in my throat will dissolve and a cry will erupt.

I know it in my bones: the madness will only end if I stop running. If, one of these days, I surrender.

# CORONADO

*1 day after*

Once day broke, I made my way over to where the truckers convened, searching for a ride to San Diego. Some brushed me off; one gave me a once-over with his offer, which I declined. It wasn't until later that afternoon that I finally encountered a woman with short dark hair and thunderous boots who agreed to give me a ride, without asking questions, a courtesy I greatly appreciated.

Ten miles out, I reached into my backpack to see if I had any spare cash to offer her and realized what had been left inside. There it was—the handgun, the murder weapon. It burned hot in my hand, like it had just been fired. So hot, I wondered if I was imagining things, reminding me of what it—what *I*—was capable of.

As my hand brushed against the gun, I had to force myself not to react to the emptiness of Arthur's promise. He wasn't going to protect me. He'd sent me into a den of wolves ready to feed. He'd run away and left me on my own, just like before. I was no longer his muse.

I was his way out.

IT WAS TWILIGHT BY THE TIME I MADE IT BACK TO CORONADO.

The shattering of glass came to me again, forcing me to remember it all: the squeeze, Max's vacant stare, the sticky pool of blood. Standing on our street between our yellow bungalow and the Fowlers' pink house, I panicked that the visions might never go away.

"Lucy?" I heard a voice call out—a man. Could it be? No, I was back on our little island. "Lucy?" Again, I heard it. My palms were clammy as I turned toward the source. I was surprised to see Theo burst through the gate of the pink house's white picket fence. "Lucy! My God!" He sprinted across the sidewalk. "Are you okay? Damn . . . the whole city . . . the whole country . . . We've been looking for you for weeks. For months." Theo reached forward, like he had to make sure I was real.

I flinched at first, my body on high alert. "Sorry, I . . ."

He held up his hands, coming in peace. "Don't apologize." His square face softened with concern. I marveled that my absence had had the power to make him worry. "Your mom's out canvassing with my dad, but my mom's inside, running phone trees. Come on, she'll know what to do."

The concept of the Fowlers collaborating with my mother surprised me. I couldn't picture Mom teaming up with anyone. "Please," I said. "Not yet." I looked down the street, the one I hadn't realized I'd missed all this time. Suddenly, I felt the need to immerse myself in the ocean waves, to dig my heels into the wet sand, to start over, to right the wrong. Looking at him under the glow of the streetlamps, I was struck by his presence, the path I did not take. "Let's go to the beach."

Theo examined me, looking me up and down, making sure I wasn't bleeding somewhere. "Your mother's worried sick. She's hysterical. We need to find her, so she knows you're safe."

"I'm not ready yet," I told him. "Please. I'll face it all soon. My mom's out, right? Can I just have one moment of peace before I have to explain everything?"

He rocked back and forth on his heels as he mulled it over. "Okay," he said, relenting, and began walking toward the ocean cautiously, watching me in his periphery. "I came back from training this weekend to see if I could help. I didn't know if I was ever going to see you again. I can't believe this."

When the beach came into view, deserted apart from the resort guests down the way in front of the lit-up Hotel Del, I asked him, "Have you ever done something bad?"

Theo looked both ways before crossing the palm tree–lined street. "What?"

"Something that you couldn't take back," I explained.

We paused to remove our shoes before stepping onto the cold sand and then passed by the lifeguard stand. I was comforted by how common the ritual felt.

"We all do things we regret." Theo trudged across the sand toward the dark ocean waves.

"But have you ever done something bad?" I watched him recoil from my interrogation, imagining what he saw in the film reels playing in his mind. Was it a flash of a memory like mine? The grip on the handgun, the moonlight hitting Max's face, the fire aglow in the rearview mirror.

"Anything you might have done to get back home will be forgiven. I don't know where or who—"

I stopped him. "I think there's something wrong with me."

"There's nothing wrong with you, Lucy."

The ocean played its melodic beats. I curled my toes deeper into the sand, wishing I could stay there forever—never having to face the consequences—but I wasn't the girl I was before, who rejected the dark-haired, brokenhearted boy by the ocean. I was someone new. "You know what? I think it's time to go swimming."

Without hesitation, I unzipped my jean shorts and shrugged them off my hips with ease. I didn't try to cover my body, but maybe I should have. I stood there in my mismatched bra and underwear and felt Theo's eyes on me. Odette must have felt like that often, and I reveled in the power of being noticed in this new way. Now I realize Theo was taking in the consequence of what I wasn't able to see on my own. I was all bone, unwell, but I wasn't able to feel the pain, not yet.

I charged into the ocean, letting the cool water cover me. I pushed forward against the tide and dove into the water. It had been years since

I'd allowed the water to cover the top of my head. I waited for the panic to barrel toward me, but a tug pulled me to the surface.

Theo stared at me from beneath his dripping lashes, treading water. "Jesus, are you okay?"

I laughed, delighted I was able to unnerve him. "Why wouldn't I be?" I couldn't help but be amused watching his expression shift from shock to relief. His eyes wrinkled, and he let out a laugh. I lingered on the strong curve of his naked neck, his Adam's apple bobbing as our laughter danced on top of the cascading waves.

I could lose myself in him and nothing would matter again. Foolishly, I thought it was that easy to erase the whole summer in the magnetism of his skin against mine. When he let go of my arm, I grabbed him back instead, pulled my body against his, testing him, what damage he might do. How far he'd go.

Our laughter stopped, and then it was only our breathing. Lapping water. Muscles straining. Twin pulses dashing. His hand found my waist to support me, as the other found my center.

He wanted me in the way I needed him to want me. The animal impulse emerged, carnivorous, savage. My lips found his neck, then my teeth his lips. He mended my broken pieces back together.

In turn, I tore him apart.


"THIS IS THE CORONADO POLICE." THE WARNING BLARED THROUGH A MEGA-phone; then came the flashlights. "Please exit the water. I repeat, exit the water."

We parted slowly, coming to the realization that we'd been caught.

"Fuck," Theo cursed, refusing to look in my direction.

As I exited the water, a heavy-duty flashlight shone right into my face. My identity as the missing girl was quickly confirmed. My whole body pulsated with an unfamiliar fatigue. There was a disconnect—I couldn't match what my body was experiencing with the emotional gravity of the minutes spent in Theo's arms.

"Lucy!" It was uncanny—the call of my mother.

"Mom?" I searched the dark shapes on the beach, flashlight beams cutting through the sand. She found me and wrapped my shaking frame in a blanket.

"I'm here, I'm here," she repeated, rubbing my goose-bumped arms.

Behind me, Theo scrambled onto the beach and raced to his pile of clothes, abandoned on the sand.

"Stop right there," the voice from the megaphone ordered.

Theo wrestled himself into his boxers, this innocent young man, guilty of being in the wrong place at the wrong time. As soon as she saw him, Mom detached herself from me, charging Theo. Her scream ripped my chest open. Colin stepped out from the darkness and tried to pull her back, but there was no use. A mother's fury knows no limits.

"Theo!" Mom shrieked. "What have you done?"

# CORONADO

I STROLL ALONG THE SHORELINE AS THE CAMERA'S TRAINED ON ME. It's the worst time to film, with the sun at its highest point, but that doesn't dissuade Isaac. He pedals backward with the rest of the crew as I slog forward through the sand.

"You make it sound like you wanted to drown yourself," he says.

I stop. The crew follows suit. I imagine I'm the conductor and they're the orchestra, poised to crescendo at the flick of a wrist. "I don't think I wanted that," I say, though it's still impossible to untangle the web of emotions I felt that night.

"What about Theo?"

I close my eyes, remembering the flashlights skirting the surface of the water. Perhaps I was destined to hunt him in the dark waves like a shark ticking, detecting blood, breaching the crest toward the late-August moon. I remember his touch, the old memory I return to, one I attempt to replicate time and again. In bar bathrooms and hotel suites, with whatever john is eager and willing. "I needed to prove that I could do whatever I wanted, without anyone telling me I couldn't. I wanted to make up my own mind. And there he was. This sad, elusive boy who couldn't possibly have fathomed where I'd been for those eight weeks or what I'd seen. He was looking at me like I was a miracle. If things had gone differently . . ." I hold my stare on a teenage boy surfing across the way, his full lips pressed together in concentration. "Theo was only guilty of being a hormonal eighteen-year-old looking for a thrill. I was the girl to give him one."

"How do you feel now about the Fowlers?" Isaac asks. It's maybe the third time he's asked me this, and each time, I realize I've given him a new answer.

"We all make mistakes, just like Theo said that night. The Fowlers are far from perfect," I say. "But did they sign up for their whole lives to implode for the entertainment of housewives in the grocery store checkout line?" I think back to reuniting with Theo. I remember his plea for peace anew. This time, I force myself to sit in the discomfort. "Of course not. That choice was made for them, and I can't deny the part I had in that." The admission doesn't melt away the lingering guilt, not entirely, but I find a sense of relief in saying this aloud.

We make it to the lifeguard stand. It's been painted, updated, but there's no mistaking it. "This is where we came out of the water." I'm amazed that the stand is still there, bewildered that the chaotic energy of my rescue didn't break down its molecular structure.

"Why were you surprised Diana looked for you the way she did?" Isaac asks. "Don't you think any parent would move heaven and earth to find their missing child?"

"Knowing Mom cared enough to search for me, it felt like the proof of her love I'd always wanted." I swallow, unsure if I still believe what I'm saying after Friday night. "She didn't want to lose me."

I squint at the tourists, the locals filling the sand, and spot a dark-haired girl of about twelve peeling an orange on a towel. For a split second, I see Odette in her place. I remember the days we spent out here, alone, while Mom was away, jet-setting, having her own adventures without us. I ruminate on my sister's plea to open my eyes, to see our mother for who she really is. To confront her about her connection to the Oasis, I would need evidence so undeniable that she couldn't twist it in her favor.

# PAPER CUT

THE CREW LOADS THE EQUIPMENT INTO THE VAN IN THE BEACH parking lot. I tell Isaac I'd rather walk. I ask Sloane to join me, and we promise to meet at the house.

"Want to grab a coffee somewhere?" Sloane asks as she wipes a ripple of sweat off the back of her neck. "We have some time to kill while the crew sets up."

I glance at the van, then back at her. She nods, receiving the message that I will not elaborate until we're out of earshot. We set a quick pace on the sidewalk, arms pumping, like we're just a pair of Coronado moms on a power walk. When the coast is clear, I lay it out there. "I need a favor, but before I tell you anything, I need to know I can trust you."

"A hundred percent," Sloane replies. "Lucy, I'm here for you, whatever it is."

I take a deep breath. "I can't hold it in any longer."

"What is it?"

"I feel like I'm going to lose it, if I haven't already, that is."

Sloane grabs my wrist. "What are you saying, Lucy?"

"He left a gift for me at the hotel."

Sloane raises her eyebrow, then lets go. "Tex followed you here?"

"I just need to take control over *something*. I'm supposed to sit on camera with my mom today," I say. "After what I saw on Friday night, I can't face her like this. I can't show up empty-handed."

"What did you have in mind?"

"If there's one thing I know for sure, Diana Golden never throws out a photograph," I tell her. "No matter the subject. If there's any proof that she knows more about what went on at the Oasis than she's letting on, it has to be in her studio in the carriage house, but I can't do it alone."

Sloane lights up, thrilled I've decided to pull her into my investigation, so thrilled she divulges part of Isaac's plan for the day. "The crew will be setting up for the next hour; then Diana is set to arrive. Isaac's conducting a solo interview with Diana first. I'll have him stall as long as he can while we look."

As soon as the plan's hatched, the house comes into view, the bougainvillea as bright as ever, and the fear of what we might find spreads through my chest like a virus. Suddenly, the need to know feels dire. Thankfully, there's no sign of Mom's car yet. Our spare key's burning a hole in my pocket. "We'll have to act fast."

"Let's get you what you deserve," Sloane says, racing ahead to meet the crew van as they turn onto the street.

"Hey, Sloane!" I call out to her. She whips around, and I recognize the pain in her expression when she looks at me. It isn't pity. It's something else. "Thank you." She smiles, tight-lipped and serious.

While Sloane confers with Isaac, I turn away from my childhood home to get a good look at the pink house and see who is lucky enough to live there now, eager to daydream about a better fate than my own, just like I did twenty years ago.

But it's not pink anymore. The new owners, whoever they are, painted it white, stripping it of all its magic. Now it's just a house. The garden beds are full and bright, and hummingbirds flock to the feeders, but it's not the same as it once was. It's changed.

THE CARRIAGE HOUSE BOASTS THE SAME WIDE-PLANKED FLOORS, but Mom has upgraded the drafting table and the technology in the years I've been away. Sloane and I work in tandem. She pulls out boxes. Some are labeled; most are not. I sort through binders of film negatives, copies of shots, original prints.

I scan the dates. I look for Max and Arthur. I look for the Oasis.

An hour into our search, we hear Mom's car pull into the driveway. My heart stops. We freeze and wait as we listen to Isaac greet her. The front door opens, then swings closed. A minute later, we look at each other and get back to work.

The next hour passes too quickly. I can sense Mom's presence through the walls. The panic that she's going to catch us searching her archives inspires me to move faster. If I'm discovered and my suspicions are wrong, this mission will be the nail in the coffin of our relationship, already on life support.

I'm packing up another box of dead ends, negatives from ten years ago, when Sloane calls my name from the darkroom.

I find her on her hands and knees in front of a dusty cardboard box. The label reads "2002." My chest tightens. Sloane's big brown eyes narrow. We drag the box across the weathered floor into the main room, with sweat on our brows.

We slow our pace to inspect each item carefully, tearing back the layers of the past. There are hundreds of photographs of Judy solo. Some with her friends. I find the original photograph of me from the party, the one on the missing poster, stuck to a folder. I peel them apart, then set the photograph aside.

Next, I pull out a chubby manila envelope, the corners soft with age, addressed to my mother. My throat closes when I see written in marker on the back in her messy scrawl: Research for *Before and After*, her famous series about her infamous daughter.

Sloane rests back on her knees patiently, letting me do the honors. I topple back onto the floor, hands shaking as I undo the envelope's brass clasp. We both hold our breath, like we're about to plummet down to the ocean's floor and we don't know if we'll ever come up for air.

I only have to pull the first item out of the envelope to find it.

All the proof I need to know, for certain, that my mother is a monster. She's been a monster all along.

# CORONADO

*2 days after*

Much later, I woke up in a hospital bed. With strained effort, I turned and saw Mom in the hallway speaking with a police officer.

I squeezed my eyes shut, like a little kid who didn't want to wake up yet, feigning sleep. Arthur hadn't mentioned anything about the police.

Suddenly, I remembered my backpack on the beach—containing my notebook and the gun. The gun that killed Max. It was only a matter of time before they looked through my belongings and found it.

If they hadn't already.

AFTER COMPLETING TREATMENT FOR DEHYDRATION, I WAS DISCHARGED AND permitted to return home later that day.

"How did you find me?" I tried to piece it together as Mom drove to the house. "How did you know where we were?"

Mom flipped her mirror down and wiped under her eyes with her ring finger. "The whole neighborhood watch was out looking for you. We've *been* looking for you. Damn it, you need to take responsibility for what you put me through." She plowed through a yellow light. A van crossed behind us only a moment after. A near collision she hadn't even registered.

I tucked my knees into my chest, a gnawing feeling in my gut, disheartened that she still hadn't asked me where the hell I'd been. We turned onto our street and stalled behind a long line of cars. "What's happening?"

Mom ignored me, laid on her horn, and maneuvered around the traffic. The cars parted, letting her pass.

"Mom, what's going on?"

Then I saw the news vans. The appalled faces of the drivers, jaws dropping, cameras flashing as we passed. The reporters and their microphones and cameramen. Hordes of neighbors and spectators. Some held signs that read, WELCOME HOME, LUCY!

As we pulled into our driveway, Odette emerged from the house and elbowed her way through the reporters. "Back up!" She met me at the passenger door, looped her arm around me.

The swarm yelled their questions in my direction. They called my name out, over and over, until it all began to blur.

"What do you want?" I asked weakly.

"Back up!" Odette yelled again. My knees wobbled on the porch steps. She ushered me inside and slammed the door. I sank into the couch, flushed and lightheaded.

Odette flipped on the television set. The local station cut to footage of our street, our house. I saw myself on the screen, the news crawl announcing my mysterious return.

They wanted me. They wanted my story. They wanted to understand how a girl like me could disappear for eight weeks, then show up in the ocean with the boy from across the street. My pulse raced at the possibility. *The world wants to hear what I have to say.*

"Wait, Mom's still outside."

Odette poured herself a generous glass of vodka from the bar and pointed to the TV. "Mom can take care of herself."

There she was, Diana Golden, on our front porch steps, answering questions from the press. An assortment of microphones marked with various news stations were held out in front of her.

"We are so lucky to finally have our girl back home," Mom said. "We kindly ask you to respect our privacy at this time as we unpack the unusual circumstances of my daughter's disappearance and return. It's time now for healing. Thank you for your prayers, your diligence, the Coronado Police Department for their cooperation and professionalism . . ." Mom paused, like she was looking for a face in the crowd. "I also want to thank our friends Colin and Melissa Fowler for their efforts. Above and beyond. Who says good neighbors are hard to find?" she joked, breaking into a soft laugh that eased the tense crowd. Then Mom's voice caught, her eyes misting. "Thanks to you, we never gave up hope."

"Jesus," Odette said. "You got to be fucking kidding." It was a mystifying sight, witnessing Odette pace the living room. "Theo was the last one to see you and then he's there when you're found. Mom's out there praising his parents for putting up flyers? She's cracked!"

"Stop, Odette. Theo doesn't have anything to do with where I've been." I didn't know how to begin to explain to her all that had transpired.

Odette rummaged through her black-fringed purse for a pack of cigarettes. "Yeah, well, they brought him in for questioning that night."

"What?" I shrieked. "But he didn't do anything!"

Odette tapped the bottom of the pack against her palm, and I saw her hands were shaking. "He'll be fine. They just have to go through the motions. I'm sure he's already back home right now. Shining his halo."

I put my head in my hands and rocked back and forth. The nausea returned, along with another surge of fatigue.

Odette abandoned her cigarettes and hugged me. "You know, you really scared me. I thought I'd lost you. What the hell happened?"

"I'll tell you everything, I promise," I told her, nuzzling into her chest, her racing heartbeat like a metronome, and it occurred to me what it would mean if I did. "But for now, can we just not talk about it?" I felt Odette nod and thought of how we used to be—our little hard bodies warm from a shared bubble bath, our hair still wet on the ends as Mom clicked the shutter on her camera, our clammy hands intertwined on the porcelain beneath.

LATER, I WOKE UP ON THE COUCH, DISORIENTED. ODETTE'S CAR WAS ALREADY gone from the street. Back to Los Angeles she went. A handful of reporters and spectators lingered, but they wouldn't get a real scoop until later that night.

Peering through the window, I noticed a cop car parked right outside by the mailbox. In the driver seat, the officer from the hospital scribbled notes on a pad furiously.

Heat rose up in my body. I sprinted to the bathroom and vomited into the toilet. I despised throwing up, fearful something inside me would emerge that wasn't supposed to be released and I'd find a spleen in the toilet bowl. I lay on the cold tile floor for a long time, using my hands as a pillow. Shuddering, I didn't feel like myself and I didn't understand why.

I splashed some water on my face, then went to my bedroom. As far as I could tell, nothing had shifted in the two months since I'd last been there. My dress from the night of the party was still draped over my desk chair. I touched the clean notebook I'd purchased for the first day of school, which I'd missed.

I sank into my sheets and pushed down another wave of nausea. My mouth brimmed with saliva that tasted acidic and rancid, but I couldn't bring myself to get out of bed. It would be too much effort.

"Mom!" I called out.

It took her only a few minutes to appear in the doorway. "What is it?"

"I think there's something wrong with me."

"You just need to sleep."

"On Friday night, did you answer the phone?" I scrounged every bit of energy within me to sit up, searching her face for a hint of recognition. "Did you hear me when I called?"

She didn't flinch. "What are you talking about?"

"Did they find my backpack yet?"

"You need to let it go," Mom snapped. "This is serious. Get your story straight. If you mess up a detail, if you contradict yourself, they'll paint you as unreliable. They'll discredit you in a second."

"What do you mean?"

"The police station called again." She sighed. "They need your statement tomorrow."

If only telling the truth wouldn't be so damning.

BEFORE MY VISIT TO THE POLICE STATION, ANOTHER MARK OF THAT SUMMER'S bite made itself known. While I was hiding out in my room, contemplating what I would say to the police, the lone paparazzo who hadn't retreated for the evening captured a career-making shot. Out on our porch, well past midnight, Diana Golden was photographed straddling the lap of Colin Fowler. The nature of my mother and Colin's relationship had finally been confirmed. I ached for Melissa, for Theo too, for believing the pink house would provide them with a clean slate, only for their reputations to be muddied by the Golden women and broadcast for the world to witness.

The affair ripped through the news cycle—the famous photographer's illicit involvement with the married father whose son was the last to see her missing daughter before she disappeared. The husband of the great Samaritan who had spent the last eight weeks canvassing Southern California looking for a lost little girl. When the news broke, Mom showed no remorse, offered no apology. "I'm not the married one," she said with a shrug.

It didn't take long for the less-than-reputable tabloids to dig into the Fowlers' history. Colin's former mistress, back in New York, cashed in and sold her story, complete with receipts and letters from Colin promising to leave Melissa. The mistress claimed she was the reason why Colin wasn't at his office in the Twin Towers that day. Colin's extramarital activities saved him from succumbing to the same fate as Melissa's brother, Graham, business partner to Colin, who perished in the stairwell. The man who I saw in the Fowlers' wedding portrait was memorialized anew, lauded as a fallen hero of 9/11.

After his uncle's death, Theo found out about his father's affair and swore to keep it a secret from his mother. He went through a rough patch, getting himself into all kinds of trouble. They put him on and off medication to combat his behavior. At first he seemed like a troubled adolescent, angry and grief-stricken, traumatized by the tragedy of 9/11. His acts of rebellion were minor until he planted a firecracker in a team-mate's gym locker. Only it wasn't his teammate who was the victim of the childish prank but the school janitor. The explosion damaged the nerves of his right hand, rendering him unable to work. The Fowlers buried the incident with three sizable checks: one to the janitor, another to the prep school so that Theo could graduate with the rest of his class and maintain good standing with Stanford, and the last, a down payment on a home far, far away from their native Manhattan.

A perfect pink house on Coronado.

Once the tabloids lit the match, the Fowlers' escape plan went up in flames. Theo's past transgressions did nothing to help his reputation, even when the police cleared him of any involvement in my disappearance. The public had formed their opinion already. The perfect family in the pink house never existed. The press sharpened their teeth on the Fowlers' tragedy as they waited with bated breath for the whole story, the one I wasn't sure I was brave enough to tell.

### 3 days after

Mom dressed up for the occasion, her vintage Dior shift hugging her curves. She looked impeccable, her tawny-brown lipstick applied perfectly, like she hadn't lost a moment's sleep.

As she drove us to the police station, my eyes darted around the crowded street as though I were a rabid animal. If I had trusted her decision to keep me from Max, everything, my whole life, would be different. It was strange thinking back to who I'd been before I ever went to the Oasis, when all I cared about was impressing her with a piece worthy of her stamp of approval, so I could belong to her. I saw that naïve girl as a slight silhouette of the monster I'd become.

As the pink house shrank in the rearview mirror, I contemplated if I would go back, given the chance.

"What do you think is going to happen with the Fowlers?"

"They'll move on, honey," she told me. "People always do."

Terrified of what was ahead, with my new notebook hugged to my chest, I pictured what it would be like to read the statement I wrote in front of an audience instead of officers in an interrogation room—to receive enough praise to justify the wreckage.

I could almost hear it, the ovation growing louder. The *thud-thud* of the imaginary applause and my heartbeat—I couldn't decipher which was which. Yet I knew this to be true: The rare moment when creativity is expressed, when art is on display, when the perfect string of words hits you, a brief and brutal charge bursts through your system, an electricity of sorts, but it never lasts. Artists spend their lives breaking themselves to create something, to elicit that half-second response that is once revered and then can never be repeated. The connection between your soul and a piece of art is fleeting. That's what makes art heartbreaking. That's what makes it beautiful.

*My little poet.*

When we pulled up to the police station, the officer from the hospital was waiting outside for us. Two men in suits stood by her side.

As Mom parked the car, she said, "Don't say anything until the lawyers get here." Her urgent whisper jabbed at my sides. She fiddled with her keys in a nervous way I'd never seen before.

Underneath the blazing California sun, the officer's eyes appeared as cold as a merciless rattlesnake's.

In her hand, she held my backpack.

# CORONADO

I CHARGE INTO MY MOTHER'S BEDROOM AND FEEL AS THOUGH I'VE stepped back in time. The canopy bed, the vanity, the settee remain exactly as I remember. Upon my entrance, Isaac and the crew stay trained on their subject, Diana, lounging on her chaise. Her dark red waves coiffed with precision, a midnight-blue dress striking against her milk-white skin. She's in the middle of discussing her next project: a portrait collection of small-town pageant queens. She gabs about the stage moms, the glitter, the pathetic carpeted convention centers.

"Isaac, you'd get a kick out of it," she says. "It doesn't get more desperate than that."

I sneer at her comment, her insinuation that Isaac is inspired by desperation—namely, me. She appears utterly assured in the spotlight, but she has no idea what's coming her way.

Sloane slips past me, whispers to Isaac, then moves an armchair into frame. I will cue her when I need her. Coursing with adrenaline, I take a seat as the crew adjusts the lighting.

"So, you finally decided to grace us with your presence," Mom says.

I take in my cruel, beautiful mother. *The* Diana Golden. The idolized, the feared. Something about the throne from which she reigns and the past three and a half decades of casual torture propel me to the point of no return.

"I want you to tell me your side of the story about what happened that summer."

Mom laughs at my serious tone. "Darling, what's this outburst?"

"I want to hear it from you, right here and now. How did I end up at the Oasis?"

She makes a face at Isaac, insulting my intelligence. "Lucy, you told the whole world how you got there." Right in front of me, all her beauty and mystique disappears. Slowly, then all at once.

"But you were a part of it, weren't you?" I challenge her. "You planned for me to go to the Oasis."

I nod at Sloane, who doesn't miss a beat, retrieving the manila envelope from her bag and handing it over. Without taking my eyes off my mother, I slip my hand inside and remove the proof: Arthur's black Moleskine, the elusive one he always carried in his pocket. In the slanted, blocklike handwriting that once graced the margins of my pages, Arthur detailed every interaction we shared, from the moment Mom introduced him as her apprentice until the day he brought Amber to the desert. He recorded everything, every minute of his manipulation, every stage of my descent, every step of the plan they devised together to initiate me into the Oasis. It was Diana who orchestrated everything—she sent me to the Oasis on purpose. The package my mother didn't bother to throw out is postmarked August 2002, a month after my initiation. Arthur must have sent it to my mother as proof of his job well done. I hate to think about the dozens of notebooks that must have come before me, detailing his other conquests solely for Max's amusement, and it guts me more than I care to admit. I am not special to him; I never was. I consider the notebook he started after me, the green one I noticed by the fire the night he returned to the Oasis with his next target in tow. A final, failed mission.

Stuck in the pages of the notebook, there's the photograph Arthur showed me in the carriage house the night of Mom's party and swore she would never see.

Me, just shy of sixteen, the wool blanket around my shoulders, my first night at the Oasis. Beneath it, there's a stack of others I don't even remember him taking.

Me, in the back of the truck at twilight—a long exposure blurring my movement.

Me, inside the greenhouse, lying on the circular stone platform, the sprinklers at full blast.

Me, with the desert sky looming above.

A portal back to my former self, and in each frame, I'm naked and so, so young. My eyes are hooded, the ends of my hair limp and unwashed, my ribs protruding from underneath my skin. My body's a thin shell of itself. I knew I'd lost weight that summer, but it was far more drastic than I'd remembered. Seeing that poor innocent little girl, I finally understand, and for the first time, I recognize her. She is more than skin and bones and desert dust.

She is a victim.

"Care to explain why you have this?" I glower at my mother, teeth bared. "Why Arthur sent this to you. Why you kept it. Why you never turned it in to the police. Why you pretended to look for me when you knew exactly where the fuck I was because you sent me there."

Mom extends her manicured hand and takes the notebook. Her emerald eyes darken. The facade begins to crack.

"Research for *Before and After*, was it?" I point to the envelope. "Who knew I had such an influence on you?"

She tosses the notebook aside and picks up her martini. I watch her every move, slow and performative. I'm a captive audience, her favorite.

"After everything I've done for you . . ." she says, even and cool as heat rises within me.

"Excuse me?"

"You wanted to have something to say," she mutters. "You were the one who begged me to help you find your voice."

"Are you seriously implying I asked for this?" I steady myself—the room turns with the enormity of this revelation. "You arranged for a man nearly twice my age to kidnap me—"

"Oh, don't play that game. You went willingly. You were infatuated with Arthur," she says. "I did what I did for your benefit."

"My benefit?!"

"Do you think for one minute you could have written *Rattlesnake* if you hadn't gone to the desert that summer?" She puts her martini down next to her. "Do you think you'd have the money, the success, the *fame* if it wasn't for me looking out for your best interests? Don't bite the hand that feeds you."

If it was anyone else's mother, I'd fail to comprehend her reasoning, but I know all too well that she justifies her evildoings all for the thrill of strangers knowing your name.

"You started a national search for me," I say. "You played the hysterical, grief-stricken mother—"

"The Fowlers were the ones who led the search. That tart Melissa and her neighborhood watch had a field day." She scrunches her forehead like she doesn't understand the big deal. "What kind of mother would they think I was if I didn't play along?"

"I don't know. Maybe the kind who abandons her fifteen-year-old daughter in the desert where a cult leader was systematically—"

Her haughty laughter cuts me off. "You've got it all wrong! When I was at the Oasis, it was an artists' colony. A harmless little haven for hippies—not some hellscape. It all started one night in Topanga Canyon when my friend Ivy and I met Max."

"Did you say Ivy?"

"We were both young mothers who needed a miracle when he asked us to join him in the desert. Max gave us refuge." She reminisces through rose-colored glasses. "After Jesse died and I had my first photography show, I needed time away from the public eye. I had to grieve Jesse and find my bearings as a mother to Odette. But poor Ivy, her lost soul . . ." She shakes her head, pitying her old friend. "Her son's father was never a part of his life, so Max stepped up and raised that boy like one of his own. Arthur always thought he hung the moon."

I inhale sharply as the dots connect. My mother hadn't met Arthur in the fall of 2001; she had known him since he was a child. Ivy Peters was not only my mother's friend. She was Arthur's mother. I catch a glance between Isaac and Sloane as the weight of this admission collapses around us.

"Max was so generous," Mom continues, gushing. "For a while, the Oasis was everything I needed. I slowed down enough to hone my craft. I raised Odette. She loved it there. I indulged Max's crush. We had a little fling, but I couldn't survive in the desert forever. You understand I need to share my art with the world. So, once I found out I was pregnant, I left and took Odette with me. No punishment to be had. Ivy decided to stay behind with Arthur. She chose that life of her own accord. We were always free to go, just like you were."

"But I—"

"You were always whining, why weren't you enough, why weren't you as talented as Odette, why didn't you have what I had." She doubles down. "At fifteen, you didn't know pain. You were headed nowhere. You weren't going to make art that mattered if you failed to live a life that made an impact." She studies me, as if I'm alien to her. "I never saw myself in you, you know. I never thought you had *it*. So, I took the risk for you. If you had any shot in hell of reaching your potential, I thought maybe the desert was the answer. Max was agreeable to the arrangement. He always wanted you to go to the Oasis. I saw the way you looked at Arthur the second he walked in the door; you'd do anything to be chosen by him. You and your blatant desperation made it easy."

Rage consumes me. Blinding rage. "I was a child! How can you not see that Max was a delusional cult leader drunk on power? Arthur was a pawn in your game, doing your bidding and Max's dirty work. But *you*, you made a damning, awful choice as a mother."

"You want to talk to me about choices?" She guffaws. "Maybe I should have given you more credit after all. I trusted Max to keep you safe, but I didn't think I had to worry about his safety around you."

"Do you even hear yourself?" I shriek.

"Look, maybe it got messy, but you still have a camera pointed at you. So it paid off, didn't it?" She pleads her case to the poker-faced crew. "I sacrificed everything for her!" The vein in her forehead bulges. She turns back to me in tears, which have sprung from no-where. "Don't you know how hard that was for me? I was there for you that fall, when you couldn't get out of bed, nursing you back to health after—"

"Don't even go there," I warn her, a wail at the base of my throat. She's the only person who's ever known how much I truly lost in the months that followed my escape, and now she has the audacity to hold it against me.

She shakes her head. "I never imagined you'd take Max's little mus-ings so seriously."

My chest rises and falls. "What do you mean?"

"Darling, you've always loved making up stories." She smiles. "To this day, they've never found the bodies," she says, staccato, belittling me with each syllable. "Do you expect me to believe every word of *Rattlesnake* is true? Where's the art in that?"

"Didn't you ever wonder what happened to your friend? To Ivy? Max killed those women!"

"Whatever sells you more books, doll." She shrugs, still refusing to believe me. "All I'm saying is I pushed you when you needed a push." She takes a feline sip of her martini. "That's what a good mother does."

"You used me!" My mind races back to the drive to the police station when she instructed me to get my story straight. To the *Before and After* collection that garnered her critical praise and commercial success. "You used my tragedy for your own benefit. You ate it up. You always acted embarrassed about my career, but you'll do anything for the world to remember you. You'll manufacture tragedy and exploit your own daughter. Sell her up the river, then call the fucking press!"

"You are so ungrateful!" she yells back. The glass ashtray rattles on the table; her martini sloshes onto her lap. Then come her pitiful whimpers. "For you to treat me this way breaks my heart, Lucy. There is nothing I wouldn't do for my daughters. Nothing."

I glare at her. She ceases to be the beautiful artist-muse I've placed on a gilded pedestal. No, she's the ugliest person I've ever seen. Twisted and cruel, believing she's a victim, arrogantly believing she can still play me like a fiddle.

I know there will be a long road ahead to forgive myself for all the evil I have done to gain her approval, but I can't help feeling a rush of pride. The camera pans up to capture this moment. Isaac may think I'm performing for the documentary—like mother, like daughter—but really, I'm the rawest I've ever been.

"When I get back to LA, I'm putting your shit on the curb," I announce, hard-hearted. For the first time in my life, I don't give a damn what Diana Golden thinks when she looks at me. "I am no longer a daughter of yours."

# THE TRIAL

At first, I floundered. The walls of the windowless interrogation room closed in on me. My voice sounded unrecognizable as I pleaded.

The police recovered the backpack on the beach the morning after they found us—along with the gun and my journal, all entered into evidence. Theo had been the one to inform them I'd been carrying a backpack. The police, graciously, did not linger over our adolescent lapse in judgment, our tryst in the ocean. The tabloids did that work for them, casting me in the national conversation as a sexual, violent deviant.

Eventually, the important details tumbled out of me. I recounted Max's twisted theory and urged them to find Eden's body, and all the bodies, the slain mothers of the New Kind. The officers blinked at me like I was Abigail in Salem, a girl possessed. They spoke in circles around me, and before I knew it, I came undone.

"I had to kill Max," I told them. "I had no choice."

At the time of this writing, the bodies have never been recovered. I think about it often, retracing the steps. How long had Max kept me hostage in the greenhouse before Arthur appeared? How long could it have taken Arthur to bury Eden? Had he buried the others? The unsolved mysteries plague me still.

It was Amber who broke. Not yet molded by Max and his theories,

Arthur's latest recruit saw the events of that night with clarity. She knew something had gone terribly wrong. The following night, when the others had gone to sleep, Amber stole Max's truck. She didn't stop driving until she reached the main strip of Joshua Tree and collapsed in front of a crystal shop.

When the police arrived at the Oasis, they found the women and children holding a vigil in the greenhouse over Max's decaying corpse. They had moved him from the damp floor onto the stone platform and wrapped him in the wool blankets. Later, Fiona told the press they were honoring Max's journey, witnessing his soul's return to the Light.

The Oasis was effectively dismantled. A land deed for the plot on which the Oasis stood had been forged. The children were handed over to Child Protective Services and entered the foster care system. The remaining women scattered. Amber described Arthur's truck as best she could, but the search for him amounted to nothing. He was long gone.

Full of regret that she wasn't able to protect me from Max, Mom remained my one constant during the aftermath. Even when the press butchered her for the affair with Colin and clamored over her outrageous courtroom ensembles, she stood by my side, shielded me from reporters, answered on my behalf. She hired a pair of sought-after lawyers, Ben and Brad.

The prosecution charged me with first-degree murder. My lawyers assured me it was only a sensationalized ploy to make an example out of me, given the public interest in the case. To prove I acted in self-defense, they strategized to establish that Max was a danger to society.

The proceedings stalled time and again due to Max's half-dozen aliases. No family members came forward to claim him. He was the most dangerous kind of con man—a chameleon with charisma. One afternoon, Ben and Brad showed me the long catalog of Max's crimes. Among them, kidnapping, tax evasion, coercion, wire fraud, child endangerment. Matching up these criminal terms with the father figure I thought I knew made my stomach turn. Max was no longer there to face the consequences of his actions.

It was cleaner to pin it all on Max, to maintain that Arthur was yet another victim of his coercion. Without any hard evidence of Arthur's crimes, the charges against him were eventually dropped. Nothing could stick. The warrant for his arrest was nullified.

Six months after I escaped, the trial began, giving the prosecution plenty of time to sharpen their knives. The lead prosecutor, Beth Kerman, wore dated pantyhose with runs up the back. Her lack of attention to detail ended there. But, with her narrow way of thinking, she failed to comprehend the nuances of my case. She painted me as a spoiled, social-climbing fame whore who invented the murdered women to make myself appear more like a victim and less like a villain.

Then there was, of course, my journal. My deepest, most private thoughts were broadcast into the court record for the world to devour, along with all of Max's manic fables. Of course, there were the things I never had the chance to write down. The night in the greenhouse, the critical missing entry.

Midway through the trial, I smiled when Odette took the witness stand. My Cheshire cat grin, the press dubbed it, an uncanny copy of my father's, was plastered across newspapers and magazines. After that, my lawyers encouraged me to maintain a neutral expression when the cameras were rolling.

Odette's appearance in court, where she acted as a key character witness, transformed her into a pop culture icon and launched her music career. Soon enough, the attention prompted a shiny new record deal. The red plaid jacket she wore on the stand sold out everywhere. Her subsequent hit inspired by the whole summer, named "Golden Gun," topped the charts for eight consecutive weeks, as long as I'd been in the Oasis, a chilling coincidence. I read somewhere that Colin Fowler called Odette's music success "a disgusting display of fame begetting fame."

Once the press reported on the nature of my relationship with Arthur, fan clubs formed. Deranged romantics longed to bring Arthur and me together, a modern-day Bonnie and Clyde, Sid and Nancy. The Lolita comparisons were relentless and disturbing to the point where I inconceivably found myself wanting to defend Arthur. An equally powerful group supported Max as the innocent one, a casualty of a deranged Manson girl. They joined the naysayers who believed I'd lied about the missing bodies, purporting that the women never existed at all.

Two women from the Oasis testified for the prosecution, one for the defense. Fiona swore I was never held against my will and maintained that Max would never hurt a living thing. My lawyers successfully discredited her and exhumed her sizable criminal record—two charges of possession of crystal meth, one charge for prostitution, three for petty theft.

When Ronnie entered the courtroom, I barely recognized her. Her wild hair was pulled back into a simple bun, her freckled skin bouncy with hydration. I was grateful to see her alive and well after all this time, grateful she had escaped the horrors of that night, but as she spoke, it was evident the damage had been done. Ronnie detailed the abuse she endured as a member of the Oasis and the night she finally fled for good. The prosecution harped on this point—if Ronnie was successful in escaping, why wasn't I? There were no barriers to overcome, after all. My lawyers argued that Max's brainwashing made me believe the negative ramifications an escape attempt might bring were enough to keep me caged in.

It was Amber who became my most vocal advocate, deemed credible due to her wealthy Orange County family's status and her enrollment in UC Irvine on the premed track. It was an error on Arthur's part. He'd chosen the wrong girl. The tenacious woman on the stand was strong enough to point at Max's photograph and convince the jury that he was dangerous. "Lucy acted not just in self-defense, but she saved all of us. I wouldn't be here today if she didn't stop Max," Amber said. "She's not a criminal. She's a hero." She cleverly borrowed Max's language, the same language he stole from Jungian theory and twisted.

In the closing argument, Brad appealed to the jury's sense of morality. I was a young, naïve girl who wanted to get to know her father. I trusted two men whom I should have been able to trust—a colleague of my mother's and my own father. They said I was a victim who fought for my life, an unlikely hero who saved children and women alike.

At last, the verdict was read into the court record.

*Not guilty.*

The courtroom erupted. An uproar that paled in comparison to the applause I had hoped for. Relief never came. Even now, I remind myself I won, but it doesn't feel like winning, because Eden and the others, whose names I'll never know, aren't here to tell their stories. I was too late.

My father once told me if a rattlesnake bites you to stay calm, so the venom takes its time traveling to your organs. I think about that often. My father's evil worked its way through my system, his fabricated theories like toxins rushing toward my vulnerable heart. It was only in that moment in the greenhouse, when all became clear, when I found that calm, that I could slow the process, but I could never stop it. Traces of the poison remain. Not even time can expel it.

You may call me a hero, but I only did what I had to do to survive.

# CORONADO

"AND THAT'S OFFICIALLY A GONER!" SLOANE ANNOUNCES AS SHE pours the last airplane bottle of vodka into my glass.

I propose another toast. I've lost count of how many we've made in the last hour.

"To freedom from mind fuckery!"

"Hear, hear!" Sloane cheers, her cheeks rosy in the lamplight.

We down our drinks. After the catastrophic parting with Diana, I couldn't be alone tonight. I convinced Sloane to stay over and insisted it would be more fun for the two of us to enjoy my newly upgraded suite.

Sloane skips over to the entryway console and plucks Tex's gifted champagne from the bucket of melting ice. "Ooh, should we open this?"

Anger tears through me—I would have thought the hotel staff would be smart enough to toss the champagne given the tantrum I threw over its presence. The unsettling white noise of the hotel billows in my ears as I search for an excuse not to open it. I consider that maybe I'm just being paranoid, but accepting anything from Tex may be tempting fate.

"Better not," I say, pointing to the time. It's just past 1 a.m. and we have a shoot in the morning.

My stomach's bloated from the truffle fries and ice-cream sundaes we devoured on the eight-hundred-thread-count sheets. Commemorating the official umbilical cord–cutting of mother and daughter called for such indulgences. My heart hasn't stopped racing since. I pull the hotel robe around me and fall back on a pillow. Sloane follows suit. The two of us, room-service trays at our feet, participate in a type of pillow talk this luxurious suite has never seen. This place is the stuff of wedding anniversaries and sultry affairs, not macabre celebrations like ours.

I can't stop myself from sorting through the depths of Diana's betrayal, unnerved by how deftly she'd deceived me all these years. Instances when I believed she genuinely cared for me appear distorted in this new light. I'm lost in thought, unable to find my words, when Sloane grabs my hand.

"I'm really sorry about this afternoon, Lucy." She shakes her head. "I can't believe Diana did that to you. You know you can tell me anything, right?"

"Judy was right," I say, without thinking. "She was right about Diana. Maybe she's right about me too. About all of it."

Sloane doesn't press me. She only squeezes my hand in response.

My stomach drops. Her touch, her empathy—it's something new. Somehow more intimate than any of the sex I've had with nameless men over the past two decades. It's not about status, attraction, or even companionship. No, it's something else entirely.

The only friend I've made in years might see me for who I really am. Nothing's ever been more terrifying.

CAFFEINE FUNNELS THROUGH MY SYSTEM, AND THE URGE TO GET out of this town is impossible to ignore. Sloane rubs her temples behind the camera. I'm impressed she woke up early this morning to clean up our mess before shooting began. Isaac acts like today is business as usual, dragging me through details of the trial I'd rather forget, as if he didn't happen to capture Diana Golden's downfall the day before.

"The moment you heard those words 'not guilty' you were finally free—"

"But that's the thing you have to understand," I say, cutting him off. Here's Isaac's blind spot. He fails to grasp these nuances because of the way society treats boy geniuses like him. "The public put me on trial too, long after the verdict was read in that courtroom. I may be beloved by one group, the feminists, the ones who believe Amber and me, but there's an equally vocal and spirited group who loathes me and views me as a hypersexual, violent man-eater because they're too scared to question themselves. If they did, they would have to rearrange their own understanding of what it might mean for them to be wrong. They'd have to deal with a threat to the systems they think keep them safe, systems that allow men like Max to act without consequence."

"Now, given the revelations your"—he hesitates, and I taste the relief of disowning the woman I called my mother the day before—"Diana brought to your attention yesterday . . . you said she was your one constant during the trial and the months that followed. Can you elaborate?"

"There's not much more to add," I say coolly. I'm not going to divulge anything he doesn't need to know. My most private grief has no place in this documentary. "All you need to remember is the fact that her series *Before and After* marks her biggest sales to date."

When the crew wraps up, Isaac smiles at me sheepishly, like he's concerned I might collapse. I consider the possibility that there might be someone underneath the hipster haircut and Hollywood tactics, someone with good intentions.

I PROMISE ISAAC I'LL BE READY AND WAITING OUTSIDE AT THE Mojave Sands Motel in Joshua Tree tomorrow morning at 9 a.m. sharp. Despite his hesitancy, he concedes. Sloane offers to join, even drive us herself, but when we part ways at the rental car lot, I tell her not to worry.

I need to do this drive on my own. It's a challenge to shake off the astounding intimacy we forged last night in the Hotel Del. I hate that I allowed myself to reach a level of such vulnerability in Sloane's presence. The fact that I even slipped off my mask for a moment worries me. I've made it this far keeping my secrets from her, and from Isaac too, but the end of the documentary's looming. Diana's confession will have to be enough to satisfy Isaac's hunger for "new developments" in the case. He's never going to find the bodies anyway. Soon he'll be forced to call it a wrap.

The breeze tangles my hair as I barrel down I-15 with the soft top of my rented Jeep Wrangler down, afternoon sun pinking my fair complexion. I turn up the stereo, sing along to the soundtrack of my road trip to the past, trying to dispel all the energy zinging through me. I lay on the gas and zoom past fields of windmills, back to where I once belonged.

### Pioneertown

"ANOTHER." I GRAB THE ATTENTION OF A BARTENDER IN A PATCH-work vest at Pappy and Harriet's. He slides a glass of Bulleit over the bar. Tonight, this tourist attraction will serve as a much-needed detour before I yield to my final destination.

Tonight, I should behave, and I could, but I don't want to.

It happens all too easily, this well-known dance of seduction with a stranger. It begins with a charged exchange of looks, a lighthearted quip about the oldies playing. When he asks if I'm from around here, his firm, calloused hand presses into my lower back and tests my vacillating boundaries. His whiskey breath radiates heat and nonsense into my hair. The setup is so trite, it's practically choreographed. The flirtation tempts me with the seductive promise of feeling nothing, of forgetting.

I tell the stranger to meet me in five.

# PAPER CUT

In the bathroom, I crash into a pack of twentysomething girls on a bachelorette, gossiping, swiping glittery gloss on their lips, adjusting their strapless bras and newly bought cowboy hats. They glare at me as they pass; a grown woman in head-to-toe designer silk must look absurd in this Hollywood replica of the Wild West.

One girl wearing molten copper eyeshadow whispers to her friend, "Isn't that Lucy Golden?" The door swings closed before her notion is confirmed.

I study my reflection in the bathroom mirror. I try to see who it is they see. I wonder what it might be like to no longer find the phantoms of my parents staring back at me. There's his nose. There's her fair complexion, the fairest of them all.

There's his wickedness.

There's hers.

I need a surgery to remove them: the weight of my envy of her, the mass of my anger toward him. They are toxic cancers I must expel, so the infection can no longer spread and affect the way I function. The trouble is what I might find underneath.

Three taps on the door. The stranger steps inside and flips the lock, so we won't be disturbed. I catch his reflection in the mirror, beaming at his dumb luck. In this moment, as he unravels me, I tell myself he's no stranger.

I imagine he's Arthur. I imagine it's the two of us, reunited after all this time.

The wolf in me takes over, grabs him by the collar, and pulls him to the wall, so I can feel his crushing frame against mine. The old me, the destructive beast, wants this. I wish I didn't want Arthur, now or then, to want me, but, ah, there's the rub of adolescent infatuation. As much as I wish I could lose myself in this stranger's grasp, I can't. Nothing could feel as cathartic as the fantasy of Arthur's touch. I was nothing but his conquest, one of many. Only a fool would believe our connection meant more than it did. Yet here I am, trying to replicate the past anyway.

This stranger is just another one of the vultures I give myself over to in search of escape, ever since those cool nights spent in the Airstream. Disgust surges through me—the shame, the agony of what I've put myself through time and again—and I realize I can't go through with it. I'll be sick if I do. I refuse to let my body be a pawn in my own twisted games, for another anonymous man's pleasure. Not anymore. This ends now.

I pull away, but the stranger pins me against the wall. "Baby," he calls me. I squirm against his chest. "Come here."

"I'm sorry," I say as I button my blouse, even though I'm not. "I changed my mind." I duck under his arm and square off against him. "This was a mistake. It's not about you."

"Just relax, beautiful." His cheeky grin radiates desire, like he's turned on by my reluctance.

I ignore his useless pandering and pace back and forth on the tile. "God, why do I do this to myself? Over and over again. This is the last time. I'm done. Fuck, I don't even know your name!"

"It's Tex."

I freeze. "What did you just say?"

"You said you didn't know my name."

I face him, and he shrugs, like it's no big deal and he's just trying to score a point with me with this meager offering.

I don't recognize this man at all—not from the conventions, not from the online profiles, definitely not from my past. He's not Arthur. It makes no sense.

"Tex?" I ask unsteadily, backing away. Could it be a coincidence? "Watson?"

"Yeah, so?" He crosses his arms. "Do we know each other?"

With my back against the wall, panic courses through me. He's blocking the only exit. I have to play this right. "What do you want?"

"I just want to have a little fun." The stranger tries to grab my waist, but I swat his hand away.

The peculiar thing is, I believe him. He doesn't seem to recognize me either. My suspicion grows. "Did someone put you up to this?"

"I don't know what you're talking about."

I grab his wrist, hard.

"What the fuck?" He glares at my nails digging into his wrist, then back at me. He shakes me off. "Fine, shit. Yes, okay? It's not worth it. I did not sign up for this."

"Start talking."

"Look, I just thought it was a joke, like a prank between friends," he rambles, like a little boy who's been caught. "I was told I could take the money, mess around. I wasn't supposed to tell you the name until after the fact. No harm, no foul. Obviously, I was mistaken. I don't want to be involved."

"Too bad—you got involved." I shove past him and unlock the door. As we exit the bathroom, a young woman's jaw drops as she realizes why she wasn't able to use the facilities. "Now, who roped you into this? Was it someone here, at the bar?"

"Maybe, yeah." The stranger rubs his wrist like a newly released prisoner and turns his back to the crowd.

I spin him back around to face the throng of bargoers. "Who was it?"

"Can't you just let this slide?"

"Do I seem like the kind of person who lets things slide?"

He bites his lip and scans the loud, swarming bar. I grind my teeth, determined to find out for certain, once and for all, if my suspicions are correct, if it's been Arthur all along. I hunt for my tormentor slowly, carefully. I'm more than ready to take my shot once my target's been secured.

That's when I see Tex, the real Tex. Plain as day. Alone, at the far end of the bar. A wrench twists in my gut, hard and fast.

The stranger confirms my worst nightmare, one I never could have imagined. "Right over there." Before I can find the words, he rushes out of the bar, desperate to extricate himself from my mess.

I push through my heart-pounding disbelief, whip out my phone, and fire off one last message to TexWatson86, just to break her like she broke me.

I know who you are.

I'd know that shock of blue anywhere.

I WATCH IN HORROR AS SLOANE'S PHONE LIGHTS UP ON THE BAR top. She reads the message and looks up warily. When our eyes meet, the bar's roar morphs into a blare.

Tears sting my cheeks, and I'm confused by my body's reaction. I'm not sad. I'm furious. Everything she told me was a lie. She dangled a carrot in front of me, swearing her friendship was sincere, and I ate out of her palm every time.

I shove past tourists and locals until I meet the frigid air outside. To think what I could have told her in the Hotel Del . . .

"Lucy!" Sloane calls out. "Wait!"

I weave through the cars parked in the lot. I hear Sloane's footfalls on the gravel right behind me.

"I know how this looks," she manages between breaths. "But it's not what you think."

I can't find the words to respond, not yet. I'm trembling as I dig through my purse for the car key. I frantically press the lock button to locate my rental.

She catches up to me and touches the back of my arm. "Give me a chance to explain, please."

I yank my arm away and twist around to face her. "What the hell is wrong with you? God, I thought I was going crazy! But it's been you all along? Stalking me, threatening me, pulling your clever little quotes from *Rattlesnake*. Pretending to be Max haunting me from beyond, huh? 'You can't let your shadow win'? Pretending to be Arthur, on a warpath with wildflowers and champagne? I thought Tex was going to hurt me. For what?!"

"You have to listen to me now, Lucy." Sloane's eerily calm tone irks me the most. "Trust me."

"Trust you?" I can't help but laugh. "I don't even know who you are."

Her big brown eyes water. She opens her mouth to speak.

"Well?" I scream at her. "Who are you?"

Sloane tears at her scalp with her ragged nails. "I was only trying to—"

"Whatever you think you have up your sleeve, it's over." I finally find the Jeep and unlock it.

"But I can explain."

"No, I don't want to hear a single word you have to say!" I throw the door open and climb inside. "You know the worst part? For a moment there, I actually thought you were my friend."

I pull the door closed and hit the lock button. I keep my gaze straight ahead as she pathetically tries the door handle. Her muffled pleas are the last thing I hear before I drive away.

As I race down the dark desert highway, regret takes hold. My recklessness is to blame. I cringe remembering how eagerly I soaked up a fan's praise; how desperate I was for connection that I let my guard down.

This is why I can't break my own rules.

Never trust anyone, but most importantly, never, ever trust myself.


A HALF HOUR LATER, I TURN RIGHT OFF TWENTYNINE PALMS Highway and park in front of the steel gate of the Mojave Sands Motel. I'm still trembling as I lug my suitcase across the courtyard complete with a koi pond and a native-desert garden. I'm disappointed by how easy it is to see inside suite five, made of various panes of glass, some transparent, others clouded and colored. So much for privacy. I spin around the courtyard to make sure Sloane hasn't caught up to me, but all I hear is the blurring traffic from the highway.

Fury festers in my gut at the lowly assistant's gall to pull off such an elaborate scheme. It's painfully obvious that she just wanted to insert herself into the narrative, *my* narrative. She thought she could pull a fast one on Isaac and get to the bottom of my case herself. But she is nothing. She means nothing to me. She never did.

I unlatch the metal gate of the small patio. I set my purse down on the antique table and let myself in per the booking reservation's instructions. The suite is long and skinny, retro and sexy, with concrete floors and warm mid-century furnishings. A kitchenette and bench with a record player make up the main room. Past the dark nook of the bathroom, I step up into the bedroom and face-plant onto the wooden platform bed.

I can taste it—the desert dust. It's the most memorable sensation, as recognizable as the lies rotting inside me all this time, petitioning to be thrown out for good. I'm not sure how long I lie there, curling into myself, cursing the only friend I've made in years, before I hear it. The outside world clawing its way in.

The sound of her voice snaps me clean in half. I keep my body perfectly still, but the lights give me away.

She knocks softly. "Let me in." She sounds even calmer than she did in the bar parking lot, an unsettling thought. "I want you to know I've only had good intentions from the start. I want what's best for you, for both of us."

I creep down to the main room, where I can make out her shape through the tinted windowpane. I forgot just how dark the night can be out here. Terror burns bright and wild in my whiskey haze. I tiptoe behind the kitchen counter, where there's a clear pane of glass. I catch a good glimpse of her outside the door. I notice something bulky in her jacket pocket. Maybe it's a gun, and this was her plan all along.

She jiggles the doorknob and shuffles side to side. "I'm not going to hurt you, Lucy."

I work up the nerve to respond. "What makes you think I can trust anything you have to say?"

"Because I know you," she says. "I know you better than you think."

My throat feels like it might close. I watch her through the windowpane, panicked, out of my depth. She takes whatever's in her jacket pocket and passes the object back and forth between her hands. I squint, trying to make out what it is. Once my eyes adjust to the darkness, I recognize it: circular as a globe, a smooth navy velvet base, a deep grooved pattern in the glass, a silver sphere top.

Odette's perfume.

The bottle I stole from her room twenty years ago. The scent I wore the night Arthur robbed me of my innocence. The distraction I pushed into the hands of a little girl before my escape.

Before I assess the risks, I open the door. The pendant light above the doorway creates a hazy halo around her blue mane of curls, and the effect is almost angelic.

"Where did you get that?"

"You gave it to me."

I see her anew. Behind her blue hair, behind her tough exterior, behind her producorial methods, I see the woman standing in front of me as that same little girl with wide brown eyes who wondered about the outside world, who wanted to taste snowflakes. The innocent child I "saved" from the rattlesnake during my initiation. I promised her everything would be okay if she would just be quiet and take the perfume like it was her own, if she promised to forget whatever it was she might have seen that night and never tell a soul. The eldest of the New Kind, after me.

*Susanna.*

"But how could you . . ." I hesitate. One ragged breath. Then two. Then three. "You can't be."

Once and for all, she discloses why she put me through all the torment. "I need to know what happened to Ivy Peters. I need to know where she is."

My head's spinning as I put it together. In a trance, I recall the photograph of Ivy, her round face, her soft curls. There had been something so familiar about her. Now I knew why.

"You're Ivy's daughter?"

Sloane confirms this piece of the puzzle. "I'm your sister too." She follows me inside. The door clicks shut behind her.

I take another step back, running into the concrete wall behind me. I wince at the contact. I remember us only yesterday, knee-deep in my mother's archives, looking for clues, and last night, at the Hotel Del, fast asleep beside each other. All the while, she was keeping her true identity a secret. She isn't just Max and Ivy's daughter. She's Arthur's half sister too.

"You scared the hell out of me," I tell her. "What kind of a person would come up with the whole charade of TexWatson86 just to torture their own sister?"

"I'm trying to tell you, Lucy," Sloane says. "I never meant to hurt you, but it was the only way I could think of to get your attention. I needed you to be worried, so worried that maybe, just maybe, you'd tell the truth this time. Maybe you'd grow to care enough about me to give what I need." She twirls the perfume in her hand, the bottle now empty. It catches the light. I envision her younger self dousing her wrists with it in the aftermath of the Oasis's collapse. "You're the only person who can help me."

"Whatever it is you think you know, you're confused," I snap. "You were just a kid."

"Ironic, isn't it? You of all people gaslighting me. You'd think you'd know how harmful that can be." Sloane sighs. "When the Oasis was raided, I was put into the system. I was the oldest of all the kids. No one wanted to adopt a ten-year-old raised in a violent cult. I spent the next eight years in and out of foster homes. Each one worse than the last. I was told to forget what happened to me. If I didn't, I'd scare off any potential parents. I'd isolate myself even further from what was considered normal. I was told repeatedly that my version of the events of that night could not be trusted. I was a kid, after all, right?"

Max's arrogant resolve flares in her—how had I not seen it before?

"Meanwhile, you had everything," she continues. "You had the famous family, the resources, the fancy lawyers, the headlines." She counts my good fortunes on her fingers. "I tried to contact you countless times throughout the years, but every single time, you dismissed me. You said it yourself: *People like that just want their fifteen minutes of fame.* The only way I could get through to you was as a fan, so I started slowly. I created TexWatson86 to stay in your orbit, to keep tabs on you and wait for the right opportunity. When I saw Isaac's documentary on the Buckhead Butcher, I knew that was my chance. So I brought him your case. Of course, the boy wonder's clout convinced you to sign on. You leapt at the first chance to stay relevant."

I kick myself now for how easily I gave in and trusted that Isaac's Midas touch would turn me back into gold. "Wait, what exactly did you tell him? What does he know?"

"Look at you, squirming." Sloane takes a seat on the bench, and up close, I can see that her nail beds are destroyed, raw and scabbed. "I convinced Isaac that investigating your case would be worth it."

"Isaac knows who you are?"

"Of course." She smiles eerily, like it's a preposterous question. "He knows everything. He's known about it all from the beginning."

"TexWatson86 too?"

"We needed to wear you down somehow." Sloane shrugs.

I look down at my hands, embarrassed to meet her gaze. So it wasn't all in my head. Isaac's precious process was designed to distress me for a reason. TexWatson86 was manufactured to push me closer to the edge, so Isaac would only have to give me a nudge, call action, and I'd freefall on cue.

"It was my idea to befriend you," she says. "After all, I always wanted to be your sister. I always wanted to get to know you. Sure, at first, I knew you were only using me to fan your ego and dig up dirt on Isaac. You think I didn't know you staged our run-in at the yoga class? Tell me, Lucy." She cocks her head to the side, like I'm daft. "Did you really think I had no idea that you were the one who *drugged* me that night at Bar Stella?" She laughs to herself. "I have to applaud you for that one. I didn't think you had the guts. You thought you covered your tracks so well, but Ivy's father called us five minutes after you had the audacity to pose as a producer on our team. What did you call yourself? Liza, was it? Such a talented sleuth, aren't you?"

I feel the color drain from my face. I was always one step behind. Shame fills me as I realize how foolish I really was. She knew, all along, I was using her.

"I'm sorry, Sloane"—I hesitate—"Susanna. I shouldn't have, but—"

"I would have done the same thing." She waves me off. "I guess it was wishful thinking. I hoped maybe if you learned about Ivy and her story, you would care. You might consider someone other than yourself."

"I do care—"

"It took a while, but eventually Tex caught up to you. My little scheme worked. You ran straight to me, just like I planned. You wanted me to comfort you and reassure you. Your guard was coming down. So I was patient. I knew I'd earned your trust when you asked me to help you search Diana's archives. Last night, you were *this* close to admitting what you've been hiding."

"You're wrong," I say, backpedaling. "I don't know what you want me to tell you, but you need to leave me alone."

Sloane ignores my plea. "You know exactly what I want. That's how I convinced Isaac to do the documentary. I simply explained there is more work left to do."

"What work?"

"It's time," she says, the phrase a discomforting echo from the past. "I want to find my mother. I need to find her."

"I can't help you."

"Because I'm nobody, right?" Her voice breaks. "Only an assistant, a fan, an internet troll whose attention you take as evidence of your outrageous level of fame. Just a little girl you abandoned in the desert."

I want to tell her to surrender to a lifetime of uncertainty. Finding Ivy's corpse cannot rewind the horrors of Sloane's life and return the mother who was taken from her. What remains of us after death is inconsequential. I realize I'm rationalizing, like Max, recalling his convenient theory that our bodies are only temporary vessels.

I thought I was almost done. I thought the revelation of Diana's involvement would suffice, but the threat of Sloane's remark sears into my skin. The shiny new package of the documentary isn't enough to disguise the fact that I'm telling the same old story. If I continue as planned, I'll remain a one-hit wonder, mediocre at best, but Isaac and Sloane want more. They're out for blood.

"The truth will set you free," Sloane says. I shudder, remembering Tex's message before I knew what it meant, before I knew whose hands were typing on the keyboard. She sets the perfume on the kitchen counter and turns to go.

"Wait." I have to ask her, though it's a futile request. "What does Isaac have planned?"

She looks back at me, her hand on the doorknob, but never answers my question. "Maybe now you can be the hero. That's what you've always wanted, right?"

WE DRIVE THROUGH THE CENTER OF TOWN PAST A FUNKY COLLEC-
tion of vintage shops, rock collections, organic grocers, vegan cafés. I
search the faces on the street as if I'm already haunted by what's bound
to happen, wary of the ghosts I fear I might confront today.

The highway stretches out before us, and forty agonizing minutes
later, the crew van dips as it makes a wide left turn onto an unmarked
dirt road. A dilapidated mailbox points us in the right direction. We all
hold on as the van rattles down a hill toward a ranch at the bottom of
the slope.

The run-down house looks like it's being held together by peeling paint. An assortment of junk overflows the narrow porch: wind
chimes, large crystals and boulders, a broken tricycle. Dried-up overgrown brush and weeds fill the poorly constructed garden beds lining
the side of the house.

In the rearview mirror, Sloane watches me intently as I take in
the scene. We've said nothing about last night to each other, but the
revelations hang in the air like smoke, choking me with the potential
consequences of all that's occurred. I'm not sure I can go through
with this.

"What is this place?" I ask, despite knowing full well that Isaac
wants to capture my reaction in real time. I assumed we were headed
to the site of the Oasis, but I don't recognize this at all. "Where are
we?" No one acknowledges my question.

The driver shuts off the engine. The crew unloads. Paralyzed in my seat, I watch the café curtain on the front window of the house sway in the breeze, expecting it to shift and reveal who is inside. Thankfully, I don't have to wait long to find out.

A lone woman emerges from the front door. She's only a few years older than me, but her hair's streaked with gray, hanging in two braids down to her waist. A ratty pair of men's overalls drape over her gaunt frame. When she grins at Isaac, I recognize the gap in her teeth.

Fiona.

DUST RISES IN THE AIR AS FIONA MOVES A STACK OF OLD ASTROL-ogy books off a yellowing futon and plops them down by her defunct fireplace. Gingerly, I take a seat on the futon, annoyed that my new silk skirt will need to be dry-cleaned after coming into contact with this filth. Isaac's crew and their camera equipment take up every available inch of the packed front room. Discomfort twinges on their faces as they negotiate space with the waste, far past hoarder status.

From a tattered recliner, Fiona glances at me in between each row of her knitting. Sun-spotted, she's aged in a way that I find alarming at first, but then I reconsider. Perhaps she wants to embrace the years she has suffered—and it's reasonable to assume she has suffered all this time from the looks of the battered old shoebox she calls home. As Isaac films, she never stops knitting, her cracked hands always in motion with the marled wool yarn. It's perplexing to be this close to her, to watch as she weaves each row with meditative precision.

Isaac asks, "Fiona, how old were you when you first came to the Oasis?"

"Sixteen," Fiona states for the record. "I was there nearly three years before the first of the New Kind returned." She points at me with her knitting needle. The last time I saw her, against the flames, she charged right toward me with that same intensity, a blunt knife in her hand instead. I shake off the memory. *She's changed, I'm sure of it*, I think, trying to comfort myself.

"I see," Isaac says. "Can you tell us your experience of that summer?"

Fiona only hums oddly, the first few notes of the lullaby I can't forget.

"Where you went after?" Isaac prompts her.

"Nowhere."

Isaac pivots. "Are you still in touch with anyone from back then?"

"Well, the cowards decided they'd be better off in the outside world. They tried to turn us against the cause and thought we'd just pack up and go." She harrumphs. "Well, not me," she says proudly. "Not Beatrice."

"What cause is that, Fiona?" Isaac asks.

"The Oasis, of course," she spits back at him. Isaac licks his lips, like he can taste a savory rave from the *Hollywood Reporter* on the tip of his tongue. I shift on the futon, an uncanny dread dispersing through my veins.

"According to official records, the Oasis disbanded back in 2002 after the killings," Isaac states.

"Just because we don't live on that land anymore doesn't mean we gave up." Fiona never acknowledges the killings. She only goes on the defensive. "We do our part. We're almost there."

"Almost where?" I interject, though I'm petrified I already know the answer.

"To the Light."

It's impossible. Has nothing about that fateful night made a difference? The aftermath, the press, the trial? I picture Fiona: in the cowboy tub, floating alongside her; in the greenhouse, handing her a packet of seeds. I resist the urge to shake my old friend and tell her she's got it all wrong. Before I can, a leggy teenage girl appears in the doorway, barefoot and rail thin. Her hungry eyes bounce between me, Fiona, and the camera like she's watching a tennis match.

PAPER CUT

"Is that . . ." I say aloud, befuddled, like I've seen a ghost. "Be-atrice?" The girl's her spitting image.

"You fool!" Fiona laughs, jarring and high-pitched. "She's one of the New Kind."

I attempt to catch Isaac's attention, to make sure this is really happening, but he's zoned in on Fiona's manic cackle, nodding at Derek to zoom in. I lock eyes with Sloane and realize they designed the shoot to capture precisely this moment. "But you said Beatrice . . ." My pulse races as I conceive the worst. "Is she . . . ?"

Fiona lunges forward. I flinch, afraid she's coming for my throat, but she's only getting out of her recliner. "Beatrice made it to the Light," Fiona declares. "I've almost made it through to the Underworld—twice, if you must know—but he says my insides must be rotten, can you believe that?" She grabs a pail by the front door and goes around to the numerous houseplants one by one. All the plants appear to be long dead, curled over with parched, diseased leaves. Like a shadow, the teenage girl follows Fiona. I realize there's no water in the pail at all. Fiona's just going through the motions, pretending to water the plants. "He promises me it will happen. One day, soon, I'll make it there too. I'll join the others. You'll see."

"Fiona . . ." I tread carefully, absorbing my building fear. My stomach turns. If Beatrice made it to the Light, someone sent her there. Someone fathered her child, this teenage girl, one of the New Kind. "Who are you talking about? Who is *he*?"

Joy cascades over both their faces. "Our hero," they say in unison.

Fiona waves us down the hallway. "He's waiting for you."

Isaac gestures for me to follow them, and I'm about to protest, but I know I have to see this for myself, like Sloane said. I spot a rack of clothing—faded, moth-eaten, splitting at the seams—alongside a pile of dusty blankets and a landline phone handset dangling off the hook. All feeble attempts to re-create the past.

A trace of mold crawls up the paper-thin hallway walls. We pass a kitchen on the left. Inside, there's a broken window, dingy with filth, and grayish scum clinging to the floor beneath the busted fridge. A twentysomething woman with dark circles beneath her eyes is splayed out on the floor, trying to pry open a can of processed soup with a dull knife. A fly circles her as she works the blade, but she ignores it like she ignores us. On the right, there is a bedroom with stained, threadbare blankets scattered on the floor. A little boy sleeping naked turns onto his side, and I can't tear my eyes away from his protruding spine, his scabbed elbows, infected and yellow.

Everywhere I turn, it's obvious this place, this "new Oasis" has spoiled, gone past its prime, but I can't stop looking.

"Here we are," Fiona, my former guide, announces, as she pushes through the back door and beckons me to follow. I feel the heavy awareness of Isaac's cameras behind my shoulder taking in the horrendous sight ahead.

The yard's littered with tarps, heaps of trash, and hubcaps, but that's not what I notice first. It's the children, a handful of them, loitering in the rubble, fatigued, only skin and bones and brittle hair. They glare at us, this troop of foreigners, with something inconceivable in their expressions. The children of the Oasis I once knew obeyed their leader and his rules without rebellion, but they were still curious. They wanted to know what snowflakes were like. They wanted to know what was out there. But these children are fully surrendered.

They know nothing of the outside world.

I clench my jaw when I see the shape of a man emerge from behind a tarp in the distance.

This man is nothing like I remember, apart from his stone-gray irises—the only feature I recognize. He is not the broad-shouldered, formidable, smoldering artist I spent my youth pining after. He is not the seducer with the bobbing Adam's apple, magnetism, and stature.

This man's hair has grown long, past his shoulders into tangled, limp curls of white and gray. Ragged and worn, his leathery skin is encased in a layer of dirt. When he smiles at me, his rotten teeth betray him. He is no wolf. This man who broke my heart a million times over is no hero either. He can't be.

"My little poet," Arthur says, stealing my father's nickname for me. His once-familiar rasp slices me in two. "Welcome home."

I take a step back. Arthur's harrowing rip-off of the Oasis is nothing like the utopia my father promised. An image of my younger self in those long-lost photographs flashes in my brain—my slight frame, ribs protruding from my skin, that same surrender in my expression as these children have. I wonder if my memory failed me, if I ever recognized what was right in front of me as wrong. If I only conjured up the hazy, picturesque daydream of that sun-soaked summer. If paradise never existed at all.

I have to get out of here. I have to end this. I whirl around, charge through the camera crew, shove past Fiona, race through the house the way I came, and make it to the front porch, winded.

Instinctively, my hand flies to my stomach. I try to catch my breath, but I can't. I hear them, like a mob chasing after me, pitchforks in hand. My mind is swimming with thoughts, but I can't hold on to anything. I'm sinking.

"Lucy?" Sloane bursts through the front door and finds me first. "Are you okay?"

"I've had enough." I wrap my arms around myself and pace the front yard, shuddering. "I quit. I'm not doing it anymore. I will not be subject to this torture. You can't do this to me." I look at her, the person I thought I could trust. She's my sister, after all. "How could you let this happen?"

Sloane grabs my hands to still me, then whispers, "Don't you see why it's important that you keep going?" She gestures to the side yard behind her. I glance at the lot of them: Isaac, the camera crew, Fiona, Arthur, the children. They stand by, eyes wide and eager, anticipating instruction.

A pretty young woman pokes her head through the huddle and strains to get a better look. Arthur waves her through to the front of the pack, stands behind her, and places his hands on her delicate shoulders. Her frail arms cradle the unmistakable swell of a pregnant belly.

She's growing the next of the New Kind—Arthur's kind. That young woman is next too, next to brave the Underworld, to make it to the Light, to reach wholeness, to be the hero.

She is next in line to die.

# JOSHUA TREE

DRESSED IN ONE OF DIANA'S ROBES, THE LAVENDER ONE WITH LACE trim, I make coffee in the suite's French press while I wait for the outdoor tub to fill. I watch the desert sky stretch and yawn, pink and gold, unwittingly partaking in the culmination of Isaac and Sloane's little experiment on my psyche for the content-hungry world's satisfaction.

After yesterday's failed visit to Arthur's compound, I know today is the day I'll return to the Oasis, the one I knew. Now is the moment to decide, for better or worse, if I'm brave enough to withstand one more day of torture or if I'll crumble under the pressure.

On the bench, by the record player, Arthur's old Moleskine sticks out of my bag. As I smooth my hand over the cover, I imagine the weak pulse of that girl in his photographs. Somehow, she's still hanging on. I stuff the Moleskine back inside the manila envelope and seal the clasp.

I read over the draft of the foreword I stayed up all night writing and rewriting. I was like a hamster in a wheel after witnessing the state of Arthur's compound. I kept lingering over the children's faces, the novelty in the young pregnant woman's expression, Arthur's steady voice. I kept trying to make sense of what I know now.

Scanning the page, I catch myself painstakingly trying to craft a new angle to make my version of the truth marketable, fresh, sensational. Mostly, I see the untold story I'm too afraid to tell hidden in the blank spaces between the lines. I drop the page and watch, repulsed, as my pedestrian attempt at genius flutters to my feet.

Before I can think it through, I grab Odette's perfume bottle from the counter and hurl it at the concrete wall.

When the glass breaks, a howl escapes my body. Pieces scatter in every direction.

I kneel down to clean up the mess I made. Using the foreword as a broom, I sweep the broken glass into my palm. Searing pain pierces my finger pad. A hiss slips from my lips. I dump the glass back onto the concrete floor to assess the injury, but then I see it's only a tiny nick.

A paper cut.

The invisible wounds we inflict on ourselves—the white lies, the split-second, life-altering decisions, the raging, quiet regrets—damage us the most. All these years, I've lied to protect someone I once loved and soothe truth's brutal sting. It was the only way I believed I could live with the monster inside: forget what she did and forgive what she failed to do.

I abandon the wreckage on the floor, head past the bedroom, and push through the metal door to the private patio in the back. I crank off the tub faucet, the hot water now to the brim. Suddenly, the whole desert falls silent, but I can hear my heart straining in my chest, pounding beat after beat. I'm still here. *I'm still alive.*

I slip off the robe, step into the tub, and let the steaming water remedy the paper cut. With my head halfway underwater, I scowl at the inspirational quote carved into the rusted sign on the wooden fence, likely picked up at a roadside sale on some old desert highway.

*There's no way out but through.*

As the tub faucet drips, I realize I disagree. There is another route. I go over each turn in my head. The steps of the winding path I did not take. Then again. Then once more.

# PAPER CUT

## *The Oasis*

THE DRIVE TO THE SITE OF THE OASIS IS SILENT. AFTER WITNESSING yesterday's display, the crew finally shuts up and pays me some respect. I wonder if they think of cults differently now that they've observed the lives on the line.

During the ride, Sloane briefly grabs my hand on the seat between us. I can't look at her, not now. I'm so angry with her for keeping all her secrets from me, for keeping me in the dark about Tex's true identity, her true identity. I'm angry with myself that I never gave her more credit. She was never a powerless assistant. She had the deck stacked the whole time. Even though I'm furious, I understand that returning to this place must be just as difficult for her as it is for me. Maybe it's even crueler. No one took her seriously all these years, and that's because of what I did.

Once we arrive, I'm surprised to see neighboring houses spread in all directions. The patch of land once known as Max's kingdom is now only a shell of what it was. The women's adobe house has been boarded up, deemed unlivable, while the only evidence that Max's adobe ever existed is a slight slope in the dirt where it once stood. Part of the greenhouse's frame still remains—but of course the glass has been removed, after it shattered that fateful night. The cowboy tub is rusted and turned over. Desert weeds climb up the sides, likely a nest of rattlesnakes roasting underneath it, riddled with the poison unique to this land. Arthur's Airstream is long gone.

The crew gets to work setting up, but I stay in the van and wait for Arthur to arrive. I hear Isaac promised to personally drive him to the shoot.

I never thought Arthur would get this far. For decades, I've imagined him, how his life turned out, where he went when he ran away and broke his promise that he'd return for me. I imagined him surviving off the grid in the Pacific Northwest, falling in with a crowd of thru-hikers ranting conspiracy theories. I imagined him working an oil rig in Alaska, his rough hands on a local barkeep during the offsea-son. I fantasized he'd be an artist, branded with a new name, running a small, respectable gallery on the main street of some Hudson Valley hamlet. Most recently, I thought of him as Tex Watson86, stalking me all over Southern California, spewing hate online, sending me another bouquet of wildflowers, twisting my own words for his pleasure.

I never once considered this would be his fate. I'm astounded he's only been down the road from where it all happened. He's spent the last twenty years collecting women and children like trophies and be-coming Max 2.0. A twisted part of me feels validated by the role I played in his eventual outcome. I always feared I was a forgettable blip on his radar, but I was much more than that.

I was his catalyst.

Another car carves through the dirt, kicking up rocks and sand in its wake, and I know Arthur's inside. Watching from the van, without thinking, I say his name aloud, to no one, and it tastes bittersweet on my tongue. With each day that passed in the two decades since I saw him, I lost another inch of our memories, but being out here, observ-ing him as he sets foot on this soil and takes in this land, everything comes flooding back with reckless abandon. Every touch, every whiff of his musk, every lie we told.

A tap on the car door startles me. It's only Sloane beckoning me to take my place, just doing her job. As I obey her commands, avoid-ing Arthur's gaze, I think about their mother, Ivy. I consider what it must have been like at seventeen, coming home pregnant only for her parents to throw her onto the street without mercy. I understand how easy it must have been to find refuge in a place like this after eight years of struggling to raise her son on her own. I don't blame her for believing in a man who promised her everything.

Isaac directs me to take a seat next to Arthur in the out-of-place director chairs angled toward the camera, staged in the center of camp, where the fire pit used to be. Sloane ushers me to the seat like she's worried I'll make a break for it. I watch carefully to see if Arthur recognizes his half sister, but it appears he's too preoccupied with his own agenda to notice.

Arthur's oddly comfortable in the spotlight, like it never crossed his mind to consult a lawyer about the possible ramifications of his film debut. I'm at a loss for what it means for him to agree to be filmed so openly and relive that summer on the record. I thought if I ever reunited with him, if he ever agreed to sign up for Isaac's project, he would be cagey and defiant. On the contrary, he appears to have no qualms about his indiscretions. He's not just talking. He won't stop.

"The beginning of something grand, I'm telling you," Arthur goes on. "Divinely designed. Once you're aware, I promise you'll be freed. Just like I was." It's unclear who exactly his soliloquy is aimed toward. Even now, he's campaigning for a new convert.

"Arthur." Isaac tries to get his attention. "All we want to do here today is tell your story."

"The story of the hero," Arthur says. He catches a new wave of focus and wants to ride it to the end. "Well, you see—"

"No, our story," I interject. "I was fifteen when we met, and remind me, how old were you?"

"Can't say I recall." He scratches his neck with his ragged fingernails, and I marvel at how our skin-to-skin electricity used to hold me hostage.

"Twenty-five," I clarify. "A full decade older than me."

"Age is only temporary," Arthur replies. I can only imagine the media storm that will brew once that comment airs. "The body is temporary."

"Right." I concede so that I can watch him relax, then counter with my next point. "But back then I was not a consenting adult when you groomed me, kidnapped me, and manipulated me for sex and whatever else Max commanded."

Arthur doesn't skip a beat. "Now you're in your shadow, my little poet. Remember: there are no victims."

For all the evil he's done, I appreciate that Arthur was a victim too.

I know this. Like the potter on the wheel, Max shaped Arthur, crushing a sense of right and wrong out of him with the heel of his vile palm, when his mother had brought him here looking for sanctuary. But Arthur needs to take responsibility for his part: for failing to break the mold, for perpetuating Max's evils, for spewing the same jumbled jargon even now. At some point, Arthur must have crossed over from innocent victim to guilty perpetrator. Discerning where that line lies is a moral quandary for philosophers, law enforcement, and, undoubtedly, armchair detectives to debate.

"Tell us, Lucy." Isaac steps in to redirect the conversation. "What happened that night?"

I glance down at my hands, at the paper cut from the morning, inflicted by the account I planned to tell once again, but another version of the events needs to be told.

The remedy is the truth. Only then can time form the wound into a scar, so it can never be forgotten.

"I am not the hero the world thinks I am." The confession melts like cotton candy in my mouth as I speak it into existence. "I am not responsible for the collapse of the Oasis in 2002."

"My destiny, written in the stars . . ." Arthur mumbles incoherently.

"Lucy," Isaac says. "Tell us what you mean."

"The story I told in *Rattlesnake* was just that—a story, a lie," I tell them. "I was too enmeshed with Max and brainwashed by his teachings to take action that night or any night. I would never have betrayed him." As I shoulder the shame, it miraculously shrinks with every word spoken. "Max was my hero, my god. I believed in him. I believed every word he said." I turn to Arthur. "I believed every word you said too."

"Start from the beginning," Isaac instructs me.

I face the camera. "After Eden gave birth to the New Kind, I did as I was told and took the children back to the women's quarters, but I wanted to do more. I wanted to witness Eden's journey to wholeness. It was all we talked about, you know? It was right there in front of me. I had to record it for Max, like I'd been doing all summer. So I turned around.

"I went back to Max's house, and I offered to do my part," I say. "Max instructed Arthur and me to take care of Eden's body. Somehow, this didn't deter me. We were always told that bodies were temporary. As I understood it, this was the moment we'd been waiting for. Eden's soul was on its way to the Underworld, and from there, she would go into the Light. I thought I was helping her."

I tear up, remembering the surprising heft of Eden's small frame, the stench of the dried blood from the birth, the soreness in my muscles as we carried her across camp to the greenhouse.

"I thought I was giving her what she wanted. You have to believe me," I say, despite knowing how deranged I must sound. "I thought I was being a supportive sister, one of their own, Max's dutiful servant. Then Max took off in his truck. He said he had to take care of things, make sure the outside world was sealed off before Eden's soul could descend. Arthur and I got to work burying Eden, but when we noticed a light on in the women's quarters, Arthur sent me to check it out. He said it was important that the women and children remained inside and oblivious. So I went over there and found Susanna in a state of confusion. I gave her a distraction, made her promise to keep whatever she might have seen to herself, then sent her back to bed."

From afar, I spot Sloane's lips curve up, just like our father's, cracking me open as I take on the role of truth-teller.

"Arthur and I finished burying Eden. Once Max returned, he had me copy down the ritual of the birthing ceremony for the Oasis records, just like I wrote in *Rattlesnake*." I take a breath and prepare for what I'm about to divulge next. "But I didn't kill Max. As much as I wish it was true, I am not the person responsible for my father's death."

There's a heavy pause. For a moment, no one speaks. The desert wind ripples through the crew and sends a stack of call sheets flying across video village. No one rushes to retrieve them.

Isaac breaks the silence. "Well, then who did?"

I keep my voice steady, setting the pace, just like Diana taught me. "It was Arthur," I admit, at last. "Arthur killed Max. Arthur shot him in cold blood in the greenhouse the night of Eden's murder. I saw it happen right in front of me, and I did nothing to stop it."

Isaac shifts to the side, so the camera's no longer obscuring his face. I can see it in his demeanor, in his awestruck expression, in the charged look exchanged between him and his assistant. He thought I'd admit to knowing where Eden's body was, because that's what Sloane must have told him. She must have seen us dragging her body out of the house, heard Max's truck start up, and surmised we'd driven off-site to bury Eden. They thought if I came clean that I knew where she was buried, they'd be the heroes and the documentary would be deemed a success. But *this* confession was never part of Isaac's process; this was not the new information he planned to reveal. It's better—it's *much* better. In the right place at the right time, the boy genius captures lightning in a bottle, and I let him.

In my periphery, I notice Arthur sitting up straight, like he's just now pulled his head out of the clouds and started to pay attention to what I'm saying.

"At first, I thought maybe we were all headed to the Light, right behind Eden." I tell it all to the camera, but finally it doesn't feel like a performance, because it is fact. I shed the layers, and it feels triumphant, weightless, even. "But I was too programmed to understand what exactly Arthur had done to Max, what Max had done to Eden, what crime we'd committed by burying her. Arthur told me we had to run. I believed him, even though I was devastated to leave them all behind. I was hysterical. The Oasis was everything to me. I didn't understand the gravity of it all until Arthur dragged me out of there. When we got to the truck stop, he explained everything."

As I twist my braid over to one shoulder, I remember how his fingers felt running through my unwashed hair as I sat in the passenger seat. Breathless, I'd held on to his every word.

"Arthur told me when I reported his fault of breaking the Oasis's rule to keep me pure, Max tried to break him. In the days and nights that followed, Max became determined to make Arthur a leader and show him what it really meant to go from the Underworld to the

Light. Max revealed his plans: how he had Arthur lure young girls to the Oasis for this purpose, so Max could teach them his ways and send them on their journey. At first, Arthur thought this meant Max had finally accepted him, but once he witnessed Max suffocate Eden, once he agreed to get rid of Eden's body and saw where she was headed, it became clear he had been controlled from the start. There was no enlightenment on the other side, only death. Only a corpse that needed to be disposed of. When Arthur was fifteen, he believed his mother had gone to the Light after she gave birth to his half sister Susanna. But that's only what he was told. Arthur pieced it together that his mother was the first woman Max killed. A woman named Ivy Peters."

Across the way, I see Sloane drop her shoulders in relief.

"That's not why I did it," Arthur says, interrupting me. I only needed to hand him the shovel and stand back to let him dig his own grave. "I *had* to help Max, so I could step in as the next leader of the Oasis. It was my destiny. I sent him back to the Light, where he belongs, where all of the heroes belong."

I shake my head at his delusions. "Maybe that's what you tell yourself now, but I swear, Arthur, you had a moment of clarity. That night, you saw Max for who he was—a murderer. That's why you killed him. You wanted to avenge your mother's death. You protected me. You got me out of there."

Arthur rocks back and forth, his head in his hands. "No, no, no."

I ignore his denial. He's only had decades of convincing himself otherwise. I know better than anyone what that's like. "At the truck stop, you convinced me to take the fall. You swore I'd get off easy—as a minor, as a girl, as the daughter of an evil cult leader, I would be forgiven. I'd even be praised for my bravery. The law would grant me immunity and see the act as self-defense. You told me I'd ultimately have a story to tell, something sensational to write about. You told me I could prove my worth to my mother back home. I was naïve enough to listen when you swore it would be the best decision for us, and you'd come find me, so we could be together when all was said and done. The moment I realized you left me with the gun, I knew you never planned to come back for me."

"Max was a hero. A hero, a hero . . ." Arthur repeats over and over, his deluded loyalty as strong as ever.

"I knew you'd manipulated me to protect your own interests and buy yourself time to get out of Dodge, but still, I realized I had a choice," I continue, high off the release of the lies, electrified by the cameras trained on my every movement. "I could tell the truth to the police and walk away with not only the stigma of being a foolish, blind victim, but with the scarlet letter of an accomplice. I'd be pitied, punished, or worse, forgotten. My story would end there. Or I could take a risk. I could say, 'I killed my father.' *That* was a story that would garner attention and attract an audience. How taboo, how radical, how brave. It was a gamble I took and reaped the benefits of. I shared that story with the world because I believed the version with me as the hero was the remedy. Telling that lie gave me a platform, a career, an entire life—one I never imagined would get this far, but now I see the Oasis is still out there. It's still alive, helmed by someone far more dangerous than Max ever was or might have been. I won't stay silent any longer."

I turn back toward the camp, what's left of it, hoping what I'm about to say will bring me closer to the hero I claimed to be. "Say what you will about Max, but he kept to his land. Sure, he let a precocious teenage girl divulge his little theories in her diary, but he didn't invite a swarm of cameramen and a hit filmmaker into his operation. Sometimes I think he wanted us to fear the outside world because he feared it himself. He couldn't control it. That's why he made it so unfathomable to leave. Maybe he wasn't so indestructible after all. But you . . ."

I turn to Arthur, his half smile crooked. "You want to be memorialized. You're delusional enough to believe you may even find a new recruit. As much as I wanted to blame you for standing by Max, I understood the strength of his power. I understood he made you question yourself; he made you beg for his attention through actions he demanded of you—waving his staff whichever crooked way he wanted you to follow. Back then, you didn't know another path existed, but then you kept going. Now you can't stop, can you? You're still manipulating those women, promising them the heavens as you trap them in a hellscape Max designed and you perpetuate. You're starving those innocent children."

"I would never endanger my children," Arthur protests. "The New Kind are our only hope."

"What about her, then?" I point to Sloane and wave her over to join us. Her face reddens, but she stands. The crew members, aside from Isaac, look at each other, confused, as Sloane brazenly takes her cue and comes forward. "Susanna. Your sister. Why didn't you protect her?"

"Susanna?" He breaks into laughter that quickly morphs into a desperate cry. "It's you? The second of the New Kind." He drops to his knees at her feet in reverence and grabs her wrists. "I can guide you to the Light," he says, completely delusional. Sloane blanches and looks to me of all people to save her.

"Let her go," I tell him.

Then he turns to me. "My little poet," he says. "You trust me, don't you?"

He releases Sloane, and in one fluid motion grabs me gruffly by the neck. Sloane shrieks, hitting his back to try to force him off me, but he's too strong. There's no stopping him.

He tightens his grip on my throat. I want to believe there's remorse or leftover affection behind those wolf-gray irises that once caused me to doubt if I could ever be loved by anyone else, but that's only wishful thinking, an unlucky penny tossed into a wishing well.

I start to panic. I can't get enough air.

Isaac breaks his own rule of appearing on-screen for my well-being. He abandons his post in the director's chair and charges into frame to stop Arthur. The crew quickly follow suit and rush over to help, leaving the cameras rolling.

Isaac and his crew pry Arthur off me, and I finally break free from his grasp. I heave, bent over, sucking in the desert air in quick gulps.

The crew restrains Arthur as best as they can, but he is a force of nature. With all the adrenaline pumping through him, he takes off toward the horizon line. Derek bolts after him. I hear the camera assistant dialing the police.

"It's time," he says into the phone, doing the job he's paid to do. "Send them in. He's running."

Sloane cries openly, freely, her face as pink as when I gave her the stolen perfume. I thought I convinced her whatever she saw that night never happened, but it was that pivotal moment that propelled an obsessed assistant twenty years later. She listened to her gut. Sloane approached Isaac determined to grant the women of the Oasis peace. Maybe she even predicted this scene playing out, cameras rolling, sound still speeding, police on standby. Thanks to me, Isaac's process worked, but I will play their success to my advantage.

This time, I won't let anything stop me from telling the truth.

In the distance, Derek catches up to Arthur and wrestles him to submission, his nose to the ground. In the distance, sirens wail.

I feel sorry for Arthur, I really do. There's not a shadow of a doubt in my mind that he honestly believes what he's saying is true. He's too far gone. He'll never come back, but those manipulated women, those malnourished children, that innocent unborn child cursed with his blood, they will have a fighting chance this time. I'll make sure of it.

This time, the hero narrative will prevail.

# THE OASIS

THE BULLDOZER TEARS THROUGH WHAT'S LEFT OF THE DILAPIDATED greenhouse's frame and pushes it to the side. The sound of metal being crushed is so loud, it makes my skull vibrate.

Isaac and his crew film as I watch the search-and-rescue team do their work. Police cars line the perimeter. This is a crime scene, after all, and we serve no official purpose. We're only here to capture what remains.

For decades, naysayers assumed I was making it up when I said Max killed those women. It's true crime 101, after all: no body, no crime. Even Diana Golden said as much. Many believed those nameless, faceless women just disappeared; their lives were considered meaningless because of the way they chose to live them. Runaway girls are easy to eulogize, memorialize for their beauty and wasted potential, discard for their frivolity. But it's the mothers they become who are the easiest to forget, the ones your glance skips over without thought. There will always be pieces of those left behind. No one can ever wholly disappear. The mark we make stays embedded somewhere in the earth. If you look hard enough, if you care to find the evidence, you will find a trace of each individual's unique impact.

When the police arrived on the scene two days ago, the sheriff took Arthur away, and a pair of detectives stayed behind. After they took our initial statements, I walked them over to the greenhouse.

When the compound was searched after Max's death, authorities were too stunned by the scene of the followers worshipping Max's rapidly decomposing body staged on the stone platform to consider what might be underneath it. If they would have thought to remove the platform, they'd have discovered the long-defunct well beneath. This is where Arthur and I buried Eden. Inside the well, the bodies of all the women who sacrificed their life force in exchange for birthing Max's children, the New Kind, were tossed out and abandoned. One on top of the other. Water and women give us life, even in the harshest of deserts and most disturbing of circumstances. I suppose this twisted logic is why my father named this unholy place the Oasis.

The police brought me to the station for questioning, where I repeated the truth about the events of that summer night. I didn't skip a single part, despite knowing the possible ramifications for my role in not only burying Eden, but in concealing evidence and withholding the location of the missing women's bodies for decades. Resigned to whatever punishment the police deemed suitable, I understood there was no going back. I was surprised when I was dismissed with only a thank-you for my cooperation with the investigation into Arthur's offenses. They understood I was the brainwashed victim; I'd had to play my role to save myself, while Arthur's evils had surpassed victimhood a long time ago.

The authorities took Arthur into custody, and the state charged him with a litany of crimes, a list that seems to expand by the hour. Despite it all, I'm grateful to Arthur for doing what he did twenty years ago, for pulling the trigger when I couldn't and dragging me out of there. I like to think maybe I've already paid my penance in my own way. I'm sure it's only a matter of time until my new lease on freedom will rile up the haters online once again.

It will take hours—days, more likely—to recover each corpse from the bottom of the well, the dark abyss that transported the women to the depths, like Persephone's passage to the Underworld.

It will take weeks to identify each of the mothers' bodies, using dental records, DNA, and old case files.

It will take months to track down the surviving members of their families. Some, like Sloane, have been waiting eagerly for that bittersweet reunion, to lay to rest the mother she never knew. I allow myself to hope that the children of the others, the first wave of the New Kind, will come out of the woodwork and reveal themselves at last. Others, like Ivy's father, will have to make peace with the fact that his daughter *was* susceptible. She was one of the cult girls, after all. The grandson he never knew is a monster; his granddaughter took part in his downfall by way of showbiz manipulation.

It will take longer, much longer, to reconcile myself to the fact that I am the reason this recovery is beginning twenty years too late.

Two nights ago, as Arthur's followers were enacting the sunset ritual, his compound was raided. The women and children were promptly taken to the local hospital to receive treatment for a host of maladies. I imagine those children in that sterile environment, awestruck by the outside world they never knew existed. I shiver wondering how Arthur will show up in their lives as they get older. I pray they won't look too closely in the mirror.

"Any news on the baby from Arthur's camp?" I ask Sloane.

She turns away from the greenhouse to answer me, using her hands as a shield against the persistent sun. "Any day now," she reports without emotion.

I can't help but toil with the fact that it could have been me birthing Arthur's offspring.

Soon the whole world will know I told the truth—just not all of it.

I told the entirety of what happened that fateful night, but I decided to keep one final piece of the puzzle for myself. In grappling with the past, I have to take apart the fiction I convinced myself was true and separate it from the cold, hard facts. After all, I am the only one who suffered because of it. If you forget the mother's misery, as so many do, miscarriage is a victimless crime.

After I returned to Coronado, I miscarried at eight weeks. I had only just discovered I was pregnant the week before I lost it. I thought my body had been reacting to the trauma of what had happened. The nausea, headaches, and missed period hadn't fazed me—but there was, of course, more to it than that. I wasn't listening to the messages my body had been giving me. We were still awaiting the trial when Diana took me to the doctor, and we learned the truth. I marvel that I only knew for one week. For those seven precious days, it felt like I'd lived another lifetime, consumed by the possibility I might be capable of loving another so completely. I fantasized I was having a daughter and maybe, just maybe, she'd turn out differently than I had. When I started bleeding and the monotone doctor explained the pregnancy was no longer viable, I said I was surprised. When the doctor scraped my insides to ensure I was clean and pure again, I cried like it was a shock. But deep down, I already knew. I knew something was not right.

Forget the science. Forget how *normal* everyone says it is. Forget the likelihood that an embryo made by Arthur and me was corrupted from the start. Every time I tried to picture her, my daughter, I couldn't. I knew she was never meant to see the outside world. If she did, she'd have to understand where she came from, who she came from, and neither of us could have survived that.

Besides Diana, I've never told another soul. That fall, she nursed me back to health, never scolding me for what happened, but never asking the questions I wanted her to ask. Now that I know the scope of her role in all of it, I understand she kept my secret not out of love for me, like I thought, but to protect herself. It was in her best interest if my pregnancy and miscarriage disappeared into thin air. And so it did.

For years, I stalled the grief by playing out a fantasy that my daughter was off somewhere making her own mark, forsaking every cell of hers that stemmed from her lying, scheming father. The idea soothed me, and even now, I can't bear to admit what happened. If I tell the world about her, she won't be mine anymore. I'll have to let her go for good. I'll have to admit my worst fear might be the reality: maybe I'm not good enough to be a mother.

The world certainly thinks so, as so many vipers online can attest. I know they would only double down on their assessments of my deficiencies if the news broke. For so long, I told myself I shouldn't want to try. After the mistakes I've made, I didn't even deserve to want a child of my own, so I let the years roll by. Now here I am, nearly thirty-six years of age, constantly hounded with all sorts of risks and frightening statistics about conceiving at my advanced age, and I still want to know. I want to know if I am good enough. I want to find out for myself if motherhood's the path I'm meant to take.

Ivy found this place when she had nowhere to go, when she was a single mother raising her young son as best as she knew how. She died while her womb was still healing from the birth of her second child, one she would never hold, just like Eden. What might that be like, to slip through the threshold into nothingness, without the gnawing discomfort of the wanting, without the monotonous nights drowned in the blue light of the television set, tasting your own bad breath? They didn't disappear—they're there, in that well—but my baby did. She passed through my body with my tainted blood.

If my daughter was lucky enough to be born and get paper cuts and suffer through school assemblies and decipher instructions on that folded piece of paper inside a tampon box and fall in love and fail, I would love her. I would tell her that she is beautiful and smart and worthy. I would love her if she never got a song on the radio, if she never made a theater of thousands applaud. I would love her if she made mistakes, if she told lies, if she trusted the wrong people. I'd tell her she mattered. I'd pray she'd love herself fiercely and I would love her because I wouldn't know how not to love her.

Out in this desert, I can sense my father's presence, stewing in the heat. To him, I was the first of the New Kind, the one to thank for the inspiration behind his grand plans. Maybe Diana leaving the desert gave him the deranged idea to keep the mothers stranded here forever, so they couldn't walk out and bruise his ego. I could have been the reason he wanted to cut off the Oasis from the outside world, as if the one that existed had to be burned down and started from scratch. I imagine this place now as Diana described it—a hippie commune—and wonder how blind she may have been to Max's burgeoning narcissistic tendencies. I guess we'll never know what exactly happened during those six odd years until the second of the New Kind was born. I consider how painstakingly Max developed his depraved theories in that time, picking up a Jungian paperback at a garage sale and twisting the language for his benefit, pacing back and forth in this dirt, testing his methods on Ivy and Arthur. It's funny—in some strange way, I understand why Max fabricated his doctrine to justify his evil actions. He thought he could eliminate the sacred bond only a mother could have with her child—a bond superior to whatever power he believed a father could exert over the next generation—but he made a serious miscalculation. Maybe my mother took that bond for granted, squandering it for her own benefit, but I am a descendant of theirs in equal measure. Together, they gave me life, but I know now I am whole only on my own.

We hear a commotion from the search-and-rescue team. A few shouts that are indecipherable. The bulldozer operator adjusts his position and lowers the machine's arm, struggling to get a firm grasp on the round stone platform in the center of the structure. With strained effort, the machine knocks the stone platform loose at last. I realize I've been holding my breath. Sloane and I lock eyes for a moment. When she turns her attention back to the greenhouse, I exhale, but I find I can't stop looking at her. She cries tears of relief, a strange smile on her face.

Somehow, I feel myself smiling too. I don't edit myself. I claim our father's Cheshire cat grin and let it be what it is—mine.

It's beautiful out here, and I feel a rush of contentment that the beauty of the desert was as real as I remembered it to be. Bold and daring, serene and comforting—a landscape of contradictions.

The lullaby comes back to me then, washing over me anew. I can hear it, haunting and feminine, blowing through the branches of the Joshua trees and whispering through the juniper bushes. The voices of those we lost and now found carry up from the well, along with their long-forgotten wishes to be free of it all. To be free of the wanting.

I hum the melody, but I think I'm going to change the words.

EVEN THOUGH I'VE ALREADY LIVED IT AND SEEN IT COUNTLESS TIMES in the editing room as a producer, I sneak into the back of the Theatre at the Ace Hotel to catch the final scene of Isaac Coleman's latest and rumored-to-be-finest work yet, *The Stories of Lucy Golden*. The audience doesn't notice my entrance—they're focused with rapt attention. I relish it, their delectable, bated breath.

There I am, up on the big screen, back at the loft, months after Arthur's arrest, after my infamous confession, reading the foreword of what became the bestselling anniversary edition of *Rattlesnake*, complete with a new ending: the truth. Once the news broke, the demand for appearances skyrocketed. Podcast offers, speaking engagements, the works. Now everyone wants a piece of Lucy Golden, and I'm hard-pressed to say no when opportunity strikes.

It's heartening to see this image of myself, framed by the velvet red curtains, flanked by the ornate moldings of this storied venue. I appear so assured in my own skin, wearing a contentment I thought at one time could be found only in a faraway desert. Dare I say, I resemble the star I never believed I could be.

"When I was a little girl, I made up stories," I recite to the camera with the papers on my lap. I knew it by heart. "For years, I convinced myself that everything I wrote in *Rattlesnake* was true because I wanted to believe it was. I, the strong feminist, eliminated an evil predator preying on women and children. To admit I was the fool who failed to heed the warning signs was not an option. To admit the mistake of doing what I was told was too much to bear. The only way I knew how to survive? Lie. To the world and to myself. But there was someone else that night who witnessed me carrying Eden's body out of Max's house. I made her question her own reality and put her in a position in which she was never believed."

I spot Sloane and her new purple hair in an aisle seat, beside her grandparents Helen and Doug. Last I heard, she was crashing with them in Brentwood while prepping for the feature she sold to Isaac's streamer. As she listens to this message from me, she leans forward, and I smirk, imagining she's trying with all her might not to bite her nails.

We haven't seen each other since that day in the desert. She decided not to stay on the project through postproduction, citing a need to focus on her own work. We have exchanged calls every now and then, but we never manage to speak directly. Ignored calls result in paranoid ramblings in voicemail messages. Questions and half-hearted apologies ping alternately in our email inboxes. Neither of us is ready yet to face the other, in the new iterations of ourselves, but I like to think we're taking steps toward some semblance of a sisterhood.

"I am sorry for what my lie did to Susanna," I say on-screen, with hard-earned sincerity. "By coming clean, I hope she can move on from that night too. I hope she'll forgive me."

In the theater, she appears to sense my stare on her back as she turns in my direction. She nods at me in the dark, an acknowledgment of the latest offering I've left at her feet. As soon as I smile in response, she swivels back around to the screen, and I wonder if she saw me at all or if I only imagined it.

"It will take time for me to relearn my history and come to terms with it all." I watch as the version of me on-screen holds back a tear, smiling through it, like the now-canceled and widely despised Diana Golden taught me. "The woman who raised me led me to believe I wasn't capable of being a great artist if I didn't take risks. I believed her, and it nearly cost me my life. Lately, I've been rethinking what being an artist demands of you. I have to believe you can create art without destroying your sense of self and replacing it with a mask you're told to wear. Authenticity is more powerful than performance. I'm telling the truth now, so all the young girls out there who are told to be anything other than their true selves know that it's okay to speak up, to fight back, to own your experiences. You are the only person who can tell the world who you are."

I deliver this line with such conviction that I'm reminded of the celebratory call from Julian when he read the foreword for the first time, ecstatic about the new angle.

"Brilliant," he exclaimed. "You've done it again!"

Now it's time for me to do my job. I slip out the back doors. Malin's waiting in the lobby to escort me backstage. You might think it would be more terrifying to step onstage than it was before, but it's liberating to have butterflies. The good kind.

We make it to the wings just in time for the last bit of Odette's latest hit song, triumphant yet haunting, scoring a montage of old photographs taken by those who hurt me most. Updates on the case roll alongside the images of my former self. All of the satisfying "where are they nows," Arthur's life sentence, then, one by one, a list of the women we lost, starting with the first: Ivy Peters.

I peek around the curtain and recognize some misty-eyed fans in the front row. Isaac appears at my side and tips his fedora. I'll be sure to tease him for wearing it after our sold-out Q and A.

"Trust the process," he whispers. I roll my eyes at him as the final note plays.

Ready to take a bow, we wait for the applause we deserve.

# ACKNOWLEDGMENTS

A FEW YEARS AGO, I CAME ACROSS A BOX OF KEEPSAKES FROM MY childhood. Inside, I found an old school project titled "All About Me." Curious to find out how self-aware I may or may not have been at the age of seven, I turned the page and laughed out loud when I read: "I like to write. I like to make things."

Before selling this book, I often questioned if I'd ever accomplish what I spent as long as I could remember trying to do: *Write. Make things.* There have been countless occasions when I doubted my writing and equated its merit with my self-worth; something that's reflected in Lucy's story. But somehow, this book was not made out of construction paper crookedly stapled together, and lucky for me, it was not made alone. I'd like to thank the people who lent a hand in making that little girl's dream come true and realizing this Capricorn's ambitions.

So, thank you:

To Madeleine Milburn, my legend of an agent, for digging me out of a slush pile and changing my life overnight. Your expertise and kindness are unparalleled. To the team at Madeleine Milburn Agency: Hannah Ladds, Giles Milburn, Valentina Paulmichl, Hannah Kettles, Georgia McVeigh, Saskia Arthur, and Meghan Capper for your dedication.

To Josie Freedman and CAA for seeing a life for *Paper Cut* beyond the page.

To Danielle Dieterich and Sarah Hodgson, my brilliant, divine editors! You both understood my vision from the beginning and guided me with clarity, passion, and a sense of play. Our conversations always leave me feeling seen and inspired. Thank you for taking a chance on me.

To the team at William Morrow: Liate Stehlik, Kelly Rudolph, Robin Barletta, Marie Vitale, and Grace Vainisi. Special thanks to Kathleen Cook for the thorough, thoughtful copyedit.

To the team at Corvus in the UK: Dave Woodhouse, Anne Bowman, Felice McKeown, Aimee Oliver-Powell, Laura O'Donnell, and Holly Battle.

To the teachers who instilled a love of craft and storytelling in me: Sue Ellis, Lori Hewett, Jane Graham, Kathleen MacManus, William "Electric" Black, Joe Vinciguerra, Drew Perry, and Doug "Doom" Kass. To this day, I often hear Electric's exclamation in my head: "Where's the *story*, Rachel?!"

To my bosses, mentors, and champions throughout a decade of working in the television industry. To Nahnatcha Khan for my first gig in Hollywood. To David Baggelaar for seeing something in a pilot script. To Tommy Schlamme and Julie DeJoie, for the indelible mark you made. To the many talented writers I've worked alongside for the invaluable lessons.

To the brave survivors who speak up about their experiences in high control groups and the filmmakers and journalists who amplify their lived experiences. Your offerings were crucial to my research.

To the generous group of actors who lent their talents to a nascent version of *Paper Cut* way back in 2019, my community in the audience, and my alma mater, Elon University, for hosting us. Heaps of gratitude to Samantha Lubben for an actor's perspective on Lucy, continued spiritual guidance, and our soul sisterhood.

To the early readers who empowered me to keep going: Leah Konen, Michelle Richmond, Barry Gribble, and Jordan Overstreet. To *The Shit No One Tells You About Writing* podcast, particularly CeCe Lyra, for the advice and feedback.

To my dear friend Amanda Pellegrino for answering every author question I've ever had and spending countless hours brainstorming, reading, and rereading. If I had a nickel for every time I've uttered the words "Well, Amanda says . . ."

To my support system of wise, willful, wonderful women who cheer me on daily, I'm lucky to know and love you: Callen Olsen, Susan Griffiths, Eugena Neumann, Sarah Papineau, Jen Gresenez, Tanza Loudenback, Carling Andrews, Katie Burris, Chloe Waibel, Valerie Reich, Sarah Pickett, Logan Baker, Caroline Haye, and Georgia Loftis. Lots of love to Lindsay Friedrich, who reads every draft with unmatched enthusiasm and still asks for more!

To my family: the Taffs, Peacocks, Bishops, Boyles, Morrows, Prendergasts, and Prices for your steady love. To my late grandmother Dadie for inspiring me with her lifelong pursuit of self-discovery and Jungian studies. To Brian Boyle, the other writer in the family, for showing me what's possible, getting me started, and letting me use your washing machine (and occasionally live in your guest room) during my "starving artist/assistant" days.

To my sister, Elise, for the endless inspiration. I wouldn't be the person (or writer) I am today if it weren't for you performing your heart out from a young age, making the world your stage. There's nothing I love more than talking story with you.

To my exceptional parents, to whom this book is dedicated (*I swear they do not resemble Max or Diana!*) for always supporting my goals and providing me with the education and opportunities to achieve them. Mom, thanks for showing me what it means to live a creative life, comforting me when I need solace, and emboldening me when it's time to grow. Dad, thank you for being the best coach and business manager. For better or worse, I'm pretty sure I get my work ethic from you. I hope I make you both as proud as you make me.

To my handsome, hardworking husband, Evan, for giving me a little honey every day. I'm so proud to call you (and Maggie) home. I love you.

And finally, to you, dear reader, for spending your precious time with this twisted tale. Thank you, thank you. Please come again soon.

# ABOUT THE AUTHOR

RACHEL TAFF is an author and television producer. Most recently, Rachel was the Director of Development at Dynamic Television, known for *Ginny and Georgia*, where she sold projects to Amazon and Hallmark. Previously, Rachel worked for Emmy-winning director Thomas Schlamme's Shoe Money Productions, where she developed projects for FX and managed a production slate including *Snowfall* and *The Plot Against America*. Additional credits include *SMILF*, *American Dad*, and *Fresh Off the Boat*. Rachel earned a Media Arts & Entertainment degree at Elon University. After a decade in Los Angeles, she now lives in Atlanta with her husband and their Portuguese water dog. *Paper Cut* is her first novel.